The Jihad Ultimatum

JOHN D. RANDALL

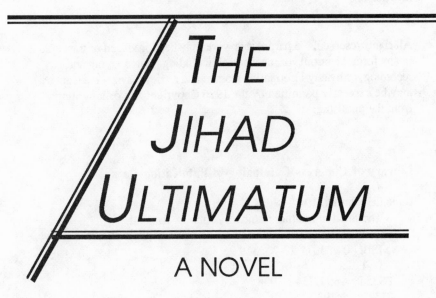

THE JIHAD ULTIMATUM

A NOVEL

Saybrook

Publishing Company

Dallas   San Francisco   New York

THE JIHAD ULTIMATUM is a work of fiction. Although some of its
characters are actual historical persons, the words and deeds ascribed to them
are purely fictitious and do not in any way record actual words and deeds of
said persons.

Library of Congress Cataloging-in-Publication Data

Randall, John D., 1944–
    The jihad ultimatum : a novel / John D. Randall.
        p.   cm.
    ISBN 0-933071-23-X : $19.95
    I. Title.
PS3568.A4957J54   1988
813'.54--dc19

                              88-14109
                                 CIP

Saybrook Publishers
4223 Cole Avenue, Suite Four
Dallas, Texas 75205

Distributed by W. W. Norton & Company
500 Fifth Avenue, New York, New York 10110

To my wife, Linda

CONTENTS

CHAPTER 1

Scotty's Dive

NEW YORK CITY

Murphy Monahan stepped out of his office and scanned the nearly empty bullpen. It was a quarter to Miller time, yet the day was only half finished. It was part of the Never-Ending Work Day, the Week That Wouldn't Die, The Month Without Rest, the Year Without Pity—take your pick.

Halfway across the office Monahan spotted a tall young man sitting at a small desk cluttered with paper. He was out of place. Desks were organized by order of seniority, with the closest filled by the newest of rookies. Grizzled veterans got the window seats around the corner, out of eyesight and certainly out of earshot. The more seniority someone pulled, the further away from the boss they got.

"Coldsmith!" shouted Monahan. "What the hell are you doing over there?"

A hundred years ago Monahan had been in Coldsmith's position. He knew what drudgery the boy was going through. He was probably completing a stack of routine reports for one of the more senior agents, reports that no agent had the time to do and that no supervisor would ever read.

What a waste of time, thought Monahan. No matter how hard he'd tried in his five years as Special Agent in Charge (SAC) of the FBI's New York Regional Office, Monahan had been unable to change the Way Things Were Done. Rookies still stayed late and did meaningless grunt work.

"I've got an opportunity for someone, Coldsmith," Monahan bellowed.

Scotty Coldsmith looked up from the paper-strewn desk, then looked around the empty office. He was the only one there, and the only one named Coldsmith.

"Sir?" he replied.

"Yes, you, Coldsmith. Thank you for volunteering. I've just received a telex from Paris. There's a Soviet courier by the name of Rostov on Air France flight 10. He gets here in an hour and a half. Give him a heavy tail."

Coldsmith looked up at his superior with semi-glassy eyes. Doing Campo's paperwork wasn't his idea of fun but at least it had the promise of being completed before seven. Going to Kennedy in rush hour to tail a Soviet courier meant the whole evening, possibly the entire night, was gone. Not only would it kill the rest of the day, it would more importantly destroy a promising date with a buxom and willing Columbia graduate student named Leslie.

"Do you know what that means?" asked Monahan.

Coldsmith sighed to himself, then answered with a rookie's smile. "Yes, sir. Make sure the mark knows he's being followed. But, sir, my unit has two espionage cases, six . . . maybe seven . . . whitecollars, and the big case with Civil Division. And I've got all these reports for Mr. Campo . . . they've got me running . . ."

"The plane lands at Kennedy in an hour and a half. Be there," were Monahan's last words.

Monahan threw the memo slip down on Scotty's desk with a practiced fling. The piece of paper made two full turns and came to a stop right in front of Scotty's hand. It was all in the wrist. There was no appeal. Monahan was in charge. He was the Supreme Allied Commander (SAC). His Manhattan Regional office was the largest of all the 59 field offices, largest in the FBI's network of over 400 locations across the country. It was a pisser of a job.

Scotty looked at his watch. An hour and a half? Even on a good day it would take him that long to get there. As he cleaned and locked his desk, Scotty made a quick call to his hot date. Just listening to her voice made him horny.

Maybe the Van Wyck would be clear. *Sure . . . you bet,* he thought sarcastically. Bridge or tunnel? The thought of driving to Kennedy was totally depressing. He looked over his shoulder and saw Monahan standing in the doorway watching him leave.

Surveillance was a pain in the ass. It was a 25-hour-a-day job and incredibly boring. The FBI just didn't have enough people. If it was just the Russians it might be one thing, but no—the FBI had to watch the Czechs, the Poles, the Germans, the Chinese, the Cubans, you name it. And the U.S. government made it so easy—the god-damned treaties made it so easy for every hostile nation in the world to send their best espionage agents to New York under diplomatic cover. How could the FBI cover them? The answer was they couldn't. How difficult was it to follow someone in New York City? Close to impossible. It required long hours by very skillful men and women to keep on the trail of a

3

gle foreign agent. Once having given them the slip, a foreign agent could meld into American society with ease. All he needed was a source of money and the ability to speak English. The U.S. was an open country with no checkpoints between the various states and cities. Anybody could get a Social Security card, driver's license, credit cards—instant identification. Even after deregulation the telephone system was the best in the world. So was the postal system. Calls could be made without fear of being tapped, and letters were mailed and delivered on time, without fear of interception. The transportation system was incredible. Anybody could get anywhere anytime, no questions asked. No patrols, no passports, no ID checks. All a KGB agent had to do was look and act like a normal person, have money, speak reasonable English, and stay out of trouble. In short, it was a bitch of a job.

After fifteen minutes Scotty, 25 years old, six months out of law school and into the first phase of his intensive FBI training, finally made his way down the slowest elevator in all of New York to the cramped underground parking garage. It was dark and dingy. Scotty half expected some nights to get mugged going for his car. FBI agents could get mugged, too. But not very often. Most times you could park your car wherever you wanted, flash a badge, and nobody would give you any shit. *Back off, Jack, this is the* F *god-damn* BI.

Once into traffic, Scotty mumbled to himself. *Face it Coldsmith, whatever decision you make tonight is bound to be wrong*. The bridge had been OK, but his decision to cut down to Bushwick Avenue had been a bummer. Traffic was backed up wherever he went. The problem was, there was no quick way to get to Kennedy. Maybe the plane would be late. With the window down, the cold, damp January air ripped through the old Mustang. Scotty loved the cold air. It was a good thing, because in the wintertime rookies got plenty of cold air.

Scotty had done surveillance before. Diplomats and couriers can do almost anything. They could carry bags of dope, concealed weapons, national secrets, anything . . . and, they are immune from prosecution or arrest. Actually, just from prosecution. They *can* be arrested and deported.

All Scotty had was a brief description and a seat number, 5B. The man was white, five foot ten or eleven, middle-aged, slight build, no facial hair. Probably only twenty percent of the American population fit that description. If Scotty didn't get there and follow the man from the time he got off the plane, then he might as well forget it.

Alexander Rostov, senior European agent of the KGB, looked at his watch. The plane was on time. It was time for his adrenalin to kick in. The slim, young Arab he'd been ordered to tail was eight seats behind him. Would anyone be meeting him in New York? The thought gave Rostov indigestion. Following someone was difficult work anyplace— but in New York, it was especially difficult. *Is anyone going to be there to help me?* Rostov thought.

Three days ago, with no explanation, he'd been pulled out of his normal routine and ordered to find a group of Arabs who had been seen entering France through the port city of Marseille. One of the group, a man known as Ysed Bandar, had been captured by the local police. Rostov had been incredulous when he'd received his instructions— *infiltrate the police station and obtain enough information to find the others!* The orders had come directly from Stephan Baykal, the Soviet Ambassador to France. Whatever the reason, the information apparently had been worth risking the life of the top KGB agent in Europe, a man who was the control point for seventy-eight Soviet agents and nearly three hundred French, Swiss, and German citizens who were under an ironclad reign of terror—people who had made a mistake and now paid for their sins by supplying information to the Soviet government.

It had taken every bit of Rostov's skill to pose successfully as an attorney for the Arab, convince the captured man that he was a friend, get his instructions, and then kill him—right under the nose of an INTERPOL inspector, a rotund bureaucrat named Marmande. He wished he could have seen Marmande's expression when he found Bandar. The Arab functionary had given him the names of Khalid Rahman, Aziz al-As, and Bafq el-Rashid. They meant nothing to Rostov. He assumed they were terrorists.

Bandar had openly, and stupidly, told Rostov that all he knew was that they were going to Geneva. What a dunce the man was. He had had no choice but to kill him. The second piece of his instructions had been—*no one is to know who this man is. Kill him.* And kill him he did, with a curare-tipped dart from a gas-pressured plastic tube, the simplest of devices. Point and shoot.

Rostov had tracked the Arabs to Geneva, where they spent two nights. In the intervening day the man known as Rahman spent most of his time inside a bank, while the others loitered. Yesterday—no, it was today—Rostov had followed them to De Gaulle airport in Paris, where the group had split up. The frustration of trying to follow three men, obviously taking different paths to the same place, was tremendous. From a phone kiosk in the Air France terminal Rostov finally reached Ambassador Baykal.

"Atlanta? Khalid Rahman is going to Atlanta?" was Baykal's response.

"Yes. On Delta. Aziz al-As is going to New York on Air France. And the one called el-Rashid is boarding British Airways to Heathrow. I don't know where he's going from there."

Rostov remembered Baykal's pause.

"Follow al-As to New York. When does he leave?"

"Forty-five minutes," had been his reply.

"What gate?" asked the Ambassador.

"Twelve."

"You will have full courier status before then, including passport and papers. Stand by the gate," Baykal ordered.

And it had been so. Five minutes before the gate closed another agent from the French embassy ran up and handed Rostov his papers. It was official. He was a courier for the government of the Soviet Union.

The flight had gone well. Aziz al-As had hardly moved. Rostov knew he had the advantage. He'd been to New York before. Three years ago the Soviet delegation at the U.N. had undergone some internal strain—there had been defections. Rostov had been chosen as the one to bring two of the weaker members back in line. It had been messy. Ambassador Korz had given him the most evil of evil eyes when the task was done. The Ambassador did not like to expose his

There was no way the young Arab could have been to New York before. Aziz al-As would be forced to spend most of his energy simply getting around the strange country and very alien city.

Rostov was first off the plane and half way up the jetway before the second passenger said goodbye to the attendant. He hoped there would be a contact waiting for him, what with the crowd of people and the need for trailing the Arab. He didn't relish the idea of following him in a cab. Rostov had nothing but a small cloth overnight case and a virtually empty diplomatic case handcuffed to his wrist just for flashing to the customs officer.

While the Arab queued for his luggage, Rostov went for the customs line.

"Diplomatic pouch," he said as he handed his passport to a man with worn-out eyes. A scowl crossed the customs official's face.

"How long will you be here, Mr. Rostov?"

"Perhaps a week."

"You are not to leave the New York City area for the duration of your stay, you know that?"

"I am aware of the rules," replied Rostov.

"Smile for the camera, Mr. Rostov," said the official.

The customs agent noted Rostov's name and destination and waved him through after taking his picture. Rostov glided over to a nearby pillar, positioned himself and kept his eye on the young Arab still waiting to go through customs.

— • —

Scotty zipped in front of a cab to a curbside parking spot and hit the street running. The hack gave him an Italian fist and shouted an obscenity Scotty couldn't hear.

"Hey, you can't park here . . ." yelled the airport security man.

Scotty shut the man down in mid-sentence with a flash of his badge.

"Don't let anybody touch that car, you *hear*?" he yelled as he ran into the terminal.

Scotty wasted no time as he barged right up to the front of a line and got the immediate attention of a reservation agent, "FBI. The Paris flight. Gate number."

"Twenty-three. It's landed," was the reply from the desk attendant.

"When?" demanded Coldsmith.

"Five minutes ago."

"Damn! Which way to customs?"

He had a choice, run for the gate or wait for his man at customs. The one thing Rostov did have to do was pass through customs, register himself, get photographed, and get the INS lecture on travel restrictions. The process took five minutes.

Going to the plane was out of the question. Maybe Rostov was carrying luggage. That would slow him down for sure. Scotty took off in a dead run. He was six-five, all legs, and he could cover a lot of ground easily. He seemed to lope through the terminal, gliding through and around the incredible mass of people crisscrossing their way to different destinations. The international terminal was the gateway to the U.S. from Europe, and as a result, in the babble of voices could be heard the ancestry of America.

The baggage area was packed with Europeans. Suddenly, the luggage from several flights started to offload at once. People milled and crowded around as the bags dumped out. The noise level increased ten decibels as a planeload of Oriental passengers came in to wait. After the people got their bags they then stood in line waiting to pass through customs. Every line through customs was busy.

"I'm looking for a Soviet courier named Rostov. Have you seen him? I need to follow him," whispered Scotty to each customs agent as he went from line to line.

"You just missed him," said the sixth agent, temporarily distracted from his luggage search. "He went through here not three minutes ago. Wait a minute—that's him over there! By the pillar."

Scotty turned as the customs agent pointed. Rostov was standing against the wall on the opposite side of the room. He appeared to be waiting for someone.

— • —

From behind Rostov came a soft female voice that startled him, "Alexander Rostov? Don't turn around . . . please. There is an FBI agent coming this way. He is looking for you. You don't have much time." The soft voice turned icy, "There is an old Chevrolet, blue with white top, parked in the passenger loading area directly behind us. Go through the double doors to the street level. You will know it is the car by a red playing card taped to the window of one passenger-side rear door. Get in. Remove the card. I will take over surveillance and report to you later. Who is your mark?"

"He's in line six, about ten back from the customs agent. He's carrying two suitcases," said Rostov.

"The young man, five-eleven, tanned skin, yellow shirt?"

"Yes."

"Please go now," she said.

Rostov looked around and spotted a young man advancing toward him through the crowd. Tall, neatly groomed, clean-cut—he looked like he'd come out of the FBI mold. Rostov gave him a cold stare then quickly headed toward the street exit, dodging around several slow-moving groups of tourists heavily laden with luggage.

— • —

That's Rostov? Fairly nondescript, even for a Russian. A grey character if ever I've seen one, thought Scotty as he slowly moved through the the milling crowd of people. Rostov leaned to his left as if someone on the other side of the post was whispering to him. Then Rostov looked up, turned in Scotty's direction and made eye contact immediately. From across the room Scotty could briefly see Rostov's icy intensity. He tried to get closer to the Russian, but Rostov turned and quickly made his way to the street-level exit.

Scotty turned on his lope and hurried after him. Outside the terminal Rostov went right for the back seat of an old car. A Chevy of some kind, Scotty thought as he ran to his own car. Where was it?

"Where's my god-damned car?" he shouted.

It was gone! Towed! *They towed my god-damned car,* he thought. *I'm the FBI, they can't do that!*

It was too late to worry about the car. Cutting in line he took the first cab, pushing two startled businessmen out of the way, parting them like the Red Sea with the magic words, "FBI, out of the way!" As he got into the back seat he pointed to the Chevy pulling away into the traffic. "Follow that car," he instructed the cabbie.

He'd always wanted to say that.

SOVIET MISSION TO THE UNITED NATIONS

Rostov had been taken directly to the headquarters of the Soviet mission to the United Nations on 67th Street between Third Avenue and Lexington. There he had been escorted to a room and had somewhat reluctantly relinquished responsibility for tracking al-As. After eating and concluding that no one was going to see him tonight, Alexander Rostov went to sleep. It had been a difficult week.

— • —

"So, Rostov, we meet again. I hope you had a good night's sleep. Today is a new day, one I'm sure you will not forget. Your mark is covered. However, unlike our last meeting, it appears I am now responsible for you," said the fat minister, his jowls shaking with the beginnings of an evil laugh.

"I am only here on an assignment, Korz," replied Rostov.

"All that changed while you slept last night. As I said, today is a new day. Today, you are mine," the laugh finally escaping.

"No, they would never . . ." Rostov's thoughts were incomplete. "My networks . . ."

"Moscow has ordered," Korz said with finality.

Alexander Rostov was stranded in a foreign country and under the control of a man he had nearly brought down by accident. It hadn't been Rostov's fault that two of Korz's staff had defected.

Korz shifted his bulk and looked out of his twelfth floor window down the corridor of buildings toward the East River. He smiled. Rostov saw how precarious his position was. Decisions were out of his control, and he didn't like it. Born in Paris, in 1944, Alexander Rostov was the progeny of a French seamstress and a Russian intelligence officer. His mother died in childbirth, and at the end of the war, his father returned to Moscow with his son. Colonel Rostov was a strict disciplinarian. At an early age Alex learned that misbehaving or a drop in his school grades would mean several licks from his father's razor strap.

Growing up, Alex had no caring women in his life—only a senile grandmother and an indifferent housekeeper. His father had several mistresses—none of whom stayed for long. The colonel showed little respect for his women, a trait he passed on to his son.

In school, Alex did well in his studies, especially in foreign languages—learning both French and English. He also excelled in contact sports, outmaneuvering his opponents with a keen sense of anticipation and quick reflexes. Encouraged by his father, he joined the Party at age fourteen. He spent the next four years at an academic military school, which prepared him to follow in his father's footsteps as a member of the KGB.

Korz turned around, his contemplation over. His pudgy fingers played with a single sheet of paper.

"Instructions from Moscow require no explanations. You will continue to follow this man. His name is Aziz al-As. He is a member of Zaid abu Khan's Islamic Jihad. There is a connection between Khan and Qaddafi, but there are no details," Korz paused. "It says here that I am to be your new control, that I am responsible for the execution of these instructions and whatever may follow. Given the nature of our past relationship, this makes me somewhat uneasy. Do you understand my concern?" asked Korz, shifting his bulk again.

"Believe me, Korz, I don't care for this any more than you do," replied Rostov, ignoring Korz' title.

After a brief pause, Dimitri Korz continued.

"His passport and hotel registration show he is travelling under the alias of a British subject named John Smithton Ramsey."

"Hotel?"

"Yes, we have kept track of Mr. Ramsey. Unless he is very good, he knows nothing of us. We have him under close surveillance," said Korz. "The other man, the one who flew to Atlanta—his name is Khalid Rahman. He is Khan's second in command. We were unable to follow him in Atlanta. Khan is obviously planning some kind of terrorist act in the United States. Moscow wants to know what it is."

There was a brief period of silence as both men settled into their chairs and superficially adjusted themselves. Korz stared at the agent from across the polished desk. They were both KGB but there was no trust between the two. Korz hadn't risen to the top of his profession by trusting anyone. The same applied to Rostov.

"I know what Moscow thinks of this," Korz continued. "You are expendable, but you know that. It comes with the territory. If you ever want to see France again, you will do what I say. Cross me, my friend, and I will cut you off at the knees."

"Don't threaten me, Korz," Rostov replied, near anger.

"There is no threat, comrade," Korz replied. "I have assigned someone to work with you."

"I work alone," Rostov snapped.

"While you work for me, you work with whomever I assign. The only thing I know of you is that you almost cost me my career. Then, you reported to Moscow. Now, you report to me. I could have you killed as retribution. But, I won't. Moscow has too much interest in this, and unfortunately, your skills are required. Regardless, as of now you have a partner. Her name is Katrina Tambov."

"Her?" asked Rostov, obviously upset.

Korz leaned over the desk, slightly red around the collar, and gave Rostov the evil eye, "Because, comrade, she is my best agent. Your new partner is Katrina Tambov. Have I made myself clear?"

Rostov had no choice. Korz continued, "You must find out if Khan, or Khan and Qaddafi, are planning the usual terrorist irritants: airport bombings, assassinations, kidnapping; or, are they planning something unusual? I, we . . . Moscow . . . wants to know. Do you understand?"

"Yes," answered Rostov dutifully.

"Then I'd like you to meet your new partner."

Rostov turned around just as a tall, raven-haired, young woman entered the room, draping a winter coat over a tall-backed chair. She wore high black boots with three-inch spiked heels, a plain brown wool skirt with a dark red, almost burgundy, long-sleeved blouse. Her hair was tied back to the right in a semi-ponytail. She was striking. The silky blouse clung to the top of her breasts, clearly outlining the fact that she wore a low-cut brassiere. The blouse then was severely drawn over her front and tucked into a narrow waistband. The tightness of the blouse and the sheerness of the bra made it impossible not to notice her firm breasts and raised nipples. Rostov estimated that she was probably his height, five-eleven or so. He smiled to himself. This was no pantyhose woman. He shook off a mental image of her, half-naked in a domineering leather outfit, whip in hand, ready for a strange, dark party.

"This is Katrina Tambov, my best agent," introduced Korz.

There was no attempt at a handshake or greeting.

"We met at the airport," was her unsmiling reply.

"You?"

"Yes," replied Katrina. "Are you surprised?"

Surprised? The first voice he'd heard had been soft, almost like it had come from a different woman. This was not the voice he remembered.

Rostov turned back to Korz.

"I will need some equipment," he said.

"What kind?" replied Korz.

"Surveillance, listening devices, short-wave radios, a weapon, ammunition . . . standard supplies . . . vehicles."

Both Korz and Katrina Tambov laughed dryly. Korz spoke.

"Only in America. We have access to most modern equipment here. And, almost everything can be ordered by mail!"

Korz rolled his big body into a deep laugh.

"That which we can't get by mail can be obtained at trade shows or by other means. All it takes is identification. You will have the best."

Without waiting for Rostov to comment, Katrina spoke. Rostov looked at the above-the-knee slit in her skirt as she briefed him.

"Last night we followed Aziz al-As, alias John Ramsey, to a hotel at 50th and Third, room 12D. He paid in cash. He has been out once already this morning to purchase American clothes, all functional: jeans, corduroys, heavy shirts. He does not appear to be confused by the city. He uses a map and seems to read English well," she said.

Rostov was surprised. He had made the mistake of underestimating his opponent's skills, basing his opinion on what he might have done at such an age.

"How are you covering him?" Rostov asked.

"We started with a full box, but it was over-coverage. We've gone back to a half minus one."

Rostov nodded. A full box required seven people and a controller, which he assumed was Katrina. The suspect was covered front, rear, and from the opposite side of the street. In addition, coverage was provided on parallel streets. For example, if al-As walked up 50th toward Rockefeller Center there would be one ahead of him as he walked westbound on 50th, one behind him on the same side of the street, and another on the opposite sidewalk. On both 49th Street and 51st Street there would be a mirror pair in case he decided to cut through a building to escape the coverage. If, for example, al-As made a move through a department store from 50th to 51st the whole group would move. The team which was on 51st would pick him up and be the prime tail. The team which was following him on 50th would move north to 52nd Street and be the north mirror. The team which was on 49th would move to 50th and be the south mirror. In this way if the mark was suspicious he'd have to pick up seven different people, a task which is impossible. Even the most paranoid of agents would think they'd slipped a tail.

With al-As moving around town with so much purpose and lack of concern for being watched, Katrina had pulled the coverage back to a front-back-side. The four agents on the parallel streets were removed.

"He is not moving around as if he suspects someone is following him. From observing his habits, he is an organized person. He seems to be doing things in order, as if from a list. It is my opinion he is preparing to leave the city. We should be ready when he leaves," said Katrina.

"Why do you say that?" asked Korz.

Rostov interrupted.

"Because the man is not looking for a place to live. A hotel, with a public lobby, is too risky to conduct any kind of operations. If his operation, his mission, was in New York, the first thing he would do would be to look for a safe place to live, someplace where he could get out of the way."

"Comrade Rostov is correct," nodded Katrina.

There was no smile although Katrina felt some degree of satisfaction with Rostov's unsaid approval of her logic.

"It is time I resumed my hunt," said Rostov.

Rostov got up, nodded in Korz's direction and walked out. Katrina gave Korz a long look, then followed, catching up with Rostov in the hallway.

"We must leave separately. The mark . . . ," started Rostov.

Katrina interrupted, "He is a ruthless killer, a leader of the future in Khan's army. Like all of Khan's men he is willing to die, but only for a reason. These people are extremely violent. He is known to have the impetuosity of youth, which on the one hand gives us an advantage, but on the other makes him very dangerous. We can most likely depend upon logic in his movement but be prepared for random events in times of stress."

How does she know all this? wondered Rostov, who wasn't used to such intelligence from a woman.

"Where do we meet?" he asked.

Without batting an eye or changing an inflection, Katrina picked up where she left off.

"Aziz al-As is at a nearby hotel on 64th Street. When you leave the building, walk three blocks south, then one-and-a-half blocks east. His hotel is named the Lyden Gardens, it is halfway down the block on the north side of the street opposite a hospital. Two of my agents are set up on 64th, one is on Third Avenue, another on Second Avenue. It's only four blocks from here and I suggest we walk. I can have automobile support within minutes if we need it, but walking gives us a better opportunity to melt into the crowd if the FBI has someone waiting for us . . . and I assume they will. This building is watched closely twenty-four hours a day. Here, you will need this in case we get separated."

Katrina handed Rostov a small walkie-talkie. The unit was not much larger than a standard belt-strapped paging device.

"We have modified it slightly for two-way communications. The red button for talk, the black for listen. Press the red once, wait for a black response, then talk. We change the frequencies daily," said Katrina.

Rostov strapped the device to his belt without comment. They continued down a hallway to an elevator, then to the street level of the 67th Street mission.

"Do you know the city?"

"I know where we are going," replied Rostov.

"Fine, then. I suggest you wait ten minutes or so and leave through the door in the side of the building. We may or may not be followed, but we must leave separately to ensure at least one of us moves freely. Do you know where it is?"

"I know where it is, Comrade Tambov," Rostov said more tersely than necessary.

Rostov didn't like taking directions from a woman, not even simple directions.

The Soviet Mission to the United Nations occupied most of the block on 67th between Third Avenue and Lexington. Other than the fact that there was a large concentration of New York City patrolmen on the street, clusters of FBI in the construction shed at street level, and twenty-four-hour CIA coverage from the buildings on the north side of the street, 67th Street was just like any other street in that section of the city. It was tree-lined, narrow, and very upscale. The street out in front of the mission had been under construction for so long that it was a running joke to the KGB inside. What started as simple remodeling to a building near Lexington had turned into a permanent affair. The construction trailer had been taken over by the FBI so that the agents didn't have to stand out in the cold of winter or heat of summer while waiting for this or that KGB agent to leave the building. The trailer was manned twenty-four hours a day.

The entrance to the mission could easily have been mistaken for a posh hotel or apartment building . . . except for the two burly KGB agents standing just inside the heavy, bullet-proof, plate glass doors. Just outside the doors were the duty cops from New York's finest. Directly across the street, four stories up in a well-maintained brownstone, were the CIA operations. They monitored the KGB, the police, the FBI, the staff, the transmissions from the antennas and satellite dishes on the roof, and anyone who passed by who simply looked curious or out of place.

On Lexington between 67th and 66th was the wonderfully rustic 7th Armory, home for the Army weekend warriors. Directly opposite the Armory on Lexington was a police kiosk. In between the buildings of 67th and 66th Streets was a narrow walkway. It would almost be considered an alley except that it was too narrow for vehicles. From the kiosk, one went down a short series of narrow concrete steps then walked fifty feet to the "back door" of the Soviet mission. It was this back, actually side, door which Rostov would use while Katrina Tambov went out the front.

"Remember, use your walkie-talkie if you have to."

Katrina put on her coat, turned and walked toward the front entrance. The heels of her boots clicked in rhythm as she crossed the marble foyer.

Ten minutes later Rostov left through the rear entrance. It was the last time either of them would see the comfort of 67th Street.

— • —

Scotty followed Rostov to the mission by cab, then reported to The Shed, where he turned in his description of his mark to the team of agents assigned to surveillance and spent the night scrunched up in a too-small cot, his six-foot-five frame overhanging the six-foot cot. Considering the level of street noise, it felt like he'd spent the night sleeping out in the middle of Lexington Avenue. Rostov had been added to the long list hanging in The Shed of people to follow. With its Lexington at 67th Street location, The Shed could see both the front and side entrances to the Soviet mission. Normally one agent watched each entrance and rotated surveillance on an hourly shift. It was difficult to pay attention for more than an hour.

In the morning, Scotty's first thought was that his car was still impounded somewhere in Queens. But, as he joined the men on surveillance, he heard one of them say "Damn! She's a good-looking woman."

Eyes went to the east window and watched Katrina Tambov walk away from them toward Third Avenue. The cold wind blew her coat open, revealing a slit skirt and skin nearly up to her thigh. She packed the skirt well and it was easy to see she was in shape. Her calf and thigh muscles were well defined.

"That would be some ride," said another agent.

Scotty, a fresh cup of hot coffee in his hand, leaned over the shoulder of another agent just as the skirt went around the corner.

"Who was she?" he asked.

"Katrina Tambov, personal attaché to Korz," said the agent on watch.

"How'd you like to have that kind of personal service?" said another.

The men laughed. For a moment they each had a short, action-filled fantasy, then snapped back to business.

"Who's that?" said the agent posted on Lexington.

His shiftmate looked through his binoculars out the dirty window down Lexington and saw the face of Alexander Rostov at the police kiosk.

"Hey, kid. I think this is your mark. You'd better hustle buns if you're going to stay with him," shouted the agent.

"Where?" asked Scotty, spilling some of his coffee on his leg as he got up.

"He's heading down Lexington. You'd better hurry."

Scotty looked through the window at the retreating Rostov, then followed the agent's advice and hustled out the door, throwing on his coat and scarf in the process. It was a miserable day in New York. It was the kind of damp cold New Yorkers wanted to see only from the heated safety of their apartments. It was the kind of cold which soaked through gloves and could penetrate any overcoat. It was the kind of damp cold that always came before a good snow—and Scotty Coldsmith had wet pants. In minutes the hot coffee would be only a memory. The wet patch would follow him like a winter's cold.

Scotty crossed Lexington, dodged a group of army privates detailed to gopher coffee at the corner deli at 66th Street, then picked up Rostov as the Russian strode purposefully along the four-lane avenue.

The man must be cold, thought Scotty. He's only got a light jacket with no hat or gloves. He's got to be cold. Scotty wore his heavy winter coat, Thinsulate gloves, and scarf. Even so, he could feel the cold. He looked more like the young lawyer he was than the FBI agent he wanted to be. *Rostov must come from Siberia and thinks this is Miami,* thought Scotty.

Scotty kept a half-block distance between himself and Rostov, although he doubted if Mr. Monahan would have called that "heavy coverage." Rostov didn't turn around to check his coverage and didn't seem to care if he was being followed. Maybe he was just out for a walk—or to get a paper. Why risk getting caught when the *New York Times* just might print it for you.

He was probably going out for a bagel. *That's it! Even Soviet agents like bagels and cream cheese,* Scotty thought. He cracked a smile just as Rostov turned left onto 64th Street and seemed to pick up speed as he went uphill along the shaded street toward Third Avenue. Wherever Rostov was going, he knew the way.

The smile from Scotty's lips faded as he risked life and limb to cross Lexington against the light and keep up with Rostov. Then at Third Avenue, Rostov ducked into a small pharmacy on the west side of the corner. Scotty stayed on the north side and waited for the Soviet agent to reappear. A long thirty seconds went by as Scotty fidgeted, wondering what to do. On the opposite side of the six-lane avenue the waiters were setting up tables at a fashionable Italian restaurant. It was the kind of restaurant design that was popular in New York. The outside wall was all glass. This meant that people could be sitting one pane of glass from the sidewalk. Disgusting, thought Scotty.

Not a day went by when he didn't say to himself that "this isn't Kansas, Toto." Born and raised in Laramie, Scotty had gone to the University of Wyoming but had majored in the Cowboy Bar and Grill before getting bit by the law bug. The Grill was one place which didn't cotton to strangers. You had to be invited by a regular and even then you never knew when someone might not like the way you walked or talked and would want to roughhouse a bit.

"Bullshit," he mumbled to himself as he crossed 64th Street and walked toward the pharmacy. It was time to let Rostov know he was being followed. Scotty walked into a pharmacy that was nothing more than a home for dirty books just as Rostov walked back out into the cold. Scotty saw the spy from up close. He was older than he looked—

lighter, and tougher. His eyes and brows were dark, his skin tan and drawn.

Rostov seemed to *like* the cold. For a brief moment the two men made eye contact—Rostov giving Scotty the fish eye as he left. The look made Scotty feel like he'd been stripped clean. *He knows*, thought Scotty. *Damn, he* knows! *I'm a trainee and he's a professional spy. Jesus, this man is* out of my league.

Scotty watched Rostov cross Third Avenue and waited until the Soviet continued down 64th Street before he left the warmth of the drugstore and did the same. Rostov then went into the atrium of nearby New York General Hospital and stood mingling in the crowd of patients waiting for their rides to pick them up.

Coming up the street from her unknown hole, somewhere down on the grounds of New York General on York Street, was the 64th Street baglady. Residents along the crosstreets in New York could set their clocks by their baglady. Pushing one or two heavily laden carts, the women would slowly make their way from the grates along the East River up toward Central Park. They were protected not only by their zone of odor but even better by the sounds they projected—shrieking unintelligibly, spewing obscenities at everything and everybody in their way. A baglady could clear space faster than a fart in an elevator. Scotty just shook his head and walked across 64th Street, out of the woman's path.

However, she *was* entertainment. Watching the baglady briefly kept his attention off the cold and the fact that a Soviet agent was standing in the warmth of the hospital atrium, clearly *not* in distress. He was waiting for something or somebody.

Then he remembered the Russian's eyes. Scotty had *no* confidence in his ability to follow the man, if Rostov decided to lose him.

— • —

Aziz awoke from a restless sleep to the raucous sound of New York City getting up for another day. Between two and four there had been a lull in the number of emergency ambulances coming to the hospital, but at four they started to arrive with regularity. At four-thirty the hospital's garbage was picked up with excruciating slowness but with a maximum of noise. From then on the noise, the shouting, the banging all made it impossible to sleep.

By seven o'clock Aziz found himself to be very hungry, but as the Lyden had no restaurant he got dressed and walked out, pausing only to be buzzed by the night clerk still on duty. New York City was a totally alien place, but even so, Aziz had recognized that the city was a perfect place for him and others like him. There were so many different kinds of people . . . and nobody seemed to pay attention to anyone else but himself. People snaked their way along crowded sidewalks with only the narrowest of personal space. New York was a perfect place for the son of an Iranian coastal fishermen, now turned terrorist, to do his business.

Aziz had a natural ability to pick up languages. English and French were the languages of choice for terrorists and Aziz was glad that Khan had made him develop his natural skills. The ability to order a croissant and orange juice in three or four languages, or exchange money correctly without thinking, was a skill highly prized in his business.

At precisely nine-fifty Aziz bundled up and walked out into the grey New York morning a second time. This time he turned right and headed up toward Third Avenue. He was not distracted by the flow of people into and out of the hospital across the street. Aziz did not like sick people, nor did he like to be around them. Sickness was not tolerated in Khan's camp. To be sick was to be weak.

It took Aziz four minutes to walk the short half-block up to Third Avenue then down one block to the Citibank branch at 1062 at the cross of 63rd Street. He waited the extra six minutes until the guard opened the door. As the bank opened, the first flakes of snow fulfilled the grey promise of the morning. Aziz was glad to be inside. He walked to the rear of the bank where a prim secretary fended off and protected bank management from misdirected customers, allowing only those with prearranged business or those with clearly defined needs which only management could resolve to enter the inner sanctum.

"I need to see the bank manager, please," Aziz spoke to the woman, who was nicely dressed in a conservative blue suit and white blouse.

"Do you have an appointment?" she asked, primly.

"No, I need to have an international transfer arranged this morning. Here are my papers."

Aziz handed the secretary the authorization from the Bank of Geneva, the account information, and the list of authorized signatures. The secretary looked at the paper, then at Aziz.

"Please wait here, Mr. Ramsey. I'll get the manager."

The secretary walked to the bank manager's desk which was semi-concealed behind a glass partition. The manager scanned the documents then walked out to meet Aziz, glasses and paper in hand. He shook hands with Aziz.

"How much do you plan to transfer, Mr. Ramsey?"

"Only five hundred thousand . . . today."

The casual delay of the word "today" was not lost on the bank manager.

"How much cash will you need?"

"Not more than two thousand, in traveler's cheques. Fifty and one-hundreds please."

There was much administrivia which had to be done. However, with a half-million-dollar transfer, which would net the bank a tidy sum in interest, Aziz found that much of paperwork was quickly cleared.

"It should take no more than a half-hour to obtain the confirmation from the Bank of Geneva, Mr. Ramsey. Please come into my office and have a seat. Would you like coffee?"

"No thank you, I don't drink coffee," replied Aziz.

"Tea?" the manager asked.

Aziz shook his head no. The manager went about his tasks. At ten-forty-five he came back.

"I believe we're ready, Mr. Ramsey. Here are your traveler's cheques, and these are your bank drafts. Please wire me personally if you would like to arrange another transfer. This is my home telephone and this is our Western Union address," said the manager, handing Aziz his business card.

Aziz pocketed the money, the cheques, and the bank drafts and walked toward the door. Everything was so efficient. He walked back to the Lyden Gardens, took the elevator to his room on the sixth floor, picked up his small case and returned to the checkout where he paid for his night's stay in cash.

It was time to go. There was much to do and just enough time to get it done.

— • —

"What the hell's going on here?" Scotty mumbled, stamping his feet trying to stay warm.

What was Rostov doing? He wasn't on a dead-drop, and he hadn't met anyone. All he'd done was to stand around in the hospital for twenty minutes then walk two blocks, then start back again to the hospital. He'd retraced his steps exactly. It was eleven o'clock, and Scotty was cold. Although his hands were warm, the rest of him was freezing. The area below his coat felt like it was naked to the wind. His coffee stain had frozen before it had evaporated. It was 20 degrees and a fine, light snow blew down through New York City. Miserable weather for man or beast . . . especially man.

What's happening here? Why is Rostov standing over there? Is he trying to trick me?

At that moment Rostov burst through the hospital's double doors and headed down the street.

He has a walkie-talkie! He's tracking someone. He . . . they . . . are following someone. Damn! How could I have been so stupid? thought the young man.

Scotty wasn't stupid, just inexperienced. Rostov headed up 64th Street toward Second Avenue, then, using a garbage truck as a cover, crossed the street and dashed down the northern sidewalk toward Second Avenue. Scotty was on the run now. He had no walkie-talkie.

When Rostov reached Second Avenue, Scotty stayed on the opposite sidewalk. The north-south sidewalks of Second Avenue were crowded with people walking quickly to their midday destinations and waiting for buses.

The light changed and Rostov dashed across toward the pharmacy on the other side, then jumped out into the middle of 64th Street and maneuvered around the construction. Scotty ran for the intersection and hit it just as the lights turned green. The downtown traffic rushed at Scotty. A car stopped, the driver cursed. A cab breezed by, missing him by only inches. A delivery truck bore down on him. He jumped out of the way just in time. When he got to the other side he looked through the snow and saw the courier.

Rostov was following another man, and the man had just gone into a Hertz office. Rostov went to his walkie-talkie, looked down 64th at Scotty's position, then resumed talking. Scotty started to get weak in his legs. Something was happening and it wasn't good. Wherever there is a yellow Hertz sign there seems to be a red Avis and a green National sign—and 64th Street between Third and Second Avenue was no exception.

Scotty's instinct told him he was about to need a car and need one quickly—either that or a cab and a lot of money. His odds were much better going for the car. Catching a cab in New York in the beginning of a snowstorm was nearly impossible. Rostov held his position west of the Hertz desk. Scotty ran for the Avis office.

Inside he was struck by the incredible warmth and the crowd of people waiting in the single line to rent and/or return a car to an overworked and underpaid desk clerk.

There was no time for the social graces.

"I'm with the FBI—I need a car, right now!" Scotty said with unused authority as he bumped the last man in line and barged his way to the front. Outside he could see an undistinguished car pull up, the driver get out, and Rostov take his place in the driver's seat.

Damn! thought Scotty.

"I'm sorry, sir, but you're just going . . ." the clerk started to say.

Scotty banged his fist on the counter, leaned over and snapped his wallet out. His very official FBI badge flapped open and his very, very upset voice shut up everyone in the room.

"My name is Coldsmith and I'm with the FBI. I'm in pursuit of a criminal and I want the next car out of the garage! And I want it now!"

Scotty grabbed the contract and the keys from the woman's hand, turned to his left and went through the glass door to the garage.

"Where's this car?" he shouted to the attendant while flashing his badge.

The attendant pointed to the car directly in front of the garage doors. Scotty got in, fired up the red Mustang, and revved the engine.

"Open the god-damned doors!" he shouted at the attendant.

The attendant looked at the clerk, who gave a nod of approval just as Scotty shouted in final anger, *"If you don't open the door, I'm going to drive right through!"*

The door rose just in time for Scotty to see Rostov accelerating up 64th Street in a black Buick Century. Scotty peeled after him, his rear tires bouncing and slamming over the curb. He kept his eyes on Rostov who had just crossed over First Avenue heading for York.

The light turned yellow well before Scotty got to the intersection and was red when he ran the light, horn blasting. The northbound traffic on First slammed to a stop as Scotty bounced through the pot-holed intersection bounding after his prey. He still had no idea whom they were following. Rostov was after someone and he was after Rostov. And, someone else was working with Rostov.

The snow appeared to come down a bit harder as the two cars turned right onto the less-travelled York Avenue and headed toward downtown. The pause in traffic was temporary as Rostov turned right and followed what appeared to be a dark blue Cutlass onto the lower deck of the Queensboro Bridge.

Rostov bore into the left lane as the Queensboro divided on the east side of the East River. Here the major artery, which led out of what many would call the world's most important city, simply ended in the borough of Queens, tucked under the steel girders of the elevated bridge. Unlike Manhattan, Queens appeared at first glance to be a semi-normal city.

Led by a seemingly uncaring blue Cutlass, Scotty followed Rostov out Northern Avenue past the Ronzoni macaroni plant and eventually found a left onto the Brooklyn-Queens Expressway and a right to the Grand Central Parkway. The merging traffic at Boody and 30th was heavy. Rostov piled through it, but Scotty yielded to the exiting cars.

When Rostov turned onto the bridge he had knowingly violated the terms of the diplomatic agreement between the Soviet Union and the United States. Up until that moment Rostov had been a diplomat. Now he had *officially* become an agent, a spy . . . an enemy of the United States.

Now what? wondered Scotty. *Pick him up or let him go? Who is the guy in the blue Cutlass? Why is Rostov following him? What am I going to do?*

SOUTHERN CONNECTICUT

Rostov cracked the corners of his chapped lips in a self-satisfied smile. The FBI agent had rented a car from Avis, therefore he had no communications with the outside world. Yes, he would have the license number of this car, but so what? All Rostov would have to do is make a switch and get another car. The woman was out there someplace.

I guess it's good I'm not alone, Rostov thought to himself. And, the thought of a close encounter with the long-legged attaché was a pleasant one.

Scotty had skillfully followed Rostov out of the city, past the stadium with the incomprehensible orange and blue sign "Baseball like it oughta be." Rostov knew English fairly well, but the word "oughta" made no sense. The roads around New York were in terrible condition, as was the traffic. Following al-As was easy. The terrorist seemed to have no idea he was being tailed, so Rostov could keep track of him well in the rear.

Does the young FBI agent know I am following someone? Probably, he thought as he drove over the potholed grey Whitestone Bridge. One of the three lanes was under construction, which made for very slow going. He paid his toll, and bore off to I-95 to New England. This was the America he had seen on Soviet television. Junk. Deterioration. Trash littered the poor highway; bits and pieces of worn tires made an obstacle course of the remaining good lanes. At bridge undercrossings the left lane was closed more often than not because of construction. In many places lanes appeared to be permanently closed because they were dangerous. There was too much to be repaired.

Yes, New York and the surrounding area reaffirmed Rostov's feelings toward the United States and the superiority of the Soviet system. This was a nation of decay. New York's polyglot population had to make synergism of the nation's will impossible. A nation's strength was in unity. If New York typified the United States then Soviet domination was inevitable. The decay was obvious.

North of New Haven Rostov got a buzz on his CB.

"I have you both. I also see al-As. Back off and let me follow him," came the female voice.

It was Tambov. He looked in his rearview mirror but couldn't pick out which car she was in. Rostov smiled.

The smile was short-lived.

At exit 70 on the east bank of the Connecticut River, al-As and the blue Cutlass exited.

"He's getting off!" said Katrina. "I'm behind you both. I'm going to have to lay back."

Rostov enjoyed the hunt. It had been easy to follow on the freeway unobstructed. Now surveillance would be more difficult. Driving with his left hand Rostov opened a map of the area with his right, trying to locate where al-As was headed. The Long Island Sound was to their right. They were in a low-lying tidal delta area at the mouth of the Connecticut River, state highway 156. Up ahead were several possibilities to lose the FBI, thought Rostov. This must be a summer resort area of some kind, although it was difficult to tell. It was also difficult to tell why al-As had pulled off the main highway onto this back road.

They crossed over a set of railroad tracks and passed a place called Kelly's Silo Inn. A picture-perfect white scene opened up as Rostov came out of the snow shower and into sunlight. To his right, at the mouth of the river, was a white lighthouse out on a sand spit with snow-colored seagulls flying lazily overhead waiting for their next meal.

"Are you ready to pick up al-As?" asked Rostov.

"Yes. It will be no problem. He has no idea the three of us are back here. Your young FBI agent knows nothing of me, as well."

"There are two roads up ahead which appear to lead back to the interstate. I will lose him at one of the two. What kind of distance does this frequency have?"

There was a pause.

"I don't know," replied Katrina Tambov. "What do you think he is doing."

"I don't have the slightest idea."

She sounded as if she was in the back seat.

"I'm going to take the second road that leads back to the highway. I will go east. It appears as if al-As will continue on this road along the coast, at least to New London. If I lose the agent, I will monitor the exits along the highway and meet you near exit 84. It is vital you follow al-As."

"You don't need to tell me my job, Comrade Rostov," came the cold reply. "What do you plan to do with the American agent?"

"I will kill him, of course."

MOSCOW

"I don't know. I will try to find out. What was said was between the two of them. Qaddafi was overheard shouting once—something about bombs. My men were unable to understand the whole conversation. Khan also at one point raised his voice, but it seemed as if he were berating the Colonel. But, I . . . we . . . think an agreement has been reached. Khan is not a frequent visitor here. He does not get along with Arafat or Arafat's lieutenants."

The speaker was Major Alexei Vilyev, chief Soviet attaché to Muammar el-Qaddafi, responsible for all direct contact between the Colonel and official Moscow. While the outside world might consider Libya to be a puppet state of the Soviet Union, no one in Vilyev's office or in the Politburo considered it so. Vilyev was at the top of the Soviet organization in Libya. He controlled the eight-hundred-fifty-eight Soviet "advisors." Most were Red Army technicians, aviators, instructors, and heavy equipment maintenance supervisors who had dotted-line responsibility to Vilyev but who received orders from, and reported to, Moscow. Vilyev was KGB.

On the other end of the phone line, overlooking frozen Dzerzhinsky Square and a thirty-eight inch accumulation of snow, was Major General Gregori Bodnof, Vilyev's direct supervisor and head of the First Directorate. Of the four major Directorates, the First had complete responsibility for all KGB activities outside the Soviet Union, including assassination, infiltration, disinformation, and sabotage. The other Directorates and Departments, with the bulk of the KGB's manpower, dealt with the internal security of the Soviet Union. Bodnof reported to Viktor Chebrikov, First Commissioner and head of the KGB and a long-time winner in the brutally tough Communist politics. Chebrikov had risen to the top job after Andropov left it to assume overall power, taking his job.

In 1985, and the years since, Secretary-General Gorbachev had gradually streamlined the top-heavy organization within the Kremlin and had greatly reduced his span of control. Departments were consolidated, duplicate functions eliminated. The one department Gorbachev had been unable to reorganize was the KGB. From almost all viewpoints the attempt had been very painful.

Since assuming power, Gorbachev had tried without success to split off the First Directorate from the KGB and have the operations controlled by his hand-picked successor Eduard Shevardnadze, foreign minister. What Gorbachev wanted was for the ambassador to a nation to be the one in charge of all operations, including all aspects of spying. Instead, the ambassador reported to Foreign Minister Shevardnadze, while the KGB officer reported up to Chebrikov through Bodnof's First Directorate. Thus in a foreign embassy, the KGB officer had responsibility for monitoring "internal" security and at the same time ran the external networks of spies within the country. Oftentimes the KGB officer and the ambassador or his staff were at odds over mission and objectives. It was a wasteful use of men and materials.

"Did you say bombs?" asked Bodnof.

The built-in propagation delay, forced by taking land line signals, converting them through encryption devices, then sending them to a COSMOS satellite, then re-converting the signal in reverse at KGB HQ, made the pause in the communications even more pronounced.

"I . . . we . . . believe that Qaddafi has assembled a limited number of low-grade atomic weapons, and has given some of them to Khan," returned the attaché through the static of the connection.

"Given?" replied Bodnof.

"Bad choice of words. Qaddafi would not 'give' anything. If there has been a trade, it has been to his advantage, for sure. If Qaddafi has indeed gained atomic weapons, and in turn negotiated with Khan, then Khan is on a mission of destruction that is beyond the scale of anything any rebel or misfit of his ilk has ever tried. Whatever he is attempting, it is very, very dangerous. The repercussions could be global."

"Thank you, Major. We are aware of the implications. You will call me directly with any information, no matter how insignificant it may seem," replied Bodnof.

Bodnof hung up. Chebrikov would want to know where Khan and his men were. Coded bulletins were sent by courier or encrypted transmissions to all Soviet embassies and field agents.

> URGENT TO ALL FIELD PERSONNEL. TRACK AND
> REPORT WEHREABOUTS OF ALL KNOWN MEMBERS
> OF IRANIAN REBEL ZAID ABU KHAN. TOP PRIORITY.
> MAINTAIN SURVEILLANCE.

SOUTHERN CONNECTICUT

"What is this son-of-a-bitch doing?" mumbled Scotty.

It wasn't really a question. Scotty knew what Rostov was doing. He was following that blue car which was a quarter mile ahead. But why was the blue Cutlass taking the scenic route in the middle of a snowstorm? Scotty didn't mind the snow so much—after all he'd grown up where the winters were six months long—it was the vehicle he drove that made him nervous.

Out West he was used to driving trucks; the four-wheel lane-eaters, the kind that came with a gun rack, a slobbery dog, optional baseball cap, six-pack of Bud, and a pretty sandy-haired girl with freckles. Not that Scotty was ever a yahoo—but he could have been. It would have been easy. Not that such a life would have been so bad—it was just that it would have been too hard to leave the Cowboy Bar and Grill routine once a few years had passed.

Scotty, Rostov and the blue Cutlass passed a Chevron station on the left, then slowed down for what Scotty thought was a restaurant in Old

Lyme, but which turned out to be the police station that housed the resident state trooper.

Should he stop? *Damn, damn, damn! Make a decision, Coldsmith... make a decision ... too late. You'll regret it.*

The three cars passed the station, slowly passed a closed George's Seafood, then suddenly hit a stretch of twisty road . . . and a patch of the snowshower.

Waitaminute! Damn . . . waitaminute!

"You son of a . . ." Scotty mumbled.

The black Buick had accelerated down and around a bend in the road, then up over the next hill. He was out of sight in an instant. He'd been daydreaming! Scotty got to the top only to see the next bend and no black Buick.

Jesus, how could he have lost . . .

He came over a hill and could see a marked intersection ahead with the familiar blue and red interstate sign, directions to I-95 and the Connecticut Turnpike. There was the blue Cutlass! But where was the goddamned Buick? Where was Rostov? *God-damn, god-damn!* Scotty swore to himself as he hit the wheel of his rental car with the palm of his hand.

Should he try and follow? Go back and . . . and do what? Tell some Connecticut trooper that a Soviet agent is on the loose?

Follow the Cutlass was his only choice.

"Follow the Cutlass, jerk," he berated himself.

He'd lost Rostov. Just like that, he'd lost the agent. It was so easy. *What a jerk I am,* he thought.

Rostov was out here following the blue Cutlass. This is the same guy Rostov was following in New York City. Scotty squinted through the white glare of the no-sunset afternoon. He couldn't read the license plate. At least he had had the presence of mind to jot down the plate of Rostov's car . . . big deal . . . it was probably a diplomat car. So what? So what if it was found? Even with Rostov in it . . . is the State Department going to deport someone because he took a drive to Connecticut?

But Scotty's gut feeling was that there was something here which could be out of the ordinary. Rostov was following someone. Rostov did have some help. Scotty looked in his rearview mirror. Was there something back there? It was hard to see. No, probably not, was his inexperienced opinion.

NAGS HEAD, NORTH CAROLINA

The trip odometer on Khalid Rahman's powder blue Ford Fairmont read 586 miles as he pulled into the nearly empty parking lot of the Armada Hotel, located in Nags Head at the entrance to the Cape Hatteras National Seashore on the Outer Banks. The air smelled of damp salt, and there was a cool ocean breeze. The breeze was crisp on his cheeks as he got out of the car and closed his eyes for a few seconds to let the wind wake him up. It felt good after the terrible day he'd had. He was very tired, depressingly so, even more so than he wanted to admit—and this was only the start of the journey, the single most important operation ever attempted by the Jihad, certainly by Zaid abu Khan. The mission was historic.

It must be jet-lag, he thought. *No, it's probably from the concentration of having to navigate in the land of my enemy. Everything is so different.*

The trip had started well. He had arrived in Atlanta at eight, cleared customs, and had no difficulty in renting a car. He had stayed at a nearby Days Inn motel and had relished the feeling of elation of having beaten the Americans at his entry. They were such fools. They were always looking for drugs. He wore a nondescript but clean jacket and slacks, a light coat, and carried only one small suitcase filled with the usual things of travel. There had been no question about his length of stay or his destination, which of course had been false.

His confidence took an emotional toboggan ride when at 8:30 this morning he started his drive through Atlanta. Atlantans laugh over the tale of the five pigs let loose in what is now central Atlanta and the mad dash of the city roadbuilders to follow the pigs with the construction of roads. The city is a nearly incomprehensible patchwork of one-way streets which defy logical direction, layout, and naming. Directions of "north" "south" "east" and "west" have no meaning in Atlanta, not in a city where roads bend, turn and most often run northeast-southwest or southeast-northwest.

Faced with a self-imposed deadline of conducting his banking business and getting on the road by eleven, Rahman found himself in the middle of the never-ending construction of Interstates 75 and 85 through the city. Based on the premise that no freeway will be built unless it is already obsolete, Atlantans have for the last thirty years faced interminable construction delays and have created the twenty-four-hour rush hour.

Even though his map was marked with his destination, it took Rahman nearly two hours to find his way through the Atlanta maze to the Bank of Georgia. By then, he was in a foul mood. Luckily for him, and probably for those in the bank as well, he received excellent service, and he held his composure long enough to complete his transactions. But it was noon before he managed to negotiate his way back to the roller-coaster-like interstate and head north past the Georgia Tech campus and the multi-storied Varsity Grill.

Leaving Atlanta Rahman's spirts started to rise again as he drove north on I-85 through rural Georgia and South Carolina. The road was good, the countryside beautiful, and the prospect of delivering a blow to this obnoxiously proud nation was very pleasing to him.

The most difficult part of the journey is over. Once inside the country it will be child's play to execute Khan's plan . . . whatever it might be, thought the Iranian.

By late afternoon Rahman entered the populated sections of North Carolina. The interstate highway became older and more heavily used. The expansion belts in the concrete, now contracted by the winter's cold, made the ride rough and bumpy. Construction between Greensboro and Raleigh made the ride even worse. But the most tiring part of Rahman's day was the last 190 miles, mostly driven over two-lane highway—and in the dark. The going was slow, and Rahman had to be extra careful to obey the speed limits in every small village along the way. On the open road it was easy . . . but passing through the back-country towns took extra attention. He didn't want to be stopped by some local patrolman—and end up having to kill him.

It was nearly ten when he crossed over the McIntyre Bridge which connected the mainland with Roanoke Island and the city of Manteo. The city of two thousand was sound asleep . . . its lights long since turned to blinking yellow. Rahman continued over the low-lying Baum Causeway from Roanoke Island to the town of Nags Head on one of the fragile barrier islands which make up the Outer Banks.

The night clerk was dozing in the small office behind the registration desk and seemed to resent the intrusion of a paying customer. Rahman registered quickly and let the boy continue his sloth. The room was well-appointed but the smell of the ocean was pervasive. Rahman opened the sliding doors with difficulty, their runners rusted with salt accumulation and caked with fine grains of sand. In an instant the room was filled with the cold air. Leaving the door open, Rahman undressed until he was naked, then got into bed. Within minutes the temperature in the room was a brisk 35 degrees and Rahman was asleep.

NIANTIC, CONNECTICUT

From her bundled vantage point in the Dodge Caravan, Katrina had seen the snow stop falling at two in the morning. She had barely been able to keep awake, especially knowing that Rostov was warm and sleeping on a comfortable bed in the Rocky Neck Motel, only four miles away on highway 156. Rostov had changed shifts with her at one-thirty. He seemed impervious to the cold.

"Nothing, they are both asleep," she had said.

"Keep your radio close by, comrade," Rostov had replied. "We will have to leave on short notice."

"I will sleep with it," she had said, giving her seat to Rostov while stepping out into the snow-covered street.

The black embassy Buick softly idled behind the van. It promised warmth and sleep. Rostov didn't answer her statement but thought of the walkie-talkie under her nightdress and how warm it would be, tucked between . . .

Snap out of it, Rostov! How long had it been? He had been too busy for anything more than a whore for the last three years. The last one had been in December, the week before the New Year's celebration, the week of the Christian Christmas. He remembered because he'd beaten her badly when she failed to perform *exactly* what he'd wanted. He'd gotten into an unreasonable rage, one which was brought on by one of his irregular and infrequent bouts with the bottle. He'd hit her hard, knocked her to the floor, and kicked her several times. The sight of her almost naked body writhing in pain, unable to scream, but able to try and squirm away across the rug had finally driven him to erotic excitement. He had caught her, ripped off her panties, and raped her from behind . . . although it was difficult to see how a whore could be raped. He had left her lying on the floor crouched in a semi-fetal state and had casually flipped her payment onto the floor beside her as he left.

This hadn't been the first time. Although Rostov realized this was irregular behavior, certainly abhorrent to many, he simply didn't care. He had to periodically clean his body and mind of misdirected energy and beating up on whores was his way.

He doubted if he could dominate a woman such as Tambov, although the attempt would certainly be worth the effort.

Rostov's mind did not linger on the thoughts of Tambov's warmth, but instead went to that of the FBI agent and Arab terrorist sleeping in a small inn in a small American village on the cold coast of Connecticut.

Why was Aziz al-As here? Where was Khalid Rahman? And where was Bafq el-Rashid?

At six-thirty the sun came up and the young FBI agent came out of the inn. He cleared off his car, warmed it up, and drove around the block to a point only four hundred yards from Rostov's van.

"Wake up, Tambov. It's time to go to work," he radioed to his partner.

"I'm on my way," came her quick and surprisingly alert response.

She was like him. One of the things which had made him successful was his ability to sleep when the opportunity arose. Rostov could sleep on the edge of consciousness and awake as if he was still in mid-stride, his senses fully honed, his wits about him. It was a talent which had saved his life several times and undoubtedly would do so again. Apparently Tambov had the same body clock. Although it didn't change his opinion about working with a woman, nothing he'd seen in her so far had made their partnership unworkable. If it had, he would have killed her rather than risk losing al-As. But everything she'd done so far was professional and clean.

At seven-thirty al-As came out of the inn and was momentarily blinded by the reflecting sunlight on the new snow. From behind his sunglasses Rostov could hardly believe what he was seeing. The Arab seemed oblivious even to the possibility that someone might be following him, much less a small caravan. Whatever Khan was planning he certainly was doing it with inexperienced help.

By eight o'clock al-As was back on Interstate 95. A half-mile behind him was the FBI agent, followed by Rostov, then Katrina Tambov in the black embassy Buick. There was a reasonable amount of traffic, including the usual number of trucks, enough that the pleasant ride through the beautiful Connecticut countryside would make the multiple surveillance possible without much effort.

This parade can't go on much longer without being noticed, thought Rostov. *The FBI agent needs to be put away.*

NAGS HEAD

Jacques Marmande had failed to do two things that he had promised René Chatillion he would do: report the presence of Khalid Rahman to the U.S. Customs Service, and update his superior with his location. Not only could he have done them both, he should have. The "should-have" feeling nagged him as he patiently followed Khalid Rahman around the American coastal communities. But his pride—his ego—prevented him from doing what he promised he would do and what as an INTERPOL inspector he was trained to do.

The Americans should have been notified.

Three days earlier Marmande had sat in his Paris office, wading through the four-inch case jackets containing the backgrounds and known crimes of Zaid Abu Khan, Khalid Rahman, Fazluh el-Bakr and several other leaders of what INTERPOL and European governments thought was the heart of the various Jihad movements. The more he looked the angrier he got.

Why was Bandar, an Arab terrorist linked to Zaid abu Khan, entering through Marseille customs like a normal person? It wasn't their routine. It was out of order. Criminals were remarkably consistent and rarely changed habits. Marmande had been successful in his career by capitalizing on his ability to establish the routines and habits of his cases. This one didn't make sense. And the fact that it didn't make sense was significant to Marmande. Something out of the ordinary was happening. The problem was, he didn't have the slightest clue what it was.

And then the terrorist was killed in the Marseille jail after Marmande had taken charge. *Nobody kills someone in my charge,* he thought. The police captain had railed at him, made him look foolish. Unfortunately, he was right. It was an embarrassment. Jacques Marmande did not like to be made the fool. He had personally taken the lawyer back to Bandar's holding cell, then left him alone while he went back to check on the lawyer's identity. Less than ten minutes later the prisoner was dead and the lawyer gone.

Why was the man killed? Bandar was a soldier, nothing more. Marmande scribbled down a list of words on his desk-sized pad. Revenge. War. Secrets. Who killed him? He jotted down another list. Israeli. Khan. Personal vendetta. ? It was the "?" that bothered him. Who would go to the effort to kill a minor terrorist? My God, the risk! Whatever the reason, the man posing as a lawyer had taken a tremendous risk to walk into a well-guarded police station and assassinate a man in broad daylight.

What would have happened to Bandar? He would have been in jail for a good long time. His dossier was well documented. If the Israelis could have tied him into any of their hundreds of other bombings he would have been extradited then executed. But even though the French government had changed its ways, the process of the law was slow. Bandar would have stayed in Marseille for a long time. But then again, the Israelis were a patient lot. If they wanted him, there would be little nationalistic self-satisfaction in murdering the terrorist in a foreign prison. No, the current government in Jerusalem would need a bigger show and tell. Marmande scratched "Israeli" off his list. A personal vendetta against the terrorist was unlikely. Marmande also circled the "?". An outside force, which at the time didn't or wouldn't make any sense, was always a possibility. He went back to Bandar. Why was the man in Marseille, and why was he dressed in the clothes of a business-man?

Terrorists don't take vacations. Marmande wrote another list. Messenger. Mission. ? In this case the "?" was the least likely. Bandar was either taking a message to somebody or he was on a mission. If "mission" was correct then it was likely there were others involved. If "messenger" was correct then where was he going?

Marmande wrote down Destination? Marseille. Paris. Geneva. Spain. The list would be too long and not meaningful. He scratched the list.

Marmande subconsciously ran a hand under his armpit and over the medium-sized roll at his waist. His overweight was not due to lack of exercise, but due to his fondness for wine. One of these days he'd quit smoking, too. He'd been hooked on American Winstons for the last ten years, almost two packs a day. Filthy habit. But none of his habits prevented Jacques Marmande from being one of the best detectives in INTERPOL.

At forty-eight Marmande had risen as far as he'd wanted to. The next level was captain and he didn't want it. The extra pay wasn't worth the headaches. Being a captain meant sitting behind a desk and having to listen to everyone's complaints. Captains don't solve crimes, they stay in their offices and administer. Inspectors investigate. He might be a bit puffy around the waist and cheeks, but he still was one damn good inspector.

"Francine, bring me the other folders please," he asked his secretary.

"Do you want them all?" she said with resignation, fully knowing what the answer would be.

"Yes, thank you."

It took several trips and a half hour, but by the time she finished, Marmande's desk was covered with blue and red folders, some were on the floor, some seemingly abandoned in the nearby comfy easy chair. Marmande was in full motion. He ripped through the jackets, each a known member of the Islamic Jihad, removing good photos, and noting the names. There were different reports, but most people agreed upon the number eight hundred as the number of active Arab terrorists in various training camps in Libya and Lebanon. No one knew how many terrorists used Iran as a base. The faces in the photos all had the same burning look of committed hatred in their eyes. Most had a moustache and/or a beard and would look like completely different people without them. And these were only the ones with dossiers! There was no way to keep up with them. In the long run they would get what they wanted. Wars of attrition were like that. They had the backing and mission and purpose of their religion. He only had the backing of the European police. There was a big difference in commitment.

Marmande's boss, and INTERPOL's Chief Inspector, was René Chatillion. Marmande had spent nearly two hours debriefing him. It had been painful. Marmande was good and Chatillion knew it, but this had been a blunder. The Marseille chief of police had captured an Arab terrorist. True, he had been lucky, but luck was something never remembered after the fact. The chief could have connected the terrorist Bandar to anything, tied him to any number of unsolved crimes of terror. The slate could have been cleaned on cases which were unlikely to be solved but for political reasons he was unable not to close the book. Unsolvable acts of terrorism stole valuable detective time. Capturing Ysed Bandar had presented the chief with an opportunity to tie the terrorist to many of his worst outstanding cases. But a dead terrorist could not be questioned or go to trial. It had been INTERPOL's fault. What had made it worse was that the chief had waited nearly five hours for Marmande to get to Marseille from Paris. Then in less than a half hour the terrorist was dead and his murderer was gone! Not only had he escaped, but Marmande, the Great INTERPOL Inspector, hadn't been able to come up with a clue. Marmande had been quick to leave. The longer he might have stayed the worse would have been his blame.

Marmande's dark thoughts were interrupted by a young officer who knocked first but entered without stopping. In his hand was a crumpled copy of the composite photo. His face showed wide-eyed enthusiasm.

"Sir! Inspector Marmande! They've found one of your suspects!" the young man exclaimed.

"Where?" asked Marmande, getting up from his old chair.

"At De Gaulle, not more than fifteen minutes ago. They've followed your instructions and not detained him."

"Where at De Gaulle?" pressed Marmande.

"Delta Airlines. It's this man."

The crumpled copy landed upside down on Marmande's desk with the picture of Khalid Rahman circled in red. Marmande grabbed it, then snapped orders.

"Don't do anything to make him suspicious. I want that flight delayed. I want a first-class aisle seat and I don't care if someone gets bumped. But I want it done quietly! Understand? Move!"

The young detective moved. Marmande shouted after him.

"Where is the flight headed?"

"Atlanta," he shouted back to Marmande.

Atlanta? In the U.S.?

Marmande unlocked the top drawer of his four-drawer filing cabinet and, like a magician pulling a rabbit from a hat, came up with a mid-sized airline travel bag. Placing it near his coat and scarf, he walked outside, then down the hallway toward René Chatillion's office. On the way he stopped at his secretary's desk.

"Francine, get a helicopter ready for me in five minutes. I need to get to De Gaulle. Delta. They are delaying the flight. I need some American dollars. Two hundred will do."

Marmande checked his wallet. American Express. VISA. A few Francs. While she called for the helicopter, Marmande pointed to Chatillion's office.

"Is anyone in with him?" he asked.

Francine shook her head no as Marmande knocked and entered.

"They've found one of my men. It's Khalid Rahman. He's boarded a flight to America, to Atlanta on Delta. I'm going to follow him."

It was a statement, not a question. No approval was being asked for, although it would be granted.

"Khalid Rahman? Have the Americans been notified?" asked Chatillion.

"No, not yet. There isn't time. I'll notify them when I reach the United States. I don't want the FBI simply picking him up. Rahman and this Bandar are both Zaid Khan's men. I don't know why or how, but I know Bandar's killer is connected to Rahman. Somebody is following these Arabs, and it's my murderer."

"Jacques, you must notify the Americans," replied Chatillion.

"I will, René, but that man was my prisoner and he was killed. It was my fault. The killer could be Israeli, Libyan, German, or MI5 for all we know. I don't care. No one kills someone in my charge. René, I've got a feeling about this. This Arab is my only link to the killer."

Francine came to the edge of the doorway with two folders. Marmande saw her and waved her in. She gave Marmande the money and

Rahman's blue INTERPOL folder. Marmande pocketed the money and quickly rifled through the folder. After a minute he gave the folder back to Francine.

"The helicopter is here, Jacques," she said.

"René, I'm going to find my killer. Please don't notify the Americans. Trust me on this one. Please let me get this man. I'll tell the FBI when I find him. I will, really."

Marmande turned around and hurried toward the door.

"I'll let you know where I am," were his last words before the elevator doors closed.

Marmande inserted a key into the elevator's lock. He was now express-bound for the roof. In less than 30 seconds he was through the door and into the bitter cold February afternoon. The helicopter was ready. Ducking down, he ran for the opened passenger side door and slid in next to the pilot. The helicopter flew off backwards and up, and in an instant was above the beautiful city's skyline headed on a ten-minute flight to De Gaulle airport.

For a moment Marmande's mind was lost in the sight of the city—his city. He'd flown these kinds of flights before, and every time he thought the same thought. Was this the last time he'd see Paris?

No, of course not. He'd be back. But the thought wasn't convincing. He didn't feel right about this one.

"Don't be stupid, Jacques . . . you don't believe in premonitions," he mumbled softly to himself.

— • —

In Nags Head, Marmande's feeling of dread had been replaced by fatigue. As he studied his map, he could see that Rahman had done the same. The land called the Outer Banks consisted of a barrier island as wide as three miles and as narrow as several hundred yards running one hundred fifty miles from the suburbs of Virginia Beach south to Cape Hatteras, then southeast for another sixty miles back to the mainland. At Cape Hatteras the Outer Banks were twenty-five miles from the mainland out into the Atlantic Ocean. From Virginia Beach the land went unbroken through the North Carolina summer resort cities of Kitty Hawk, Kill Devil Hills, and Nags Head. South of Nags Head the land was owned by the U.S. Department of the Interior in the form of the Cape Hatteras National Seashore.

— • —

While Marmande had spent a restless night and awoke feeling incredibly disoriented, Rahman came down at seven-thirty, ate a leisurely breakfast, read the Tuesday edition of the *Coastland Times*, then proceeded to drive around for the next three hours as if he was just another tourist. Marmande knew the man was simply doing what needed to be done; the first thing one does when in a foreign country is to get the lay of the land. While there wasn't much to cover, Rahman was very thorough. He drove north on Beach Road the full eighteen miles from Nags Head to Kitty Hawk, stopping every few miles to make notes of this and that. The road was very poor, obviously battered from ocean overwash and simple neglect.

Rahman stopped in several stores but bought nothing. Each time he left he spent a few minutes furiously scribbling notes to himself on a small pad. Seemingly satisfied, he crossed the causeway to Roanoke Island and turned left at the first traffic signal. Marmande looked at the map. There was only one road on this part of the island so there was no need to tail him tightly. The road snaked its way past the outdated water pumping plant and a radio station. The land was marshy on both sides of the road. After two miles, Marmande entered the fishing village of Wanchese. In an attempt to vitalize the fishing industry in North Carolina the state government had pumped in nearly ten million dollars to provide the fishermen with a Seafood Industrial Park, a place where fishermen could dock, offload their fish directly into packing plants, and get repairs when needed. It was nearly deserted.

There were no more than ten or twelve local fishermen, proud families who had fished the waters off the North Carolina coastline for two hundred years. The idea behind the park had been to provide the northern fishermen with a good place to base their operations in the winter months when it was too cold to fish up north. The idea had been good, but the execution had been poor. The nearest open water to the Atlantic was through Oregon Inlet. Even with constant dredging it was nearly impossible to keep a clear channel through the inlet, a channel deep enough for 82-foot trawlers. Too many boats had been lost, shoaled on the shifting sandbars of Oregon Inlet—so many that the northern fishermen no longer used Wanchese as a port.

Marmande slowly drove through the dying village; one eye searching for the blue Fairmont, the other on the town itself. Most of the homes were the tidewater type; clapboard built on above-ground cinderblock base, a tin roof, a front porch grooved with the path of many years of wear and tear, and littering the front and side yards were the dead bodies of every car ever owned in the family, the parts long since stripped for use elsewhere. Elegant weeping willows were mixed with the tall sycamores.

The fishing village was a mess of old and new. Everything was used until it either rusted out or was broken, then abandoned where it last lay. Old fishing boats were simply left in the last slip they were docked, some sank in the harbor, others were destined to follow when their hulls rusted through. Only three or four fishing companies seemed to survive.

Marmande parked his car, got out and walked around the side of one of the fishing companies. To his left was the trawler *The Wancheseman*. Across the channel was the freshly painted green and yellow Army sidecaster dredge *The City of Newport News*. Most of the slips along both sides of the channel were empty. Further down the channel to his left was the boat repair facility. It, too, was empty. Finally he spotted the blue Fairmont near the harbormaster's building, and in a few minutes out came Rahman.

This is no tourist, thought Marmande as he hurried back to his car. Khalid Rahman was setting up a base camp.

WANCHESE, NORTH CAROLINA

"My name is George Dijon and I represent clients who would like to use this port as a base for a research project," said Rahman to the white-bearded harbormaster.

"Research project, you say?" he questioned. "We don't get many research boats down here. Get a few treasure hunters, though. You wouldn't be one of those, would you?" he quizzed.

"It doesn't look like space is a problem here," returned Rahman, ignoring the harbormaster's probe.

The old man saw that he wasn't going to get meat on his hook, but at the same time he didn't get a denial from the foreigner. He let it drop.

"How long do you want and how much are you bringing in?"

"Several months. Our first boat should be here within two weeks. Just to be safe, I think we should have space for all three."

"Three . . ." repeated the harbormaster.

"Yes . . . we'll be offloading a lot of equipment, then there's the surveillance boat, the supply boat . . . they'll be coming later."

"What's the name of the boat?" he asked.

"I don't know who will be first. I'll let you know later this week."

Rahman signed the paper, paid for a month in advance, then left. It was only the first day and already things seemed to be moving well. He smiled as he left.

The next step was to get out of the hotel and create a base camp. There was much to acquire, much more than he wanted to move into and out of a hotel room. He needed to rent a house.

Renting a house on the Outer Banks in February was not a problem. There were plenty of homes. By the end of the day Rahman had a four-bedroom, two-bath, oceanfront home in South Nags Head, three blocks south of the Armada hotel and only six miles from Wanchese. He had been very specific about getting a home with a telephone and about not being near people. There were no renters within four homes on either side of Rahman.

Yes, things were going well.

NEW BEDFORD, MASSACHUSETTS

How long was this going to go on?

So far Scotty had learned almost nothing about the man he was trailing. The man's name was John Ramsey. He seemed to have a penchant for taking the slow road to nowhere. This wasn't the time of year people visited Rhode Island and the coastline of Connecticut and Massachusetts. Yet Ramsey had gone into almost every small village along the coastline, sometimes parking his car and walking about the towns as if he was sizing them up for a purchase. The two-and-a-half-hour trip from Niantic to New Bedford had taken all day.

Where was Rostov? Scotty felt uneasy not knowing where the Russian agent was.

You never wanted to admit to a hunch unless it panned out. He hadn't wanted to talk to Murphy Monahan, but he didn't have any choice. When Ramsey had stopped for breakfast in the beautiful village of Mystic, he'd had a chance to call in.

"Connecticut? What the hell are you doing in Connecticut, Cold-smith?" said Monahan, not angrily.

Monahan knew the task was difficult, nearly impossible. The Soviet had been an active agent, apparently sent on some specific job. There was no way a trainee would be able to keep up with an experienced KGB agent.

"What should I do, Mr. Monahan?" asked Scotty.

Monahan looked out into the chaos of his organization. He had experienced agents working sixteen hour shifts, seven days a week. The morale of his squads was somewhere between exhaustion and resignation. His turnover rate was twice the national average and there was nothing he could do about it. He needed more men, more equipment, and more authority to kick ass. Instead, he had to deal with the cost-cutting political bullshit of Congress and the bureaucrats within the Hoover Building in Washington, staffs manned by former agents, who once they got a taste of the high-profile work, seemed to forget where they came from and what the mission of the agency was. The FBI was a vital national resource, but it seemed that when good agents went to HQ they automatically got sucked up into the bureaucracy and national politics of the city. New computer equipment always went to HQ first, never the field. But it was the agent in Omaha, or Albany, or Portland who needed the god-damned computer. It was the field agent who needed quicker access to computer data and communications with other computers—not some HQ staffie who used it to do calculator work. HQ just didn't understand—or worse, didn't care.

"Go ahead, Coldsmith . . . follow your hunch. But I can't afford to send anyone to help you. Do the best you can," said Monahan with a resigned sigh.

"Yes, sir."

Scotty had spent the rest of the day tailing Ramsey up the Connecticut coastline into Rhode Island and finally into Massachusetts, with side visits to Misquamicut, Quonochontaug, Narragansett, Sakonnet, Acoaxet, Nonquitt and other wonderfully unpronounceable villages. He watched the bare oaks and maples of Connecticut turn to the dark green evergreens of Rhode Island and Massachusetts. With the new snow the countryside was quite beautiful.

At dusk they arrived at New Bedford—a city in deep, deep trouble. Divided by Interstate 195, to the north was the old section of town, rich with Greek and Basque heritages. To the south were the wharves and the heart of the New England fishing industry. The abandoned build ings, mostly of carefully laid stone, told a story of what could have been. They provided a perfect but eerie backdrop for New Bedford's last attempt at self-preservation.

The town had had more than its share of grief in the last twenty years and had ridden an emotional rollercoaster as interest rates drove the family fishermen out of their historic business and into "tenant" fishing for large corporations. As larger and larger trawlers fished the Atlantic beds the New Bedford fishermen were forced to purchase bigger and bigger trawlers, which by the end of the 1970s and early 1980s, were impossible to buy and maintain because of high interest rates and incredible insurance premiums. As a result, families of proud men and women became paid laborers for Boston and New York conglomerates. A New Bedford fisherman was no different from a Nebraska wheat farmer who had to sell out because of low prices and high interest.

An attempt was made in the mid-80s to make New Bedford a tourist attraction; complete with pseudo-traditional trinket shops, piped-in sailing music, cobblestone narrow alleys, and new facades on old businesses. Only the exterior had been completed when the fishing industry was killed by strikes and labor actions against the fishing companies and corporate greed and pride by the out-of-town owners.

It wasn't at all unusual in America to find a large town with a disproportionate number of Americans of European or Asian descent. In New Bedford's case, over half the town was Portuguese, which was logical since the Portuguese have been fishermen of note for ten centuries or more. America was lucky to have the skills of an untold number of Portuguese generations. But unfortunately this February evening the nets of the large trawlers hung dry, the holds empty. With fuel costs so high, the large companies found it more economical to leave the 80-foot trawlers in port. In the mid-80s the fishermen had gone on strike for higher wages, won most of their demands, yet ended up with fewer and fewer boats to man because the companies couldn't afford to use them all. It was a cycle which was typical in many American industries. The fishing industry was almost at the point where it was cheaper to *import* fish from Europe than to use American resources to fish the waters off the coastline of the United States. All in all, it was an incredible situation.

Scotty watched Ramsey register at the Holiday Inn, eat a leisurely dinner, then leave for the center of what mainly was a deserted downtown.

— • —

"If he gets out of his car, he's dead," said Rostov in a cold voice.

Katrina only nodded. Lights out, the dark van slowly bumped over the cobblestones along Pleasant Street.

"He's stopping. Where is al-As?" whispered Katrina.

"He doesn't matter. Al-As will return to his motel room. This agent will not. Weapons," demanded Rostov.

Katrina reached under the back seat and slid out a metal compartment. She pulled out a 92F 16-round Beretta handgun for herself and a more sophisticated 20-round 93R for Rostov. Both fired 9mm bullets. Rostov's gun could throw out single shots or a three-round burst and came with a collapsible shoulder brace so the revolver could be used like a rifle for sure shots on a running target. Like the U.S. Army, the Soviet mission to the United Nations had chosen the Beretta as its weapon of choice. They were so much easier to get from the Army than from anyplace else.

Each in turn pulled on sure-grip gloves and quietly snapped a six-inch silencer on the Beretta's custom-designed barrel. They got out of the van and headed up the street. Rostov pointed for Tambov to take the west side of the street while he would run through the shadows of the east side. Although Katrina had changed shoes, she still made a click-click sound on the cold cobblestones. They sounded like castanets to Rostov. It was the first irritating thing she'd done.

A half-block ahead of them the FBI agent paused, then turned around the corner and headed down Union Street out of sight toward the darkness of the wharf.

— • —

Scotty parked his car well behind Ramsey and followed him through the clean but deserted downtown area; past banks which could loan no money, stores which had no more credit, and empty buildings with new facades, which at one time offered promise and now only collected dust. He turned left onto Union, crossed the street and headed downhill toward the four lanes of Route 18, Water Street. The only light came from the corner streetlamps and from the red-and-white neon sign of the National Club, a bar which like the Cowboy Bar and Grill in Laramie didn't cater to strangers.

Ahead of him Ramsey crossed the four-lane highway against the light. There was no traffic headed in either direction. Scotty thought he heard the sound of someone moving from behind him. He pressed against the side of the building and looked up Union Street. The soft clicking of odd shoes on the cobblestones stopped. Perhaps it was the echo of his own feet.

He could hear music coming from the National Club. It wasn't rock. Foreign. He couldn't understand the words, but a bar was a bar.

There it was again! Someone was following him.

He turned around to see the faint bright orange of Rostov's 93R automatic 9mm rip off two bursts of three shots each.

"Rostov . . . !" Scotty exclaimed.

Four of the bullets ricocheted against the brick facade behind him. Two found their target; one nicking his left arm, a second grazing his right side. As Scotty lunged for protection between two parked cars another bullet, this one from up the street, smashed into the metal of the parking meter not two feet from his head.

Just at that moment, four toughs, obviously drunk, poured through the doors of the National onto the street, all talking in a language Scotty didn't understand. Finally able to get to his shoulder-holstered .38, Scotty drew it out and searched for Rostov and the other unseen Soviet agent.

"Get down!" he shouted back to the four drunks.

One of them was struck by a bullet in the leg and cried out in pain. The other three were instantly sobered. They weren't kids. They were men in their forties and fifties, each with muscles honed by years of difficult work at sea, fists toughened by brawls ashore, and minds hardened by the prejudice against foreigners. They saw Scotty and assumed that he had shot their friend. Scotty's .38 was still in his right hand when the three remaining men, their jackets and clothes oily from working on the docks, fell on him and began to hit him with their fists. Scotty tried to struggle free. His .38 fell under the parked car. He fell into the middle of cobblestoned Union Street and the three men began to beat and kick him.

"No . . . No! You don't understand . . ." he shouted as he tried to protect himself.

It was true. The men didn't understand. Again and again they kicked. He was losing consciousness. Two had him by his head and shoulders, another by his left leg. They were dragging him across the road! As they did he could see the shadow of Alexander Rostov standing near the corner, his frame obliquely lit by a yellow streetlamp.

No—no—no! He couldn't shout. His voice was gone. The men continued to beat Scotty with their free hands as they dragged him into the shadows of the wharf. One man said something which Scotty didn't understand. There was a brief argument, then apparent agreement. They dragged him down further into the darkness, away from the falsely renovated section of town and into the shabby piers of old New Bedford.

Oh God they're going to throw me into . . .

Scotty felt the three men lift him up and with a concentrated effort throw him over the edge of the old pier and into the 35-degree water of the Acushnet River.

CHAPTER 2

My Name
is Charlie

"Those . . . those shoes . . ."

Rostov was so angry he could hardly contain himself, his words sputtered out of his mouth.

"Rostov, it's not my fault. You had the clear shot and you missed him. From point-blank range you missed him. How could you?" she questioned, ignoring the deep anger in his face.

"If it hadn't been for you . . . if I had been here by myself and not tied down with . . ."

"Oh, shut up Rostov! I don't want to listen to your whining. The question is . . . is he dead? Did they finish off your job?" she said with unconcealed sarcasm.

She turned and started to walk away. Rostov, livid with rage, grabbed her shoulder and spinning her around, he struck her across her face with his open hand.

Katrina hardly flinched although the left side of her face had the red imprint of his fingers. Anger boiled up within her. She lashed out at him with a strong right hand, returning the slap across his cheek. If anything, hers was the more powerful of the two blows.

They had left the wharf area when the trio of thugs had dragged the FBI agent away. Their only other choice would have been to kill them all, but that would have meant a blanket of police and FBI, they had decided. No, this was better. The agent would simply disappear. The men would take care of their wounded companion; no doctor, no police reports.

They'd come back, registered as husband and wife in the same motel as al-As, rotated the COMEX towards al-As's room and gone inside. If al-As decided to call anyone, or received a call, the machine would pick up every detail.

Rostov was surprised at the stinging blow Katrina returned; not only at its power but also by the fact she had the gumption to strike back at a man. His anger became mean. She was a tall woman, nearly five-ten, he a little under six feet. Her 145 pounds was well spread out over her frame. More taut-figured than slender, Rostov outweighed her by only twenty pounds.

He struck her across her chest, feeling her firm breasts as his hand slapped across her nipples.

"You son of a bitch," she cried in anger. "Don't you think you can do this to me!"

Shoes off, she kicked at him with her stocking foot. Her foot nearly found its mark between his legs, but not quite. Rostov had turned slightly to avoid the direct hit. He was also quick enough to grab her leg and throw her off balance. She fell backward and down to the floor, grabbing the end of the bed to cushion her fall.

"Bastard!"

Rostov jumped on her and began to beat her around the head with his closed fists.

"Slut . . . you cunt!"

He could barely speak, the anger and frustration spit out of his mouth in dribbles.

"No!"

Although on the bottom and in a poor position, Katrina covered herself up as best she could so that Rostov's blows were deflected by her arms. She then gave him a weak uppercut to the jaw and a more powerful straight right hand to his sternum, which temporarily knocked the breath out of him. Katrina scrambled up from the floor. Her skirt was up to her thighs and exposed a patch of smooth white skin above her black stockings, which were connected to a thin black garter belt around her waist. One of the stockings was already torn.

Rostov recovered and lunged at her as she tried to scramble across the bed to the relative safety of the other side of the room. He tackled her around her legs, his hands under her skirt and on her thighs. She turned and hit him across the head with her right arm. He reached for her supporting arm, found it, and pulled it out from underneath her. She fell to the bed. This was what he wanted all along.

"Now you'll pay . . . bitch!"

She struggled but he was clearly getting the better of it, now on top of her legs. She was twisted and turned, now on her stomach. She tried to flail at him but she had no leverage. Her legs were pinned with his weight. Her skirt was bunched up above her waist, her sweater rode high in back, exposing the thin black brassiere. Grabbing a fistful of her black hair he slammed her head down onto the bed and climbed higher, now well-positioned on her buttocks. She could struggle but not move.

"Now!" he grunted lustily.

His hands went under her sweater and quickly pulled the material up to her shoulders. Her arms and head were extended over the edge of the bed. She was pinned. He pulled the sweater up but not all the way over her head and shoulders, trapping her arms. No matter how she would struggle, the sweater would not come off. He hungrily groped her body, his hands slipping underneath and probing her breasts. She cried out in protest.

"No, Alex . . . no! Please!"

Her objections only fueled him. He unbuttoned his shirt and his pants, his erection finding space at last. Shifting his weight he removed one pantleg, then another, while she continued to struggle. He could feel the movement of her buttocks against his erection as she tried to get away from him. Her soft, cotton bikini panties rubbed against him. He straddled her and urgently started to probe.

Her panties were in the way. He ran his hand up underneath the material, bunching it and twisting it in his fingers as he did so, then roughly pulled the right side down over her buttock. He shifted his weight and did the same with the left side. He couldn't get them down! With a pull he ripped the material over her feet, then roughly spread her legs out. His erection found her now-wet sweetness.

She moved with his urgency. She'd never been dominated like this before. She'd always been in control, always on top, always bringing herself off before her mate. There was nothing tender between the two of them. Just as she started to get into his movement he pulled her sweater completely over her head then got off her legs.

"Up!" he commanded.

She got up on her knees as he demanded, then bent forward, her weight on her elbows. Then he was on her again, rutting her from behind. She still had on her brassiere, garter belt, and stockings. He roughly slid his hands under her bra and cupped her breasts as he pumped her from behind, grunting with satisfaction at every stroke. In . . . grunt . . . in . . . grunt . . . in.

Releasing her breasts he grabbed her hair and pulled her head back, enough so there was pain.

"Come on, bitch! Hump!"

He struck her rump with his free hand, hard. He hit her again, his fingers leaving a red welt on her soft white skin. She did as he told her . . . moving, sitting back into his forward stroke.

He released her hair but continued to urge her on. Slap . . . slap against her buttocks. His grunts were mixed with hers as they now entered the final stage of their lust, neither caring if the other came.

"No . . . No!" she shouted.

She could tell he was reaching the end. His grunts had the urgency of pre-orgasm. She wasn't ready. He went back to her breasts, roughly tearing at her bra. With four animal surges he came. They collapsed on the bed. He was finished; she was tired, hurt, and not fulfilled. It had been unlike any sex she had ever had.

He pulled apart and almost instantly fell asleep. She stayed awake for another half-hour, finishing for herself what he had started.

Somehow, they'd each gotten what they wanted.

— • —

They resumed their teaming arrangement as if nothing had happened. While Katrina followed al-As back to the waterfront, Rostov carefully searched his room and found nothing. Katrina, in the Caravan, followed the young Arab when he left the motel and headed back to the waterfront. Neither spoke of the events of the previous night.

Al-As went directly to the parking lot at the pier along the Acushnet River. There was no evidence of the trouble of the previous night, nor any indication from al-As that he was even aware there had been a killing. The wharf area consisted of three typical wooden piers and the parking lot, which had slips all along the outer edge. Almost every slip was occupied by a commercial trawler. Some crews sat in the harbormaster's hut and played cards, others talked, still others aimlessly did work which didn't need to be done, but was done in the interest of killing time.

Aziz al-As eyed the boats, then walked out to the end of the parking lot to a clean, red-trimmed boat, the *Bedford Clipper*. He went aboard and spoke to the captain. From her position in the van, Katrina pointed the COMEX toward the pier and recorded their conversation.

AL-AS: *Hello!* [Sound of unintelligible mumbling.] *Hello aboard the* Bedford Clipper! *Are you the skipper?*

CAPTAIN: *Aye.*

AL-AS: *Could I have a word with you, sir? Permission to come aboard?*

CAPTAIN: *Aye.*

[Sound of al-As boarding]

AL-AS: *My name is John Ramsey. I'm in the market for buying or leasing a trawler. It may be difficult to believe, but I'm a fisherman as well. My family has fished for hundreds of years, although as*

you can see it's been a while since I've made my living that way.
They said you might be looking for work, or even possibly to sell
the Clipper. *Is that true?*
CAPTAIN: *Aye.*

Al-As had to stop asking closed questions or else the conversation,
such as it was, would be ending quickly.

AL-AS: *Well . . . ?*
CAPTAIN: *My name is Carver Medway. I've fished these waters for*
thirty-five years. My father and his father and his father and
generations back to the 1820s have fished these waters. There's
no fish out there. What do you want her for? Why do you want to
buy the Clipper?
AL-AS: *I said,* may. *I* may *want to buy. I represent a French firm*
who may want to search for a missing ship. The idea would be to
retrofit a trawler with oceanographic equipment and hire a crew
who knew the north Atlantic and the coastline off the northeastern
United States. I was told not only might the Bedford Clipper *be*
available, but that so might you and your crew.
CAPTAIN: *Might. How much are you talking?*
AL-AS: *How much do you owe the bank? What remains on your*
mortgage?
CAPTAIN: *If the corporations hadn't come in here with their*
oversized trawlers, I could have made a living like my father and
grandfather did. But they came in, fished the banks dry, and I had
to get a bigger boat to compete. Then the fuel started to . . .
AL-AS: *How much?*
CAPTAIN: *A little over three hundred thousand dollars.*
AL-AS: *How old?*
CAPTAIN: *Eight years.*
AL-AS: *Then you paid, five-fifty perhaps six for it?*
CAPTAIN: *Close enough.*
AL-AS: *And you've depreciated it over . . . ?*
CAPTAIN: *Eighteen years.*
AL-AS: *If we were to make an offer it would probably be in the four-*
seventy-five to five-hundred-thousand range. Perhaps we might
lease instead.
CAPTAIN: *That would be a fair price.*
AL-AS: *When would you be able to muster a crew?*
CAPTAIN: *Anytime. Anytime. There are plenty of men in New*
Bedford who want work. Plenty. Good men, too.
AL-AS: *Captain Medway, I am on a short schedule. I have other*

ports to visit, but I will be making my decision soon. Either way I will contact you. Good day.

CAPTAIN: *You won't be disappointed, Mr. Ramsey.*

AL-AS: *No word to anyone, Captain. My backers insist on anonymity. Any compromise of their intent and our negotiations will be terminated. Am I clear?*

CAPTAIN: *Aye.*

AL-AS: *Good. I'll be seeing you, Captain.*

— • —

Things had gone well so far. He was right on schedule. He would give the captain a day, perhaps two, to stew in his juices before going back and striking a bargain. Money wasn't the object, rather the delay was necessary so that the captain would agree to the deal without hesitation, be anxious to please, be willing to mind his own business and not ask questions.

What questions? Anybody would ask several. Why would two men, obviously foreigners, charter a boat and take off for waters that are difficult to sail in good seasons, much less the dead of winter, and bring aboard boxes which may or may not contain some sort of scientific equipment.

Aziz could have simply bought the boat for cash, hired a crew, and set sail for wherever he wanted. But a purchase created a legal audit trail and took time. It involved lawyers, accountants, and banks. No, a charter was what was needed, but a charter with a captain who didn't mind keeping quiet and could hire a crew who would do the same. Once they got to sea it would all become irrelevant—moot—for the captain and crew would be killed. Their silence was only needed on shore.

Aziz went back the motel room and waited for Bafq's telephone call. Today was the eleventh. They would have to leave no later than the morning of the fourteenth.

At two o'clock the phone rang.

— • —

AL-AS [flatly]: *Yes.*

VOICE [unknown]: *It is I.*

AL-AS: *And?*

VOICE: *I have the things I was to get. Do you have a boat?*

AL-AS [hurriedly]: *Yes . . . no . . . not yet. But I will tomorrow. When can you get here?*

VOICE: *I am only a short distance away. When are you to talk to Rahman?*

AL-AS: *Tomorrow morning. I can go no further without his instructions.*

[pause] *Have you been followed?*

VOICE: *No . . . and you?*

[false laugh]

AL-AS: *No, not at all. The Americans suspect nothing. I am a foreigner with money. It is only the money they see.*

VOICE: *I will be there tomorrow night. Make sure there is a room for me.*

AL-AS: *Tomorrow night, then.*

The phone was disconnected.

"What a strange conversation," said Katrina to Rostov as they sat together in the van, recording the phone call.

"More advantage for us. Until we see him, we can only assume al-As was talking with Bafq el-Rashid. Either the two of them have never worked together or they dislike each other . . . either way, they are not a comfortable team," said Rostov smiling to himself.

"Not like us?" ruefully smiled Katrina.

Her small joke was lost on Rostov, who was too absorbed in thought.

"Where is Rahman?" Rostov mumbled, not paying attention to her.

"Rahman? Khalid Rahman?" questioned Katrina.

Rostov's attention snapped back to the present.

"Yes, Korz told me that Rahman had tried to enter through the city of Atlanta—he was supposed to make sure Rahman was followed."

"What are they doing?"

"I don't know. What I *do* know is that we . . . you . . . must report in to Korz. I don't want to be cut off here without a way home," Rostov replied angrily.

Katrina didn't try to defend her superior. Rostov had prior experience with the bulbous mound of flesh, too. Only not like hers. Just thinking about his pudgy hands on her made Katrina's flesh crawl. Although she had been forced into a semi-mistress situation, she had turned her sexual prowess to her benefit. After a while things seemed to work in both directions; he got what he wanted, and with the threat of denial she got what she wanted. Yes, Korz *would* cut Rostov off—cut him off at the knees, leave him out to be captured or assassinated.

"I will call," she said simply. "Should I tell him about last night?"

For a brief moment Rostov's face became incredulous. Why would she tell Korz of their nasty passion . . . ?

Then it dawned on him.

"Yes . . . the FBI agent. No, the agent is dead. We will be gone as soon as we know Rahman's location."

Katrina pretended to be unaware of Rostov's momentary confusion. It amused her to see what first thoughts came into her comrade's mind.

DZERZHINSKY SQUARE, MOSCOW

From the inside, Dzerzhinsky Square was beautiful at night. Those poor souls caught outside in the –28 degree temperature, with wind chills in the –40s, thought otherwise. Anyplace outside, in the middle of February in the Soviet Union, was a bitch. However, at this moment, to Major General Gregori Bodnof, outside would have been the preferred location for his hot seat. But he'd been in Viktor Chebrikov's huge, early-Russian ornate office many times before, even sometimes in the hot seat.

For many first-time sitters in the seat, it was the last time they had the opportunity to do so for a long while, sometimes forever.

Six floors directly under Chebrikov's office, and three floors underground, was the dreaded Lubyanka prison. Outside Chebrikov's office was a stairwell which led directly six floors down. Each floor down was progressively less decorated, darker, more dank. Dante's layers of hell were accurately represented. Clean palace guards were replaced by brutal thugs at level 2, who then would beat and drag political prisoners through the slime and muck to their cold, rat-infested destination.

Bodnof knew the rules when Chebrikov invited him to sit in the hot seat and not on the couch. He'd sat in the chair before in varying times in his career, but mostly as Chebrikov's Chief of the First Directorate he'd sat on the couch. Tall-backed with large oversized arm rests and a too-soft cushion, the hot seat instantly made the designated sitter feel small, insignificant, and physically very uncomfortable. As usual, the room was in semi-darkness. The hot seat was at one end of a large table. Across the table sat Chebrikov. To his left sat Eduard Shevardnadze.

This is it, thought Major Bodnof. *Succeed and I can have it all. Failure means disgrace and banishment.*

If either Chebrikov or Shevardnadze were made to look bad, then death was not out of the question. Chebrikov spoke slowly and quietly.

"Major Bodnof, the Foreign Minister and I have a number of questions regarding your operation in America."

Your operation? thought Bodnof. Even though he tried to think of the cold outside, and even though he was practiced and skilled at question gamesmanship, Bodnof started to perspire. Before he could answer "yes, sir" Chebrikov continued.

"An inaccurate answer will cause the unfortunate death of many Soviet soldiers, all needlessly. Sad to say, those deaths could even reach beyond the battlefront."

Battlefront? Bodnof was perplexed.

"I'm not sure I understand, but I will do my best, General," replied Bodnof.

"Who are these men?" Chebrikov asked.

"Khalid Rahman is Zaid Khan's number-two man," began Bodnof. "He is 48, an experienced terrorist, but one who will never rise to the top of any organization. He prefers action to politics. He is a doer, not a talker. For him there is only one cause, one leader, and that is Allah— although it appears as if Zaid abu Khan is now his representation of Allah. Before joining Khan, Rahman worked for Arafat in Lebanon, but he quickly learned that Arafat cared for Arafat first, Arafat second, and Palestine third.

"In 1982, Rahman left Arafat after a meeting in an Athens café, where Rahman became convinced abu Khan exhibited characteristics which the Prophet wanted all Muslems to show. Khan was a quietly determined leader, one who would give no quarter in battle, yet one who would not risk the lives of his men needlessly. It was this last quality that, as a lifelong warrior, Khalid Rahman respected.

"The man known as Bafq el-Rashid is a munitions expert. His speciality is bombs of all kinds. He has been tied to the murders of bankers in England and industrialists in West Germany, in addition to the almost numbing frequency of sudden deaths in Lebanon. It was el-Rashid's work that caused the American disaster in Beruit and the eventual pullout of the Marines. His age is not known, but he is believed to be in his late thirties. Where he came from is not known. He apparently joined Khan in 1983 and has stayed with him ever since, although it is not apparent that el-Rashid is a devoted Muslim. He is a peculiar man, has no friends, and even in the violent world of terrorism, is considered to be dangerous.

"Last in the group is Aziz al-As, the man our agents have been tracking for the last four days. This man . . . this boy . . . is nothing more than a young but intelligent functionary whose apparent skill is language. Al-As speaks at least four foreign languages, English the best. His good looks give him the appearance of a European playboy, although he spent his early years in a poor fishing family on the Caspian Sea.

"For the past day al-As has been in a small fishing village named New Bedford in the province of Massachusetts."

"State," corrected Shevardnadze.

"And do you still believe these men are planning more than the usual terrorist activities?" asked Chebrikov.

Bodnof pondered. It was nothing more than a gut feeling and the logical connection of the available facts.

"I do. The three men are operating independently, but in concert. We know their arrival points in the United States: Atlanta, New York, and Boston. We have been able to follow only young al-As."

Bodnof could see the storm clouds rising on Chebrikov's face, and he cut the General off before the scorn could leave his lips.

"However . . . our agents have monitored al-As's conversations, both with the captain of a fishing vessel and on the telephone. He has made contact with el-Rashid. He is scheduled to make contact with Khalid Rahman tomorrow."

"What kind of contact?" interjected Shevardnadze.

"Yes, Mr. Minister . . . he, al-As, is to make contact with Rahman via telephone. It apparently has been pre-arranged. Also, Bafq el-Rashid is scheduled to meet with him. I deduce they have been looking along the eastern coastline of the United States for some kind of safe harbor, a fishing village."

"To what end?" asked Shevardnadze.

"I think they intend to charter a trawler and somehow meet up with Khan or Qaddafi's men," answered Bodnof.

"And?" probed Chebrikov.

" . . . and . . . I think they intend to smuggle atomic weapons into the United States."

"Are you making the assumption Qaddafi has them?" asked Chebrikov.

"Yes, General. We . . . I . . . our agents . . . I believe Qaddafi has them," Bodnof stuttered.

"Why would he give them to Khan?" asked Shevardnadze.

"He owes him a debt. It was Khan who killed Sadat. It was Khan who firebombed the Americans in Beruit. It was Khan who almost discredited Mubarak. It was Khan in Chad . . . ," replied Bodnof, rattling off an impressive list of accomplishments.

"Enough. Do you feel strongly about this, Major General?" asked Chebrikov. "Be sure of your answer."

This was it! Thought Bodnof. He felt drenched. The back of his shirt clung to his skin, damp with his sweat. He was grateful his wool suit jacket hid his discomfort.

"Yes," he replied.

"If there is any information which we . . . I should have which you think may influence a decision we may or may not make, I expect you to inform me personally. You may go," said Chebrikov.

Bodnof wanted to bolt out of the room but protocol wouldn't allow it. He gave a slight bow to his superiors, then walked slowly through the door, carefully closing it behind him. Once the door was closed Chebrikov and Shevardnadze continued their conversation.

"So?" asked the KGB commander.

Shevardnadze only nodded as he pondered. Then he spoke.

"How good are your agents?"

"Rostov is second-generation KGB. He is in charge of three networks in central Europe. Korz keeps his own counsel, you know that."

Shevardnadze nodded again, silently.

"If what we think is true is actually true, then there will be a period of time when we will have a clear advantage over the Americans," said Shevardnadze.

"What are you planning?" asked Chebrikov.

Shevardnadze ignored Chebrikov's probe.

"It is important you keep me informed. Hourly. I want to know everything. What I do will be based on the information your agents provide."

It was the second time Shevardnadze had used the word "your" to Chebrikov. Just as Bodnof had been forced to accept responsibility by his superior so had Chebrikov by a peer. It was as if Shevardnadze had stuck Chebrikov with a piece of flypaper. Once on, it wouldn't come off. Once responsible, always responsible.

THE KREMLIN, MOSCOW

Eduard Shevardnaze stood in front of an oversized electronic map of the world which showed the configuration and current position of all Soviet forces. The Soviet forces were in red, the known American and NATO forces in blue. Behind an ornate wooden desk was Mikhail Gorbachev. To Gorbachev's right was Viktor Chebrikov.

Chebrikov's grandfatherly appearance belied the dread the man had over nearly every citizen in the Soviet Union. The man was short and squat and wore a suit which needed to be custom-tailored, but wasn't. The meeting could have been mistaken for a late night business-strategy session. Both Gorbachev and Shevardnadze looked like successful top managers. However, this was not the case with Viktor Chebrikov.

"Khan, with Qaddafi's explicit support, is planning an act of sabotage beyond anything ever tried before," said Shevardnadze.

"What opportunity can we gain?" asked Gorbachev.

Shevardnadze looked at the stony Chebrikov. It was obvious from the look that he was to continue.

"Several. We've followed these slugs almost since they've left Iran. They aren't very good spies, but they've been good enough to get into the United States. I think we have three options."

"Option one: we can let Khan enter the U.S., then let the FBI and the American public know of his presence, and in the spirit of Soviet-American cooperation deplore such heinous acts. We come out way ahead. The American conservatives will be made to look foolish, the liberals clairvoyant, and the president will be forced to give us concessions," said the Foreign Minister.

"And no one would complain about a takeover of Libya and the assassination of Qaddafi," added Chebrikov.

"That is correct," Shevardnadze agreed. He continued.

"A second option is to do nothing. Let Khan and Qaddafi play the hand out to its conclusion."

"What is our advantage in allowing that?" questioned Gorbachev. "In that game, whatever happens, the president and the American conservatives are winners. He can't lose. Any action he takes will be popularly backed."

"As in option one, Qaddafi would be eliminated," said the KGB officer.

Gorbachev moved in his chair, a troubled man.

"Qaddafi is the least of our problems. Libya is the least of our problems. Yes, the American public would back a full-scale assault. And they could do it, perhaps not with ease, but they could do it. What would we lose? Not much. The European Common Market would lose more in loss of trade than we would by losing an unstable ally. No, that's not the problem. It's Khan, not Qaddafi. Iran is the key. What would the president do with Iran? No, I don't like this alternative. He might think we are to blame. We would have to gear up for a response. No. We gain nothing with this alternative. We are put on the defensive with no potential gain. I like the first alternative better. Let us not lose sight of the fact that some of what we have been telling the world is actually true. We are at least providing the illusion of loosening individual liberties. But, we do need world peace—more importantly, we need to break down this choking bureaucracy we have, otherwise we will never become more efficient. I believe it deeply. We have risked a great deal, you and I, in trying to keep our country competitive," stated Gorbachev, with fervor.

"Yes, I agree. We have come a long way, but there is so far to go," Shevardnadze paused. "There is a third alternative," he said with a gleam in his eyes.

Gorbachev's contacts with the Western leaders had changed him. Shevardnadze was about to remedy that. He looked at Chebrikov and gained his tacit approval and backing.

"And what is that?" asked Gorbachev.

"At the appropriate time we take the initiative from Khan. If the weapons are atomic as we all believe, then if properly placed, considerable damage could be inflicted within the United States. Planned correctly, it would even be conceivable to disable or partially disable the American defense system long enough to seize the initiative. We would only need three or four days to take over Iran and Iraq and have a line of supply from the Caspian to the Mediterranean to the Persian Gulf to the Indian Ocean. We would have the oil the Europeans need and ocean bases for our submarines. Imagine! Soviet submarine bases in the Persian Gulf and the Mediterranean! It would be the largest single expansion of our power since World War II," said the enthused Shevardnadze.

"And exactly how would you plan to disable the American defenses long enough to accomplish this?", smiled Gorbachev.

"I've studied the possibilities. There is a way . . . . "

For the next fifteen minutes Shevardnadze outlined his plan as Gorbachev listened. Hearing no objections, he continued with the logistics.

"We have over three hundred thousand troops on the Afghan border and another two hundred thousand in Volgograd. We have supply lines which reach directly to the Iranian border on either side of the Caspian Sea. I propose we move within the next ten days. We will move Divisions 14, 19, 25, and 33 from their current positions outside the city to locations along the Turkey-Iran border between the Black Sea and the Caspian Sea, and to positions east of the Caspian. Furthermore, Divisions 1-10, 18 and 28 are to be moved to positions along Iran's eastern border."

With a light pen Shevardnadze drew three heavy lines. One line came from Afghanistan and extended to the Persian Gulf. A second came from east of the Caspian Sea, went through Tehran and into Iraq. The third came from Soviet Armenia south through northwest Iran and met up with the second line inside Iraq. Shevardnadze then continued the double line.

"Within three days, perhaps four, we could capture both Iran and Iraq, take the oil fields, and have direct access to the Persian Gulf and Arabian Sea. The American defense network will be disabled—they will be powerless to stop us! They won't counterattack because they won't be able to, and they won't know we are responsible. It will be Khan and the Ayatollah and Qaddafi they will blame. You will simply be doing the president a favor. The world will think you are a hero! You will be helping the United States in its time of crisis by wiping out one of its enemies, the cause of its misfortune. By the time they recover it will be over! Syria, Lebanon, Jordan, Oman, the Emirates, Yemen, Ethiopia . . . we control them all. We will have Israel and Saudi Arabia surrounded. It will only be a matter of time—and we will have done it without nuclear weapons."

Gorbachev pondered. There were no signs that the trouble in the Persian Gulf was any closer to a resolution. American gunboats still escorted Kuwait-owned oil tankers. Khomeini and his son, along with Abdul Waquidi, ran a government that somehow managed to wobble forward even though it was constantly on the edge of pitching into the abyss of chaos. The American development of SDI, combined with the multi-decade failure of the Soviet economy could very easily result in the beginning of the end of communist rule in the Soviet Union. There soon would be no reason, no justification for the party's existence. The beginnings of a capitalist sub-economy had already started. Except for Central America, the Party had been stagnant for nearly the entire decade. Time was slowly running out on the concept of communism. Growth was essential. Growth through inner renewal, or . . .

Shevardnadze's plan was a good one.

"It appears to be a no-fault plan. Are you sure the American defenses will be crippled long enough?" he asked his Foreign Minister.

"Yes. It's conceivable they could be partially disabled for a week, perhaps ten days."

"Partially?"

"Mostly. Enough for second-strike defense, but not for first-strike attack," responded Shevardnadze. "Their Stealth bombers will be airborne but won't attack as long as their missiles can't get out of the silos."

"We can do this in three days?" asked Gorbachev.

"Certainly by day four," responded Shevardnadze.

"Then its up to our agents," said Gorbachev flatly.

"Chebrikov's agents."

"Our agents."

There was no place else to put blame for failure. Gorbachev pondered the situation as he looked at the snow-covered streets of Moscow. The Politburo was not firmly under his control.

"We must be careful, my friend," he continued.

"Yes, but we haven't gotten this far without risk . . . great risk," reminded Shevardnadze.

"This . . . this thing we plan . . . this is different from what we have done before."

Gorbachev felt an adrenal surge of Mother Russia pride stirring in his chest. It was possible . . . very possible. The contrary Politburo would be his. His name would be mentioned in the same breath as Lenin's.

Shevardnadze only nodded. There was nothing else to say.

NEW BEDFORD

For the first time since he boarded the plane in Paris, Aziz was nervous. He hated being cooped up in a motel room. The American television was a babble of strangeness. What if Rahman had been captured? How would he know where to take Khan?

But al-As was ignoring his real fear. Very shortly he would meet up with Bafq el-Rashid and he would be in charge of the older terrorist. The phone call had not gone well. Bafq had assumed the superior position. It had only been a brief moment, but el-Rashid had turned their roles around. Aziz would make sure there was a room for el-Rashid. It wasn't much, but still Aziz was worried.

He saw the message light on his phone blink at the very instant the phone rang. Both jarred him out of his self-imposed malaise.

"Hello, this is John Ramsey," answered al-As.

It was Khalid Rahman.

— • —

"What is he speaking?" asked a disturbed Katrina.

"Farsi. They're speaking their normal language, probably with a Kurdian dialect. It's what I would do if I were talking to an agent of mine, especially if I were in a hotel room and I were talking to someone in a protected location on the other end. Why waste the effort? Words can be confused, misinterpreted. More importantly . . . the conversation is secure. Not only does the phone have to be tapped but the listener must be able to translate Farsi. This must be translated. I assume Korz can get at least this much done for us," lectured Rostov.

The small amber screen of the COMEX-100 displayed a rush of gibberish garbage as the internal translator tried to produce English characters from spoken Farsi. While the actual voice was captured, the display meant nothing.

Rostov nodded in approval as the conversation continued to be taped. It was frustrating, but Khalid Rahman was a worthy opponent.

"You must leave immediately and return to New York. I will stay and continue to monitor them. They will be here at least another two days, then I fear they will leave by this boat they are contracting. We must know where Khalid Rahman is! There must be something in this tape which will lead us to him. Korz must do something."

Katrina didn't respond immediately, but sat listening to the conversation between al-As and Khalid Rahman for another few minutes. Finally, she asked. "Where will you be?"

"Unless I am returning to France, I cannot risk going back to New York. This problem with the FBI agent may not be finished. I can't chance being tagged again."

Rostov's eyes showed concern and Katrina understood it well. Away from his home base, professionally naked, Rostov had the fear of being left out in the cold. If there was information in the message, Korz could decide to start his own operation or let Washington take control. Either way, Rostov would be on his own. Rostov's insecurity was heightened by his lack of feeling for what he really was doing. He'd been told to follow the terrorists, but he had no idea of what was happening with the information he was digging up. There was no exchange, no update. He and Katrina reported to Korz, but received no instructions other than to continue. Without Katrina, without his link to the Soviet network, Rostov was a man out on the end of a limb, on a path from which there was no return.

Rostov's confidence came back to him. Simply stated, there were no rules in his business. Korz was being told by higher authorities to keep track of al-As. It wouldn't be prudent for him to abandon Rostov . . . at least not while al-As remained in the country.

"I will be here. I will follow al-As. You must go," he said with renewed authority.

The conversation finished, Rostov rewound the cassette tape, popped it into a plastic case and gave it to Katrina. Without a word the dark-haired woman got out of the van and walked toward the adjoining restaurant where the embassy Buick was parked.

Katrina had no intention of driving all the way back into New York. She would drive to New Haven, leave the embassy car someplace on the Yale campus, then take the train into New York, so that she could arrive at the mission on foot at night. It was doubtful if Korz would have someone who could translate Farsi. The message would have to be coded and either transmitted to Moscow via satellite or sent by courier to Washington, where it was more likely to be translated.

Back in the cold of the van, Rostov's thoughts were dark. He was in a position he liked to put his enemies in—defensive, dependent on others for support. He didn't like the feeling.

NAGS HEAD, NORTH CAROLINA

Jacques Marmande had a headache. He'd had the headache since he'd left Paris. But today the pain was throbbing behind his eyes. It must be a migraine. He was letting his insecurity get the better of him. Khalid Rahman had spent the entire previous day buying things, mostly clothes . . . clothes of all sizes and descriptions; shoes, hats, gloves, coats, pants. All of his selections were typical American outdoor casual.

It was clear to Marmande that Rahman was the reconnaissance man for some kind of operation.

At one point during the day Marmande had felt confident enough to let Rahman go his own way, knowing full well that the terrorist was just out buying more of this and that, and would return to his rented home.

Marmande had procrastinated in calling René, delaying longer than he knew he should . . . because he knew he would be forced to lie, or at least stretch the truth.

"Why haven't you reported, Jacques?" would be Chatillion's first question. "What do the Americans think?" would be his second. "You did report Rahman to them, didn't you Jacques?"

A telephone call would end up in a personal disaster. His superior would flush out his failures like a dentist finds the decay of a cavity with a needle-sharp pick. He wouldn't be able to answer the questions directly. His words would end up in meaningless sentences of excuses and roundabout explanations.

Instead, Marmande sent a telegram.

> I HAVE FOLLOWED RAHMAN TO NORTH CAROLINA COASTLINE. REMAIN CONVINCED HE IS PREPARING FOR MEETING WITH HIS FRIENDS. I AM WELL, ALTHOUGH TIRED.
>
> JACQUES

There would be no telephone number, no hotel name, no place to reach him. He was playing a hunch, an all-or-nothing hunch. He knew he should have told the Americans. This was Khalid Rahman! He was Zaid Khan's number-two man!

But Marmande's pride had replaced his better judgment.

NEW BEDFORD

Carver Medway was very glad to see al-As.

"Mr. Ramsey, I didn't expect you to return."

"Why not, captain?" replied al-As.

"Oh, I don't know . . . I . . ."

"I've gone back to the people I represent and have told them I recommend your boat, the *Bedford Clipper*. There are others, you know," smiled al-As with a superiority which was threatening, but not condescending.

"Yes," said Medway, anxiously.

"But, I must see how your boat handles itself. More importantly I must see how you and your crew handle yourselves."

Medway was confused.

"You had mentioned buying the *Clipper*."

"Yes, that is true. And that is still the case. But, I don't have the feeling you wish to sell. Is that true?"

"Aye, true enough."

"Good, I . . . for tax reasons we prefer to charter your boat for an extended period of time. It has to do with depreciation," said the young al-As.

Medway smiled. He understood the IRS very well.

"But, Captain Medway, our principals are very concerned about you and the crew—concerned not only about your skills at sea, but also about your ability to keep things to yourself, under your hat so to speak. Do you understand me?"

Medway was not offended, but at the same time was not about to get into an illegal operation.

"I'll sell the *Clipper*—no, I'd sink her—before I'd get her into running drugs, Mr. Ramsey. Before I agree to anything, I need to know what it is you really want me to do."

Aziz looked around at the empty boat in the silent harbor. The wharf was ringed with empty boats.

"Captain Medway, my principals are in marine salvage, not drug running. For the time being, that is all I can say. If you want employment, I am ready to sail tomorrow . . . if not, well . . . I can find someone else. Regardless, I need a good crew which wants to be part of a team. There is money to be made by all. What we don't need are newspapers and glory-hunters. I need someone who can take control and keep his crew under hand. I thought I had that man. Perhaps I was wrong."

Aziz stepped back. The cold of the New England afternoon whipped through the port town. The cobblestones of Union Street were empty of tourists. A few men lingered around the harbormaster's house. Good and steady work was hard to find.

Even good and steady work that was obviously on the sly was hard to find. Medway was no fool. Whatever the young man was proposing, however deep his pockets were, the objective was not quite on the level.

"How much?" the captain finally asked.

Al-As nodded and smiled to himself.

"Yes . . . payment. Seventy-five hundred for a two-week journey. A trial run . . . out to sea and back. I will bring one man along with myself, and some equipment, not much."

"Where?"

Aziz pretended to hold back, linger as if he didn't want to tell the captain. The wind blew across the expanse of the Acushnet River. Both men were cold, however Medway was the colder of the two.

"Do you know the area around Sable Island?"

"Aye. I've even fished the area. Only last year I was there. Is that where you intend to go?" asked Medway.

"Yes. Do you have charts of the area?"

"It's not a good time of the year to be cruising that part of the Atlantic, Mr. Ramsey."

"Yes, I know. That's why we are going. Nobody will be there. Do you have charts of the area?"

"Aye, I have charts from Newfoundland to Florida. Are you sure, Mr. Ramsey?"

"Do you wish the charter, captain Medway?" asked al-As.

Aziz saw the doubt creep back into Medway's eyes.

"This is a charter, Captain Medway, nothing more. I need to see how this boat will handle herself in rough water."

"Aye, you will get that," responded Medway, pondering.

"Seven thousand five hundred dollars, captain. For a two-week trip. If you want to fish on the way back, it's up to you. Whatever you get is yours."

The deal was too good for the out-of-work captain to turn down.

"Agreed."

"Good! One thing, captain . . . I may not look it, but I think I mentioned before that I have the background of the sea . . . . I don't think you need to hire a full crew. I wouldn't mind working a shift or two, neither would my partner. It's up to you, we don't care. If you want to save some money, you have two extra able hands. Our principals want to make sure we have everything under control."

Medway smiled, then shook al-As's hand.

"When will you be ready to leave, captain?"

"Is tomorrow too soon?"

"No, indeed. What time is best?"

"High tide is at noon. We should leave no later than ten."

"Agreed."

Al-As looked around at the empty boat.

"Do you need an advance, captain?"

Medway smiled and shrugged.

"Yes, I suppose you do. A thousand?"

Before Medway could gasp, al-As whipped out his wallet and peeled off ten one hundred dollar bills.

"That should take care of provisions and anything you need for a crew."

Al-As walked down the gangway to the concrete wharf and his waiting blue Cutlass, confident that Medway would hire a minimum crew for such an easy trip. With two extra men, al-As and el-Rashid, even if they were the worst of mates . . . all Medway had to do was hire on a good mechanic and a combination cook/all-hands mate.

Medway smiled as he watched al-As drive out of the empty parking lot, turn right onto the equally empty Highway 28 and head north toward Interstate 195.

Things were looking up.

— • —

It was so cold . . . so unbelievably cold. It was a crypt of coldness. His hands were frozen. He tried to move them, but nothing happened. MOVE, GOD-DAMN IT! Nothing.

His legs were on fire! How could his legs be on fire and his hands frozen? How come? Why? His body burned and the pain drove through his mind like a spike. His skin was on fire. He tried to scream but there was no sound . . . no sound because his mouth was closed.

Water! The water! God, it's cold! I can't feel anything . . . grab for it! Missed! Please!! I don't want to die . . . no, please!

Scotty's mouth opened wide and he tried to scream the pain of the tortured dead. He was in hell. *Why? I only lived twenty-five years . . . I didn't do anything which deserved this. Is that what it's all about? Is this what I've lived for? What do I have to do to go to heaven? Where's the cutoff?*

Scotty could see nothing but a bright haze, a glare which was like looking at a sunrise through a blizzard.

He could hear bells and noise around him.

"Doctor . . . he's alive! He's alive! He's coming around!"

Who's coming around? Around what?

All Scotty could feel was pain . . . like a thousand needles were pricking his skin . . . poking here, poking there . . . jab, jab, jab.

It hurt. He hurt. And he couldn't scream . . . couldn't tell anyone. He heard a male voice speak and it wasn't his own.

"It *is* a miracle . . . and he's not out of it, not by a long shot. His internal body temperature was down to 63 degrees—but his skin was nearly frozen. That boy is one hurtin' puppy.

Scotty tried to scream, tried to tell the voice that he was alive . . . still inside the body . . . but he couldn't. He passed out from the pain.

— • —

Aziz came back to the motel, parked his car, walked through the lobby to the newsstand where he picked up a *Boston Globe*, then walked down the hallway to his room. The carpet needed to be cleaned. He walked in and was immediately slapped up against the wall, his head smacked against the thin wallboard, knocking askew a tasteless print of Americana that hung over the maple veneer pressboard dresser. The room was dark. He temporarily lost his senses. His eyes couldn't fo-cus. It didn't matter. Aziz was doubled-over in pain from a blow to his stomach then another to his sternum.

His attacker seemed to be able to see in the dark. Aziz could barely breathe. He went down on his knees then felt two strong hands on his shoulders. His jacket was roughly pulled down over his back and half way down his arms, bent so that his arms were pinned, like a straitjacket. He felt another blow to the back of his neck. He was losing consciousness, but not completely.

The strong hands pulled him up from the floor then threw him forward where he landed on the bed. The only sound came from Aziz as his brain reacted to the several areas of pain. The surprise had been complete. He could barely catch a breath, much less try to fight back, his arms pinned as they were. His legs felt like rubber. He was momentarily stunned.

The man jumped on the bed, directly onto his back. Aziz nearly passed out from the pain and the lack of oxygen. He felt hands around his waist, then his pants being drawn backward down his legs. His shoes were handled and dropped to the floor one at a time . . . plunk, plunk. Then his pants slid down, first one leg, then the other, and also fell to the carpeted floor. Then his underwear followed the same path.

The attacker jumped on his back again, this time bending his left leg back at the knee. He felt a rope go around his ankle and a quick but tight knot tied. In a lightening fast move the man did the same to his right leg. Still bordering on unconsciousness, Aziz felt the man release his grip but then knew his left foot was being tied to something. The man angrily grabbed his right foot and tied it to the opposite side of the bed.

Aziz was spread-eagled, face down on his stomach, hands under his body, tied to the king-sized bed.

"Wha . . . what do . . . do . . . you want?" he stammered in heavily accented English.

There was no response.

The man was on his back again, this time to roughly gag Aziz with something.

The man got off the bed and there was silence.

Then he heard one shoe drop to the floor, followed by another.

Aziz started to squirm. He couldn't speak, couldn't shout, couldn't move!

He heard the change and keys in the man's pants jingle as they fell to the floor, then the stretching sound of a shirt being drawn over a chest and head. Finally, he could hear underwear softly peeling down over the man's legs.

He felt hands on his legs! The man positioned himself between his legs and ran a rough hand up each calf to the knee, then up over the back of his thigh to cup his buttocks. His fingers kneaded, probed, and massaged the young man's skin.

Aziz's heart raced. This was the abomination of abominations! Of all the crimes of one man against another, Allah did not forgive manlove. Compliant or unwilling, it did not matter. The victim and the aggressor were just as guilty in his eyes.

Aziz was trapped. He squirmed and moved. He could feel the anger in the man as the unseen hands went from massaging to beating. The hands went under his body and felt his genitals. Aziz was not hard. This seemed to make the attacker even more angry. Aziz tried to cry out, but was unable to, even with the pain which would follow.

The attacker's left hand stayed on his penis, trying to stroke it to erection. His right hand, now lubricated with some slippery jelly, probed Aziz's anus. It was only temporary, needed so his attacker's erection could perform the ultimate violation.

Forgive me, Allah! Please, forgive me!

The pain wasn't as bad as he thought it would be, but it was bad nevertheless. The man was large, the attack violent. The lubrication enabled the rape to be complete. The man didn't grunt, didn't utter a sound. The smell of their sex was in the room. Aziz struggled but that only seemed to make the attacker enjoy his violation even more.

Then the pain was as bad as he expected, even worse. The rape was nearly complete, and he could sense the man's urgency as he approached ejaculation. Then he felt the rush as the man came. Then he was out, but the pain of his entry lingered as Aziz's colon, unaccustomed to such insertion, sent signals of pain throughout his body. *Don't do that! Don't do that!*

It was over. He felt the man get up off the bed and quickly get dressed. Then he heard the door open and close as the rapist left.

Aziz lay there, body hurting in multiple places and the man's semen oozing out of his rectum. He was humiliated. But he couldn't stay there forever. He had to get loose. His attacker hadn't made it so it was impossible to get out. It took nearly ten minutes for Aziz to get the tight jacket from around his arms and shoulders. Once that was off it was a struggle, but he managed to get to his left foot and free the knot. Twenty minutes after being raped Aziz was in the shower, lights still out. He couldn't look at himself in the mirror. His shower done, Aziz lay back on the bed, this time hunched into a fetal position.

The phone rang! It startled him.

"Hello," Aziz said weakly.

"You sound ill, Aziz al-As. This is no time to be sick. There is much to do."

It was Bafq.

"Ye . . . yes . . . I mean, no. I'm just tired."

"I will be down. We must talk," came the commanding voice of Bafq el-Rashid.

"No! . . . I mean, yes . . . give me a few minutes."

He hung up and began to cry.

— • —

A half hour later Aziz let el-Rashid into his room. The scent was familiar. Or, was it just the lingering odor of what had happened? He couldn't tell for sure if it had been him, and certainly couldn't tell Bafq anything. Khan would have supported his immediate execution even if it meant altering the plans. No, it was best to be silent. But there was no mistaking a change of attitude. No matter how hard he tried, Aziz couldn't make eye contact with the slightly larger and older man. Physically the two were equals, or at least Aziz had thought they were.

"You do not look well, al-As," said Khan's munitions man. "Has Rahman contacted you?"

Bafq el-Rashid's voice was strong and clear. His English was getting better and it sounded like he enjoyed the practice. His dark features highlighted his face, his bones were sharp, and he could have used a few pounds of weight. His sallow eyes picked and pointed, the dark irises wobbled slightly as they stared ahead.

"Well . . . what did he have to say? Where is he? When do we leave? Have you finished what you were to do?" Bafq demanded.

The questions rattled Aziz. He was supposed to be in charge of this phase of the mission. While the questions were expected, it was el-Rashid's tone of voice that Aziz didn't expect. It wasn't that his voice was threatening, it was . . . assumptive. Bafq had found a vacuum of energy and was seizing control.

"I have a boat and we are ready to sail tomorrow. Do you have the equipment?" asked Aziz.

"Yes. What about Rahman?" said el-Rashid quickly.

"Rahman is preparing for our arrival. There is much for him to do. The port is as Khan said it would be, empty. They will welcome a northern fishing boat and crew. We will be able to move freely, without suspicion."

"We must be on guard at all times, al-As," el-Rashid said sternly.

Aziz said nothing. He averted his eyes and pretended tiredness.

"What time do we sail?" el-Rashid asked strongly.

"At ten," replied Aziz.

Without a word el-Rashid turned and left Aziz's room. As he opened the door he gave Aziz one more shot.

"Don't oversleep."

Sleep? Who would sleep? Aziz sat on the edge of the bed and buried his head in his hands. His shame was complete. He knew it had been el-Rashid, yet Bafq hadn't let out a clue, not an inkling that he'd just performed an act of the unclean, an act so vile that it could not be washed from his mind. Bafq el-Rashid had taken Aziz's manhood from him.

Down the hallway, Bafq el-Rashid smiled as he fell asleep. Not only would Aziz al-As follow his instructions, but he would do so without question. Failure to do so would mean additional visits in the night.

NEW YORK

A strong hand shook the heavy, sleeping body of Dimitri Korz.

"It is Moscow, sir," said the soldier without emotion.

Korz grumbled as he slowly rolled out of his enormous, oversized American bed. It had been warm inside the covers and he had been thoroughly enjoying the satyric fantasies of his semi-conscious morning state.

"Bring Tambov," he ordered as the soldier wrapped the ambassador in a fur robe and directed Korz to his slippers.

Korz walked down the hallway to the elevator, which quickly rose to the sixth floor. A guard snapped to attention and opened the door to the lead-shielded communications room. Katrina Tambov was already there. She looked wonderful, very reminiscent of the body he'd just left in his dreams. How long had it been since he'd been with her? Too long. Things weren't working the way they did in years past.

The guard closed the door, leaving the communications officer, Korz, and Katrina Tambov inside the small, lead-shielded office. Korz nodded to the officer, who in turn activated the connection. Talking to Moscow was not one of the joys of office. First of all, conversation was rarely pleasant. The motherland was not necessarily the best place to live, and consequently, on occasion, people resented the fact that Korz was in the land of opulence while they were forced to stand in cold queues for anything and everything.

However, this was not the case this morning. In a few moments the thrice-delayed voice of Major General Bodnof was heard. Bodnof's voice was encrypted in Moscow, sent to a Soviet communications satellite over the North Pole, then down to a dish on top of the Mission, where the signal was decrypted and sent to an old Western Electric speakerphone.

This time it was Bodnof who had the advantage of the time zones. The man sounded enthusiastic, almost cheery. This was not like Moscow.

"You have done well, ambassador. The information is very timely. It confirms what we have suspected," breezed Major General Gregori Bodnof.

"Confirms what, Major Bodnof?" asked Korz after the delay, somewhat testily.

"Let me read you the transcript. Are you ready to record?"

"We are always ready to record, Major General."

Korz's comment was a not-so-gentle reminder that the recording of conversations was a way of life throughout the government, certainly in the upper echelons.

AZIZ AL-AS: *Hello?*

KHALID RAHMAN: *Aziz, is everything all right?*

AZIZ AL-AS: *Khalid! Yes! And you?*

KHALID RAHMAN: *I am safe. It is as Our Khan said it would be. And you, have you found a boat? Have you spoken to Bafq?*

AZIZ AL-AS: *Yes on both accounts! He is to meet me here tonight.* [pause] *I, too, have found this New Bedford to be as you said it would be. The fishermen are very anxious to make a bargain. The boats, Khalid! They are wonderful. They are so well equipped. What of this Wanchese?*

KHALID RAHMAN: *The port is quiet. You are expected. I have reserved three slips, one will be empty on either side of you. They are away from the fishing companies, near the center of the harbor. You should have no problem. I am not a fisherman, but it appears to be well marked.* [pause] *There are two things, Aziz . . .*

AZIZ AL-AS: *Yes?*

KHALID RAHMAN: *From what I can determine, we are safe from inquisitive local people. They have seen people seeking treasure before.*

AZIZ AL-AS: *Good!*

KHALID RAHMAN: *But . . . there is a United States Coast Guard station at a place called Oregon, your entrance from the ocean to the bay of Pamlico. Be aware.*

AZIZ AL-AS: *Thank you, Khalid. I expect to be contacted by the Coast Guard several times.*

KHALID RAHMAN: *Good. The second thing is that you should expect to see a United States Army boat either in harbor or on the waters nearby. Apparently this Oregon can be a difficult passage. You must be careful. The fishermen say it is navigable only at high tide . . . and only during the daylight hours.*

AZIZ AL-AS [pensive]: *This is good to know.*

KHALID RAHMAN: *When do you think you will arrive?*

AZIZ AL-AS: *I expect to make a deal with the owner of the boat this morning. I will tell him I will want to leave tomorrow. I want to be at Sable Island at least a day early, two is better than one . . . in case Our Khan arrives ahead of schedule.*

KHALID RAHMAN: *How long will it take you to get there?*

AZIZ AL-AS: *It is nearly six hundred miles. We will be lucky to make eight miles, perhaps ten, per hour. I would estimate seventy-two hours.*

KHALID RAHMAN: *And from there to here?*

AZIZ AL-AS: *It is hard to say. We will be going against the Gulf Stream. It is twice as far . . . six, perhaps seven, days. We should be there on the 21st or 22nd, no later than the 23rd.*

KHALID RAHMAN: *On the 21st high tide is at 9:23 A.M., on the 22nd at 10:04, and on the 23rd at 10:46.*

AZIZ AL-AS: *Praise Allah! I am ready, Khalid!*

KHALID RAHMAN: *Yes, yes . . . I'm sure you are, Aziz. You must make note of this. I cannot be waiting at the port all day long for you. I don't want to arouse suspicions. If something happens . . .*

AZIZ AL-AS: *But, Khalid! Nothing will happen!*

KHALID RAHMAN: *. . . if something happens, Aziz, I have rented a house in the nearby community named Nags Head . . .*

AZIZ AL-AS: *What?* [confused over name]

KHALID RAHMAN: *N..A..G..S . . . . H..E..A..D. Two words. It is on the beach road, oceanfront. House number 137. The local telephone number is area code 919 number 995-3481.*

AZIZ AL-AS: *I have it.*

KHALID RAHMAN: *Go with Allah, young Aziz al-As.*

"It is very important, Ambassador Korz, that you meet Zaid Khan at his destination and have him followed . . . very discreetly . . . but very closely. He must be protected at all costs."

"From the Americans?" asked Korz.

"Yes . . . from the Americans . . . and from anyone else you deem may hinder Khan's plan."

Korz was fully awake. He gave Katrina Tambov a disturbed look.

"What plan?" asked Korz.

There was a delay, longer than normal for the transmission.

"We don't know. It is your job to find out."

Dimitri Korz closed his eyes in resignation. Bodnof continued.

"Ambassador Korz, Secretary General Gorbachev is aware of this operation as is Mr. Shevardnadze. My superior . . . our superior is highly concerned that you have the right people tracking Zaid Khan and his men."

"They got you this information, Major General. They will be able to follow whatever and whomever is required," Korz said curtly.

"Very well, Ambassador Korz."

"Major General . . . does Moscow have a theory on what Khan has in mind? Has it changed in the last week?"

"No, it has not changed. However, the reason why we are following has changed. We, as a nation, are more interested than we were last week."

There was another long pause before Major General Bodnof continued.

"You must determine if Zaid Khan is smuggling nuclear weapons into the United States."

Although the room was cold, Katrina shivered from the thought that people in her homeland wanted her to follow crazy people with atomic weapons. Rostov was right. The cold of being alone was not far from reality.

"Furthermore, you must determine what Khan's objective or objectives are. If he has nuclear weapons and he does manage to get them into the United States then we must know what his plan is and when—this is very, very important Ambassador Korz—we must know when he delivers his blackmail, whatever it is, to the American president. The timing is crucial," emphasized Bodnof.

"And?" replied Korz, waiting for Bodnof to finish.

" . . . and . . . when he issues his blackmail demand . . . your agents will eliminate his men and take his weapons. That is all you need to know at this point. Do you understand your orders, ambassador?"

"They are very clear, Major General. Has Washington been notified?"

"Yes, of course. Ambassador Kemeravo is in agreement."

"Very well, then. Please convey my greetings to Viktor."

"The line has been disconnected, Mr. Ambassador," said the communications officer.

He turned to Katrina Tambov.

"This Rostov, how good is he?"

Katrina held Rostov's life in her throat. Whatever information Rostov would get in New Bedford with the COMEX-100 was now redundant. Korz could have Rostov eliminated or left in the cold to rot, to be captured or killed by the Americans, or simply sent home to France.

"He . . . he is . . . good, very good. We seem to work well as a team," Katrina answered in measured terms.

"Your . . . our lives are on the line, Comrade Tambov. I like it here, and I assume you do as well. I don't relish finishing my days out in some eastern camp."

The thought of the overweight Korz huddled around a fire or tramping through the snow wearing rags was unsettling, even though she didn't care for the man.

"Neither do I, Dimitri."

Katrina was one of the few who could get away with calling the ambassador by his familiar name.

"Very well, then. You will need assistance, a team."

Katrina was both pleased and more than a bit anxious. It was a very dangerous operation, and she would be the leader. Rostov might think he was the leader, but he wasn't. It would take all her skills to get the job done while allowing Rostov to think he was in charge.

"Where are these places . . . this Wanchese? We need a map," said Korz.

NEW BEDFORD

Alexander Rostov sat on a waist-high stack of empty crab traps and watched as Aziz al-As and Bafq el-Rashid boarded the white-with-red-trim *Bedford Clipper*. Aboard with Captain Carver Medway were two crew members; young Bennie Triolo and cook Dinghy Compton. Dinghy was known to be a bit slow.

Parked on Union Street, facing downhill past the National Club on the right was Rostov's van with the ever-present COMEX-100. There was no use monitoring it now. Whatever was being said was of little consequence. Besides, the Americans would soon be terminated once they were in open waters.

Almost at ten o'clock on the nose the mates aboard the *Clipper*, including a laughing Aziz al-As, threw the last of the lines over onto the concrete wharf and the trawler pulled out into the Acushnet River.

Rostov pushed back his cap and took what little warmth the morning sun had to offer. It was surprising how much relief he'd had when Katrina had called him with the news . . . not just the translation of the al-As/Rahman telephone call, but more importantly the reprieve from what could have been a difficult situation for him. It was a little unsettling to think that for once his life had been out of his own control.

Even if Korz had pulled the plug, he would have survived, thought Rostov. It was time to move south, time to meet Katrina and meet with his new network, a network of new-breed Soviet spies—made in America.

BOSTON
11:30 A.M.

"Congratulations, young man. You've just survived 5-2 odds against. Actually, they were higher but not after the first day. My name is Preston Hammel. You may call me Doctor . . . or Doctor Hammel . . . or given your apparent age, 'sir.'"

"Wh . . ."

Scotty's first attempt at speech was much closer to a croak.

"Where are you, you ask? Massachusetts General Hospital, in Boston. You were chauffeured up here yesterday in the best ambulance money can buy. You can afford it, can't you?" the doctor laughed. "That's all right, you don't have to answer. The next question . . . how long? It's been three days since you were hauled out of the river. You were nearly frozen, you were. We have some questions we'd like to ask you. So do the New Bedford police."

There was a definite pause as Dr. Hammel became serious.

"Who are you, son? The people in Medical Records get real antsy not knowing the name of a patient."

Name? They don't know my name? But my wallet . . . shield. God damn, they took my shield! Mr. Monahan will be pissed.

"Coldsmith. Scott Coldsmith."

He could barely get the words out through his parched lips. Scotty realized how terribly thirsty he was. Then he looked down at the IV stuck in his hand.

"You put salt in those things? I'm dying of thirst."

Doctor Hammel laughed, as did the attending nurse.

"I'm going to have to let the police know you're awake, Mr. Scott Coldsmith. They'll want to know how you got into the Acushnet River and got all those cuts and bruises."

With an effort Scotty reached over to the doctor.

"I'm with the FBI. Please call this number for me . . . area 201 553-2700 . . . ask for Special Agent in Charge Murphy Monahan. He's in charge of the FBI in Manhattan. Please."

Dr. Preston Hammel was temporarily dumbfounded.

Scotty went back under the control of the drugs surging through his body. The last thing he could remember was hitting the water; beaten and nearly unconscious, clothes soaked by the icy cold river, and sinking. His hand had struck a submerged piling and he'd grabbed for it. He remembered the slimy feeling the piling had and the difficulty he'd had in grabbing for it. The piling was the last thing he'd remembered.

Dr. Hammel spoke to the unconscious Scotty.

"We'll do it, son. The divers say they had to pry your hands off the piling. You were on that thing tighter'n a barnacle. You're one lucky fella."

KITTY HAWK, NORTH CAROLINA

"Yes, sir . . . can I . . . ?"

"I'd like to buy that one."

The salesman at Ocean Chevrolet thought he'd died and gone to heaven. Khalid Rahman had pointed to the only truck he'd had in his inventory—a new Suburban. It listed for $25,900. Rahman walked around all nineteen feet of it and nodded his head in approval. The vehicle was huge.

"I want the third seat removed. I don't want it."

"Yes, sir."

"Are the shock absorbers of the heavy-duty type?"

"Yes," said the salesman with enthusiasm.

"Good," said Khalid with businesslike approval.

Rahman sat on a beat-up metal folding chair next to the salesman's desk and watched him hurriedly completing all the forms for the order, hurrying so he could get Rahman's signature before he changed his mind.

"How much for cash? Bottom line."

"Cash? You mean you're going to pay by check? Well, we'll have to wait for the check to clear, then . . ."

Rahman put his briefcase on the man's desk right on top of the paperwork, snapped the clasps and opened it.

"Cash. How much?" asked Rahman.

In less than half an hour the forms were completed, and Rahman had gotten a 10% discount—not as much as he could have, but worth the question.

"Do you have someone . . . ?"

"No, I'll be back for my car in a few minutes. I'll take it now. I want to have it customized."

"Well, you know, we do customizing . . ."

The salesman talked as if he never completed a sentence. Rahman shook his head and handed him the address of the rental cottage in Nags Head. He didn't have to drive far, only about four blocks. The lumber and construction business was thriving on the Outer Banks. It didn't seem to matter what kind of tax laws were passed, people still wanted to come and build homes. He pulled into Guy Lumber and asked for the manager.

"Do you have a carpenter who could do a customized job on the inside of that truck?" asked Rahman.

The foreman walked with Khalid out into the breezy afternoon. The sun just couldn't seem to punch through the coldness of the wind. Two blocks away whitecaps formed on the breaking ocean waves as the wind flattened out the crest.

"What do you want done?" asked the foreman.

"I have some heavy, but very valuable, objects which I need to secure well for a long trip. Use the entire rear storage area and build five separate storage areas, each four feet tall by three feet wide, solid wood on all sides. I want the cabinets to be connected together by snaps or hooks so that they are secure, but can be removed singly if necessary. It appears to me as if you will need to run two rows of three cabinets each down the center of the truck's storage area. I'll use the last for extra storage. I want them secure on either side with some sort of brace onto the side walls. Finally, I want a hinged cover or lid for each. When all six are covered the total area should be completely flat and I should be able to store more things on top."

Rahman looked at the foreman, who was slightly puzzled.

"Expense is not a problem. Time and quality are my concerns. I want strong wood and good craftsmanship, and I'm willing to pay for it. Today is the 14th. I must have it finished by the 17th."

The foreman looked at Rahman, then at the Suburban. Things were slow. It would be an easy way to pick up some money on the side.

"Two thousand dollars," the foreman said, figuring he would settle for half the amount and still make a nice profit.

"Agreed. Here is half the amount as an advance on the materials," replied Rahman as he pulled out a packet of one hundred dollar bills, broke the seal, and gave the man ten crisp Franklins. Rahman continued.

"When you're done, please deliver it to this address. I will pay the balance then," Rahman said, businesslike.

The two men shook hands and Rahman walked back toward the smiling Chevy dealer to pick up his rental car.

Things were going well. The truck would be perfect for the mission. There would be room enough for the four of them, and five bombs Khan would bring. Khan would also bring whatever sidearms were needed, since it would be difficult to get them quickly—not impossible, just not worth the risk.

It was winter in America, the warmth of springtime was a long way away. While Rahman had no definite idea of where they were going, he had a hunch that it would be wise for him to insure that everyone had cold weather gear. It was a good hunch.

BOSTON

"I want my walking papers, doc. I'm leaving. I've got work to do."

Although he would have preferred that Scotty stay another few days for observation, there was really nothing Dr. Hammel could do to prevent the young FBI agent from going his own way. Scotty was well enough to leave.

What would have happened if the thugs hadn't come out of the bar? You'd be dead. Scotty thought. The Soviets had a crossfire and they had the experience he didn't have. But, the sons of bitches didn't get him! They had a four day start. The image of Alexander Rostov, standing backlit on the opposite corner of Union Street, came back to Scotty. Yesterday afternoon the New Bedford police had come up and interviewed him. Yes, the men had come out of the National Club. Yes, he would recognize at least two of them. Yes, those were the men. The police had shown him mug shots of four men who had been picked up. Apparently one of the men had had an attack of remorse after throwing Scotty into the Acushnet River and had called the police. It had been the police who had pulled Scotty out of the river. With or without the confession the four men would have been easy to identify. Things started to fall into place for the police once Scotty told them that someone had fired at him just before the struggle started.

"We found 9mm shell casings across the street. And one of the men had been shot in the leg. What kind of gun were you carrying?" the lieutenant had asked.

"Standard issue, Smith & Wesson .38."

"Do you know who was shooting at you?"

"Yes, but I can't tell you. It was a man I had been following. I lost him a few days ago . . . when was it? I can't remember dates. He was following another man."

In Scotty's brief career with the FBI the one thing he had observed was that an agent never offered information. An agent's purpose in life was to vacuum information for himself.

"Is that it?" asked the officer, sarcastically.

Scotty tried to get his mind back in gear. What did he need to do? He had to get a warrant for Rostov's arrest. He had to find out why John Smithton Ramsey was in New Bedford. He had to find his car. He had to get the descriptions of Ramsey's Hertz rental into the National Crime Information Center (NCIC) computer along with Rostov's black Buick. Ramsey had registered at a Holiday Inn out near the interstate. Perhaps Rostov had done the same. What rooms were they in? The rooms would need to be dusted. The Hertz computer would have to be flagged for Ramsey; either for a return or for a new rental.

"Are you going to press charges against the men?" the police had asked.

Scotty didn't hesitate. There was *so* much to do, and *he* was all right—but his face turned sour when he thought of the four men beating and kicking him.

"Yes. You bet. Those sons of bitches tried to kill me."

The New Bedford police had left with what they had come to get and had left Scotty with a longer list of to-dos than he'd thought.

One thing at a time. You can only do one thing at a time. Get organized and get going, Scotty said to himself as he pulled out a pad of paper and made a list. There would be no help from the Bureau other than the computers.

BOSTON:
  FBI OFFICE
  DISTRICT ATTORNEY - GRAND JURY - WARRANT
  NCIC - BUICK

NEW BEDFORD:
  CAR!
  HJ - PRINTS
  RAMSEY - WHY?

NEW YORK
  MY CAR
  BADGE
  CLOTHES
  HERTZ
  CUSTOMS
  SOVIET MISSION
  SCOTLAND YARD - RAMSEY
  CIA - ROSTOV

Scotty left Boston General at eleven. Behind him was the nearly frozen Charles River and the city of Cambridge on the other side. Boston was a clean, nice-looking city. The historical sites were well maintained and integrated into the city, and made the city appear to be liveable . . . as opposed to barely tolerable, which is what Scotty thought of New York. A short cab ride took Scotty to the JFK Federal Building. Everything he needed was in one building; the FBI office, the District Attorney, the U.S. Federal Court. The first thing he had to do was to get Rostov, as well as the black Buick, into the FBI computer.

His first stop was the FBI office. It was here he had his first lesson in FBI data processing, to learn the facts of life. Scotty was fortunate to talk to a rotor clerk who was kind enough to set him straight.

"Listen, son . . . we don't want to enter that here. You've got to have your office do it. Once it gets into the system only the originating office can remove the record. You'll be down there in New York and I'll be up here. I really don't want anything to do with it. Neither will the D.A. Neither will anybody in this office. Your man's a Soviet courier out of the mission in New York, not Boston. We aren't going to be following this dude. You are. Call your office and have them put a TFW into the system."

The senior clerk laughed at Scotty's confused look.

"TFW, Temporary Felony Want. You're in Manhattan? Do you know Rosemary Fielding?"

Scotty shook his head no.

"Rose and I talk all the time. Call her and tell her you need a TFW."

"But they said I couldn't call in."

"Secure lines, son. We've got secure lines between offices. Call Rose. Good luck."

Scotty stood in the clutter and bustle of the Boston office and never felt so out of place in his life.

Call Rose.

He did, explained where he was, and what he needed.

"OK, but the TFW will only stay in the system for 48 hours. Are you going to get a warrant by then?"

"Yes," said Scotty reluctantly.

He would have to go to New York, get the warrant, then go back up to New Bedford . . . this was not at all easy.

"This is a New Entry?" asked Rose.

"Yes." [ET]

"Name?

"Alexander Rostov." [Rostov, Alexander]

"Sex, male. Race?"

"Caucasian," replied Scotty. [M] [W]

"Place of Birth?"

"Unknown." [XX]

"Date of Birth?"

"Unknown." [XXXXXX]

"Height?"

"About five-ten." [510]

"Weight?"

"One sixty." [160]

"Eye Color?"

"Unknown." [XXX]

"Hair Color?"

"Brown." [BRO]

"FBI Number?"

"I don't understand," replied Scotty.

"Is this your first entry, Mr. Coldsmith?"

Rose sounded like she was easily in her fifties. Scotty felt a little silly when she called him mister.

"Yes, it is."

"The FBI number is your number. It can be from one to nine characters, alphabetic or numeric. Your name and a sequence number is OK."

"All right, use Coldsmith 0001." [COLD0001]

"Skin Tone?"

"Skin tone? What do you mean?" asked Scotty.

"Is he an albino? Does he have fair skin, ruddy complexion, sallow, olive . . . give me a color."

"Fair." [FAR]

"Scars, Marks, or Tattoos?"

"I don't know." [NONE]

"Do you have any fingerprints on this man?" asked Rose.

"Not yet. I will."

"When you do, it's very important you get the codes right . . . and in the right order. Talk to your print guy when you get them. I don't have time to give you the short course on prints over the phone."

"Social Security Number?"

"Rose, the man's a Soviet agent."

"Does he have a driver's license?"

Scotty thought that was funny. He started to laugh.

"Listen, Coldsmith, he could be using a fake ID or someone's real license," lectured Rose.

"No . . . sorry." [NONE]

"What's this guy wanted for?"

"Attempted murder, espionage, sabotage, illegal entry, flight to avoid . . . "

"OK, OK . . . you got them all." Espionage [0103], Sabotage [0104], Illegal Entry [0301], Aggrav Asslt—Pub Officer—[1305], Flight to Avoid Confinement [4902].

"Date of Warrant . . . skip it, you'll need to get that warrant, Coldsmith, or else this drops out in 48 hours."

Rose put in the Originating Agency Case Number. It was a nine digit number preceded by the office abbreviation [MAN666890]

"You've got 121 character free field for a description. What do you want?" [SUSPECT SOVIET KGB AGENT ARMED AND DANGEROUS]

Rose continued.

"Do you have any automobile information?"

"Yes, I do. He was driving a black 1986 Buick Century, license plate New York 8644NTO. [BUIC] [SKY] [NY] [8644NTO] [BLK]

"That's it, Coldsmith. Get that warrant."

ABOARD THE *BEDFORD CLIPPER*, ATLANTIC OCEAN

Aziz felt a rough hand on his shoulder. He cringed and was immediately wide awake, but did nothing to avoid the contact. Was this another beating? Was it . . . ? His heart beat rapidly.

"Get up! It is time," said Bafq el-Rashid.

Aziz swallowed hard and could feel the tears of relief in the back of his eyes.

Aziz and Bafq shared what had been a make-shift "guest" bunk in a nook off the galley. They could hear and smell Dinghy the cook preparing breakfast. The odor of fish was pervasive. It was part of every meal aboard the *Clipper*. This morning, their second out from New Bedford, it actually smelled good.

The first day had been a difficult one for Bafq. He was not a sailor by any means. The moderate Atlantic waves had been too much for him for the better part of the afternoon, but by evening he had gotten used to the rolling and pitching of the boat and his walk had changed from a stagger to something more under control. Bafq el-Rashid was a man who always insisted on being in control.

Aziz still carried the mental baggage from the night in the motel. He slept restlessly and continually kept watch to see if Bafq was watching him. Several times he glanced at el-Rashid only to find Bafq's cold eyes locked on him in return. It was unnerving.

"Get out of bed. Now!" el-Rashid ordered again.

With Bafq watching Aziz did what he was told, dressing hurriedly in the dark of the early morning. The sun would rise late this cold morning. The barest of pink tinged the cloud cover to the northeast as the *Bedford Clipper* made its way toward Sable Island, a frigid rock with an unmanned lighthouse; inhabited only by seals, gulls, and crabs.

The sounds of the galley mixed with the noise and vibration of the *Clipper*'s engines and the relentless sloshing of the waves against the boat. The smell of fish and eggs was mixed with that of diesel fumes, all masked by the pervasive taste of salt.

"Take this! You take the captain, I will take care of the other two," whispered Bafq el-Rashid.

Bafq's hand gripped the younger man's shoulder.

"Where'd you get that?" Aziz said anxiously.

It was a snub-nosed gun of undetermined manufacture.

"Just because we are in America doesn't mean you can't get a gun when you want. What do you think I did for two days, play with myself?" el-Rashid said with scorn. "Take it! The captain is at the wheel. We must hurry."

"Why not wait? We will be there tomorrow. Let them take us all the way," argued Aziz.

"Can you operate this boat, or not?" returned el-Rashid.

"Yes. A boat is a boat. This is a good one. I can sail her."

"Then do as I say!" whispered el-Rashid with a tone which implied more than a threat.

In el-Rashid's hand was a knotted leather garrote of approximately thirty inches. He twisted and wrapped one end around his left hand, then did the same to his right.

"Go!"

Aziz went. He stepped out onto the rolling deck of the *Bedford Clipper* and walked toward the ladder which led up to the pilot's house. The morning was very cold, the air damp. The trip from New Bedford had been not without its tensions. Medway's crew spoke very little. Dinghy Compton stayed in the galley and did cleanup aboard the boat. The young Portuguese, Bennie Triolo, spoke very little English, and stayed away from the foreigners. He sent signals of mistrust that were picked up by el-Rashid, and it had been the young man's obvious dislike which had gotten Bafq up in a killing mood. It had to be done sooner or later. Captain Medway had not picked up on his mates' suspicions.

Medway had picked up something, but had refused to recognize it. This was going to be a short, profitable trip, one which would help pay the mortgage on the *Clipper* as well as several months' mortgage on his small home in New Bedford. There would be *no* trouble, he had promised himself. He was humming as he piloted the boat in the early morning fog. He turned when he heard Aziz climbing up the ladder.

"Good morning, John," said Medway, smiling.

His smile was gone in an instant.

"My name is Aziz al-As and I am taking over this boat in the name of Allah himself."

Aziz pointed the evil-looking little gun at Medway.

"You're a drug runner, aren't you?" shouted Carver Medway. "You scum! Why do you need the *Clipper*? Why me?"

Carver Medway was beside himself. He made a move toward the younger man. Al-As fired a single shot which popped out of the gun and tore into Medway's left leg, splattering the meaty section of upper thigh, at once disabling the captain and at the same time throwing blood droplets everywhere within reach. The sound was like that of a bullet going into a ripe pumpkin. THWAP! Medway bent over in pain, dropping to his one good leg.

"You son of a bitch!"

Aziz, calmly as could be, pulled the trigger twice more. The first shot went through Carver Medway's stomach, the second lodged in his chest. Medway shuddered backwards, hit his head against the steel wall and fell in a bloody heap. Blood oozed from the clean wounds. His eyes glassed over as his heart beat rapidly, trying to keep up with the loss of blood and the damage done to his system.

Aziz backed out of the door and slid down the slippery ladder to the main deck. The *Bedford Clipper* continued chugging its way through the waves. He ran back toward the narrow galley where he found the body of Dinghy Compton rumpled in a pile on the floor. The gas grill was still on, burning a fish stew with eggs. Aziz turned the blue flame off, bent down to see if indeed the crewman was dead. A large bruise had started to form under his Adam's apple. Dinghy's neck lay all limp, flopping from side to side at an unnatural angle to the tune of the boat's movement.

Where was Bafq?

From below Aziz heard shouts, then commotion. Bafq must not have had the element of surprise with Bennie Triolo. From the galley Aziz rocked his way through the narrow crew's quarters then to the ladder leading to the engine room. The stink of the fumes from the diesel engines was familiar, not entirely distasteful. Aziz had spent much of the previous day getting a good feel for the *Clipper*, although it was doubtful if he would have to make any kind of emergency repairs. Once they met up with Khan, they would scuttle the Libyan boat and there would be plenty of trained crew to handle the engine.

Seeing no one in the engine room, Aziz went back to the empty cargo hold. The smell of dead fish brought back memories of his childhood on the Caspian Sea. A noise above deck! Aziz ran back toward the engine room and up the ladder to an outside hatch which led to the aft section of the main deck.

Bennie Triolo was giving Bafq el-Rashid the fight of his life. The young Portuguese sailor and the older Iranian rolled on the steel grates that covered the large hatchway to the holds. It was unclear who was in command. Aziz ran toward the fight. The two men wrestled, clawed, and rolled.

"Hold him!" shouted Aziz.

Bafq gave up on trying to get his garrote around Bennie's throat and instead concentrated on maintaining a constant position. Aziz came closer and held his snub-nosed gun not two feet from Triolo's head. At the last instant Bennie looked up, temporarily distracted from his effort by Aziz's shout in Farsi.

He saw Aziz's finger close on the trigger. A second later he was brain-dead as Aziz fired a bullet straight through his forehead. Triolo's grip on el-Rashid was instantly relaxed, throwing him slightly off balance.

Before either could say a word they were both shaken by a sudden shift in the direction of the *Clipper*. Instead of going into the waves the boat started to take the Atlantic's pounding broadside.

"We're turning!" shouted el-Rashid.

Aziz was thrown off balance and fell to his knees on the grated deck. The first wave hit the *Clipper* broadside and washed over the gunnels, splashing the two Arabs.

"A boat doesn't make a turn like that unless . . ."

Carver Medway was alive and the realization struck Aziz. They were very close to failure. Medway could sink the *Clipper* very easily by allowing the boat to be swamped. I would do the same, thought Aziz as he tried to run toward the forward part of the boat. Another powerful wave, easy to manage while going into it but very difficult when broadside, smashed into the *Clipper*, throwing a slippery mixture of froth and seawater across the deck. Aziz fell in mid-step, crashing heavily to the deck.

The *Clipper* was slowly turning. Medway had the wheel and was spinning the boat, alternating broadsides. In a short time the momentum would be ripe for capsizing. Aziz got up and struggled toward the wrought-iron ladder.

Suddenly al-As felt a sting in his leg. Looking up saw a puff of white smoke. Incredibly, Carver Medway stood at the hatch, bracing himself against the thrashing of the Atlantic, and fired several wild shots toward Aziz. Blood dripped down his arm and over the gun. He wore a wet mat of blood on his chest.

Aziz dove for the galley hatch as he heard several other shots ping against the steel masts, then the thump of bullets into the mass of hanging nets.

"Captain Medway, you can't win! Throw down your weapon. I won't harm you. You are too valuable to our mission," al-As lied.

Medway shouted something unintelligible, coughing up blood in the process. He was almost gone, but he gamely hung on as his boat slowly spun to its death.

There wasn't much time. Aziz ran through the galley, jumped over the body of Dinghy Compton, knocking the pan of breakfast onto the deck. At the forward section of the galley there was a ladder which led up into the pilot's house. This enabled crew to go from the topdeck to the engine room or sleeping quarters without going outside. Aziz hoped that Medway was too dazed and nearly dying to close the hatch cover, which would in effect lock Aziz out and force him to take the pilot's house from the main deck . . . a very difficult task as long as Medway had cover. As long as Medway had his senses a frontal assault would have the same odds of success in this battlefield as it had in past wars, very little.

The hatch was open! Aziz scrambled up. Carver Medway was on the floor in front of him, facing the aft hatchway. He was on the radio!

"Mayday . . . mayday . . . this is the trawler *Bedford Clipper*. My boat has been hijacked and my crew killed. I am at position 43 degrees north latitude, approximately 62 degrees west longitude . . . mayday . . . mayday, please assist. This is Captain Carver Medway. My trawler the *Bedford Clipper* has been hijacked by drug runners. I need help. My crew is dead . . . mayday . . ."

Aziz fired a shot which struck Medway in the right cheek. The bullet shattered his teeth and passed through his mouth from side to side. The microphone fell harmlessly to the deck as the room seemed to be instantly filled with Medway's blood. Medway's body shuddered to the left, his head slamming against the wall of the pilot house with a thud.

Aziz climbed into the pilot's house and immediately went to the wheel. The *Clipper* was almost out of control. For the next ten minutes Aziz fought with the boat to gain control, to right the boat and get her back on course.

Firmly in control, Aziz looked down at Medway just as el-Rashid climbed up to see how he was doing. The captain was still alive. His eyes were glassy. With his last bit of energy he tried to reach for a gun. Where was his gun? He floundered around, his eyesight hazy.

"I have your gun, captain Medway," said Aziz.

Medway looked up into the sympathetic eyes of Aziz al-As and the cold face of Bafq el-Rashid who stood behind him.

It was over.

He was losing blood. He could hardly feel the pain in his legs and chest as el-Rashid dragged him toward the door, leaving a trail of blood on the floor. Once at the door, el-Rashid rolled him through the opening then down the ladder. Medway fell in a messy lump.

Still awake, Medway's consciousness translated some last images from his eyes. His head rested against the pebbled steel deck. Fifteen feet away was young Bennie Triolo, dead. Next to him was Dinghy Compton. He watched as they attached something to Bennie's legs. It was a weight of some kind. And then he saw them pick the young man up and, without ceremony, dump him over the side into the Atlantic. They did the same to Dinghy.

They came to him.

Please. Please. I don't want to die. Not like this! Carver Medway couldn't say a word, he could only scream them to himself. His eyes frantically tried to communicate with the two men. *Please don't throw me overboard! Kill me first!. Please! Oh, god . . . no! Please don't throw me overboard. I don't want to die like this. Please, please!*

Then he felt someone's rough hands tie ropes around his legs. A heavy weight was placed on top of his stomach. It was an anchor to one of the nets. He didn't remember it weighing as much as it did. Then the hands, one set on his shoulders, another on his legs. Medway sagged in the middle with the extra forty pounds of steel.

They lifted him up. He was above the level of the railing. He could smell the closeness of the water, feel the sting of the spray.

Then he was falling. In the fifteen-foot drop to the top of the rolling waves, just before he sliced through the surface to his death, Captain Carver Medway asked for, and received, his forgiveness.

NAGS HEAD

Korz had given Katrina two additional agents, an odd pair referred to as Reynolds and Williams—no first names were used. Surprisingly to Katrina, Rostov felt no need to be in control of the group. He was quite willing to let her be control leader for the operation. Since it was unlikely he would ever work with these men again, it made sense for her to be in charge of the operation. As top agent for Korz, she already knew the two New York men. As far as Rostov was concerned, it was only important that he be in charge of their team. What she did with Williams and Reynolds was unimportant, as long as they didn't get in the way and were reasonably competent at their job.

They had met Williams and Reynolds at the Clara Barton rest area on the New Jersey Turnpike just north of the Delaware Memorial Bridge. Katrina had returned to New Haven where she had waited for Rostov to meet her with the Caravan. It had taken them a little over five hours to cover the distance, and they'd gotten there early. The whole trip had been through the leaden skies of New Jersey. From New York to Philadelphia the air smelled of chemicals. The smell seemed to affect everything, including what they ate and drank.

Katrina briefed the two men on what was expected and the general scope of their mission. Williams and Reynolds were as American as could be . . . in fact, they *were* Americans. Both had been turned at an early age and had worked in civilian jobs in the government for the last ten years. Both men could handle small arms as well as sniper rifles. In addition to his agent skills, Williams had a pilot's license and had fought in Viet Nam flying helicopters.

The team was a good one.

On their way to North Carolina, Katrina transformed herself from a hard-edged eastern European to a more casual, preppy American. She switched to running shoes, slacks, sweater, and parka. She softened her makeup and let her hair fall naturally around her shoulders. She also insisted that Rostov get some more appropriate clothes as well, which he reluctantly did.

In Virginia, the sleet they'd driven in since New Jersey finally turned to rain as the temperature rose to a balmy 38 degrees. With Williams and Reynolds in the lead the procession went under Hampton Roads into Norfolk, then turned at Great Bridge Boulevard in Chesapeake and headed down state 168 toward North Carolina and the Outer Banks. The traffic was negligible but the group was careful to observe the speed limit. An hour later they crossed the Currituck Sound via the three-mile-long Wright Memorial Bridge to the village of Kitty Hawk. At the welcome center they easily got their bearings from a large map, quickly locating Roanoke Island, the village of Wanchese, the National Seashore, and the route to Khalid Rahman's rental cottage. With only two north-south roads, one on the beach and the other three blocks inland, route-finding wasn't difficult.

"That must be it," said Katrina, as they made a slow pass down the beach road in Rostov's black Buick.

There was no need to linger, nor was there a need to stay right on top of Rahman. There was also no need to set up the COMEX.

"Whom would he talk to?" laughed Rostov. "The rest of his gang is on a boat somewhere in the Atlantic."

Nevertheless, Williams and Reynolds were assigned to Wanchese, making the Croatan Motel in Manteo their base. They would spend much of their time at Chuck's Crab House lingering over meals, which fortunately was busy for twelve hours a day, so it made things a bit easier for the two men. Katrina and Rostov would tail Rahman.

For the first time in two weeks Alexander Rostov could relax. It was a strange feeling and one that he would not have for long.

NEW YORK

Scotty sat in his cramped, non-smoking window seat on his peanutless Eastern flight from LaGuardia to New Bedford. You couldn't even buy peanuts from Eastern, and Scotty was hungry.

It had been a pisser of a day.

After landing he'd gone to the Queens Impound lot and paid a huge fine to free his car—it almost wasn't worth it. Then he looked around to see if there was anything else he could do—anything to put off the inevitable. He had dreaded it so . . . my, how he had dreaded going back into the office. No ID, no badge, no Soviet agent. He had been admonished when he had been given the identification to *never, never, never* lose it. And here he was, just into training, and he'd already lost it.

But things never are quite as bad as the mind thinks they will be. When he'd arrived at the office, Murphy Monahan wasn't there, so he was off *that* hook. Word had gotten back ahead of him and many of the agents had come by to see how he was doing. It made Scotty feel good. A few agents told him not to worry, they'd lost *their* badges as well . . . but they'd never lost theirs at the bottom of the Acushnet River. Several of the agents had confirmed what Rose had told him, and even gave him names, places, and the best time to see the D.A. about getting a warrant.

It was the paperwork that killed him—the forms, the rush to typing, then the dash to the U.S. District Court to meet with a D.A. who didn't know him from Adam and had no time even to eat, much less diddle around with a young FBI agent trying to find some Russian when there were so many really *serious* crimes to prosecute. Still, the "good-old-boy" network worked. As he was told to do, Scotty dropped one or two names of agents who said that mentioning their name would get Scotty the attention of the D.A.—which it did. The D.A. even went out of his way to get Scotty in front of a judge so that Scotty could ask for a Federal warrant against Alexander Rostov.

What Scotty wasn't prepared for was walking into a Grand Jury room, waiting a half-hour for a case to be processed, then having to present his reasons to an unsmiling judge while the Grand Jury listened.

"Just call him 'Your Honor,' tell him the facts, and get the hell out of here," said the D.A.

Scotty did exactly as he was told. The judge had no questions and signed his warrant. With a warrant Rose could change the message key entry from Wanted Person–Temporary Felony [ET] to Wanted Person–Felony [EW]. Rose also added a Notify on All Hits [NOAH] to the entry. If anyone else made a connection, a hit, on any relevant field then that officer was obligated to notify the agent/officer who entered the record.

Scotty also talked with the men in the 67th Street trailer to see if any of them had sighted Rostov in the last week. They hadn't.

Finally, Scotty had spent an inordinate amount of time at the 64th Street Hertz outlet trying to get a copy of the rental form signed by the increasingly mysterious John Smithton Ramsey. It had been worth the wait. Ramsey had been forced to produce a credit card *and* a driver's license. The license was international as was the Visa card. Ramsey gave an address in London. At this point they were just numbers. He didn't have enough information to query Scotland Yard.

He needed more. Where was Ramsey? Where was Rostov?

Long gone.

You can only do one thing at a time, Scotty thought to himself. *Just make sure that the one thing you're doing is at least taking you in the right direction.* Unfortunately, New Bedford seemed the only direction he could go. The thought of walking back to the wharf gave him goosebumps. But, he *had* to do it. *Face up to it! Get a grip, Coldsmith!* As the flight began its slow descent to the New Bedford Municipal Airport there was sleet in the air. Misery loved company.

SABLE ISLAND, NOVA SCOTIA

The Libyan fishing boat *Grand Occidental* had performed without a flaw, although from Khan's perspective it was unfortunate that he had been forced to use the crew provided by Qaddafi. The men had been competent enough, but their loyalty was not to Khan. More importantly, they had no sense of mission, no passion.

During the interminable ten-day trip on the *Grand Occidental*, Khan kept himself separated from the Libyans. Although there had been some grumbling, the captain's quarters had been given to him. The Libyans' crew of four, including a cook and an engineer, gave Khan a watchful eye and a wide berth.

In the cargo hold, sitting on three wooden pallets secured by heavy ropes, were five low-grade, incredibly dirty, atomic weapons. Each weapon was roughly 85% of that which was dropped by the *Enola Gay* on Hiroshima.

The polonium and lithium wafers had been the trickiest. Polonium was a natural chemical element formed from the disintegration of radium. The material was chemically formed after the decaying process from irradiating the chemical element bismuth. The solid material produced was radioactive and had an incredible ability to induce an electrical charge. Its original use was to provide power for space satellites.

Unlike the polonium, which had a high melting temperature, lithium was the world's lightest solid metal, melting at a low 178C. Pliable, like plastic explosive material, lithium was an inert substance, but one that was critical to the thermonuclear process. When the radioactive polonium and the inert lithium were put together, an excess of neutrons was generated. By itself, this process was harmless. But, when the process was started in the presence of a uranium isotope, U-235, the added neutrons, which make up the nucleus of all substances, caused the uranium isotope to break apart. The now unbalanced nucleus tries to split into two equal parts. It does, but some of the mass of the splitting atom is converted into energy.

The uranium isotope U-235 is used for this process because in its natural state it supports continual fission. So, when the splitting process starts, each new nucleus in turn splits, thus creating more energy, etc., etc. Once the nucleus-splitting process begins, it continues until there are no more atoms, until every chemical atom has been converted to energy. It turns out that about fifty pounds of processed U-235 is required to provide enough critical mass to produce an atomic bomb.

Each of Khan's bombs contained fifty-eight pounds of processed U-235.

The bombs that Qaddafi had been able to assemble were relatively simple. Inside a heavy, stainless steel ball-like container was the majority of the uranium. The detonator could be of any design, as long as the lithium and polonium wafers were not next to each other. Qaddafi's scientists had designed an odd-looking contraption, but one that was well built. On top of the container, approximately one and a half times the size of a basketball, was an extension two feet long by four inches in diameter, also constructed of stainless steel. It looked like a short arm. The joint of the arm and the container were double-welded. At the tip of the arm was an inch-thick threaded cap. In the center of the cap was a quarter-inch flat metal screw, three inches long.

Inside the arm were the timer and detonator. Of all the materials, the timer had been the hardest to obtain. The processed uranium had been stolen from a French think-tank company which had been arranging an illegal trade with the South African government. The polonium had come from India, and the lithium from a source in Ethiopia. The timer was from West Germany, a miniature device that combined radio and computer technologies. A 256K microprocessor chip had been inserted into what had been the internals of a standard travel alarm which could be set for any date in the future. With three of the clock's five small buttons, an alarm could be set for any year-month-day-hour-minute and second. It was a terrorist's dream come true. Bombs could be planted anyplace in the world and there would always be time to escape.

Under the timer were three four-inch detonators buried in a gooey batch of plastic explosive and five pounds of processed uranium. Under it all was the wafer of inert lithium. When the electrical charge is given to the detonator, the lithium-tipped uranium is fired down the short barrel into the radioactive wafer of polonium. The two wafers meet, excess neutrons are generated, and the uranium isotope starts its irreversible process of fission. The fifty-eight pounds of processed uranium is converted to energy in one hundred-millionth of a second and an explosion roughly equivalent to one megaton is the result.

Detonated from the top of the JFK Federal Building in Boston, the weapon would turn every building in a half-mile radius to radioactive rubble—from Columbus Park to Paul Revere's house to the Boston Gardens to the Shriner's Hospital for Crippled Children to the Old South Meeting House . . . all would be gone. The blast, followed by dirty radioactive fallout, would kill or incapacitate millions of people.

Left in the back seat of a parked car on South Capitol Street the bomb would level the U.S. Capitol, the Botanic Gardens, the Supreme Court, the Department of Labor, and all of the House and Senate office buildings.

The physical devastation would be greater in certain cities. Clearly, if Khan wanted to kill *people*, he would take his series of nasty little bombs and secrete them in the center of cities where a compact explosion would do the most damage: New York, Boston, Washington, Chicago, Dallas, Houston, Atlanta, San Francisco. Five weapons properly placed could kill over sixteen million people and permanently injure, disfigure, or give cancerous levels of radiation to many millions more.

It could also start World War III.

With the expected retaliation, it certainly would mean the permanent obliteration of Iran, and most likely Libya, and every other country who could be remotely tied to the bombing. Anyone could be a terrorist. All it took was a mean heart and a willing purpose. You didn't need brains, nor necessarily courage . . . as witnessed by some of the stupid acts of random terrorism by Khan's contemporaries.

No, you gained someone's attention not by striking angrily at him but by driving the stake of fear through his heart. Khan's objective was not to destroy the heart of the United States, not to anger the monster, but rather to bring the country and its leaders to its collective knees. Mere death and destruction were not the way of Zaid abu Khan.

Khan and the Libyans arrived at Sable Island at 4:00 A.M., Atlantic Time. The sun was a long way off. A front, which had swept up the American coastline, had brought patches of rain and sleet into the area. As instructed, the Libyans kept the fifty-mile-long island between them and the mainland of Nova Scotia and the curious ears of long-distance sonar, although it was unlikely any normal measurements could pick up the boat since Sable Island was nearly 150 miles off the coastline.

At eight o'clock the Libyan pilot turned to Khan.

"Ahead," he pointed to the southwest.

There would be no radio contact, although all normal channels were open in case it wasn't al-As. Twenty minutes later the *Bedford Clipper* pulled alongside the *Grand Occidental.*

"What a boat they have found!" said the smiling Khan to the surly Libyan captain. The captain was ready to get rid of his cargo and return.

The two boats danced closely to each other. Although the weather was miserable, there was fortunately not much wind, and consequently not much wave action. The Libyans secured a wooden gangway between the boats and Khan quickly boarded and clasped Bafq el-Rashid's hands with his.

"Well done!" he shouted up to the smiling al-As in the pilot's house of the *Clipper.* "We must hurry before the weather changes!"

Although a minor point in his plan, the transfer of the six weapons from the *Grand Occidental* to the *Bedford Clipper* was no easy task. Potentially, it was as tricky and difficult as anything they would try. Rocking with the waves, al-As and the Libyan pilot kept the two boats from smashing into each other, yet close enough that the gangway would remain secure. Since they were el-Rashid's bombs, the wiry Iranian led the Libyan deckhands in the transfer of the bombs, one at a time, from the hold of the *Grand Occidental* to that of the *Bedford Clipper.* After el-Rashid secured his weapons and made an inventory of the required accessories, he and Khan returned to the *Grand Occidental.* Khan was in very good spirits.

"Are you and your crew ready?" he asked.

"Yes, we will return immediately. We have been paid. I and my men want nothing to do with whatever you have planned. We are going home."

The Libyan seaman had no respect for Zaid Khan, either the man or his politics.

Khan kept his outward expression impassive. There *was* no return. Everyone on this mission was on a one-way trip. There could be no return to Tripoli or Algiers where word of Khan's secretive Atlantic meeting could possibly reach Western ears, certainly not before the Ultimatum was ready to be delivered.

Bafq el-Rashid prepared for what Khan was going to do, and turned to the hatchway ladder just as Khan lashed at the Libyan with a knife which seemingly had come out of thin air. The knife cut a swath, slicing across the man's hand, arm, chest, and up to his neck. For a second the wound seemed to pucker, then a ribbon of blood appeared which quickly turned to a flood as it gushed from the exposed skin. The pilot was speechless, dumbfounded at the swiftness of the attack and the severity of the wound. The pilot clutched himself, not knowing which was the worse of his injuries. In a blur, Khan whipped a second slice that cut the man's neck from side to side in front. The jugular was ruptured. The man would be dead within a minute.

El-Rashid quickly disabled a second of the Libyans who had climbed up the exterior ladder to the small landing area outside the pilot's house. He simply tossed the man over the side and down the fifteen foot drop to the main deck below. The man fell heavily and did not get up.

El-Rashid looked at the *Bedford Clipper*, which was slowly starting to drift away from the *Grand Occidental* as the Libyan boat no longer had someone at the wheel.

"You must hurry, my Khan!" urged Bafq.

Khan realized the problem and quickly followed el-Rashid down the ladder to the main deck. The second sailor was groggily coming around from his fall. Khan ran for the gangway as el-Rashid stopped to deliver a forceful kick to the head, then followed Khan over the wooded platform to the relative safety of the *Clipper*.

Bafq el-Rashid did not stop to see if Khan was all right. He realized what needed to be done and ran instead ran toward the hold of the *Clipper* and found the boxes of ammunition, wooden crates with Soviet SVD sniper rifles, and box after box of hand grenades. He stuffed several in each pocket then ran back toward and across the gangway, grabbing a rifle at the last second.

"Bafq!" shouted Khan.

El-Rashid tossed the rifle to Khan as he rushed for the unstable gangway. Aziz was doing a masterful job of keeping the *Bedford Clipper* close by. The two other Libyan seamen only now realized what was going on and rushed to the main deck. As they did so they were immediately killed by a barrage of 7.62mm bullets fired from Khan's rifle. Down into the black hold of the *Grand Occidental* went el-Rashid. He could feel the boat starting to list to one side, into a broadside state. Once that happened the *Clipper* would not be able to keep up with the *Occidental* and Bafq would be trapped aboard.

Inside the hold, el-Rashid quickly made his way back to the stern of the boat. A fire was not what was needed. The *Grand Occidental* must sink. The smoke from a boat on fire could be spotted. On his hands and knees el-Rashid wedged three grenades near the hull of the boat. He looked behind him. He had a short run then a twelve-foot ladder to the main deck. He would have to pull the pin on the grenade then get up the ladder to the deck to have an even chance of getting off the *Occidental*.

El-Rashid did what was needed, and did it without thought.

He pulled the pin on the Soviet hand grenade and ran for the ladder, hoping that the Minsk-made grenade was not defective. A premature explosion would kill him.

The rungs of the ladder were slippery and el-Rashid struggled up the steps three at a time, reaching the top just as the grenade exploded. Shrapnel ripped into his feet just as the other three grenades were detonated from the first. El-Rashid was on deck, slipped and fell, as the *Grand Occidental* was rocked by the force of the explosions.

Ahead he could see but not hear the shouts of encouragement from Khan. The boat rocked again as the Atlantic rushed into the hold. It would be a matter of minutes. The *Occidental* started to list and pull away from the *Clipper*. The gangway was nearly stretched to the limit. Aziz was trying to keep the gangway in place. At last, el-Rashid staggered to the gangway and with a tremendous effort launched himself down the wooden planks just as the the *Occidental* started to sink. Khan and el-Rashid grabbed the heavy man just as the gangway fell into the now turbulent water.

He was aboard, and safe, and out of breath . . . and wounded. Khan congratulated him and expressed concern for his injuries, but el-Rashid brushed him off saying "My wounds are minor. I will heal by the time we land."

With al-As's attention solely on the *Clipper*, the two men watched as the *Grand Occidental* sank into nine hundred feet of cold Atlantic water.

NEW BEDFORD

There was more work in New Bedford than Scotty had counted on. Upon landing last night he waited a half-hour for the New Bedford taxi cab to take him to the Holiday Inn on I-195 and Route 18. For the time he spent he could just as easily have walked it.

"Mean night, ya' know," the cabbie had scowled when Scotty had grumbled at him.

The whole East Coast was under the spell of the winter miseries— from rain in the Carolinas to sleet and snow in New England. It was warmer outside the Cowboy Bar and Grill than it was in this depressing city, thought Scotty, checking into his room. Of course, it always was warmer at the Cowboy.

"I'm with the FBI. I need to talk to a manager," he had said when he arrived at the motel.

"Is there something wrong?" asked the concerned clerk.

"Let me talk to the manager, please."

Scotty was escorted into the office behind the desk where he talked with a young woman no older than he.

"On February 10th a man by the name of John Smithton Ramsey checked into this motel. He was here at least one night. I need to know what room he was in. I need to see his folio, and I need to have his room dusted for fingerprints."

The girl—young woman—didn't bat an eye, but instead turned around and tapped a few keystrokes into her IBM PC/XT.

"The 10th, you say?" she asked.

"Yes."

"Here it is. He stayed three nights, checked out the morning of the 13th, and paid in cash. He was in room 128."

She tapped in a few more codes.

"You might be in luck, Mr. Coldsmith. As you can imagine, we don't get much Cape traffic in February. The room hasn't been rented the last three nights."

He smiled and she smiled. *Don't start up, Coldsmith*, he thought to himself. Instead, Scotty pulled out the Customs picture of Alexander Rostov.

"I need to know. . ."

"Yes, I recognize this man. He was here as well. With a woman. *I* checked him in personally, and I checked him out. Also on the 13th . . . I'm sure of it."

She went back to her PC and busily attacked her database file.

A woman!

"Yes, here it is. I remember it because it was very unusual. He insisted on paying in cash. You know we need to have an imprint so we can be protected against fraud. But, I don't think he *had* a credit card. I told him he couldn't have room service without a credit card but that didn't bother him any. So he paid in cash."

Rostov! *You son of a bitch*!

Scotty could barely conceal his enthusiasm.

"Somebody's in the room tonight, I'm afraid," the manager said.

"That's unfortunate. I'm afraid we're going to have to inconvenience them. Not only will they have to be moved, but they'll also have to be fingerprinted. That room must be sealed off as soon as possible. May I use your phone?"

Scotty dialed the police station and talked to the lieutenant who had come up to interview him in Boston.

"Listen, I need a favor. I'm out at the Holiday Inn and I need two rooms dusted . . . tonight. It has to do with the shooting. I'll be by tomorrow to make a statement against those thugs."

An hour later Scotty, the hotel manager, a bellhop, and a disgruntled New Bedford policeman all converged on a couple in room 152. Once the couple had been fingerprinted, moved and apologized to, the manager gave them two bottles of wine and a chit for a free dinner to smooth over any bad feelings.

Scotty stayed with the policeman until both rooms had been done.

"I'll give you an analysis tomorrow," the policeman said.

"I'll need to send a copy of them to Washington," replied Scotty.

Scotty had gotten to bed late and slept late, which didn't matter since the New Bedford taxi didn't function before eight A.M. anyway.

After checking out of the motel, the first thing Scotty had to do was find his rental car. An hour and fifty dollars later, Scotty finally said goodbye to the New Bedford taxi and had his Avis rental back. At least Avis would be happy, the car appeared to be in good condition. From the lot he drove directly to the wharf, where he had last seen Ramsey the night of his attack.

John Smithton Ramsey, if that was his name, had been headed down Union Street and across Water Street to the wharf. Ramsey hadn't gone to the wharf for a walk-away shrimp cocktail, that was for sure, thought Scotty as he pulled in past the red brick harbormaster's house and parked in one of the diagonal spaces. There were only a few cars in the lot.

"Damn!" he shouted.

Parked right ahead of him was the blue Cutlass! It was Ramsey's car!

Scotty got out, pulled his notebook out, verified the license plate number—yes, there was the yellow Hertz sticker on the lower right front windshield.

He checked out on the 13th and he drove here. Scotty couldn't believe his luck. He went to the public telephone near the harbormaster's house and dialed the police.

"No, I'm not rushing you for the report. I need you to do another job. It's a car . . . a blue Cutlass and it's parked at the wharf. I need it impounded and dusted for prints."

If he hadn't been so sore and so bundled up with heavy clothes Scotty would have done a backflip, he was so happy.

"*You son of a bitch,*" he muttered to himself as he walked into the harbormaster's office.

The harbormaster, the essence of a crotchety, grumbling, old seafart, had no intention of giving Scotty even a look. He could see Scotty standing there from his peripheral vision but had no intention of asking him what his business was. Three unemployed fishermen sat around smoking, drinking coffee and talking in Portuguese.

"Are you the harbormaster?" Scotty asked politely.

The old man looked up and gave Scotty the evil eye, then returned to his paper.

"I said, *are you the harbormaster?*" he repeated, this time more loudly and with less patience.

"Aye," he said without looking up. "You don't have to shout."

"Well, that's nice. I'm with the FBI and I'd like to ask you a few questions," said Scotty, his voice mixed with irritation and sarcasm.

The attention of the harbormaster and the three unemployed fishermen had been gained.

"As a matter of fact, *I'm* the one some of your friends tried to kill the other night . . . so let's get one thing straight, I may look young and inexperienced . . . but looks *can* be deceiving. If you clowns don't cooperate, I can make your next few days *very* busy."

The threat had been delivered at just about the right level. But it had been the fact that Scotty had been the one the boys had thrown into the river that brought them around. If it had been otherwise, the harbormaster would have told Scotty to take a leap.

"Good. Thanks for your cooperation. First, how long has the blue Cutlass been there?"

"I don't know. Do you think we keep track of everybody who comes and goes around here?" returned the harbormaster, with equal sarcasm.

"Yes, I think you do. How long has it been there?"

"A couple of days now. I don't know, maybe three."

"Who left it?" asked Scotty.

"A man, I don't know," the old man shrugged, got up and filled his coffee cup.

"This man, where is he?"

Silence.

"How would all four of you like to spend a day in Boston in front of a Federal Grand Jury? That's the next step. If I don't get answers—and the right answers—you'll be up in front of a very unhappy judge, a judge who will want to know *why* you weren't cooperating with the FBI. I repeat—where is he?"

"He left on Carver Medway's boat, the *Bedford Clipper*."

Each question had to be asked. These people weren't going to give *anything* unless it was pried out of their mouth.

"*When* did the *Bedford Clipper* leave?"

The old man opened a book. There had been so few boats leave that the *Clipper*'s entry was on the first page.

"Ten A.M. on the 13th."

Scotty sighed.

"*Where* was he going? What was his destination?"

"Didn't say," replied the harbormaster.

"What do you mean, 'didn't say'?" asked Scotty, full of doubt.

"I mean exactly what I said . . . he didn't say."

"Doesn't he *have* to? Doesn't he have to file . . ."

"What? A *flight* plan?"

The harbormaster and the three fishermen laughed out loud.

"That's a good one, Caleb . . . a flight plan," said one of the fishermen as he slapped his knee.

"Yeah, something like that," replied Scotty.

"Doesn't work that way with fishermen, young FBI man. A fisherman doesn't say *where* he's going, just that he *is* going. If a man knows where there's fish, he's not going to tell anybody. He doesn't have to say he's going anywhere, or where's he's going if he's going . . . he just has to tell me when he's coming back, so's I've got a space for him when he comes back."

"When is the *Clipper* coming back?"

"Let's see . . . Medway said he had a ten-day charter. He'll be back on the 22nd."

"Charter? You mean he wasn't fishing? Who chartered the boat?"

"The blue Cutlass, there . . . he chartered it. All we saw was the two of them carting boxes and crates aboard."

"Two . . . there were *two* of them? Two?" questioned Scotty in amazement.

"Aye, two. Never saw the other one before. He just showed up and left. The Cutlass had been here talking with Carver Medway once or twice before."

"What did the second man look like?"

"Didn't get a good look," shrugged the harbormaster.

"Tall? Short? Blond hair? Bald? Fat? What?"

Scotty held out his hands in a motion to the old man, asking him to give him *some* sort of clue.

"He was taller than Cutlass, maybe leaner . . . hard to tell with the jacket . . . had kind of a hard cut to him, know what I mean?"

Scotty did.

First a woman with Rostov, now a second man with Ramsey.

"Where did they go?" Scotty repeated, slowly.

"I don't know," said the harbormaster.

"Does Medway have any family?"

"Yes, a woman and a couple of kids," said the old man, indicating with a look that the wife wouldn't know squat.

"A crew. He must have had a crew. Who went along with Medway?"

"Dinghy Compton's always been his cook, and I think he took Bennie Triolo as a first mate. The kid comes cheap. Medway knows his way around a dollar bill, he does."

That comment got several 'ayes' from the listening fishermen. There wasn't much more to get from the men other than the addresses of Medway, Triolo, and Dinghy Compton. He got them, then stepped back into the cold winter air.

First of all he had to go to the police station and make sure that the 9mm shell casings from Rostov's gun were included in the package which would go to Washington, to the gnomes in the Identification Section on the third floor of the Hoover Building in Washington. Although gnomes should always work in the basement, these gnomes could work *wherever* they wanted. The guys in IDENT could give you the suspect's mother's maiden name if hard pressed.

— • —

"Mrs. Triolo, my name is Scott Coldsmith and I'm with the FBI."

Maria Triolo looked at Scotty as if he'd just stepped out of a spaceship. She neither understood why a good-looking young man was on her front stoop nor the words he said. She just shrugged, said something in Portuguese and closed the door in Scotty's face.

Scotty stood on the stoop, then looked around to see if anyone else was watching. Several heads ducked behind drawn Venetian blinds. He smiled to himself. No sense threatening the woman. Just tuck that one away as Followup-When-There's-Nothing-Else-To-Do.

MANTEO, NORTH CAROLINA

It had been a miserable day on the Outer Banks. A second low pressure system had followed the first, which was now in the waters off Long Island. The new front had come in and sat heavily off Cape Hatteras, spinning its nasty northeast winds into the coastline from Delaware to South Carolina. It was 38 degrees and pouring. Farther north, the coastline counties of Maryland and Delaware were getting another dose of wet, sloppy snow.

It was late in the day and, with the bad weather, darkness had fallen early. Rostov and Katrina were both tired from the close tail they'd put on Rahman. All day long Rahman had been buying this and that—foodstuffs, clothes, a radio—and he wasn't very organized. After every purchase he would drive back to his rental house, wait a while, then make another trip.

But, at least they had someone to follow. It had only been a day, but Williams and Reynolds were about to go stir-crazy watching the dull community of Wanchese become even duller.

"This is probably his last trip out today," said Rostov, with a tired voice.

With only a routine job to do, knowing that Khan wouldn't be here for several more days, his mind had a very difficult time telling his body that he had to be sharp.

"Things do close down early around here. Not like New York," said Katrina.

Rostov smiled. Nothing was like New York.

They found that talking via the walkie-talkies was something which made the time pass easier as they waited in their separate cars.

Rahman had parked his car in the renovated section of downtown Manteo. Rain pelted the new waterfront townhomes, mostly unrented, and the gift shops, mostly closed. Water rolled off the slotted wooden walkway into Shallowbag Bay. Through the mist and rain could be seen the small Elizabeth II, a carefully-constructed, handmade replica of one of the boats which in 1586–87 braved the unknown to bring the first settlers to the area from England. The boat had been built for the quadricentennial celebration. Local officials had been more than slightly embarrassed to find out that when the boat was completed, the channel leading out of Shallowbag Bay to the Pamlico Sound wasn't deep enough, so the boat stayed where it was until the channel was dredged deeper.

There were no visitors to the Elizabeth II this afternoon, nor were there any visitors to downtown Manteo. Only a few local regulars parked their cars and ran to the safety of the Duchess of Dare restaurant or the town's movie theater across the street.

"It's your turn, Alex," said Katrina.

Indeed, she had followed Rahman as he'd gone shopping in the Ben Franklin store. At least that was inside, thought Rostov, muttering to himself as he got out of the car.

While Katrina sat comfortably in the van, Rostov wearily set off down the street, ducking under protected awnings and eaves whenever possible. It was difficult to follow a man when you were the only people on the street. Rahman seemed to be in a world of his own.

He crossed Budleigh Street to a series of shops with covered roofs that partially extended over the sidewalk. He followed Rahman down Budleigh, just within sight of Katrina.

— • —

Marmande had been tailing the Arab all day. He stopped under an awning to light a cigarette while Rahman diddled around in a sporting goods shop. Marmande looked up and noticed a man crossing the street, perhaps thirty yards in front of him. The walk was familiar. Marmande's body surged with adrenalin. Could it be? Marmande's senses honed in on the man's body language.

It was him!

Wait a minute! Could it be? Are you sure? It is! It's the lawyer! It's his killer! What luck! And he walked right by me. Marmande's heart surged with adrenalin. Damn, what a detective! He knew it all along. That son of a bitch, whoever he was, was tracking Rahman and his men, too. *It's him! What intuition! What a detective!*

Marmande wanted the man's head on a platter. It was time to settle old debts—arrest him and turn him over to the Americans. He would certainly be extradited to Paris to face trial. He'd hang for the murder. Marmande smiled at the thought. The Arabs would just be a bonus for the FBI.

Look at him. He's cold and unpretentious. This wasn't a master spy he'd trailed, he was nothing more than a cold dog in a rainstorm.

Marmande flipped his cigarette onto the wet street and slowly followed the lawyer. The wind smacked him across the face, blowing the hood to his rainjacket back onto his shoulders. In an instant his face was wet, his glasses streaked and blurred. Glasses were one of life's major difficulties. Now that they were nice and wet the next stage was for them to fog up. And of course there was nothing to dry them with, so he half looked through them, half looked over them while he slowly moved up the street behind his killer. Hood up, head down, and glasses fogged, Marmande made his way toward Rostov. There he was. He had him! Half way across the street Marmande's right hand moved to his holster and unconsciously released the snap.

Now!

You bastard, I've got you.

— • —

Katrina leaned back against the headrest and closed her eyes. She wasn't used to this kind of work. She was used to getting information out of horny attachés at cocktail parties, not slopping around in the rain after some Arab. Well, Rahman wouldn't be long. The sidewalks in Manteo were nearly half empty, and it was just about six o'clock.

Who is that? At once Katrina was alert. She gripped the steering wheel and peered out through the rain-streaked window. She saw Rostov huddled at the corner. *Who is that? Is someone following Rostov? Who is it?*

She fumbled with the Caravan's door, opened it, and stepped outside into the nasty, cold rain. Thankful for wearing sneakers, she ran toward the intersection, making no noise. A half block away she could see the other man reach for what she knew was a gun in a shoulder holster.

"Alex! Alex! Watch out! Behind you!" she shouted through the rain.

Rostov turned around and couldn't believe his eyes. For a split second his mouth dropped in disbelief. It was the fat INTERPOL inspector!

How could it be? He had followed him! How was it possible?

Abandoning his sentry post, Rostov quickly turned the corner and raced down Budleigh Street temporarily shielding himself from Marmande's direct view. As he ran, Rostov turned his head and saw he wasn't putting any new ground between himself and the French detective. For a fat man, Marmande could move well. If Katrina hadn't been there, Marmande would have walked right up to him. He was getting old, thought Rostov. How could he let something like this happen?

Rostov suddenly turned right down a small alleyway and was immediately into the residential lanes of Manteo. The cold rain had kept everyone off the street. His objective was to circle back around to the car. The fat man would have to give up. But what then?

The police. Marmande would get the police.

But, why weren't the police already here? Where were they? Marmande must be following Rahman, as well.

"Damn!" muttered Rostov, realizing what had happened.

The Frenchman was after him!

Maybe it was best he let Marmande get closer. Rostov eased up the pace and took a peek behind him. Marmande was lumbering after him, still maintaining his pace. Not bad. Rostov hustled down Raleigh Way and back to Budleigh Street. Marmande had dropped back only slightly.

Katrina drove by in the van. Instead of jumping in, Rostov deliberately ran past it, giving her the eye on the way by. She ducked down. Marmande ran past the Caravan. The two men got to their respective cars at just about the same time. Rostov was first to jump out of his parking spot, followed by the panting Marmande.

— • —

These damn glasses! he thought. *They've fogged again.* Throwing them on the seat beside him, Marmande squinted at the car speeding ahead. He could hardly see.

That was a woman's voice he'd heard! It had come from behind him someplace.

The lawyer had a partner.

Marmande reached for his notepad to make note of the license plate. He always kept a notepad attached by large rubber bands to the driver's side visor. The pencil fell out, bounced on the seat, then to the floor.

"Damn it!"

As the cars motored back over the Baum Causeway, with his free hand Marmande fished through his pants pocket.

Nothing.

His coat! Everything was in the outside pocket of his raincoat. Spilling out onto the seat came a dark plastic key chain with two sets of keys to the rental cottage he'd taken only yesterday, a house catty-corner to Rahman's only two blocks away. The keys slipped down into between the seats. Also spilling out was the rental ticket for the car, his return airplane ticket, a handkerchief, and two half-eaten rolls of mints.

And a pencil! Scribbling furiously, he noted the license plate of Rostov's car and, as was his habit, returned the pad to the visor.

"I've got you, you son of a bitch!"

— • —

The two cars turned right and entered the Cape Hatteras National Seashore. Trailing by a half-mile was Katrina. There was no traffic on the two-lane road. Driving with reckless abandon, they approached seventy miles an hour.

Ten miles south Rostov hardly slowed as he went over the Bonner Bridge crossing Oregon Inlet, past the Coast Guard facility and the last outpost of civilization for twenty-five miles to the south. Ahead was nothing but sand, wind, and more rain.

Rostov looked in the mirror. How far could this go? This was as good a place as any.

"How far back are you?" he radioed to Katrina.

"I'm a half-mile behind you both," she replied through the static.

"I'm going to slow down. Can you force him off the road?"

There was a pause.

"Yes," came her cold reply.

Rostov slowly brought his speed down, allowing Marmande not only to catch up but to slow down as well. Katrina quickly made up the ground.

Ten miles south of Oregon Inlet, glasses now defogged, Marmande noticed a mini-van of some type behind him; driving in the middle of the road, its tires slicing through the highway, spitting up splashes of puddles as it rapidly approached him.

Marmande stepped on the accelerator, but the van still seemed to be gaining.

Was it the girl?

Was it his imagination?

From her position in the middle of the road, Katrina braced her left hand and arm against the steering wheel, ensuring control of the speeding car. With her free hand she reached down into the concealed drawer under the back seat of the Caravan and pulled out a Beretta M12S, 32-round, 9mm submachine gun.

She placed the gun on the passenger seat, then fumbled with the center console and lowered the front passenger window. Rain poured into the van. With a slight adjustment to the driving wheel she pulled into the northbound lane and accelerated, pulling even with Marmande. Up ahead Rostov tapped his brakes lightly, forcing Marmande to pay attention to what was in front of him. With her left hand she held the steering wheel straight. With her right she lifted the Beretta and rested the barrel on the sill of the open passenger window. Now even with Marmande, she only had to make a slight adjustment to position the gun correctly, while still having relative control over the van.

Marmande looked to his left and saw the ugly end of the gun's black barrel. He hit his brakes just as Katrina pulled the weapon's hair trigger. Two bursts of four bullets each ripped through Marmande's window and through his body. The third and fourth burst only did damage to the car's windshield as Marmande had slumped to the right, held in place only by his seat belt. His foot still on the accelerator, the car shot off the highway and into the sand, where it hit a small sandy bunker and came to a sudden stop in a big clump of sea oats.

On the other side of the highway, Katrina found herself jerked to the left by the recoiling of the repeating gun. Although somewhat in control, the Caravan skidded off the left edge, started to fishtail, but finally came to a stop sideways on the highway. All that could be heard was the patter of the rain on the hood. A mist rose from the Caravan as the cold rain hit the hot engine.

Rostov looked up at the very instant Katrina nearly took Marmande's head off. He saw Marmande's car shoot off the road. Rostov slammed on his brakes and skidded on the wet road. Coming to a stop he threw the gearshift into reverse and sped backwards up the highway toward the wreckage. Stopping, he reached into the glove compartment for his Beretta. Then he was out of the car and running back toward the Caravan.

"Are you all right?" he shouted as he got close.

"I'm all right!" she waved, pointing to the spot where Marmande's car ran off the road. "Make sure he's dead!"

What Katrina had done had taken a combination of physical and mental skills which many agents never master. Rostov ran as best he could over the wet sand toward Marmande's car. He heard the slam of the Caravan's door as Katrina followed him. He heard her shout.

"Hurry, before someone comes!"

Rostov dashed through the cold rain, oblivious to the smashing of the Atlantic's wild surf not one hundred feet away on the other side of the sand dune. Katrina's shots had done severe damage to the car. There wasn't a sliver of glass left on the entire left side of the car. Inside he could see the bloodied body of the police inspector.

How did he track me? he wondered.

Rostov's skin was tingly with anticipation. He had to do something quickly. Even in a rainstorm in winter someone would come along the highway, perhaps even a ranger.

What to do? They needed time. They couldn't take Marmande's car.

Take the body!

Rostov opened the car door, its handle cold as ice to the touch. Steam rose from Marmande's hot body as the warm blood met the cold air. Rostov struggled with the big man. He was heavy. His whole left side seemed to be bloody. In moving him, Rostov was instantly covered with the inspector's blood.

Too heavy! He'd never get the man back.

"I need help! Help me move him!" he shouted to Katrina.

She was out of breath. She stood there for a second, debating the decision.

"What are we going to do with him, Alex? Leave him! We need to get out of here!"

As she spoke, a Ford Bronco came over the slight rise and seeing the three cars skewed all over the highway, came to a stop. Out jumped the driver, a big man. In the passenger seat was a woman, probably his wife. In back were two children and a large spotted cocker spaniel.

"What happened?" shouted the man.

The man couldn't see how bloodied Rostov was. Rostov walked toward the man, Katrina back toward the Caravan.

"There's been a terrible accident," Rostov shouted back to the man, who now started to advance toward him. "The pavement, it was so bad. He lost control. We collided. He needs help," answered Rostov.

The man waved to his wife to stay inside. The wife, not wanting any part of bodies and bloody people, looked at Rostov, then turned to her children to reassure them. The excitement of the children, the barking of the dog, and the pouring rain all combined together to steam the inside of the Bronco almost instantly.

On the other side of the road the two men walked back toward Marmande. Katrina was back at the Caravan.

"Are you all right?" asked the man.

"Yes. I'm covered with his blood. He's a big man. I don't know, maybe he was drunk."

Rostov pointed to Marmande's car. Things were turning badly. They would get worse. From the south came a green U.S. Park Service police car. The ranger pulled past Katrina's Caravan, stopped in front of the Bronco, jumped out of the car and ran toward Rostov and the man.

"What happened . . .?"

They were the ranger's last words.

The rain and darkness did little to hide the muzzle flash from the Beretta. Katrina drilled the park ranger, who tumbled onto the pavement flat on his face, as if he'd been shoved from behind. Out in the sand both Rostov and the man saw what happened. The man was dumbfounded.

"Wha . . .?" was his last word.

He never got a chance to turn back to Rostov, nor back to his family. By the time the ranger hit the pavement Rostov had his gun at chest level and pulled off three rounds into the man's upper body. At such close range there was no chance for survival. There was a great bloody hole where his heart and lungs used to be.

Rostov and Katrina, thinking the same thing, advanced toward the Bronco. The wife had heard the popping sound from Katrina's blast, but couldn't see through the fogged window. She desperately tried to clear the windshield, and did so just in time to see the body of the ranger. Her husband was lying on the ground to her right.

The woman was terrified.

Struggling to get into the driver's seat, she reached for the ignition keys.

The dog wouldn't stop barking, nor the kids stop crying. She felt like she had lead in her pants.

She couldn't move, couldn't climb over the between-seats console of the vehicle. As she struggled her passenger door opened and she felt Rostov's strong arms grab her by the legs and yank her toward the wet sand. She tried to scream but nothing came out.

The children screamed.

Katrina opened up the driver's side rear door and pulled the little girl, then the little boy, both between the age of five and seven. They were terrified. The spaniel got out and ran for the dune, happy to get anywhere outside the crowded back seat.

"No . . . no . . . please, no . . . not my children," pleaded the woman. "My children, please no, not my children," she cried.

It was the last thing she said, as Rostov calmly shot her twice in the head at short range. The woman slumped to the pavement. Rostov got up, walked around the Bronco just in time to see Katrina snap in an eight-inch cartridge of 32 bullets, then fire two rounds of four at short range into the children. The shots drove them both backward ten feet, clear off the highway.

The stony-faced Katrina turned back to Rostov.

"Leave them where they are. Hurry!" she directed. "We must strip the cars. Now!"

Without questioning her, the two of them ran through the sand to the dune. Marmande's blood was turning rusty brown. Katrina went to the car, while Rostov went through his clothes. Katrina found the rental car agreement, an airplane ticket, a half-empty pack of Winstons, a handkerchief, two half-eaten rolls of mints, his raincoat, the car keys still in the ignition. There was nothing in the glove compartment. Removing the car keys she opened the trunk. Nothing. She left it open and went back to Rostov, who was struggling a bit with the big man's body. He had found his wallet, a pencil, change, and his watch. There was nothing else in his pocket.

"I've got to get the plates," shouted Rostov.

"Hurry Alex! Please hurry!"

Please no more innocent people, she thought.

Fishing through his pocket he pulled out an all-purpose knife and began working on the Georgia license plates.

Georgia?

Had Marmande known? How could he? Finishing the task, he looked inside again but found nothing. It was almost dark. He looked around. There were too many dead people, but more importantly, there were too many automobiles. No matter what you did, once you got attached to an automobile there was no way to shake it. There was always some way for somebody to trace it. An automobile was like the sticky paper he'd seen restaurants use to catch flies. The analogy seemed appropriate. If he took the ranger's car, he'd have to take the ranger as well. The family would stay where they were, regardless.

His eyes fell on the Hertz sticker in the lower right hand corner of the front windshield.

"Damn!" he said with vehemence.

Rostov scrambled through the glass to the passenger seat, mindless of the cuts to his knees and legs. Time was running out. He could feel the urgency of Katrina behind him. With his fingernails he scratched at the two-inch-square sticker. Even with the poor light he could see the number 2848 above the words HARTSFIELD INTERN'L AIRPORT, which identified the registration location of the vehicle. Somebody would soon discover this carnage and want to know who the people were and why they were murdered. Rostov didn't care about the family or the ranger, but Marmande . . . Marmande he cared about. Why was Marmande here?

The sticker seemed to be permanently sealed to the glass. Rostov scratched and scratched, at first only managing to rip the corners, then the back of the sticker. His fingernails were caked with the gummy substance.

"*Come on, come on!*" he shouted to himself.

"Alex!" Shouted Katrina. "What are you doing?"

At last he got to the front surface of the sticker and started to mutilate it. It came off in bigger chunks. After a minute there was nothing but sticky remains. Now on a thought process, Rostov first opened the passenger door then looked at the side panel of the driver's side door to see if there were maintenance stickers. There were none. Where else?

Hurry! The dashboard! Rostov ripped off a small plastic sign which advertised Hertz's toll-free 800-number for service. There might be something else . . . but there was *no* time.

Gathering everything in his arms he sprinted as best he could to the Bronco, where Katrina had already started.

The children had no ID. Katrina had the woman's purse. She'd been a pretty woman.

"Go!" shouted Rostov.

Katrina ran for the Caravan.

From behind the bushes came the old spaniel. He had done his business and came back to find something was terribly wrong. Sniffing the air, he went from the bodies of one child to the other . . . back and forth twice. Something was wrong. In distress, he barked and whined. Then he saw Rostov and barked in anger, in protection. In a near frenzy, the dog ran around the other side of the Bronco to the body of the woman, his woman. He sniffed her body as well, then nosed her arm. There was no reaction, no reassuring pat of his head.

Rostov walked around the other side of the Bronco. Rain poured down over his already-soaked shoulders. Without a thought, without remorse, he leveled his gun and shot the dog.

Rostov ran for the Buick. He made a U-turn and headed up the highway with Katrina following. The carnage behind them was awesome.

The lights from the three vehicles splayed in three different directions. The cold rain covered the bodies with a wet sheet. The wind blew the ranger's hat into the dune. The little girl's pink dress, stained brown with blood, flopped with the gusts. A ghost crab, searching for his home for the night, dug his small hole near the left arm of the little boy. The wife's dead eyes were open as if looking for her children. The man lay on his back, his face caught in a final pose of confusion and pain.

Jacques Marmande's instinct had been right. He wouldn't see Paris again.

— • —

An unlucky fisherman from Pittsburgh was the unfortunate person who stumbled upon the scene. Coming back from a bad day's fishing at Cape Hatteras, he'd almost run into the back of the park ranger's car.

For a few moments he sat stunned in his car, not believing the horrible sight in front of him.

Finally he managed to drive around the bodies and make his way to the Coast Guard station at Oregon Inlet, where the OOD had to calm the man down enough so he could get the information. Twenty minutes later, an hour after the murders, the first police were on the scene.

The first to arrive was Dare County Sheriff, Bart Claiborne.

"Jesus . . . H . . . Christ," was all Claiborne could mutter. "Rope the area off! Close the highway! Jesus . . . H . . . Christ."

He could hear the sounds of someone retching. Turning around he saw one of his men had discovered the children.

"Jesus . . . H . . . Christ. What happened here?"

Bart was a single-phrase man when under pressure. He went back to his car and radioed dispatch.

"Clancy, there are six bodies out here. I want the entrance to the Seashore closed. I want you to radio Reilly and have highway 1200 closed to northbound traffic from Avon. I want Hatteras Island closed down. Radio the Medical Center. I'm going to need three ambulances." Claiborne paused. And call J.J. Carteret. One of the dead men is a U.S. Park Service ranger."

NAGS HEAD

Katrina managed to contain her emotions until they were back in the motel room. Once inside she sobbed uncontrollably. This wasn't something Rostov was used to, or enjoyed—or was any good at. Not the killing, but the consoling.

It was hard, no question about it. It didn't matter that they were in a dangerous situation far from the safety of home. Killing was still killing. Killing a spy was OK. Killing a five-year-old little girl wasn't OK. Killing five-year-olds wasn't the reason they became spies. They weren't trained for such situations, and didn't want to be. Rostov could understand Katrina's distress but he wouldn't allow himself to feel compassion for her.

"I didn't want to kill them! I didn't want to kill them!" she cried, distraught at murdering the two innocents.

"Listen to me! *We* had to kill them. It was either you or I, Comrade Tambov. If you didn't, then I would have. We can't afford to be recognized. Not now."

At arm's length, Rostov shook her hard, but she was nothing more than a rag doll. Katrina's head rolled from side to side but the tears didn't stop. He slapped her hard across the cheek. The sound reverberated against the sparsely decorated walls. The crying continued.

"No, Alex . . . please, don't . . . not again . . . please . . . I tried . . ."

Indeed she had done more than try. She had been very good. If there was only some way he could get the *woman* in her out of her system—or out of *his* system.

Her nipples pointed at him through her still-wet blouse, whose top two buttons were now open. Striking her had started his arousal engine again. She wanted to be held, to be touched, for these few moments to be *cared* for. He wanted nothing of it. Caring was something which had been carefully removed by his finely-honed instinct for survival. Caring was not only weak, it was foolish. Caring for this woman would be a mental burden which someday could cost him his life, perhaps someday very soon. At *no* time did he want to be in a situation where his reactions stemmed from emotion rather than from instinct. The Plan, The Objective—*they* did not require caring, they required simple execution. There was no *time* for caring.

Katrina cringed and begged, closing her eyes to what she expected would be another brutal assault. She didn't have the strength to resist. *Hold me*, she thought.

He found strength in his rejection of her need. With a wordless sneer on his lips and a near-painful grip on her shoulder he ordered her. "Take off your clothes."

"Alex?"

"I said, TAKE THEM OFF!" he ordered again.

He released his grip and watched as she slowly shed her wet clothes. Wearing no bra, she dropped her blouse, revealing young breasts which ached to be touched. She glanced at him and found a return stare which bore right through her. There was no warmth there, no compassion, only anger and purpose. She kicked her shoes off then released the catch on her skirt. She wore no slip, only the soft bikini underwear. She looked up for a reprieve and found none, so she slowly pulled her wet panties down over her hips and let them fall to the floor in a clump.

She was naked in front of him. She felt his strong hands on her shoulders as he forced her to her knees.

"Oh, I . . . no . . . please, Alex!"

Katrina knelt before him. Rostov slowly unzipped his pants and with a motion released his erection. Then he put both hands on her head, tangling her hair in his fingers, and firmly pulled her toward him. There was no doubt what he wanted and she felt too weak to defy him. Closing her eyes she opened her mouth and began to move her lips up and down his shaft, taking as much of him as she could.

Get it over with in a hurry, she thought. *He* doesn't care how long it takes, just that it gets done. His hips moved back and forth, in rhythm with her effort. He made no sound, but still she could tell he was more urgent. She tightened her lips and sucked, her saliva greasing his way to climax. Up and down and up and down and up and down. She could taste the bitterness of his semen as he began to come. Rostov refused to release his grip on her head, not even when he grunted and came in four bursts into her mouth.

"Well done, Comrade Tambov," Rostov said with a smirk as she wordlessly cleaned herself up.

She hated him. She hated not being able to control him.

She went to the bathroom and started a shower while Rostov resumed talking in his normal tone of voice, as if nothing had just happened, either in the sand dune or on the floor of the room. While she ran the shower, Rostov went back to the situation.

"The man's name was Marmande. Chief Inspector Jacques Marmande, INTERPOL. He was the policeman I tricked into letting me inside the jail to first interview, then kill the Arab."

Rostov's face reflected admiration.

"In all my years . . . . I've never known a policeman to guess like that. He couldn't have known. And if he did know, then where are the Americans?"

Rostov was puzzled. It made no sense. Why hadn't the FBI swarmed over them?

"We . . . you . . . need to warn the others. We need to tell Korz, but we must be careful, comrade. We don't know what they . . . Moscow, Washington, New York . . . are planning. What we don't want is for them to drop us cold, throw us over the side."

Katrina turned the shower off, opened the curtain and began to dry herself.

"Korz wouldn't . . . ," she started to argue.

"Wouldn't what?" Rostov said harshly.

The coldness was back in his eyes. They were the same icy eyes which had forced her to the floor.

"The Arabs are too far along. We're the only ones who can help them, whatever it is that they're doing. We *must* let Korz know."

"Tomorrow. We'll tell Korz tomorrow. Tonight we must protect ourselves. Call in the others. There is no time for sleeping, comrade. We must move quickly," ordered Rostov. Katrina, bone-weary and drained emotionally, sighed to herself but gave nothing of her feelings to Rostov. She knew he admired her for her "manly" skills as an agent but, as a woman, she was only there as a receptacle for his needs. There was no sense pretending that she would be able to control Rostov as she controlled other men, Korz included. Rostov was different than any man she'd ever known, and she loathed him for what he'd done.

Plan or no plan, if he tried the same thing again, she'd cut it off.

ELIZABETH CITY, NORTH CAROLINA

Special Agent John James Carteret, nicknamed J.J., had lived in North Carolina all his life, as had his wife Nancy. Their two sons were now out of house, out on their own, and the home he'd lived in for the last twenty-five years had gotten bigger than he'd thought it would. Their marriage was disintegrating into terminal comfortableness, a stage where neither one developed new goals in life, but instead fell into the rut of work, drink, TV, sleep, get up, etc.—a routine which would slowly wind down to apathetic neglect. Recently, he'd spent moody nights parked behind a newspaper while the mindless conversations of TV sitcoms protected them from conversation. J.J. realized he no longer loved his wife, and it made him sad.

And, he didn't know what to do about it.

Except for one year in the Raleigh area office, J.J. had spent his eighteen years as the FBI representative for eastern North Carolina— basically the area east of I-95 and south through the tidal and coastal areas of the state. To the south, his good friend Jim Pierce led three other agents in Wilmington—to the north was the much larger Norfolk regional office. Although J.J. reported to the Charlotte office, he was considered a "regular" in Norfolk, especially when he wanted to use the services of a "real" office—sophisticated resources like copying machines and computers.

Over the years J.J. was constantly amazed at the aura of invincibility the FBI had. Much of the image had been provided by the late J. Edgar Hoover—but just as much by the old TV show with Efrem Zimbalist. Not only were the agents infallible, but the agents always seemed to have this incredible array of technology behind them. A criminal just didn't have a chance!

Unfortunately, what was true was that criminals ended up being chased by a huge bloated elephant. After a long while the elephant would lumber its way, taking its slow old time, backtracking over ground already covered . . . but eventually, the elephant would get the criminal cornered. If the tip of the elephant's trunk was the agent, the rest of the elephant, of course, was the bureaucracy which J.J. and other field agents had to carry with them—a bureaucracy which provided tremendous service, such as IDENT, but only at a cost of having to deal with Regional Offices, HQ, staff, and massive paperwork.

In the end, crimes were solved by individual hard work, persistence, and luck.

The typical field agent in a small town, the "lone rangers" of the Bureau, were almost forced to become good-old-boys. An agent relied on his own network of contacts. If you needed telephone records and you didn't want to go to court to get them, well—you developed a contact at Carolina Telephone who gave you what you needed, a fellow good-old-boy who understood the realities of bureaucracy. These kinds of contacts don't come easily.

The trunk of the elephant was always on the search . . . always sniffing for new information. What slowed the elephant down was the fact that he had to bring along the rest of his fat body. Top leaders in Administration—Administrative Services Division, Records Management Division—and most of all, Technical Services Division had promised for fifteen years that field agents would be provided with the most modern of support equipment available on the market. They had been promised the Star Wars equivalent of computer equipment.

Nonsense.

What J.J. needed was an easy way to access computers, send mail, and distribute pictures of evidence; simple things that state and local agents have at their fingertips. J.J. and other Special Agents were working in the technological equivalent of the Stone Age—hammers and chisels on stone tablets. The Mafia was better equipped. The Mafia didn't have to go through the Federal procurement system. The Bureau had started with grandiose plans for automation several times, only to find that by the time the procurement lumbered through the competitive process—only HQ personnel got the terminals. What started out with simple requirements always seemed to get incredibly complex as top FBI managers added this bell and that whistle. The technology never filtered to the field agents like J.J. It just made his job that much more difficult, and it was embarrassing to have to use the equipment of the local police—even though J.J. had excellent rapport with them.

J.J. had never considered moving, although it had been suggested to him many times. J.J. loved the tidewater area around the Albemarle and Pamlico Sounds—and he wouldn't leave his favorite fishing spots on the Pasquotank River for anything. As a result, J.J. wasn't exactly high on the Bureau's promotion list.

Always a hard-worker, J.J. had over the years developed good professional relationships with the local police, the Coast Guard, and the local community government leaders—which like many places in the south, changed little from year to year. J.J. was comfortable in his job. He was comfortable in his marriage.

Why then, did he feel uncomfortable about life?

When the phone rang J.J. was sitting in his favorite easy chair, about halfway down the tunnel toward sleep—dead sleep was only a half-manhattan away.

"J.J., this is Clancy in Manteo."

Clancy didn't need to identify himself.

"I know who it is, Clancy. What's up?"

Clancy was particularly excited. J.J. could feel the tension through the phone.

"We've got six people murdered down here, J.J."

"Jesus—" exclaimed J.J., sitting up.

"That's what Bart said," replied Clancy. "He told me to call you, so I'm doing it."

"But why me, Clancy?"

"They've killed six people in the Seashore, J.J. One of them is a Park Ranger . . . and, two kids! Two kids, J.J.!"

"Get me a room at the Armada, Clancy. I'll be down as soon as I can," J.J. replied, trying to clear his head.

It took J.J. nearly an hour and a half to drive the eighty miles to the Seashore. Most of the Outer Banks was long since closed. There was very little traffic all the way down. He got to the scene at 10:45.

It was more than just a little eerie. Nothing had been touched. Temporary lights had been put up, casting unnatural shadows in all directions. Dare County, state police, and the U.S. Park Service were all there, some twenty-five people in total. Police cars with their red and blue flashing lights clashed with the powerful kliegs. The cold rain sizzled and spat as it hit the hot arc-lit lights.

The rain dripped down over the stiff bill of Bart Claiborne's hat as he greeted his friend.

"Hello, J.J."

"Mean night, Bart. Hello, Bob," said J.J. to one of Claiborne's men. "What's happened here?"

"We've left everything as we found it, J.J. It's terrible. Cold-blooded murder, no doubt about it. From the shell casings it looks like they were using 9mm sidearms."

"They?" asked J.J.

"I think so, J.J. At least two. The position of the bodies . . . it's hard to figure with just one. The two kids are over there. It'll make your stomach turn. They even shot the dog. It makes me sick."

"Who's over there?", asked J.J.

"Henry. I hope you don't mind. With the wind and all, I wanted to get Henry out here to get whatever footprints he could before they're gone. The rain helped us, dampened the sand."

"I want to see everything, Bart."

"I knew you would, J.J. That's why we left it like this."

Harris Steel, Chief of the Outer Banks Medical Center and unofficial coroner, stood in the southbound lane. Behind him were three ambulances and as many teams of young men and women ready to cart the bodies away. J.J. turned to Steele.

"Have you looked at them?"

"Yes. They're all dead, if that's what you mean," answered Steele.

"No, I can see they're dead. Any estimate of time?"

Steele looked at his watch.

"I got here at nine. They couldn't have been dead more than two hours. I'd say between six-thirty and seven-thirty, maybe seven-fifteen," answered the coroner.

"Are they in their exact positions?" asked J.J.

"Yes, even the dog . . . we've marked them all. Other than Steele looking at them, they're in the same position," answered Claiborne.

"I won't be long. When I'm done, you can have them," J.J. spoke to Steele. He got a nod in return.

J.J. went first to the Park Service ranger.

"His name is Jerry Catchings. He'd been in the service for twenty years," said Claiborne.

Claiborne was acting as J.J.'s notetaker. They'd long ago gotten over the personal pride issue of who was in charge of what. They cooperated with each other. Bart needed the resources J.J. could get from the Bureau and J.J. needed Bart's men to do the usual legwork involved in solving a crime. There was no glory in solving this type of crime. There was nothing but long hours ahead. Being an elected sheriff, Claiborne didn't want the sole responsibility for having to solve the crime by some artificial deadline that the press might assign. He was glad to have J.J. there.

J.J. bent over the body. Catchings had taken the brunt of a 9mm repeater directly between the shoulder blades.

"Shell casings?" asked J.J.

"To your right. Over by that set of skids," answered the sheriff.

J.J. got up and walked over to the set of skid marks that ran off the left side of the highway. Empty shell casings littered a small part of the road. He picked one up and rolled it around between his fingers. Military 9mm.

Is this the work of a nut? he wondered.

J.J. went back and knelt down beside Catchings. Then he looked up at the car in the sand dune ahead of him, then at the Bronco. Catchings had stopped, gotten out of his car . . . drawn by something happening over in the dune, the car . . . the accident.

Somebody had been in a car, the car which was off the road. Somebody had been in it, had gotten out when Catchings walked toward the accident, and had murdered the ranger from close range with a submachine gun.

J.J. motioned for Steele to come over.

"I want to know how tall this man is, and I'd like to get the angle of penetration," said J.J., pointing to Catching's body.

"I'll try, Carteret. It won't be easy," said Harris Steele.

"He didn't draw his gun," commented J.J.

Park Service rangers who went to Enforcement School in Georgia were issued standard Smith & Wesson four-inch barrel .38s.

"Didn't even touch his gun—and he didn't call the Park Service dispatch," answered Claiborne.

"Really?" questioned J.J.

That was odd. Why not? If their positions had been switched J.J. silently hoped he would have called for help before getting out of the car. But, maybe not. Catchings had been driving north and had come upon a terrible accident, or at least what he thought had been an accident. He'd certainly never seen what had hit him, or who. J.J. got up, motioned for Steele to take over. In turn, Steele motioned for the boys with the body bags.

Still on the road, J.J. walked down the highway a few feet. He thought he saw something which might be skid marks.

"Can you turn those lights down there?" he shouted.

The technician moved one of the klieg lights so that it reflected south down the highway. Sure enough. There was a long skid mark. A car had gone sideways, fishtailed, it looked like.

"Have Henry see if he can pull any off of that. I'll need rubber samples and pictures of both sets of skids. Measurements, too," J.J. pointed to the skid marks. "Tonight."

J.J. walked toward the two dead men and the car. This mess is a good fifty feet off the highway. If the sand bunker hadn't been there the car might have ended up in the Pamlico Sound. Catchings must have been walking toward this when he'd was shot in the back. *Ugh*, thought J.J.

The younger of the two men had been shot with a hand gun, also 9mm, close range, once in the chest, once in the head. The other man, the heavier and older of the two, had been mutilated by a gun which ripped through the car and his body. With the number of bullets and the damage to the car, it must have been from a submachine gun . . . some sort of fast repeating-action gun. J.J. would have bet anything that they would find 9mm shells inside the car. He wondered if the killer could be in the military.

"Do you think we've got some military on the loose, Bart?" asked J.J. "I'll call Lejeune in the morning—and Norfolk."

Bart shrugged his shoulders. The Marine base was a two-hour drive south, as was the Norfolk Naval Base to the north. J.J. hated military cases. The conflict over jurisdiction—the constant hassle with procedure—was maddening.

So there were two killers: one at the road, one in the sand. J.J. studied the footprints in the sand around the car. The big guy had been dragged out of the car. He must have been too heavy to move any further. Why drag him out? He *must* have been dead already. There was no evidence of secondary shots having been fired. The killers wanted to get rid of the body but couldn't. They changed their minds . . . or, more likely, someone came along. Catchings. Or the family.

"This man knows our killers," J.J. said to Bart, fingering the bloodied collar of Marmande's jacket.

The heavy-set man was the key. Who was he? Why was he here?

J.J. walked over to the car, a white Mustang, and looked through the broken window. It looked like there were nine tons of broken glass inside. If the shots hadn't killed the big man, then the flying glass would have. The inside had been stripped, glove compartment open. He could see the trunk was open as well, and there was nothing in the back seat. Brushing aside some of the glass, J.J. leaned over to get a look inside the glove compartment. It was empty. His hands came down on something. Jumping slightly he looked down. It was a pair of glasses. He'd broken one of the stems. He handed the glasses to Bart. It was unlikely he'd get any prints.

Next, he walked around the car. There was no license plate. No telling where the car came from. Prints? Probably. *The car has to tell us something*, thought J.J. J.J. looked at the two dead men, then at Bart.

"So, this guy is driving down the highway in his Ford Mustang when somebody comes along with a 9mm military submachine gun and gives him the business. Happens every day, right? Are you sure we aren't in New York? Sounds like the mob to me. I thought we had the drug trade pretty much under control, Bart," said J.J. sarcastically.

"Come on, J.J. . . . . we've never had Mafia down here. It's always been the small-timers."

J.J. just nodded in agreement. But still, it didn't *feel* right.

He walked back to the highway. On the southbound right shoulder lay the woman, scrunched up with her face down on the pavement next to the open passenger door of the Ford Bronco. Her back legs were bunched up and underneath her, in sort of a semi-fetal position. She'd been murdered with a blast to the back of the head. There was no identification on the woman, no bracelet, no watch, nothing.

Next to her was the body of a beautiful dog, a family friend. J.J. felt a well of tears rise up in the back of his eyes. He fought off the desire to cry. They shot the damn dog! Who would shoot a dog? The feeling of tears changed to anger.

The rain intensified as J.J. walked around the back of the vehicle, across and off the highway into the sand on the ocean side. He shook his head as he approached the children. On the ground were more shell casings. No need to look at them any closer. Jesus, what animals would kill two kids and a dog?

Walking back down the highway, J.J. made the entire circuit again, making sure that he had the scene well in his mind. The ranger's Jeep hadn't been touched. No reason to. He and the Bronco family had stumbled into something. Drugs probably. A smuggling attempt gone bad? Gangland slaying? J.J. wasn't getting the right mental image of what happened and more importantly, why.

Everything had been destroyed, the people callously killed. J.J. walked back to the Bronco. The dog had a collar and the collar had a tag.

TAG #124
MY NAME IS: CHARLIE
I LIVE AT: 1851 ELM STREET
IF I GET LOST CALL: 442-3487

J.J. knelt beside the body of the dead spaniel.

"Good dog," he said as he patted the soft fur of the nearly-cold body.

Tears welled behind J.J.'s eyes as he remembered too much of his youth. The rain and wind picked up in intensity. Tiny bits of sand flicked against his hand as J.J. rubbed his hand across the family's good friend. With the touch, J.J. began to cry at the senseless death.

"You son of a bitch . . . you're going to pay . . ."

CHAPTER 3

Massacre at the Eads Street Bridge

NEW YORK

"Yes, that's my assessment of the damage. It's contained for the moment. The appearance of the INTERPOL Inspector was unexpected."

Dimitri Korz could feel the pressure starting to build. He could hear the strain in Major General Bodnof's voice. There was something big happening, and they weren't letting on. All they wanted to do was to suck him for information. The four-agent mission was under Korz's control.

"What about our people?" asked Bodnof.

"I have provided my best. It does us little good to soak the area with agents. Khan won't be arriving until sometime later this week. We have the port covered. We have excellent communications. When they arrive we will be able to hear their every word. When my agents know, you will know. Whatever Khan's plans are, you may be sure, Major Bodnof, that I will relay them to you within minutes. Is there a critical time which I should be aware of?"

The static on the line was delayed longer than the encryption process normally took. Korz smiled. Moscow was playing this very close. There was another delay, then Bodnof spoke.

"Ambassador Korz, do you have a weapons specialist?"

"Weapons specialist? What do you mean? All my agents are weapons specialists," replied Korz.

"No . . . I understand that," returned Bodnof. "What I mean is, do you have someone who could program an atomic weapon?"

The light clicked inside Dimitri Korz's brain and he didn't like the smell of the burning cells.

"You have the records, Major. You know the background of my men as well as I do . . . Moscow knows. I have several agents with general explosives skills, including agent Tambov. But no one with the knowledge of nuclear weapons," returned Korz with some disdain.

Another pause.

"We don't believe the weapons will be complex, ambassador. If Khan is bringing atomic weapons we believe they will be low-grade, dirty—almost of the homemade variety."

Korz's reply was caustic.

"We are spies, Major Bodnof—not terrorists. Are you asking me to do more than spy, to provide you more than just information? What is it you want? And, yes, agents Tambov and Williams have the skills you need. I don't know about Rostov." There it was. This was way beyond what was expected of him. "Are you telling me that we—my agents—will detonate an atomic weapon inside the United States. Are you telling me that, Major Bodnof?" Korz continued with rising anger.

"Yes," was Bodnof's reply.

"Not on your authorization, Major General," Korz said with scorn. "Don't you have someone you can send from Moscow?"

It was Bodnof's turn for anger.

"We don't have time to send someone from Moscow, Ambassador Korz." Again a pause. "Your people must be prepared. For the time being, that is all. If anything changes . . ."

Bodnof's voice trailed off as completion of the sentence was not required. Korz understood. He was on the hot seat.

CAPE HATTERAS NATIONAL SEASHORE

J.J. awakened from a dead sleep not knowing where he was. He'd dreamed the dream of dread, one where the faces of the dead children were somehow superimposed on his own children. He woke up feeling tired, not rested at all. His neck was soaked as was the back of his pajamas. In fifteen minutes J.J. was up and out.

His was the only car in the Armada's parking lot. There weren't a lot of tourists walking the windswept beaches in 43-degree weather in a damp, heavy mist.

While Highway 12 leading into the Seashore had been reopened, all cars had to make a stop at the Park Service kiosk and register. The same applied for down-county people living on Hatteras Island, who were going to Manteo or the mainland. The Park Service guard politely told each car that there was an accident site twelve miles down the road, and that there might be a delay in passing. But anyone who turned on a radio or read a newspaper knew of the tragedy on the Outer Banks. The pressure would begin to build, immediately if not sooner.

J.J. had driven through the Seashore many times. The accident—

murders—had taken place in a portion of Hatteras Island known as Pea Island. The northern tip of Hatteras Island had been designated as a Wildlife Refuge in 1938 and named for the wild snow peas that grew on the sand dunes. Snowy egrets, terns, herons, pelicans, and geese could be seen various times during the year.

The site was a mess. Thankfully, Harris Steele had taken the bodies away. The green Park Service car and the Ford Bronco had been removed. The white Mustang was still embedded in the sand dune, its trunk opened. The two long stretches of skid marks were roped off, leaving only a narrow path for cars to slowly make their way past. A Park Service ranger directed traffic on both sides.

Bart was there, as was Henry Onslow. Henry had been to the FBI-taught class on fingerprint identification many years ago and had passed his skill on to several policemen in Dare and other surrounding counties. Although most of the crimes committed on the Outer Banks were DUIs (Driving Under the Influence), there were at least two murders every year and enough robberies in which fingerprint identification was needed.

J.J. pulled over to the side of the highway and parked. The rain had stopped but the heavy mist was enough to fog J.J.'s glasses. J.J. had never even considered getting contacts, the glasses simply seemed like part of his body. Unfortunately, he was at the point where bifocals weren't out of the question. Glasses did become a giant pain when he had to be out in the wet, or at the beach. The salt in the air could cake a pair of glasses with a slimy coating within five minutes. He was forever trying to keep them clean. This morning he had both, so it was fruitless. As he approached, his vision was clear enough to see that Henry's number one priority was to identify footprints.

"Good morning, Henry. Is it safe to come on out?" shouted J.J. from the highway.

He got a nod from Henry and a good-morning from Bart. While he had been sleeping the two policemen had spent the night out in the cold rain. Neither man gave J.J. much of a greeting.

"Been here all night," confirmed Henry.

"Towed the cars over to Cruikshank's and left a guard with them, until Henry can get to them," said Bart.

The cars would be safe, out of the way. Harley Cruikshank ran a Gulf station and auto parts store over on the Wanchese road. He also had the license for picking up illegally parked and abandoned vehicles.

There were cars scattered all through the pine trees behind the station.

There were people like Henry Onslow all over the United States in various sections of law enforcement. People who did things very well, slowly, but very well. People who did things well also seemed to enjoy it. Henry would be one of the few people he'd ever met who would enjoy spending a night out in a cold rain on his hands and knees.

"I'll get to the rubber after I finish the footprints. Don't want to let the wind help these two bastards."

Henry's voice was hard. Like Bart, Henry was a lifetime resident of the Outer Banks. Bart was an elected Sheriff, Henry was a career policeman; politeness and politicking were not his long suits. The murder of the two children had affected everyone who had seen them. Reading about a murder was a lot different from seeing a murder victim. You could always skip over to the next story in a paper. You couldn't erase the memory of blood-stained, mutilated tiny bodies.

"One of them's a woman—either that or a small man wearing a woman's running shoes," Henry continued.

Henry hadn't yet looked up at J.J. The area around the white Mustang was filled with puddles of drying mould compound. Henry had taken pictures of each print, measured it, then carefully mixed and poured the compound into the footprint. Henry finished one of the prints, then from his kneeling position looked up at J.J.

"The woman killed the kids, J.J. Can you believe it! A woman!" The thought was obviously beyond Henry's scope of reference.

He went back to work, but a moment later said:

"I've pulled up a lot of footprints, probably even yours. What's your shoe size?"

"Eleven and a half," replied J.J.

Henry noted it on a pad.

"What kind of woman could kill two children?" muttered Henry.

J.J. couldn't imagine such a cold-blooded woman either, and instead of answering Henry he turned to Bart.

"We need those prints as soon as he can get them," said J.J., knowing full well Henry was working as fast as he could.

J.J. walked back to the chalked outline of the fallen Park Service ranger Catchings. He turned round, and walked back toward the wreck. A woman? If the woman shot the children then probably she had killed Catchings. That meant she had been driving . . . no, wait a minute. J.J. was having trouble picturing the scene. She didn't have to kill the ranger, did she? That meant she would have been in the vehicle which skidded off the left side of the highway. But what happened to the Mustang? J.J.'s mind was racing. Could the woman have killed everyone? What am I really dealing with here?

The damage to the windshield and driver's side windows was more horrible in the light of day. The man never had a chance. J.J. opened the door and peered inside. For some reason his eyes went right to it. The visor. Around the visor were two heavy-duty rubber bands. J.J. reached in and flipped it down.

A notepad! Jackpot!

Watch for prints! In his inside coat pocket J.J. pulled out a large number 10 business-size envelope and with the tip of his pen pushed the small notepad out from under the grasp of the rubber bands and into it. On his way back to his car J.J. pointed to the Mustang and asked one of the patrolmen:

"When are you going to move it?"

"Sometime today, sir."

J.J. got back in his car. Very carefully he opened the notepad, again with the tip of his pen. There, in a scribble of a man writing while driving, was what appeared to be a license plate number: 8644NTO. Was it a license plate? Was it the plate of the man(woman?) he was following? Perhaps the pad belonged to someone else.

It was a start. Please let it be a license plate number, prayed J.J. But there was no state.

NEW BEDFORD

"Ayeh, I've got a clear set."

Scotty *knew* he couldn't lose his cool and go bananas in front of the New Bedford sergeant. But his heart pumped with the news. Damn! He was going to get that bastard—*those* bastards.

"Actually, I got two clears and a partial, maybe more."

Jesus and Mother Mary, thought Scotty, trying to remain calm.

The crusty New Bedford policeman showed Scotty the originals of what he'd managed to come up with in the HoJo rooms and the blue Cutlass. The first were those of the man who called himself John Smithton Ramsey. *A lying son of a bitch,* thought Scotty. *Who was he?* Scotty'd almost been killed following him. Rostov wanted him. Some other agent wanted him. A woman? Ramsey was with another man and they'd chartered the fishing boat *Bedford Clipper* for a fun-filled cruise in the middle of the winter to the North Atlantic.

"Ayeh, they's plenty of prints, but there's a clear match from the steering wheel of the car to the ones from the motel room. It took some dusting, but I could match every one. Your Washington boys at the FBI don't have to do much on this one."

Scotty just nodded his head. The sergeant wasn't through.

"The other room . . . the one where this Rostov character stayed—I didn't have anything to go on, nothing to match—but, I've got prints— I don't know, there's so many of them. But I came up with a list of partials. This is something your people in Washington will have to do."

"How many?"

"Fifty-two," was the sergeant's reply.

Fifty-two? The sergeant could see Scotty's hang-dog face.

"But most of them are old. I've marked them. Less than half are recent. You should be able to come up with a composite, something reasonably close."

Reasonably close? Scotty thanked the sergeant, signed for the package, and left the police station for the airport.

He had a long way to go.

MANTEO, NORTH CAROLINA

J.J. showed the notepad to Claiborne.

"Could be the car we've got, or it could be the one we don't," said J.J.

"Or it could be something completely different," reminded Bart.

J.J. gave him a disgusted look.

"See if there's a hit on the license," said J.J.

The Dare County police station was in the middle of sleepy Manteo. Except for the four-hundred-year-old remains of Ft. Raleigh, Claiborne's office was in the oldest building in town, the two-storey red brick Administration Building, built in 1904. Attempts had been made to make it as modern as possible, by adding such conveniences as air conditioning, without much success. The building was a relic and people seemed to like it that way. Of course, in the mornings you had a choice of having either Mr. Coffee brewing or the lights on in the ladies' room, but not both. In the summertime, court sessions on the second floor tended to be short, as did the tempers of the circuit judges and attorneys hearing and presenting cases in hot and stuffy courtrooms.

Bart's office was halfway down a well-worn wooden hallway on the left, opposite the men's room. Attached to the Administration Building was a more modern addition that housed the actual police station, including dispatch, a small kitchen, a crash room for sleeping, and four detention cells.

It was a never-ending sore point for J.J. that he had to use the computer facilities of the local police, but in this case it made sense. Although J.J. had access to the National Crime Information Center, he would have to go to his Regional Office in Charlotte, nearly three hundred miles away, to use the FBI's terminals.

Claiborne's duty officer went through the sign-on procedure with the state computer in Raleigh. By typing PT for pass-thru, the Raleigh computer communicated with the FBI's mainframe in the basement of the Hoover Building in Washington. The communications controller in Nags Head communicated at a slow 9600 bits per second to Raleigh, which in turn had to queue up the pass-thru request along with all the other local applications, then communicate to Washington at the same speed.

Response time was somewhat slow, but certainly better than the old days where each police department had to keep all of their own records, then mail, telephone, or telex requests to Washington.

"Go into the License File first," said J.J.

NCIC's license plate file was limited to only those issued plates which were reported stolen by someone else. Using the file took some practice. NCIC had issued a four-inch binder to all users that went through the various descriptions of the rules and regulations regarding data entry and inquiry. By any casual user it would be considered user-ugly.

The sergeant typed: QV.NC1012600.??H954.??.88.PC.* which meant QV (Inquiry) NC1012600 (the identification for Dare County North Carolina) 8644NTO (the suspected license plate) ?? (Unknown State) 88 (Year of license renewal—a guess) PC (regular passenger car—also a guess) and * (no other fields in record to be scanned).

After a long two minutes came the response:

NO RECORD FOUND.

"Drop the year," asked J.J.

The sergeant moved his cursor over to the 88 and typed 00, the pressed Enter. Two more minutes went by.

NO RECORD FOUND.

"OK, it was just a shot," said J.J.

They didn't know if the license number was that of the car with no plates or something else completely different.

"Do you want any code, Mr. Carteret?"

The License Plate File, cryptically known as the $.8. program, didn't allow for much free-form description. Using fixed length records, 80 columns, there was no place to include a variable writeup of what had happened. There was a 13 character MISC field but that wasn't much.

"Armed and Dangerous," was J.J.'s response.

The sergeant typed:

EL-F.NC1012600.8644NTO.??.88.PC.030888.000000000.
NOAH.P88947

Translated; EL-F(New entry, Suspect is Armed and Dangerous), NC1012600 (Dare County, North Carolina), the license plate #, the state of registry, the year, passenger car, 030888 (date), 000000000 (case number—none assigned), NOAH (Notifiy This Agency Of All Hits), P88947 (the NCIC assigned number, by the computer).

The NOAH was the key to the record. Any person accessing the License Plate File from anyplace in the United States when reading NOAH is supposed to make contact with the originating office (NC1012600), because a "hit" may help in the investigation of a crime. Only Hawaii, Idaho, South Dakota, and Wyoming do not participate in the $.8. program.

"No, drop the Armed and Dangerous," relented J.J.

The Armed and Dangerous was J.J.'s call. Technically, it would be rash. Actually, it would be imprudent. There was no evidence that the license plate number, if it was a license plate, was involved in a crime. Since there was no state identifier, no vehicle ID#, no make and model description, he couldn't justify the call. Putting a license plate into the file and calling it Armed and Dangerous could put some innocent driver into great danger. Besides, the handwriting in the notepad was a real chicken-scratch.

Although there was a Vehicle File in NCIC, it was only used to track down missing cars. He would be breaking procedure by entering a blind record. Only the office who actually "lost" license 8644NTO should enter the data. It was a bit frustrating from J.J.'s standpoint, since it was unlikely someone even thought the car was missing. Without further information there wasn't any way he could authorize a wanted vehicle. In truth, they didn't even know it was a vehicle.

The Bronco had been licensed in Ohio. An inquiry to the state's Department of Motor Vehicles in Columbus had been sent this morning. There had been no reply as of yet.

"Let's pay a visit to Harley," said J.J.

Neither man spoke more than a few words on the short drive through the rain-soaked marshland of southern Roanoke Island. J.J. knew Bart's trouble. This was the worst crime ever committed in Dare County. Bart was an elected sheriff and next year was an election year. A few years back four people had been gunned down in a crazy love-triangle-plus-one, but it was nothing like this. Those murders had been self-inflicted and the public had been entertained, albeit briefly, by the sex and drugs implications.

These murders were different . . . completely different. An innocent family had been killed.

"Is that Henry?" exclaimed J.J.

"Yep," replied Bart.

Henry Onslow was hard at work dusting the inside of the white Mustang. Under his direction, two policemen were doing the same to the other vehicles.

"Looks like you got things under control for a change," J.J. wisecracked.

Even with the back of his mind cluttered with heavy political implications, Bart smiled but said nothing. Things *did* seem like they were under control.

The two men walked over ground packed with fallen pine needles to the white Mustang.

"Here," said Henry, handing Bart a list.

Bart looked at it.

"Vehicle IDs."

They'd need the data for the hungry computer.

Henry backed himself out of the front seat, which had been cleared of the large pieces of glass, and took off his powder-caked rubber gloves.

"This is a rental car. Whoever killed the fat guy had the presence of mind to try and throw us off the track. He really must have been in a hurry because it looks like he was clawing at the sticker in the lower right corner. All you need is a decent knife and you could get it off. He also didn't care if we got his fingerprints . . . which I have. They're all over the window and on the trunk lid. I think he's right-handed. I got a good left print on the trunk. I would assume he had the car keys in his right hand. I picked up a matching left-hand high on the passenger dashboard, several good right-thumbs and a decent middle-right. I'll have them to you tonight."

This was what Henry Onslow did best. As a result, by his choice his shift had gone from daytime to all-time.

They had most of the male killer's prints and would be able to pinpoint his shoe size by process of elimination. With the size of shoe they would be able to estimate the murderer's height and weight range. The Identification Division in Washington would be able to tell what kind of gun the 9mm shell came from. From the skid marks they'd probably be able to provide the type and make of the vehicles involved, or at least a range.

"*A rental . . .*" J.J.'s thoughts trailed off.

He hated rental cars. There was always a delay. Each of the nationwide companies had home billing offices, and, in theory at least, control over their inventory of automobiles. J.J. emphasized theory, because it wasn't always the case.

It didn't take much for a car to get lost in the system. Most rentals were in and around airport locations, within the same city or area, and returned to their point of rental. The computer was loaded with the automobile, the date of rental, and the expected date of return. For 90% of the automobiles rented, keeping track of the inventory was easy. Another five percent consisted of automobiles that were rented in one city and driven to another. A car driven from LaGuardia to Logan airport in Boston, registered in New York, would be saved by the manager at Logan for someone who wanted to return to New York . . . unless there was a shortage of cars and the car had to be rented to somebody who wanted to drive to Maine. Instead of driving to Maine, the renter drives to Bethesda, Maryland and drops the car off at a satellite rental area of National airport at a local Gulf station on Wisconsin Avenue. The gas station owner is busy and he has no computer. He takes care of the paperwork, but then immediately rents the car out to someone driving to South Carolina. In the computer, the car is still has a Maine destination. At some point in time the car will reach a location where someone will update the computer. The car will have to go back to New York, the point of registration, however it's easy for a car to be out of the system, off the map, out of sight from the computer.

At each of the HQ locations for Hertz, Avis, National, Budget, and Alamo the FBI had at least one agent who's sole responsibility was to funnel inquiries from FBI field agents to the corporation. J.J. would have to send a request out to each of the HQ offices and ask the agent to check the rental company's computer for a white 1986 Mustang with the specific vehicle ID#. Vehicle ID# was not a normal search field in computers. Without a location (airport name, etc.), license plate number, or name of renter, at least part of the search would have to be manual. White Mustangs could be searched, but then the list would have to be manually searched for the matching vehicle ID#.

It was a pain in the butt.

Leaving Henry to finish his prints, J.J. and Bart drove back to Manteo, then over the causeway to Nags Head, where they went to the Outer Banks Medical Center and the office of Harris Steele. Steele seemed to relish his job.

J.J. hated to look at dead people. Especially dead people who were cut up. Steele's morgue was crowded. Marmande's dumpy body lay under a cloth sheet. Steele uncovered the dead man's head and shoulders. It was a gross sight.

"At least eight bullets went through this man's head, neck, and shoulder. Two bullets entered through his left shoulder and were lodged in his chest. I have retrieved them for you. Two also went through his neck, one passing out through his Adam's apple the other out the back. As you can see, his head has been severely damaged. I really can't tell if there were more than four bullets . . . they all passed through his head from side to side. Other than being overweight, there are no distinguishing marks on the man, no other injuries. The entry and exit paths indicate a flat projectory."

Steele covered Marmande up and went over to Catchings.

"Park Ranger Catchings was shot four times in back from close range. The density of the wounds indicates the bullets were fired from some sort of automatic weapon. The shots passed through his body and out his chest. I really can't give you an angle, it was too close. As a matter of fact, I can't give you an angle on any of the others. Each of the victims was killed at short range."

Steele handed J.J. his report and the bullets retrieved from Marmande's body.

"Oh, yes. There is something else," said Steele, reaching under Marmande's sheet. "Here are his clothes."

"So?" asked J.J.

"Look at the labels."

J.J. fingered the bloodied shirt collar. It was a foreign label. So was the tag in the man's pants. J.J. picked up one of the well-worn shoes. Foreign.

"French?" asked J.J.

"Beats me," shrugged Steele.

"I want it all," said J.J.

"You got it."

A half-hour later the two men walked out of the OBMC and looked out to the cold Atlantic Ocean not more than a half-mile away.

"Who is this guy?" J.J. asked.

"And why did he die here?" added Bart Claiborne.

STUMPY POINT, NORTH CAROLINA

Rostov crossed the McIntyre Bridge leading from the now-dark Roanoke Island to the mainland. Following him was Williams. The two cars obeyed the speed limit, slowed down at the intersection and at Manns Harbor took the left fork onto U.S. 264 south. They immediately were off into the swampy tidal area of the piedmont.

There was really no need to spend time looking for the best hiding place. There were so many of them. A mile before the turnoff to Stumpy Point, Rostov turned left onto one of many lanes named Dead End Road. They both turned their lights out, their path illuminated by a full moon. Thirty yards from the highway Dead End Road turned to a dirt lane. The two cars continued past one or two darkened shacks down a finger of land, until they reached a point where the marsh was on three sides and the dirt turned to swampgrass.

With a towel from the Sheraton, Rostov went over every piece of the interior of the Buick, wiping any place where he might have touched. Next, he removed the license plates. Should he leave the car or try to sink it in the Pamlico Sound? At the end of the road was an opening to the water which appeared to have been used as a boat launch. Rostov opened the Buick's windows, cracked both front doors, released the brake and motioned to Williams.

"Push," instructed Rostov.

The two men pushed the Buick down the small embankment and into the muddy grasp of the Pamlico Sound. The car made an almost silent slurpy noise as it was slowly sucked into the ooze of the marsh.

Smiling to himself, Rostov and his driver Williams returned to the Outer Banks and their surveillance of Khalid Rahman.

Rostov had made a major mistake.

ABOARD THE *BEDFORD CLIPPER* — ATLANTIC OCEAN

The frontal system which had plagued the East Coast for nearly a week passed through in the middle of the night. The sunrise was beautiful. Aziz al-As had seen the sun come up but its beauty was lost on his consciousness.

Bafq el-Rashid had visited his bed twice in the last two nights. There was no pretending and certainly no apology. Aziz had done nothing; no struggle, no complaint, no cooperation. Still, the violation was the same. At the end he had asked the logical question from the stronger man.

"Why?"

There had been no answer.

What could he do? Kill el-Rashid? That was the only possibility which seemed reasonable. But it would be kill-and-be-killed. Without el-Rashid it was doubtful that the mission could be completed. Khan could try a bluff—but if the bluff was called, all would be lost. No, Khan needed the bombs to be activated in order for his plan to work. Both he and el-Rashid were needed, but el-Rashid's skills were needed more. Go to Khan? No, that was impossible. Bafq would deny it, giving that look of his, that look of incredulity mixed with disdain. Khan would have no choice but to believe el-Rashid. No, there would come a time—the right time when el-Rashid could be dealt with, and dealt with properly.

Aziz wanted nothing but his own company this morning. In a crowd, cats seem to be able to pick out the person who either hates the animals or is allergic. So it was with al-As and his need for privacy. The bridge was filled with his companions, including a rarely laughing Bafq el-Rashid. To Khan, Aziz not only seemed depressed—he seemed deep in remorse and ill-tempered. This only made the situation worse. Khan wanted nothing but high spirits and enthusiasm for the death-defying task ahead.

"What is wrong, Aziz al-As? You look terrible. Your face is drawn, tired. You must get sleep."

Aziz just nodded, hoping Khan would leave him alone.

"I will, my Khan," Aziz answered unsmilingly, moving away from the Khan and el-Rashid.

"Good!" exclaimed Khan.

Khan's mood changed quickly. He turned to el-Rashid. Fire came into his eyes and words.

"It is time to talk of what will happen."

Khan turned to el-Rashid.

"How difficult is it to change the detonation time and date once it has been fixed?" Khan asked.

"Not hard at all. The timing mechanism is nothing more complicated than an alarm clock. As a matter of fact, the device *is* an alarm clock, albeit a smart alarm clock. The clocks in these weapons are digital and actually have a 16k memory chip for simple programs. One of the programs is an extended date ability. You could set these bombs to go off in the next century if you wanted to."

The idea wasn't wasted on Khan. The thought of a permanent legacy, his legacy, was more than an interesting idea. Imagine if the American people knew there was a bomb which would go off on a certain date in the future! It could go off someplace, anyplace! Imagine the panic as the date got closer and closer. What a wonderful idea!

Bafq continued.

"When the programmed time and date are reached the battery sends a signal to the internal alarm. However, instead of triggering a bell or buzzer, the current is sent to the detonator cap . . . which really isn't a cap but rather a pencil-thin explosive wrapped in plastic. It's a bomb wrapped inside a bomb which is wrapped inside a big bomb. The plastic explodes, driving a large plug of lithium-tipped uranium down the short arm to the central chamber of the bomb. There the lithium meets an equally small deposit of polonium . . . and poof . . ." his voice trailed off.

Bafq el-Rashid leaned back on the *Clipper*'s sonar scope and smiled a black-tooth smile.

"How difficult is it to defuse?"

Bafq shrugged.

"It depends if you want a secondary trigger . . . or a third. These things can be as complicated or as simple as you want. The firing chamber, the top of the arm, has a single four-inch screw. If you wanted me to, I could wire it so that the slightest turn of the screw would detonate the weapon once I've set the time. I'm not sure I'd want to do that aboard this boat, though," said el-Rashid, smiling.

"I don't think that will be necessary. Our objective is to hide the bombs and ourselves well enough so that the president will have no choice but to give in to our demands. No choice!"

Khan's fervor started to possess him.

"We have five bombs. The first will be placed in the city of Washington and will be our calling card. We will tell them where it is. If they believe us, fine . . . if not, then they will learn the truth immediately! The second will be set in America's heartland, in the city of St. Louis, beneath the arch that symbolizes the spirit of freedom and adventure that Americans take so much pride in. False pride! The third will be in a major airport. I have chosen the one in Dallas, Texas. If the bomb is detonated, coast-to-coast air traffic across America will be severely damaged. The fourth bomb will destroy another symbol of America's pride, the Golden Gate bridge in San Francisco. America's most beautiful city will become ugly and uninhabitable—raped by the strength of the Jihad!"

Khan's eyes were glassy. El-Rashid and Aziz al-As were open-mouthed in rapture.

"The fifth bomb . . . ," Khan's attention came back to the small group, ". . . the fifth is for ourselves. It is our ticket home. You know me well enough. I don't believe in suicide missions. I have never asked you to execute a plan that had no way to come back home, and this is no different. The Americans will know the bombs are real and will ensure our safe return home. I guarantee it! The Americans will listen to me! Or they will suffer the consequences. And suffer they will!"

Khan's intensity had temporarily taken him over the edge of reality and out into his own plane of existence. He began to smile.

"They have a national song, a song of pride, called 'America the Beautiful.' In it is the line '. . . from sea to shining sea . . .' We will drive a stake of terror through their hearts . . . from sea to shining sea."

Khan paused. They could feel the vibration from the *Clipper*'s engines and the gentle sloshing of the waves against her steel plates. Khan smiled to himself.

"From sea to shining sea . . . "

NEW YORK

The NCIC classification for fingerprints is a twenty-digit field in the computer, which consists of ten sets of two characters. The characters may be either alphabetic or numeric. Every two characters in the field represent a finger, starting with the right thumb and ending with the left little finger. There are five major classification of finger patterns; arch, loop, whorl, missing/amputated, and scarred/mutilated. Missing fingers are identified as XX, scarred fingers as SR. Arch configurations are either Plain (AA) or Tented (TT). Loops are further divided into Radial or Ulnar and are entered as two-digit numerics based on the actual number of ridges within the pattern. Whorls, or circular formations, may be Plain, Central Pocket Loop, Double Loop, or Accidental and are further classified as Inner, Meeting, or Outer. Whorls are entered as two-character alphabetic.

Scotty sat at his desk and got another taste of the inefficiency of The System. There was no computer into which Scotty could enter John Smithton Ramsey's TT1648POPICI1819AA06 collection of fingerprints. Ramsey had done nothing wrong. The New Bedford police would keep a lookout for Ramsey, but they too had nothing firm on the man. Computers wanted facts, not hunches or suspects. What the computers didn't want was the clutter of man's intuition.

So, Scotty started his file. At first, it consisted only of a simple Manila folder in a Pendaflex file. He labeled it JOHN SMITHTON RAMSEY.

But there was plenty of room in Scotty's desk. This was his first case. A second Manila folder went behind the first. It was labeled ALEXANDER ROSTOV. A third went behind it and it went unlabeled. It was for the phantom woman. The woman who was with Rostov at the Howard Johnson's. Had it been a woman's heels he'd heard clacking down the cobblestones of Union Street in New Bedford?

Where did these people come from? Rostov was a Soviet agent. Who was Ramsey?

Had it only been ten days? Ten? The trails were still warm. Somewhere the trails were warm. They certainly weren't warm here.

Scotty forced himself to go back to the beginning. He'd followed Rostov from Kennedy airport to the Soviet Mission on 67th Street. The next day he'd picked up . . .

Picked up!

Rostov didn't pick up Ramsey, the Soviets picked up Ramsey. Scotty fought with himself as his logic tried to follow the obvious. Of course! Rostov had given him the eye, the eye of the all-knowing, at the pharmacy on Third Avenue. He had given him the eye because he did know everything. There had been others. *Of course there were.*

Why?

Had the Soviets been following Ramsey and . . .

Why?

Scotty's thoughts were scorching his synapses.

Why bring in someone from overseas just to add to a local trace? The embassy . . . mission . . . wouldn't do it.

Scotty kept coming back to the same thought. Rostov had been following Ramsey. He'd followed Ramsey from Paris. Ramsey had been aboard the same flight as Rostov. Scotty got up, put on his parka and headed for his car. This was not time for telephone tag.

An hour and fifteen minutes later Scotty was showing his new badge to the manager of the Air France desk at Kennedy International Airport.

"This should be easy. I want you to check to see if there was a John Smithton Ramsey on flight #10 from Paris to New York on the afternoon of February 8th."

Scotty looked across the manager's desk to the incredible ebb and flow of people through the terminal. *Everybody's an individual,* he thought. *Every one of those people has a different destination, different values, different everything. Yet they nearly share the same space at the same time . . .* Scotty's thoughts were going off into never-never land.

"Yes, Mr. Coldsmith. John Smithton Ramsey was on that flight. He sat in seat 23B," answered the manager.

"How did he pay for the flight?" asked Scotty.

"In cash, at the gate. Four hundred eighty-five dollars."

"Did he give a local telephone number, perhaps in Paris?"

"No."

There was nothing else the manager could do for him. He would have to find out how to contact the police in Paris. The drive back into Manhattan was slow, but time passed quickly for Scotty. He was deep in thought. Somebody overseas knows who these people are, and he was going to find out.

"I'm going to get you, you son of a bitch," Scotty mumbled to himself as his car limped along toward the Midtown Tunnel in the always-heavy traffic of the Long Island Expressway.

MOSCOW

The huge conference room was darkened, backlit only enough so that the dignitaries seated in the plush chairs could see each other. The lighting made it virtually impossible for the presenter to see the faces and reactions of those in the audience. Presenting was General Ivan Belogorsk, commander of the Far Eastern Theater of Military Operations (TVD).

General Belogorsk had spent most of the day flying from his east coast operations in Sakhalin nearly a third of the way around the world to the opposite side of the Soviet Union and the equally cold weather of Moscow. He had gone through eight time zones. There was one benefit. He had plenty of time on the ten-hour flight to rehearse what he was going to tell the triumvirate of Mikhail Gorbachev, Eduard Shevardnadze, and Viktor Chebrikov.

His presentation was not one of theory, nor of science, nor even one of military strategy—it was one of execution. Belogorsk was to explain how the operation would be executed—how long it would take to seize the Persian Gulf and march to Beirut—and how much firepower would it take. It would be the highlight of his career. Belogorsk and the other army generals were nearly salivating at the opportunity to wage a successful war, to get Afghanistan behind them. This was not time to be hesitant, doubtful, or cautious.

General Belogorsk was delighted at the opportunity to discuss a strategy that he had been a proponent of for the last ten years. He had received his opportunity in 1986 when his predecessor had been fired, demoted to a division command on the China-Soviet border east of Mongolia. It had been Ivan Belogorsk who had brought divisions of young and disgruntled foot soldiers home from Afghanistan in combination with a severely escalated use of armor, and more importantly, air power. While Belogorsk's Far Eastern TVD had the longest border to protect, his influence with the Politburo had been diminished by the fact that no politician wanted anything to do with Afghanistan.

Most Soviet military was located near, and strategy focused upon, that ten percent of their border with NATO countries. Three full-theater operations were conducted. Like the Far Eastern, all Soviet Theaters of Military Operations ran with a wartime command structure. The Western TVD was the point operation, including Central Europe, East Germany, Poland, and Czechoslovakia. To the north was the Northeastern TVD, to the south the Southeastern TVD.

All borders were not only to be protected, but also were to have offensive strategies for conquering adjacent foreign nations. Just as there was a plan to rush through West Germany to Paris and the Netherlands, there was an offensive plan to capture Helsinki and Lapland.

Belogorsk stood behind a podium that had an electronic display screen which could replicate the big board behind him, either as a whole or in sections. He used a light pen to activate different colors by free-form drawing. He drew a line across the 450-mile border between Iran and the Soviet Union and the thousand-mile border with Afghanistan, indicating the relative position of his troops with small boxes.

A division represented approximately ten thousand men.

"What I will need are the mobile divisions General Lyakhov currently has at his disposal in the Ukraine and at Minsk. I have ten divisions permanently along the Iranian border. Most are used for Afghan replacements.

"Because of the unique nature of desert fighting, four of those divisions are motorized infantry and another four are tank."

The motorized infantry divisions consisted of twelve thousand men: three infantry regiments and one tank regiment. The tank divisions were composed of three tank regiments and one motorized infantry with ten thousand men.

"I have five remaining divisions in Afghanistan: three motorized, one tank, one infantry. For a war of this expected duration I could move three of them to the Iranian border within days and launch an attack this way."

Belogorsk drew an arrow leading from the Zabul area of southwestern Afghanistan south across the Haumun-e Jaz Murian Desert, at which point he divided it into three smaller arrows: one each ending at the Gulf of Oman, the Straits of Hormuz, and the Persian Gulf in the Bandar-e Lingeh area. The general pointed to the Persian Gulf route.

"This consists of five hundred miles of desert. I can provide logistical support for that distance, however at beachhead I will need immediate re-supply at the airstrips in Chah Bahar, Bandar Abbas and Bandar-e Lingeh. I will need ground support teams and infantry. I will provide the infantry. We really don't want to level the existing cities, *however* I want the Navy to have the carrier *Leningrad* positioned here. It will be essential to the entire operation to have a coordinated Naval Air support from the *Leningrad* and the *Seven November*. If I have my details correct, the position of the two carriers is approximately here, and here."

Belogorsk put two dots, one in the Indian Ocean, the other in the Mediterranean Sea.

"Is that correct, Admiral?" asked Gorbachev.

"It is," was the terse reply.

Admiral Gregori Kirghiz did not like the main elements of his Navy moved around like so many toys.

"How long will it take to get them in position?"

"Three days, no longer," answered Kirghiz.

"And the support General Belogorsk needs?"

Kirghiz paused for a moment.

"General Belogorsk will get all the air support he needs for this operation."

Gorbachev turned back to Belogorsk.

"What is the American strength?"

Belogorsk flipped a switch. Instantly, the map was completed with the blue figures of the American forces, mostly navy.

"The only American carrier in the Mediterranean is the *Nimitz*, located here," Belogorsk pointed to a blue dot off the coast of Lebanon. "In the Persian Gulf is the battleship *New Jersey* and eight destroyers currently doing escort duty for the tankers. They have no capability of stopping an armored attack across either of these borders," Belogorsk tapped his wand on Iran's Soviet border on either side of the Caspian Sea. "Nor do they have the capability of delivering combat troops in sufficient quantity and quality to stop us from occupying Teheran and taking over the east shoreline of the Persian Gulf. The only thing the Americans can immediately throw at us is their naval air force, which is considerable. But, if we have the air covered, our troops should be able to strike quickly and achieve the objective with a minimum of casualties."

Belogorsk paused for questions. In the shielded darkness he could hear soft conversations between the Soviet leaders. Gorbachev shifted in his chair. Striking through Iraq, Syria, and Lebanon would bring certain Allied retaliation and an end to any pretense of *glasnost*. Once started, once completed, there would be no stepping back. There would be no way to smooth-talk the Americans, or anyone else, into believing that the objective was anything else than total world domination.

How could he even *think* of such ideas? The treaties had been signed. The reduction in nuclear weapons was real. Coexistence with the Americans was possible. There would be time and resources to concentrate on the economy, the quality of goods produced, the productivity of the workers. This plan would turn everything upside-down. Policies would change. The people would have to be convinced that Mother Russia was under attack, that the world was poised, ready for pillage and rape of the homeland.

It was almost too much to think about. The potential was so great—and he, Mikhail Sergeyvich Gorbachev, would be the leader to fulfill Lenin's prophecy.

"Continue, comrade," spoke Gorbachev. "What of the Mediterranean? What are our capabilities of striking through to the Mediterranean?" he asked.

"First, let me describe our immediate task. It is four hundred miles from the border to Teheran. There are several major highways that lead through the desert. I will need many more divisions of infantry. We will not have the cooperation of the people we conquer. I estimate we will need an additional ten divisions to seize control of the land we take and still have enough to break through to the Mediterranean. To accomplish this, I will require five infantry divisions from General Tashkent. They must be ready to launch an attack from the Iranian border in the Caucasus."

It was four hundred miles from the Caspian Sea to the Black Sea. The neck of land between the two inland seas was the Soviet land called the Caucasus. Half of the four-hundred-mile border was with Turkey, half with Iran. This operation would have nothing to do with the Turks. Belogorsk drew a thick line across the narrow two-hundred-mile border with Iran, then south through Tabriz, then west through the northern section of Iraq. There the heavy line met a now-diminished line which was drawn through Teheran from Belogorsk's troops along the northeastern border.

"Most of the Iraqi and Iranian troops are fighting near the Persian Gulf, along the Tigris River between Basra and Baghdad, well south of this operation. Neither country will be able to move sufficient troops to stop us. But—and this is very important—there will have to be massive bombing along this front line. We must throw in whatever we can, nerve and other chemical weapons are not out of the question. The Iranians have perhaps seven hundred thousand men, the Iraqis approximately the same—all are concentrated along the battlefront line near the Tigris River. It will take us three, perhaps four, days to move to a point where we would be able to isolate the front and be prepared to enter Syria. By this point we would have captured Iraqi territory down to the Euphrates River, with the exception of Baghdad. The attacks along the Tigris must be constant and indiscriminate. It would take a coordinated attack by both the Iranian and Iraqi ground forces to prevent us from taking a solid position from the Caspian south to the Persian Gulf, west to the border with Syria."

Belogorsk paused.

"We must be prepared to enter an air war with both of these countries until their military leaders surrender. While Teheran will be relatively easy to capture, Baghdad will not. We cannot be lured into a fantasy of taking both capital cities. This is the one point that is out of my control, Mr. Secretary General. You have asked me to execute a plan which will give us a position on the Persian Gulf. This I can do. I can capture land. I can hold my position. You must be willing to spend resources to wage war against two fanatical armies. This will require much of my TVD as well as troops from other theaters. It could be drawn out."

"But what of the Mediterranean?" pressed Gorbachev.

"I don't think it is possible, not unless we move every last division from along our European borders. I could make a run to the sea, but I don't think I could hold it. The logistics are too great. The Israelis would join with the Syrians . . . I don't think we would have the chance to succeed. We can, however, take Iran and a good part of Iraq," said Belogorsk, nearly spent.

"How long?" asked Shevardnadze.

Gorbachev interrupted before General Belogorsk had a chance to perjure himself. He held up his hand before the General could speak.

"Whatever time the General gives us is more than the theoretical best-case but less than what it probably will take. If it takes longer than he says, the General will have time to develop rational excuses. This operation must not take more than four days from invasion to control of the access routes to the Persian Gulf and the Iraqi lands north and east of the Tigris River. If the Iraqi territory between the Tigris and Euphrates can be captured, then Baghdad will fall as well. But, I'm not counting on this. Be aware gentlemen, what we do, we do knowing the risk of failure. On the fifth day the assault starts, we must be building air strips and highways in the Iraqi desert. The battle must be swift and complete. If we do not reach the Persian Gulf . . . if we do not take Teheran . . . if we do not isolate the battle front . . . well, we will all finish our days in cold places," Gorbachev warned, then continued.

"We will offer Hussein a deal, a restructured nation. I doubt, even with this opportunity, that we would be able to move enough men and weapons into the area to defeat both armies and capture both nations within four or five days. We offer Hussein the area south and west of Baghdad, below the Euphrates River and the oil fields of Iran in and around Kharg Island. We offer this in lieu of irradiating his country. The oil fields mean nothing to us. We are self-sufficient."

"It would be a tremendous blow to the European NATO countries," added Shevardnadze.

Gorbachev nodded silently. Indeed, it would be a blow. The Americans would blame Qaddafi for what would soon happen within the United States. The American president would strike at the target which he felt he could control and win—and gain the largest measure of political and self-satisfaction. Even with the U.S. 6th Fleet in the Mediterranean he would be helpless, powerless to do anything. Gorbachev smiled to himself. With no oil from Libya, Iran, and Iraq, the European continent would be dark within six weeks. It would be time to test the West German solution, perhaps Austria, or Finland. While the Americans might have some level of defenses up within a week, it would be months—perhaps as long as a year—before it would be able to do anything but protect itself.

The thought of being able to wage World War III on his own terms was almost beyond Gorbachev's imagination—but not quite. History was being made in this room, Gorbachev thought. He spoke to the group.

"Now let me explain why the Americans will be unable to lift a finger against us . . . "

MANTEO

The call came from one of his patrolmen.

"Bart, you'd better come and look at this one."

It took Bart nearly forty-five minutes to drive to Stumpy Point. He got there not two minutes ahead of Cruikshank's Towing Service. The day was mild for February. There was no breeze and the insects were rapidly becoming persistent. It would be a bad day for fishing unless you were wearing your coat of 100% DEET over every square inch of exposed skin.

It was low tide. Poking out of the water was the roof of the black Buick.

"Has anybody been inside?" asked Bart.

"Not yet. It's too muddy. I thought you might want to know. It might have something to do with your investigation."

"Your" investigation. Even his men were unconsciously trying to put some distance between themselves and the terrible murders.

It took only a few minutes for Cruikshank to hook up his winch and haul the car up onto the dirt lane. A small crowd of people had gathered near the highway. The car was coated with tidal slime. Three feet of water floated in the front and back seats. It didn't appear as if there were any dead people inside. Water slowly drained out through the cracked doors. Bart carefully opened the driver's door and was immediately engulfed, drenching his pant legs and shoes.

"Damn!" exclaimed Bart.

The patrolmen behind Bart looked at each other, rolled their eyes, and did everything in their power to stifle a laugh.

No body. It was a 1986 Buick. No license plate. Bart reached in and snapped the glove compartment open. Nothing. Clean. He checked the side panels for inspection/maintenance information. Nothing. Who wants to get rid of a new car?

"Get this thing out of here," Bart said to the driver.

He then turned to the patrolmen.

"Did anybody see anything, hear anything?"

"There's a colored boy who says he was wading out in that water not more than a week ago, crabbin'. Wasn't any 1986 Buick out there then."

No, there probably wasn't. Probably wasn't there three days ago, maybe not even yesterday, thought Bart. *Low tide would make that Buick look pretty much out of place for these parts.*

Bart Claiborne would have bet a month of lunches that the tire marks on the Buick would match up with one of the two sets of tracks out on Highway 12 in the Seashore. Why would whoever did this dump the car so it could be found? Why in such shallow water? And even if you were going to dump a car in the water, why do it in the same county as the investigating police department. Why?

Because they didn't know. All they had to do was to take this car across the other bridge, the Wright Memorial, and drop it off down some Dead End Road in Currituck County and he would have never seen it, nor heard of it. Whoever did this didn't realize that Dare County consisted of the Outer Banks and part of the mainland. Whoever did this was from out of town.

Claiborne radioed J.J. while he drove behind the tow truck and the quickly drying black Buick back to Cruikshank's Gulf Station and Auto Repair in Wanchese. When he got there, Henry was just finishing up the other two automobiles.

"Yes, Henry—another one," was all he said.

For the first time in the past three days Henry was a bit put out. He had another automobile to sweep clean of prints. Bart looked down through the driver's windshield and copied down the vehicle ID# for the Buick.

Maybe it was on file.

"See what you can get, Henry."

Henry stood up and gave him a folder.

"It's everything I've pulled off the two vehicles, Bart. I've got some pretty good partials on someone, but they're still just partials."

Henry looked at the destroyed Mustang, annoyed that he couldn't pull a complete set of prints of the killer, the *one* piece of evidence which would be damning, condemning some son of a bitch to eternal fire for the acts he committed.

Inside the folder was Henry's final report. It listed the size of every footprint, its location, direction, and measurements. The measurements told a story. How deep were the prints, especially in comparison with each other? Was it because the person was lighter? A woman? Old print? Henry had it all.

The woman wore a size $8^{1}/_{2}$ Nike running shoe. The man wore a size 10 loafer. There was no extra stitching around the exterior of the footprint, no nail prints that would indicate a leather sole. He wore a soft-soled shoe of some sort. There was no imprint of a label. The depth in the sand was nothing unusual. A size $10^{1}/_{2}$ indicated the man was probably five-foot-ten, 160-170 pounds.

"What kind of stride did he have? How far between . . ."

"Thirty-one inches."

"Not far . . . kind of average," replied Bart.

"He wasn't average, Bart," said Henry.

ELIZABETH CITY

"It's for you, J.J.," said Roy.

Roy Roper was J.J.'s Rotor Clerk and secretary. Without Roy, J.J. would get absolutely nothing of any substance done during the average working day. As best he could, Roy kept the bureaucracy of the FBI away from J.J. It was Roy who dealt with the Regional Office in Charlotte. It was Roy who filled the forms out which ended up on someone's desk or in one of the computers. The System *ate* paper. It created it, stuffed it, regurgitated it. Mercifully, Roy did the paperwork for J.J. In larger offices, this wasn't the case. While the number of Rotor Clerks was supposed to be one-for-one, it often wasn't. The two of them could have used a good secretary, for neither knew how to type very well, although Roy was the much better of the two.

"Carteret," answered J.J.

"This is Steve Burns in Oklahoma City. Are you John Carteret?"

"I am."

Elizabeth City must have been the absolute last place in the United States where the Federal Telephone Service (FTS) had been installed. The government used pathetically old AT&T equipment and lines for their unsecured telephone communications. J.J. had no secure lines to his office, and he used the word "office" lightly. He had had more room when he used his house as an office. Now he shared a broomcloset-sized room on the second floor of a small shopping mall on U.S. 158. The impressive emblem of the FBI was painted on the opaque glass, which effectively kept down the casual traffic of salesmen and hucksters. The people who came through the door normally had reason to seek help. Ninety—no, higher than that—percent of the foot traffic was referred to the local police department. They got everything from UFO sightings to wife beatings.

Most of J.J.'s time was spent helping the local P.D.s on the usual: drugs, smuggling, illegal interstate commerce or other activity. Occasionally there was some assistance required at Lejeune, especially if one of the men went whacko and left the base. The only reason he was involved at all in this case was that the Park Ranger, Catchings, had been on the job when he was murdered. If he'd been home and was killed by a neighbor, then it would be strictly Bart's responsibility. As it was, Bart Claiborne had primary responsibility for this case, not J.J.

"We got a hit on your vehicle ID#," said Special Agent Burns.

"Be still my heart," said J.J. with enthusiasm. "Hertz?" J.J. asked.

"You got it. They're two of us now. It's gotten too much for one," said Burns.

"What else?"

"The man's name is Jacques Marmande. He rented the car at Hartsfield International Airport in Atlanta at 8:45 P.M. on February 8th, eleven days ago. It was a white on white 1986 Mustang."

"'Was' is the appropriate term," interjected J.J.

"Is it totalled?"

"I suppose not. Needs new paint, new windshield, new seats. I can't believe Hertz would try to put it back into operation," said J.J.

"Probably not, but I've still got to let them know. You'll send me the report?" asked Burns.

"Right. I'll have the local P.D. send you a description. I interrupted you," J.J. got Burns back on track.

"Yes. There's not much left. Marmande used a VISA card and gave an address in Paris. The beginning mileage was 07435."

"Thanks for getting back to me," J.J. replied.

"You'll send the report?"

"Right."

The System still worked. Bart Claiborne's clerk, Roy, Bart, J.J., Burns, Burns' Rotor Clerk, and at least one person at Hertz would have to touch, fill out, and sign the various paper involved with the automobile. A decision at Hertz would have to be made to either write off the automobile or have an inspector come out to get an estimate for repairs. In any case, it was Hertz's responsibility to claim and remove the automobile. Just in administrative overhead, The System would eat up nearly twenty-five hundred dollars in people and travel costs. For one car! Who paid for it? Somebody had to. It was the average guy who rented cars and paid forty bucks a day . . . not the corporate salesmen who got the same car for $18.95 a day.

No matter where J.J. turned, there was a reason to be cynical.

"Call the agents covering the other rental companies and call off the dogs," J.J. told Roy.

There was no sense in having people do extra work, especially when he knew he'd need them again. Nothing soured a business relationship quicker than doing some leg work in solving a problem for someone, then getting "Oh, I got the answer from Jim" or "Gee, thanks, I guess I didn't need it after all." J.J. was very conscientious about calling off the dogs.

The man's name was Marmande and he rented the car in Atlanta on February 8th. Where'd he come from, and why? The next step was to call the airlines and have them pull up a roster list. If Marmande arrived on the 8th, then most of the computers should still have the record.

"It's Bart Claiborne, line 1," said Roy.

"Well, I've got the man's name," said J.J. to Bart.

"And I think I've got one of their cars. It was abandoned, probably within the last two days," returned Bart.

"What was the odometer reading on the Mustang?" asked J.J.

"Wait a minute. Here it is. 06625," answered Bart.

J.J. did the quick math. Eight hundred ten miles. It was five hundred sixty miles to Atlanta. Marmande was murdered on the sixteenth . . . it takes a full day to drive to Atlanta . . . that leaves seven days . . . seven into two-fifty, thirty-five-odd miles . . . Marmande wasn't doing much driving, not for a week.

"Marmande was staying here, Bart," said J.J.

J.J. could hear Bart nodding in agreement on the phone. He could hear Bart's thoughts as well. It was all a matter of priorities and resources.

"I've got some other information for you J.J.," Bart said without committing anything.

Bart described Henry's findings, especially the footprints and the partial prints on the man.

"Good work . . . very good work," said J.J., really meaning it. J.J. continued, "Look, Bart, I'll stay with finding out where Marmande came from. Maybe at the end there's an answer on why he was here. When I get that, then I'll help out trying to find out where he was for those eight days here on the Banks."

"I'll put a query in on the new car. All I've got is the vehicle ID#," answered the sheriff, and they said goodbye.

J.J. hung up knowing that the only thing they could do was to continue to dig small pieces at a time. It was persistent, boring work. But it was the only way.

NEW YORK

New York license plate #8644NTO was registered to the New York Mission of the Union of Soviet Socialist Republics. Scotty had no idea that the 'Republics' in the title referred to fifteen geographical and political districts within the huge boundaries of the country. One of them, the Russian Soviet Federated Socialist Republic, occupied nearly eighty percent of the territory and as much of the population. The rest of the republics were smaller ethnic states which had lost little of their pre-revolution look and still had a great distrust for the national Communist Party and national government.

Scotty looked at the bored clerk at Motor Vehicles and copied down the remaining information on the black 1986 Buick, including the vehicle ID. It was late. By the time he would get back downtown to the office Rosemary would be gone for the day.

He would have her revise Rostov's record tomorrow. Perhaps INTERPOL would have responded to his wire regarding Rostov and John Smithton Ramsey.

Scotty should have gone back to work.

MANTEO

A very, very tired Bart Claiborne wearily sat back from the computer terminal. His eyes were blurred, his head was spinning. This was one of those days when he felt like he'd gotten shrapnel wounds from the information explosion. There was *too* much information in those computers. He'd asked the Vehicle File for the vehicle ID# of the Buick. He'd asked the Missing Persons file for someone named Marmande. He'd gone back to the Vehicle File and asked for what they assumed to be a license plate.

But no matter how he asked it, the dumb thing always came back with the same answer.

NO NCIC MATCH.

NO RECORD FOUND.

WANCHESE

Once the Bedford Clipper had left the clutches of the northeast-bound Gulf Stream, it had made very good time. At roughly parallel with Philadelphia, Aziz al-As had brought the Clipper within fifty miles of the mainland and had steered her on a course that gradually brought the trawler closer and closer to the coastline, to a point where now, for the last eight hours, the Clipper had run smoothly a half-mile off the coast.

The boat had been hailed by Coast Guard stations in Delaware, Virginia, and now again as they approached the turbulent waters of Oregon Inlet.

"We're headed for port in Wanchese. Is there any information I should know on the condition of the channel?"

"This is Oregon Inlet. I read your destination. Are you heavy?"

Al-As paused for a second and considered the question.

"No, we're a charter. I've got some scientists on board. The only thing we're empty on is fuel, Oregon. If we don't get to port soon you may have to tow us in."

"You are at mid-tide. The channel between markers three and four will be approximately eight feet deep. Come in parallel to the shoreline and make a sharp right turn at marker six. There isn't much room at the sand bar."

"Thank you, Oregon."

The information was very useful. The pilot's house was crowded again. All eyes were on al-As as he negotiated the single most difficult stretch of water on the 900-mile journey. The inlet had been formed by a hurricane in 1846 and named for the first boat to pass through, the steamer *Oregon*. Inlets were constantly forming and closing all along the Outer Banks, mostly because of pressure from the Pamlico Sound. As a result of the constant battle between the Pamlico and the Atlantic, the tidal action between the two bodies of water was quite fierce.

Aziz brought the *Clipper* slowly along the coastline, approaching the channel markers from the north. This approach ensured a rough ride. Aziz felt sorry for local fishermen who had to endure this day in and day out. Even though the waves were small, they all hit the *Clipper* broadside. The ride was very rough. Ali Akbar held on to the railing with one hand. Aziz smiled to himself, knowing that Bafq el-Rashid was getting slightly seasick. He wished he could stay in position for another hour or so just so he'd get the satisfaction of seeing his tormentor on his knees.

Khan was oblivious to what was happening. His mind was five thousand miles away. He was on a personal high, unmatched in his life. He was the messenger of Allah.

From Cape Henry at the Hampton Roads confluence of the James River and Chesapeake Bay, south to Cape Hatteras, a sand bar ran parallel to the coastline. The Army Corps of Engineers had for twenty-five years tried to maintain a passageway through the bar by constantly dredging the channel. But it was a losing cause. At marker six, al-As stiffly turned the *Clipper* away from its broadside beating and started through the cut in the sand bar. Immediately the ride became smoother. The markers then cut to the right and snaked a small path through the mile-wide channel. Most of the water was no more than five feet deep.

Only the Army-maintained ribbon of channel was deep enough for boats carrying a draft of eight feet or more, and then they could only pass at high tide.

Directly ahead of them was the Herbert C. Bonner bridge which connected the stable part of the Outer Banks, the area of Nags Head and above, with the unstable land of Hatteras Island to the south. Aziz gave a mock salute as the *Clipper* passed the Oregon Inlet Coast Guard station on his left.

Once under the bridge, al-As followed the channel markers out into the Pamlico Sound, then made another sharp turn to the right and entered the Roanoke Channel north toward Wanchese. This passage made ocean fishing difficult. More than one trawler every season was shoaled in the low sand of Oregon Inlet.

"Harbormaster, this is the trawler *Bedford Clipper*. Do you read?"

There were no sounds other than the soft chug-chug of the *Clipper*'s diesels. The port looked dead. New Bedford looked like a New Year's party compared to Wanchese. *Was every American fishing port like this?* wondered al-As.

"Bear to your right as you enter the channel, *Clipper*. Arrangements have been made. You have three slips, #18, #19, and #20, along the starboard channel wall," answered the voice.

The port itself was well-designed, the channel deep and wide. However, it was evident that the attempts in the middle and late 1970s to make Wanchese a major fishing port had failed. The attempt never reached the critical mass required so that success was a guarantee. There seemed to be a point in any venture when the momentum gathered enough steam that even the people involved could do nothing to slow it down. The same would soon apply to Khan and his Ultimatum.

"Khalid!" said Khan, smiling as he spotted his friend waiting at the harbor.

Standing next to his new Chevy Suburban, dressed in American winter clothes, was a beaming Khalid Rahman. It took another ten minutes for al-As to gently dock the *Bedford Clipper*.

"English! Nothing but English from now on. Even between us!" Khan warned his men as they disembarked.

Then Khan bounded down the gangway and embraced his friend and right arm. He was followed by the unsmiling duo of al-As and el-Rashid. Khan's heart beat quickly with the excitement of being on the soil of his enemy and the enemy of his people.

"What is your wish?" asked Rahman.

The last ten days had gone by with excruciating slowness. Rahman didn't know what Khan's plan was—what they were to deliver, or where, but he had been told to execute a mission, and he had done so.

"We must leave as soon as possible, Khalid. The longer we stay, the better chance we have of someone recognizing us—which they *will* do at some point in time," said Khan.

Khalid could see that Khan was appraising the Suburban.

Khan's mind was moving three steps down the road. He continued. "Maps, clothes . . ."

"I have them *all*," said Rahman smiling.

"Does it have a radio?" asked Khan

"Short-wave, police band, and CB," Rahman added. "When do we leave?"

"As soon as we offload the weapons," Khan replied. "Where is the other vehicle?"

"At the rental cottage. It is on our way," said the smiling Rahman.

Khan looked across the small harbor to the fishing companies on the other side, then started walking down the concrete access path that paralleled the slips. There were only two other trawlers in port, their nets stripped and packed. To their right were the lifts of the boat-repair facility, which was empty. All around the harbor was open space, land that had been intended to have fishing and fishing-related industry built there. Instead, there was nothing but open, sandy space. At the edge of the industrial park the land quickly melted into the cattails of the low tidal marsh. Khan scanned across the harbor. There was no activity—none at all. The place was dead, nearly deserted—nothing remained but the hope of a proud group of American fishermen. Wanchese was a representation of all but a few places in the fishing industry.

"You have selected well, Khalid. We will not be noticed. Be on guard, but we should not be disturbed. Let's get started," Khan smiled to his friend.

Both al-As and el-Rashid were a bit unsteady as they walked on land for the first time in ten days. Rahman quickly backed the Suburban right up to the edge of the slip, a concrete retaining wall no more than two feet high, parking the vehicle so that no one in the boat-repair facility could possibly see what was being loaded or offloaded.

The *Bedford Clipper*'s main deck was six feet below the height of the deck. They would have to hoist the bombs up and over the wall. It took two men to carry each of the bombs, al-As and el-Rashid did the work without assignment. Rahman scrambled into the rear compartment of the Suburban and helped place the weapons one by one into their custom-designed resting place. Khan jumped down onto the deck and disappeared underneath, then reappeared in a moment, struggling with a shiny metal packing case.

"Grenades, ammunition, guns. Help me," he instructed Rahman. The highlight of the ordnance were the Soviet-made weapons; including SVD (Samozaryadnaya Vintovka Dragunova) 7.62mm sniper rifles and RPK (Ruchnoi Pulemet Kalashnikova) 7.62mm semi-automatic rifles.

Within fifteen minutes the five atomic bombs, each encased in a metal box roughly the size of a filing cabinet, were tightly housed inside the Suburban. The four men stood and wordlessly took in the enormity of the moment in time. Seagulls squawked from across the harbor. A low-flying pack of pelicans dashed across the sound. A cool wind blew into their faces, rustling and tossing their hair. They had made it. Khan was triumphant. He had penetrated the defenses of his enemy!

The feeling of euphoria was not lost on the men. Even al-As smiled at the accomplishment.

— • —

"We must go. There is much work to do. We must transfer one of the bombs into the other car—someplace between here and Washington. There will be a place."

From a hiding place in a seemingly deserted automobile on the other side of the harbor, Khan's instructions were recorded.

"They've offloaded the weapons. They're leaving. They're headed back to the cottage to pick up the other car. Then they're heading for Washington," said a slumped-down and bundled-up Reynolds.

"Acknowledged," returned Katrina, her adrenalin pumping. "It's time to go to work, comrade," she poked the sleeping Rostov. "They're here."

PARIS

The clerk watched as the new Teletype printed the message almost silently. No longer were acoustic covers needed for the ca-chunka, ca-chunka noiseboxes. The new machines seemed to glide over the paper.

People could talk in the office. They didn't have to build separate printer rooms because of 75db printer noise. The new machines were quiet.

Every half-hour the clerk tore off the message roll, cut the messages manually, then separated the messages into destinations. Those without specific destinations went down the hall to someone, a senior clerk, who made the decision where the message should be routed within the huge INTERPOL building. Perhaps the request should go to the *Sureté*, the French police. Requests came from all over the world; requests for people, places, things . . . but mostly for people—found people, lost people, dead people.

The clerk almost automatically put each of the messages into the right folder. When he came to Scotty's nearly page-long message, it went right into the North American pile. When he was done, the clerk loaded the folders into his mail cart and started down the hallway. It would take him nearly an hour to make the route through the building, perhaps more if he lingered and talked to some of the secretaries.

At 4:15 the folder was dropped on the control desk for the North American section. Information was readily exchanged between INTERPOL and the FBI, the Canadian RCMP and the Mexican State Police. It was a free two-way trade. Unfortunately, they were unable to exchange data via computer. Neither side was able to get away from the old case folder/index card approach to filing information. It was clumsy and costly. Both INTERPOL and the FBI were *gradually* changing over from the old days, but both sides were closer to the middle than the end. The FBI had many regions where criminal information was still on 3 x 5 cards, filed alphabetically. Even in large cities the FBI had to rely on the U.S. Marshall's Service, a department under the U.S. Treasury, for telecopying pictures of evidence and people. It was incredible.

The North American control desk sifted through the requests, passing Scotty's to an older gentlemen who shared the responsibility of satisfying the seemingly endless requests from the FBI with two other men.

TO: INTERPOL
FROM: SCOTT COLDSMITH
           FBI—MANHATTAN
           TELEX CODE 18-6664490
SUBJECT: REQUIRE INFORMATION ON TWO FOREIGN NATIONALS AR-
RIVED NEW YORK CITY FEBRUARY 8TH ON AIR FRANCE FLIGHT #10 . . .
JOHN SMITHTON RAMSEY BRITISH PASSPORT 443-908-0 . . . SUBJECT
FIVE NINE ONE HUNDRED FIFTY POUNDS APPROXIMATELY 28 YRS . . .

CLEAR SKIN TAN POSSIBLY SOUTHERN MEDITERRANEAN OR ARABIC NO OTHER DISTINGUISHING MARKS . . . BLACK HAIR . . . USES INTERNATIONAL DRIVERS LICENSE R3349-9984-B3T AND CITICORP VISA . . . FINGERPRINTS AND PHOTO TO FOLLOW VIA EXPRESS MAIL.

SECOND NATIONAL IS ASSUMED SOVIET SPY ALIAS ALEXANDER ROSTOV . . . FIVE TEN ONE SIXTY-FIVE SANDY HAIR FAIR COMPLEXION . . . APPROXIMATELY 45 YRS . . . IS CONSIDERED ARMED AND DANGEROUS WITH FELONY WANT ON RECORD . . . ROSTOV/SOVIETS APPEAR TO BE FOLLOWING JS RAMSEY FOR UNKNOWN REASON . . . PARTIAL FINGERPRINT AND PHOTO TO FOLLOW IN SAME PACKAGE. THXS.

The clerk thought that the name of Alexander Rostov was familiar, but the other, John Smithton Ramsey was totally blank. He went to his computer terminal and within five minutes had a partial hit on Rostov; partial from the standpoint that apparently there were no pictures of the man on file, only his name and a series of short paragraphs, entered as data appeared in various reports. The clerk printed the data. Rostov was indeed a Soviet courier but had never been tied to anything criminal. He had always been around the edges of dirty business but had never actually been accused of anything. He did have diplomatic immunity by being carried as a top-echelon staff member although there was no record of Rostov actually living at the embassy nor was there a record of Rostov actually renting or owning a place outside of the embassy. In short, the man had covered himself well.

The name of John Smithton Ramsey was not in the files. He would have to wait for the photos and prints to be telecopied. With a felt-tipped pen the clerk labeled a folder, stuffed Scotty's request and the printout inside, then pulled another folder from the seemingly endless stack of messages.

NEW YORK

"*Mr.* Coldsmith, you *cannot* enter this man into the Wanted Persons file!"

Rosemary Fielding was using her full authority as Keeper of The File to prevent Scotty from entering John Smithton Ramsey into the computer. He had everything he needed on the man, including fingerprints.

"No," said Rosemary again in her Flushing/Long Island accent, stretching a simple single-syllable word out into at least two, perhaps three. And the intonation was such that heads of other agents looked up from their desk then back down again in a covered smirk. The rookie was getting the business. If Rosemary had twisted Scotty's ear and brought him back to his desk like a child, the embarrassment would have been approximately the same.

"When?" asked Scotty.

"On page seven-dash-one it says you may enter a wanted person if the person has a mental/physical disability, is senile, their safety is in danger, they've been abducted, or they are a juvenile. This man is none of those."

Scotty went back to his desk. Where to go? He had this folder of information—half of which consisted of fingerprints from the Holiday Inn which may or may not be those of Alexander Rostov. Where to go? Going back to the bank to try to trace the money would be a waste of time and effort. There was no proof Ramsey had indeed done anything wrong. He just wanted to talk to the man.

"Coldsmith, that's the way it is. Most times you end up at a dry hole. Very few cases simply unfold in front of you. You've got other things to do. You're in the middle of training. I know this means a lot to you, especially since you got in the middle of it, but until somebody comes up with a lead on this Rostov character . . . or the car . . . you've got to put this one down and go on to other things. You've got to learn to handle ten of these at a time. You can't get emotionally attached. Get the information, pile it up . . . it's the digging that pays. But, in the meantime, you've other things to do. I'm going to give this to someone else," said Murphy Monahan.

Scotty looked at his boss in disbelief. Monahan had to be pulling his leg. He couldn't let someone else follow up on this. But Monahan's eyes said differently.

"Mr. Monahan, I've got to have a few more days on this. I can't just let you give this to someone else . . . just because it's actually turned into something. *That was me they shot at.* You told me to follow Rostov because you thought it was going to be a routine tail. But it wasn't. And I followed him. *I've seen him up close.* I know who is he is. *That son of a bitch almost killed me!*" Scotty pleaded.

Everyone in the squad room looked up. Scotty was on his feet, the papers on his desk askew, his neck and face red from the emotion.

"You can't . . ."

Scotty looked around and *heard* the silence of the room.

"You can't," Scotty repeated, his voice lower and under control.

Monahan hadn't forgotten the feeling his young trainee was going through. He was learning things early. Monahan's eyes softened slightly.

"A few more days won't hurt. This is probably as good as what you'd get in training, anyway."

Monahan started to walk away, then turned around at the now beaming Scotty.

"*Get* something on this man, Coldsmith. You can't garbage up the computer just because you *think* or *hope* somebody *might* be able to help you. You've got to have facts, information. This man who calls himself John Ramsey has been the key to Rostov. Get something you can take back downtown to the district attorney. It's your job to get the information."

Monahan was teaching. It was a situation where the learning curve had to be sharp.

"Do you understand?" Monahan asked.

"Yes, sir," replied Scotty.

"I'll give you ten days. Ten days and you're back to training," Monahan said.

"Yes, sir!" said the enthused young man.

The noise level in the room resumed its steady din as the agents went back to their telephone calls and paperwork. The mini-drama was over. What was happening to Coldsmith *was* unusual for a rookie. But during training every one of them had assisted on cases in which they'd done the dirty work and not had the opportunity to finish something, anything. Every agent in the room was silently rooting for Monahan to do the right thing. And he had.

"And Coldsmith . . . check with the Coast Guard. Call Commander Belling over on Governor's Island," was Murphy Monahan's parting advice.

Within the next five minutes Scotty was on the phone.

"Commander Belling, this is Scott Coldsmith of the FBI. My boss, Murphy Monahan, said you might be able to help me . . ."

An hour later Scotty was on the South Street ferry to Governor's Island. To his right was Liberty Island and the statue; behind him the Brooklyn Bridge and a view up the East River. An escort was waiting for him and in a few minutes Scotty was seated in Commander Belling's office—an office that had a tremendous view of the skyline of lower Manhattan and the merging of the Hudson and East Rivers into Upper Bay.

Scotty spent ten minutes and gave the Commander a brief overview of the situation. Belling leaned back in his comfortable chair.

"Well, Monahan was right in one sense of the word. I could help you . . . but only in my group. And, I'll do it as a favor to Murphy. But, you've got no real reason to detain the boat. I'll keep a lookout for it, but other than informally talking to my counterparts, the only way you're going to get a global search for the *Bedford Clipper* is to go through your headquarters in Washington. There you've got a liaison between the FBI and the Department of Transportation. The Coast Guard's tucked under DOT."

"Nothing's easy . . . " said Scotty.

Belling liked the young FBI agent. He could tell Coldsmith was just starting to get a taste for the bureaucracy he would find throughout his career in the government.

"No . . . we certainly couldn't have just anyone calling up directly, now could we?" Belling said with sarcasm at the system he'd spent twenty-five years climbing through.

"I suppose not," Scotty answered, not observing Belling's smile.

"Look, I know the Boston District Group Commander very well. We go back a long way. I'll get the word to him that we're looking for this trawler. But you're going to have to get some help from your people in Washington."

It was a cold ride back on the ferry to lower New York. Scotty elected to stay outside and let the wind whip around his ears and under his collar.

He would draft a wire, but he doubted if Monahan would sign it. There was no evidence of a crime. He had to get something hard on Ramsey. The boat was the key. Where were they going? If Rostov was following Ramsey, it was for a reason. So much of a reason that the Soviets would risk trying to murder a FBI agent. Find the boat. Find Ramsey.

The vision of Mrs. Triolo kept coming back to him. He would have to go back to New Bedford. This time he wouldn't take no for an answer. He had let the woman get the better of him before. This time things would be different. Nevertheless, the thought of going back to New Bedford for a third time was depressing.

NAGS HEAD

"J.J., Henry's found something—a set of keys. They were in Marmande's car. It looks like a set of keys for a rental cottage," said Bart.

It was reasonable to assume that if Jacques Marmande had indeed stayed someplace on the Outer Banks that he would have used the same name. Of course, the name Marmande could be an alias as well—but, one had to start someplace.

And Henry had been right about something else, as well. The tire tracks on the black Buick had been identical to the wear marks on the skid track on Highway 12. The two killers had abandoned the Buick in the Pamlico because either they thought there was enough time to get away, or they didn't know the area. J.J. thought it was a bit of both. That meant there were two cars. Our killers are now in the second vehicle, the one with the more narrow treads, the one probably occupied by the woman.

A woman! J.J. tried to picture a woman capable of doing the things which he knew had to have been done—but he couldn't. It was unlikely there were any more than two of them. With as much action as had taken place, no one would have been able to stay inside the second vehicle while all the murdering was taking place. Everyone who had been there had left some kind of track in the sand.

Jacques Marmande, who are you?

J.J. sat in Bart's beach patrol police station, a mile south of the great Jockey's Ridge sand dune, the largest sand dune on the East Coast. The beach patrol building looked like a small condominium, a series of three octagonal wooden buildings on pilings . . . an insurance requirement for any structure built on the Banks. Unlike Bart's eighty-plus-year-old office in Manteo, the offices in Nags Head were modern.

It was time to do what the FBI does best . . . call someone up and scare the pants off of them. Ninety-nine times out of a hundred J.J. could call up, identify himself as being from the FBI, ask and get the answer to almost any question he wanted. Hardly anybody ever asked for his name and a confirmation number where he could be verified. J.J. had it ready. It was a toll-free number in Charlotte. But he hardly ever had to use it. Sometimes he had to gag a laugh . . . the deadpan Joe Friday approach was the best. People would tell you anything. Yes ma'am, just the facts.

Although the list of hotels was finite, it was also very long. So was the list of rental agencies. It was possible Marmande had rented a home instead of a hotel room. By late in the afternoon it seemed as if the possibility were very real.

J.J. had been at it for nearly six hours. By three-thirty he had gone through most of the motels on or near the Outer Banks and had started on the realtors. This would prove to be more difficult, since realtors held abbreviated winter hours. Normally the owner or a family member would keep the main office open for a few hours during the day, then open up on Friday through Sunday for the weekend turnover. Rental properties were rented from Saturday-Saturday or Sunday-Sunday on the Outer Banks. He was only getting a one-in-three hit ratio.

At four-thirty he quit. There were eighteen realtors to check on in the morning. J.J. didn't want to think of the possibility that Marmande had spent most of his time in the Atlanta area and that perhaps Murder Day was the first day he'd been in North Carolina.

No, I won't think about that, he thought to himself.

WASHINGTON, D.C.

"Stay close," said Khan over the CB's channel 12 to the cars behind him.

The southbound traffic on I-95 headed to the Virginia suburbs was as bad as any in the country. Also, the organization, layout, and construction of the highway system was confusing even to long-time residents. City roads became one-way inbound or outbound during rush hours, as did certain lanes of other roads. With regard to road signs, the indecipherable were mixed with the unreadable. Bureaucratically-concise, one sign was labeled HOV-3. DOT planners were convinced that motorists driving the speed limit in darting traffic would have no problem understanding that only a High Occupancy Vehicle could travel the particular highway during rush hours, and only if the vehicle contained three people. In other locations there were signs which were inconspicuous, small green-on-green signs with polite, difficult to see, directional arrows softly pointing people to National Airport or the Pentagon.

Headed north on I-95 the caravan passed the massive Pentagon on the left, its parking lots still mostly filled with the cars of the thirty thousand or so employees of the Department of Defense. Crossing the 14th Street

Bridge, Rahman passed the Bureau of Engraving and Printing on the left, the Department of Agriculture on the right. Soon they approached, then crossed, the Mall. To their left was the Washington Monument, a mile beyond the columned Lincoln Memorial. It would be another two months before water would fill the now-drained reflecting pool between the two. To their right was the imposing view of the U.S. Capitol and the Smithsonian buildings on either side of the grassy expanse.

"This is why we have come," said Khan.

The danger of Europe, the assassinations, the hazardous boat ride, entry into the United States—it was all practice. They were in the seat of government of their sworn enemy. Less than a mile away, seated in a comfortable second-floor office, was the president of the United States. Different images and emotions ran through each of the men. Khalid and Aziz were unafraid to show their amazement and realization of where they were, while el-Rashid remained cooly silent. None was afraid, all were excited and alert.

Khan had guided them to within a stone's throw of the American leader. They had a weapon, which if detonated at this moment, would not only kill hundreds of thousands of people, including the president, but would also vaporize much of the history of the American people.

"It should be here soon. Here," pointed Khan.

The three cars queued into the left-turn lane at the corner of 14th and Pennsylvania, the Department of Commerce on their left, the block-wide parking lot of the Federal Triangle on the right, now jammed with homebound workers.

"There it is," said Khan, cooly.

To their left was the historic, be-gargoyled structure of the Willard Hotel—a building saved from the wrecker's ball in the early '80s and renewed with love and care to a point where the hotel resumed its rightful place as the jewel of downtown Washington's hotels. As they turned left onto Pennsylvania their potential view of the White House was blocked by the columns of the Department of the Treasury. Behind them on their left was the jutting discord of the Hoover Building, almost a distraction to the magnificent angle view of the Capitol. On the south side of the street were the Old Post Office Building and the "old-old" Post Office Building, now referred to as the Pavillion—an odd structure built around a clock tower.

The trio slowly made a circle around the Willard—up Pennsylvania, right on 15th, then right again on F Street.

"In here," said Khan on the radio.

Underground parking for the hotel was on F Street between 14th and 15th. For a second Khan was not sure that the Suburban would have enough overhead clearance, but it did. The three vehicles took their tickets and proceeded down and to their right, spiraling down three levels under the building before they found empty parking spaces. At $12 a day, parking at the Willard was not casually used. Khan continued until there were three adjoining slots. Rahman pulled into a corner slot up against the darkened recess of the concrete cinderblock wall. Close above him were the water and sewage pipes of the renovated hotel. With the Blazer next to it and the Suburban partially blocking the access lane, Bafq el-Rashid now could work almost unseen inside the trunk of the blue Fairmont.

Aziz provided a steady hand on a small hand-light as the Mad Bomber quickly went to work. It wouldn't take long.

"I'll do that, you go up and register," ordered Khan to al-As. "Be sure to include the correct license plate of this car. The last thing we want is for the hotel to tow it away. Do you have enough cash?"

A prepaid two-week stay at the Willard was going to cost over two thousand dollars—plus twelve dollars a day parking. Although he didn't have to have al-As register, Khan was simply being cautious.

It wouldn't take two weeks to set the rest of the weapons. This was the weapon left for the Americans. It would scare them to death. Khan smiled to himself as he watched el-Rashid recheck the time and date. Today was the 20th.

"Five days will be sufficient—February 25th, 6:00 P.M."

Bafq grunted his acknowledgement and continued his work. His fingers spun through the times and dates. He checked to make sure the time was P.M. and not A.M. He connected the detonator leads and inserted them into the plastic explosive, then finally connected the leads to the digital clock. He looked up at Khan, who was now holding the light but seemed distracted by a noise in some other part of the garage.

This is too easy, thought el-Rashid. There was no handiwork, no craftsmanship—no signature of his work. Anyone could disarm this weapon. His fingers briefly hovered over the clock, debating whether to make it more difficult. *No, this isn't the time,* he thought. The Americans were supposed to find the weapon. Perhaps one of the others.

"Finished," said el-Rashid, closing the trunk of the Fairmont.

Khan put the car keys and a three-quarters inch VHS-formatted tape cartridge under the front passenger seat, then closed and locked the door.

"Anything else?" he asked.

There was nothing. Aziz came out of the elevator, his task of registration completed.

"Move!" he ordered.

They moved.

One block to the west of the Willard Hotel was the U.S. Department of Treasury. One block further west was the White House. Another long block away was the ornate Old Senate Office Building. One block to the east and south was the Department of Commerce. Another block away was the Federal Triangle, including the Secret Service and the ICC. A third block away was the FBI and the IRS. Two blocks south, across Constitution Avenue, were two of the Smithsonian buildings—American History and Natural History. Two blocks north and west was the Veterans Administration. All these buildings were located within one half-mile of the underground parking lot of the Willard Hotel.

All would be vaporized if the Americans screwed up—if somehow they ignored his warning. At 6:00 on the evening of February 25th, come rain or snow, everything within a half-mile of the blue Ford Fairmont would be vaporized.

Within minutes they were back out into the rush hour traffic, inching their way through the K Street corridor to northbound Connecticut Avenue and the long trip to the northern suburbs. The Ultimatum had been delivered. If all else failed—if they were caught, captured, or killed—the Ultimatum had been delivered.

Khan had no need to explain his actions to the others. He sat back and with a great deal of satisfaction watched the faces of the weary rush hour travellers. Placing the weapon in Washington would accomplish more than just a dramatic notice of his intent. It bought him time. The other bombs could be placed with impunity. It would take a long, long time for the Americans to find him.

They will listen to me, he thought. *They will have to listen to me. Ignore me and they will rue the day.*

NEW YORK

"No—I do not know when they are going to issue their demands," said Korz.

He was worried and it was betrayed in his voice.

"Where are they now?" asked Major General Bodnof.

"They left one automobile in the parking lot of a hotel in downtown Washington. My agents were unable to pick up their conversations. We believe there is a weapon inside the car. I don't know where they are going next. We do know that they have five weapons—four remaining, if one has been left in in Washington."

The thought of an Iranian terrorist with five atomic weapons gave Korz involuntary shivers. They couldn't lose track of them. Five properly placed weapons could kill fifty million people and surely would start the end of the world. One was already placed in Washington.

What was Moscow thinking of to let this go on?

For the first time Korz began to think of his own life.

"What about the weapons?" asked Bodnof. "It is critical you have someone able to detonate at least two of the bombs upon command."

"It is not easy. I don't . . ."

"It is vital, Ambassador Korz!" shouted an obviously upset Bodnof.

"I . . . we don't know how complicated these weapons are. Perhaps my operative," stuttered Korz, now convinced that the end of the world was just around the corner. In the back of his mind he started to think of evacuation.

"What of his demands?" continued Bodnof.

"They don't talk much. We have the impression he may have already recorded his demands, but we aren't sure. What is Moscow's plan?" asked Korz. "What is it that we are expected to do? Will there be time for an evacuation?"

Bodnof laughed; not a hearty laugh, more rueful, ironic.

"No, ambassador, there will be no evacuation. At least, there are no plans for an evacuation. There are no plans for a general war between us. But you never can tell what the Americans will do, how they will react. I think it is time for you to understand what we expect to happen and why it is critical that we know when Khan issues his demands."

Bodnof paused.

"By sunrise on the 24th our forces will be poised to launch a three-pronged attacked on Iran; from our occupied territory in Afghanistan, and from either side of the Caspian. We will strike hard. Our forces will capture Teheran and the coastline along the Persian Gulf and Gulf of Oman. We will seize much of Iraqi territory, perhaps even drive through Iraq, through Syria, and capture Beirut."

"But the Americans won't . . ." interrupted Korz.

His large frame felt the first grip of terror. This was a different game, one he wasn't used to playing. He was a director of spies, not a war general. War was a lot different. In spying the war was individual. The ideology was personal. You turned a man because of conviction or because of greed. War was different. Many people were killed in war. Espionage could be stopped and started on demand. War could not. Once started, it played out to its conclusion. Spying could be directed like a conductor leading a symphony, or a puppeteer making a marionette jump and dance. War was a huge thing that once begun gathered a force and mind of its own. War sucked in the players, forced them to participate, then changed as the strategy of each side unfolded. There was very little control over the events, once things escalated into war.

"The Americans will not lift a finger to stop us. And it will be because of you and your men. While not foolproof, our action will not start until your team has disabled the Americans. And, Khan will be blamed. Listen closely, Ambassador Korz. This is what the Secretary General expects of you . . ."

Korz listened as Bodnof explained his specific course of action. Beads of sweat appeared on his brow and above his flabby upper lip. Bodnof continued for fifteen minutes. There was no need for notetaking as the conversation was automatically recorded. The plan was unusually bold. Simple, yet bold. More importantly, it was executable. It was very dangerous, but possible. Moscow was right, Khan would be blamed . . . at least initially. Without evidence the Americans would have no choice but to accept the surface explanation of events. Khan would issue his threats, his ultimatum, then disappear . . . killed by Rostov, Tambov and the others. The Americans would be left with threats as the main course and the waste and destruction of atomic detonations for dessert. They would have no choice but to associate the bombs with Khan's rhetoric.

And if something went wrong . . . if Rostov couldn't get the weapons, or the bombs went off prematurely, or if any number of possible imponderables happened, then Moscow wouldn't give the order for battle. The troops would be on maneuvers or war games or whatever they called them. There would be no invasion until Soviet seismologists registered the blast in the U.S., and the result was verified by satellite photos. At worst there would be a five or six minute delay. The invasion of Iran would be the least of the American government's problems.

NAGS HEAD

"Mr. Moore?"

"Yes."

"This is John Carteret of the FBI."

"Yeess?"

"Are you renting homes at this time?"

"Yes, we are . . . a few."

"Do you have one rented to a Jacques Marmande of Paris, France?"

"Is there something wrong?"

"I really can't get into the details, Mr. Moore."

"Just a moment, and I'll check."

J.J. could hear the man sifting through his rental agreements, then clumsily return to the phone.

"Yes, we do. He's in one of our cottages," said the nervous Mr. Moore.

"I think I have a set of your keys. Will you be there for the next few minutes?"

"Yeeess."

"Fine."

The rental agency was in Nags Head, less than three miles from the beach police station. J.J. called Bart Claiborne and told him the news.

"I'm sure Marmande was alone, but I think we should have some backup in any case—if you've got the time," J.J. zinged his friend.

They agreed to meet at the rental agency and they arrived at about the same time. After identifying themselves, J.J.'s first question was, "Where is this house?"

"It's in South Nags Head, oceanside on Beach Road," replied the nervous Mr. Moore.

"When did he rent it?" asked J.J.

"On February 10th. He paid for two weeks."

"So, nobody's been inside since then?"

"The cleaning crew doesn't go in until the renter leaves. No, nobody's been inside," answered Moore as he folded up his rental book.

Twenty minutes later a second police cruiser with two patrolmen joined J.J. and Bart as they slowly pulled up to the standard rental home; three bedrooms, two baths, and a common living room/kitchen. It had a small enclosed porch that faced the cold Atlantic's grey waters. The air was heavy with salt.

There was no back entrance and no appearance of any activity. J.J. knocked on the door, then opened it carefully. There wasn't much inside. It was indeed empty. The kitchen was nearly empty of food. The refrigerator had a carton of milk which was now sour. The freezer had two packages of Stouffer's lasagne. Probably only a single meal for Marmande, thought J.J. The man had been big.

"He sure traveled light," said Bart.

J.J. walked to the kitchen table, an outdoor picnic table that had been laminated with a thousand coats of enamel. In the middle sat a small pair of field glasses, neatly placed. The room smelled of stale smoke, as evidenced by the nearly filled ashtray littered with the crushed bodies of dead smokes. The window in front of the table had been recently cleaned. J.J. looked at its counterpart in the living room. The glass was caked with a salty grime, turned almost opaque with a winter's worth of salt air. The window in the kitchen area was almost clear, streaky with the hand motions of a wet rag, but still clear nevertheless.

"Marmande was certainly no tourist," J.J. muttered to himself absentmindedly, now paying more attention to the window and what lay beyond.

The policemen were finished with their short search of the house. All that they found were a few articles of clothing; no wallet, no identification, nothing.

J.J. looked out the kitchen window. Across the street were older beach homes built in the '40s with one foot already in a watery grave. Some houses along upper Nags Head and Kitty Hawk had succumbed to the relentless erosion of the Atlantic, more followed each year. J.J. looked up, then down the street. None of the houses appeared to be occupied.

"Marmande was watching something, Bart," J.J. said.

From where he was, the window was clean on the left side. Marmande was probably right-handed. He was also probably looking down the street instead of straight across.

"I want to know if there has been any activity in these homes in the last two weeks," J.J. ordered.

The houses were clearly marked by realtor. It wouldn't take long.

Twenty minutes later Bart's radio squawked. With a hand motion Bart pointed to the house two doors down the street on the ocean front. Two more hand motions moved some of his men to cover the beach access and the opposite side of the house.

"George Dijon," said Bart.

"Another Frenchman?" questioned J.J.

The two men looked at each other. What was going on here? Who were these people?

Who, and where, were the man and woman?

NEW BEDFORD

The temperature hadn't risen above fifteen degrees all day long. An Alberta Clipper, a high pressure system out of Canada, was driving quickly across the northern U.S., its clockwise winds bringing stiff, cold, damp breezes across Buzzards Bay and into Scotty's face as he stood on Mrs. Triolo's front stoop.

An equally cold, and reluctant, Patrolman Sam Benjamin stood on the steps below Scotty. Benjamin was the translator. The door to Mrs. Triolo's warm living room was cracked. All that could be seen was a slice of Mrs. Triolo's face and a glimpse of a plump, motherly body that obviously enjoyed pasta.

"When we get there, I don't care *what* you have to tell the woman. A son wouldn't leave without telling his mother where he was going. He might not tell his friends, or his wife, or his girl friend . . . but he would tell his mother."

Scotty had been very persistent and had insisted on being accompanied by someone who spoke Portuguese. Whoever came with him had to be recognized as The Law—The Man. Scotty didn't want another round of the woman's selective-hearing gamesmanship. It was a good trick—"sorry, no speak English . . . no understand." Lack of language competency was a convenient method to avoid answering questions.

"Ask Mrs. Triolo where her boy is," said Scotty.

His words were frozen by the wind, his breath showed as billows of frosty smoke.

Benjamin translated but got a shake of the head in return.

Scotty's patience with the people of New Bedford was growing thin. Everyone he'd met, from the thugs to the harbormaster to the police to Mrs. Triolo—all had been provincial. And uncooperative.

"She knows. God damn it, she *knows*!" exclaimed Scotty.

The trial of the four thugs was coming up. He *knew* it would drag on and on. The defense attorney would try to paint a picture that the men were fine, upstanding members of the community and that it was *Scotty* who had caused the problem. If a woman could get gang-raped on a pool table and be accused of disturbing the peace, then certainly an FBI agent could be said to be drunk and disorderly and had fallen into the Acushnet River by himself.

Samuel Benjamin turned around and gave Scotty the evil eye at the outburst.

"Listen to me, Benjamin. I said I don't care *what* you have to tell this woman. If I have to drive to Boston this afternoon and get a god-damned warrant for this woman's arrest, I'll do it! Do you understand? *Do you understand,* Mrs. Triolo?" Scotty pointed through the crack in the door at the obstinate woman. "*Yes,* you *do* understand, don't you?" Scotty added.

Benjamin could see that he wasn't going to get the young FBI agent off his back. There was a fire in Coldsmith, an anger that was surprising. He turned back to Mrs. Triolo and began an earnest, rapid-fire conversation in Portuguese. The crack in the door became wider. Finally she opened the door and let them inside. The warmth of the room was almost overpowering. Scotty's skin tingled, his cheeks instantly flushed. They were inside, but by no means welcome. Benjamin continued. Then Mrs. Triolo answered. The words made no sense to Scotty, but he didn't interrupt the patrolman.

As Benjamin spoke he glanced at Scotty, as did Mrs. Triolo. It was time for Scotty to remain hard, stone-faced, resolute. The woman's eyes flashed and darted, distrusting the young foreigner.

Finally she relented. The portly woman gushed out the words, Benjamin nodding as she spoke, encouraging her to continue.

"Her son told her not to tell anyone. The men who hired the boat were looking for treasure . . . treasure off the coast of Nova Scotia. The captain of the *Bedford Clipper*, Carver Medway, is known in the area as a fair and honest man. He was mistrustful of the operation but needed the work. The men needed the work."

"Where off Nova Scotia?" Scotty asked Benjamin, looking at Mrs. Triolo. "It's *important,* Mrs. Triolo. Your son may be in danger."

The woman understood his words. She spoke to Patrolman Benjamin.

"She said her son Bennie overheard Captain Medway talk of Sable Island. It's an island well off the coastline of Nova Scotia . . . nothing but rocks and rough seas. It's not a good place to go in the winter."

"Thank you, Mrs. Triolo," Scotty said as he bundled up and headed for the door.

Scotty tersely thanked Patrolman Benjamin.

"Would you have done it?" he asked Scotty.

"Hauled her in? You bet," Scotty replied, as he closed the door to his rental car.

Ten minutes later Scotty was out of New Bedford, headed for Boston and the Group I Headquarters of the Coast Guard. Scotty was starting to do what all FBI agents do, establish and use multiple good-old-boy networks. If Commander Belling had followed through on his promise, the search would be on for the *Bedford Clipper* from Maine to New York.

At 4:30 Scotty was escorted into the mahogany-trimmed office of Commander Richard Cummings. The office was a near-replica of what Scotty imagined was the captain's quarters aboard some old-time ship. The room was filled with relics of the sea, *not* including the Commander.

Scotty updated Commander Cummings.

"Yes, Belling called me. I understand you're in a bind. I think I remember reading something about someone getting thrown into the river down there in Bedford. Mean place. You say the woman specifically mentioned Sable Island?"

"I think it would have been hard for her to make up a name like that," answered Scotty.

"This is where it is," Cummings pulled out a reduced Loran Ocean Survey map, produced by NOAA.

"As you can see, Sable Island is well out of our jurisdiction. It's even out of the normal coverage of the Canadian Coast Guard. But, I can send a wire to the Canadian commander in Halifax and see if one of his boats can snoop around for us," said Cummings.

"Would you?" said a surprised and pleased Scotty.

"Yes," replied the Coast Guard Commander.

Cummings recognized Scotty was going up against The System—the Rules and Regulations of The System. He wanted to help. Scotty shook Cummings' giant paw and thanked him.

When he boarded the 7:30 shuttle from Logan to La Guardia, his spirits were up. Although he sensed it, he wasn't fully conscious of the fact that he'd done just what Murphy Monahan had told him to do. Get some facts. *Make something happen.* It felt good.

NAGS HEAD

Led by Henry Onslow, the small team of Dare County policemen had dusted nearly every piece of the cottage.

"As far as I can see there was no attempt to wipe anything clean. I've got a clear set of prints on this man," Henry had said, handing J.J. a copy of his analysis.

J.J. listed what they had.

"Whoever he is, his alias is George Dijon. He was also on the same flight as our Jacques Marmande. It's clear Marmande was following Dijon, but we don't know why. If Dijon is *not* one of the men in this picture, then Marmande could be a private detective, a policeman, INTERPOL, Israeli intelligence, or some whacko. If Dijon *is* one of the men—then, I think Marmande is either a real or quasi-policeman," said J.J.

"I'll have a warrant for the man's arrest this afternoon. I'm going ahead and putting him into the system." said Bart.

J.J. concurred. There was no Grand Jury in session. They would have to go to Raleigh to get the Federal warrant. Judge Cumberland had been notified and had given them a verbal agreement.

EW.DIJON, GEORGE.M.X.XXXXXX.XXXXXX.999.999.XXX.XXX. J.J.C0178.UKN.XXX.AA6318TTCIMI1814XI09.XXXXXX XXXXXX.HAT88987.0103.NAME ALIAS UNKNOWN SUSPECT ARAB TERRORIST WANTED MURDER.

There wasn't much they really had on Dijon, other than a wonderful set of prints. They needed more, and INTERPOL seemed the only place to get it.

"I'll take care of it," said J.J. "I think I should have sent my first wire to them. I'll include Marmande this time."

J.J. sat back in the swivel chair and looked up the coastline towards Jockey's Ridge. Brightly colored hang-gliding kites slowly circled. The morning sun reflected off their aluminum braces. At least somebody was having fun.

Evidence of something was quickly accumulating. Jacques Marmande, Frenchman . . . French what . . . policeman? A possible John Doe terrorist, alias George Dijon. Six murdered people, murdered by a pair of killers . . . one a woman. A black Buick whose tires matched a skid mark at the murder site. A partial right hand of one of the killers, the male. Shoe sizes, approximate weights and heights of the killers.

The John Doe who stayed here, *and* the killers, are long gone. The conclusion was inevitable.

Dijon had rented the house since February 9th. The killing was on the 16th. The killer's partial print didn't show up either inside Dijon's cottage. That didn't mean they weren't connected—but it didn't mean they were, either.

"Damn it!" J.J. muttered angrily to himself.

J.J. turned around and logged onto one of the Dare County computer terminals, passing through to NCIC. He muttered his frustration under his breath. He snapped at the keys, slapping at the Enter key as if forcing the computer to come up with a connection. He didn't have enough information to enter a record on the killer . . . enough? . . . he didn't have anything.

Where was the woman? In the other god-damned car. The one with the skid marks which we haven't been able to identify.

"OK, Carteret . . . back to the trenches," J.J. sighed.

John Doe alias George Dijon had stayed on the Outer Banks for nearly two weeks. Assume he got here by car. Assume also that it was a rental. Marmande was following Dijon. Check Delta's flight register. Check the rental car agencies.

Take the possibilities one at a time. Yes, the man's probably miles away . . . but he's left tracks. He had to have left tracks. Whoever these people are they show absolutely no concern for clearing the trail behind them. There has been no evidence of wiping prints or cleaning up. These people are here, doing things, and have no concern over being caught by the police. Whoever was here had not lived in a vacuum, even though he thought he had. He'd left a trace someplace. The vehicle was the key. The man wasn't on foot.

The killers had to have stayed someplace. The Buick had been discovered only three days ago.

"Bart, we need to do some legwork," said J.J.

Bart knew what the "we" in J.J.'s sentence would refer to man-hours by his policemen.

"We need to look at the registration records of every motel in this area. We need to trace every person who has spent a night in a hotel on the Outer Banks since the 9th of this month . . . up to and including today. We need descriptions, addresses, credit cards, license plates . . . you name it. We need the rental car records at the airport. Who has rented a car? While we're at the airport we should pick up the flight records for any commercial flights to and from Raleigh and Norfolk . . .

and any private flights as well. We need to see the auto dealers. Has anybody bought a car in the last two weeks?"

"Do you have any idea how many men that will take?" asked Bart Claiborne.

"When's the next election, Bart?" returned J.J., crisply, without humor.

NEW YORK

Scotty emptied the contents of his mailbox and walked back to his desk. How could he get this much mail in two days? There was *so much* internal stuff. Classes, memos, procedures . . . there seemed to be procedures *for* procedures—and memos for procedures—and memos *about* memos. He chatted with some of the other rookies, most of whom were envious that Scotty actually had *real* work to do; although *none* of them would have traded being dumped into the Acushnet River.

Getting a cup of coffee, Scotty started going through the mail, flicking one piece of paper after another into the trash can.

What's this?

TO: SCOTT COLDSMITH
        FBI—NEW YORK
FROM: INTERPOL
        PARIS
RE: YOUR INQUIRY 19 FEB

PHOTOGRAPH OF ALEXANDER ROSTOV MATCHES THOSE ON FILE. NO FINGERPRINT IDENTIFICATION POSSIBLE. ROSTOV REMAINS IN SHADOWS BELIEVED TO BE CONTACT FOR SOVIET NETWORK IN FRANCE AND SWITZERLAND.

FRENCH CUSTOMS REPORTS ALLEGED BRITISH SUBJECT JOHN SMITHTON RAMSEY ENTERED FRANCE ON 6 FEB THROUGH PORT OF MARSEILLE, EXITED INTO GENEVA SWITZERLAND ON 7 FEB, RE-ENTERED FRANCE ON 8 FEB. SUBJECT DEPARTED FOR U.S. ON 8 FEB. APPARENTLY WITH FALSE PAPERS. SCOTLAND YARD CANNOT MATCH IDENTIFICATION OR PASSPORT.

Ramsey went through France like he was on a 7-day package tour of the continent. Switzerland? How long had Rostov followed him? Ramsey had no fear of being caught—it was obvious—the passports were good, very good. There was no record of Rostov in Geneva on the same date—if he was there at all. This added a different twist. Up until now it was a mystery why a Soviet agent had been following an unknown Briton—and yet, Ramsey certainly didn't look British.

Ramsey had gone through France in order to get lost, but instead, had been found.

But now he could be put into the computer. At the very least, he could be charged for illegal entry.

"Fill out an Inter-Agency Notification Request form. I'll sign it," Monahan said. "Get down to the courthouse and get your warrant."

The request would be to the Coast Guard to formally put out a global search for the *Bedford Clipper*. Monahan initialed Scotty's NCIC form for the entry of John Smithton Ramsey into the system.

EW.RAMSEY, JOHN SMITHTON.
M.W.XXXXX.XXXXXX.509.150. XXX.BLK.
COLD0002.OLV.NONE.TT1648POPICI1819AA06.XXXXXXX.XXXX
XX.0301
ILLEGAL ENTRY & CONSPIRACY TO COMMIT.MAN667431. REF
MAN666890
COLD0001 SUSPECT BOARDED FISHING TRAWLER BEDFORD
CLIPPER
NEW BEDFORD MA ON 12 FEB NOAH.

The Xs in the first line referred to place and date of birth and eye color. None were known. His fingerprints were on the second line along with the 0301 reference to Illegal Entry.

What next? His hooks were out. The Hertz lead was in the system. Rostov was in the system. John Smithton Ramsey was in the system.

Who was the woman . . . Rostov's woman? Rostov was *not* here in a vacuum. *They* were a team. *She* was here. So was *her* transportation.

What vehicles were owned or rented by the Soviet Mission to the United Nations?

"Good question, Scotty-boy," Scotty mumbled to himself.

It looked like it would be another street-vendor lunch today, Scotty thought as he headed for the elevator and the short walk to the Department of Motor Vehicles. It may be a short walk, but it would be a long day. There was never a good time to go to DMV.

WASHINGTON, D.C.

The FBI's CID (Criminal Investigative Division) has six major departments: Front Office, White-Collar Crime, Personal and Property Crime, Organized Crime, Civil Rights, and Terrorism. Parallel to CID and reporting to the Executive Assistant Director for Investigations is the Intelligence Division (ID). ID is divided into three sections, CI-1, CI-2, and CI-3; each with certain responsibilities for protecting the United States from "activities of foreign intelligence services".

At 11:00 A.M. Scotty's wire was received by the Communications Section and routed immediately to CID. A GS-3 clerk took the wire, logged it in, and stapled a buck slip marked ACTION on the front. The wire was placed in a mail folder where it was picked up by an automated mail cart. Many Federal offices had automated the internal distribution of mail by mapping sensing tracks throughout each floor. Mail carts could then be sent from office to office without the need of a person actually pushing the cart around. The cart would move until it sensed a programmed stopping point, normally near a secretary's desk. Mail then could be inserted or removed.

The Communications clerk forwarded the wire to the Terrorism Section where it was received by another clerk, who in turn manually logged the message. For messages and information which weren't case-specific, the clerk's job was to distribute the work as evenly as possible between the special agents in the section. The agents in the Terrorism section were a crossection of young hotshots in for their two years of seasoning and old veterans who were tired of field work.

The FBI was no different from any other Federal agency with regard to the daily absenteeism of its office staff. The low clerical positions had emaciated, mundane job descriptions that offered boring work at low pay to bored people. The jobs required rote performance and little imagination or decision-making.

The clerk who normally supported the Terrorism Section was on leave. A temporary, borrowed from another department, was sitting in for the regular clerk, a woman who was home with her sick four-year old. The temporary was given specific instructions, a list of tasks to perform. One of them was mail distribution. Scotty's wire was logged and put in the mail folder of Special Agent Irwin Harding, recently of Ft. Worth, Texas, now in Washington on what his wife hoped was only a two-year assignment. Unknown to the temporary, Special Agent Irwin Harding was at home with a 102° temperature and a gripping case of the flu.

PARIS

The clerk at the American desk continued to process requests one at a time. With resignation, he picked up the stack of wires and quickly scanned his workload by fanning the papers. No long lunch today. He stopped at the third wire.

TO: INTERPOL
        PARIS

FROM: JOHN JAMES CARTERET
        FBI
        CHARLOTTE REGIONAL OFFICE

SUBJECT: STATUS—JACQUES MARMANDE

HEAVYSET WHITE MALE JACQUES MARMANDE APPROXIMATE 50 YEARS WAS MURDERED ON 16 FEB IN CAPE HATTERAS NATIONAL SEASHORE NORTH CAROLINA USA.

SUSPECT THAT MARMANDE IS FRENCH CITIZEN HOWEVER UNABLE TO CONFIRM. ARRIVED UNITED STATES ATLANTA HARTSFIELD AIRPORT 8 FEB ON DELTA FLIGHT 1046 FROM PARIS.

WE SUSPECT MARMANDE TO BE PRIVATE INVESTIGATOR FOLLOWING A MAN KNOWN AS GEORGE DIJON, ALSO POSSIBLE FRENCH CITIZEN. CAN YOU PROVIDE DETAILS?

FINGERPRINTS AND PHOTO TO FOLLOW. PLEASE RUSH. WE HAVE NO RECORD ON FILE OF EITHER.

Damn! Jacques Marmande! Dead? The portly inspector was well known within the building. The clerk took the wire directly the the fifth floor corner office and gave it to Chief Inspector Chatillion's secretary, who glanced at the wire, then seemed to be physically assaulted by the news. Her shoulders buckled and she began to cry. The clerk left without a word. Nobody liked the bearer of bad tidings.

Hiding her sobs and tears with her handkerchief, Francine opened the office door of René Chatillion. One look at Francine's face and Chatillion's heart skipped a beat and his skin began to tingle. It was Jacques. He knew that his best agent and friend was dead. Francine, red-faced and teary-eyed placed the wire down on his desk then turned around and left without saying a word. Marmande had been a friend to them all. He and Francine had joined INTERPOL within two weeks of each other, nearly twenty years ago.

René looked at the wire. It was from a man named John James Carteret, a FBI agent in the state of North Carolina in the United States. There was no doubt, no room for question. Jacques was dead. It was all there—confirmation that Jacques had not informed the Americans. Why? There would be hell to pay, and René Chatillion would have to pay it. He was in charge. Jacques Marmande had been his employee. This was no time to be contrite. Khalid Rahman was Zaid abu Khan's right hand man.

"Francine!" Chatillion called.

She had only partially composed herself.

"See that the Americans get everything they need . . . and arrange for Jacques's body to be returned," he said sadly.

He hoped they weren't too late.

NAGS HEAD

There were eight of them involved. Bart had assigned six of his twelve patrolmen, and J.J. had told Roy to come down and help with the administration and collation of the data. The amount of work to be done was massive. The prints found in the oceanfront cottage opposite the one rented by the Frenchman (?) Marmande did not match the partials Henry Onslow and his team had come up with in the white Mustang. While no presumptions or assumptions were made, J.J. had mentally shelved the possibility that Marmande's prey had been the murderer.

The man and woman had to have stayed someplace. Someone has seen them, he thought. The man Marmande was following had left in something. Someone has seen him. Both pieces were important—vital—to the solution.

It was unknown if the man and woman had been following Marmande (probable) or the mark (less probable). Even more remote was the possibility that they were completely unrelated.

In the Nags Head to Kitty Hawk section of the beach cities the identification of the rental agency was easy—each house had a sign posted with the name and telephone number of the agency. It didn't take long to determine which houses within a radius of a half-mile had been rented. Only a handful were occupied. Those houses which were privately owned and occupied were also contacted. No leads.

"It's hard to believe this many people come here in the middle of February," said J.J., as Roy tallied up a long list of motel guest registers.

Data was needed on all motel guests who had checked *in* or *out* since February 9th. Automobile data was needed as well. Two of the policemen were responsible for gathering the information. Four others, and J.J., had to verify the accuracy. They first looked for the obvious, then the less obvious. The man and woman could have registered singly or as a married couple. Computer checks were made on the vehicle, state, and license plate numbers used on the registrations. Calls were made to information operators to verify names, streets, and telephone numbers. Of course, not everyone registering in a hotel used (a) their right name, (b) their correct home address, (c) the accurate license plate number. Some people registered under their work address instead of home address. The same was true of the telephone numbers.

Two of Bart's men were busy gathering information from the Hertz and Budget offices at the airport, the airport charter records, automobile dealers, and boat charters. Who was this George Dijon? The man had come by car. What about Atlanta? If Marmande rented a car in Atlanta, then perhaps this George Dijon did as well. J.J. asked Roy to query the rental companies again, this time for a man named Dijon at Hartsfield. After fifteen hours everyone was bleary-eyed and bone-tired. Bart had four second-shift men continue with the data gathering until all the hotels and motels were closed.

The office was littered with stacks of hand-written notes and photocopies of registration tickets.

"I think we've covered all the motels and cottage rental agencies in town, J.J.," said Bart.

"What about the others?" asked J.J.

"They should be through by mid-afternoon," replied Bart.

Henry had come up with no new fingerprints. At nine-thirty the team got their first good piece of news. It came in the form of an Express Mail delivery from the Hoover Building.

"Looks like your IDENT boys came through again, J.J.," said Bart.

They all stopped what they were doing, even the men on the telephones. Roy looked up from the computer terminal.

While the Identification Division may have looked at the package, it was actually the Laboratory Division (LD) who did the work. *They* were truly the gnomes of the FBI. LD was divided into a Documents Section, Scientific Section, and Special Projects Section.

"We're looking for a late model Dodge Caravan," said Bart, beaming.

Using Henry's photos, wheel-to-wheel and width of tire measurements, and scrapings of rubber from the skid marks, Scientific Analysis had come up with the fact that the vehicle used by the killer was a Dodge Caravan.

"I don't mean to be obvious, but did any of the people we've come up with actually register using a Caravan?" asked J.J.

J.J. wasn't being flippant, nor was his question treated as such. Nobody said criminals *had* to be smart. Each of the records was searched again, even the ones which had tentatively been checked off. All that was heard was the shuffle and sifting of fingers through paper.

Ten . . . fifteen . . . thirty minutes went by.

"I found one that might be it," said one of the policemen.

The patrolman's desk was immediately swarmed. J.J. picked up the registration slip. It read "Dodge van".

"It says Pennsylvania. But there are only five numbers here . . . this is made up. It's just numbers," said J.J. flatly.

It was the Sheraton Hotel in Nags Head, not a half-mile from the beach patrol station, the photocopy read.

"It's a start. Keep going, there might be others," said Bart.

It *was* a start. J.J. and Bart left for the Sheraton.

"Would *you* put down the right state and plate number?" J.J. asked, sarcastically.

Bart Claiborne shook his head.

"Neither would I. Do you even *know* what your license plate number *is*?" asked J.J.

"*I* do, but if I was using somebody else's car, or a rental . . . no way," replied Bart.

The Sheraton wasn't doing much business. The two men went to the manager's office, introduced themselves and quickly got the manager's attention. J.J. rattled questions at her.

"This registration indicates there were two adults. They stayed here from the 15th . . . checking out on the 20th. That's five nights. How did they pay?"

"Let me get the folio," said the manager.

In a few minutes she returned.

"Cash. This is Kathy, she was the one who registered them."

J.J. and Bart looked at a girl of no more than fifteen, perhaps sixteen, years old. It would take some time to get an accurate description from the girl.

"Hi, I'm John Carteret from the FBI. This is Sheriff Claiborne," J.J. said, smiling, trying to put the girl at ease as best he could.

J.J. turned to the manager.

"Has the room been rented since they checked out?"

"No, it hasn't," young Kathy volunteered.

"Aren't you supposed to get a credit card for room registrations?" asked J.J.

"Yes, sir, but the lady said she never used credit cards and wanted to pay by cash. I told her they couldn't have room service or make long distance calls," said Kathy.

"She? The woman registered?" asked J.J.

"Yes, sir."

J.J. looked at the ticket. The handwriting was nearly illegible, as if someone was making up the words as they were being written. Which was probably the case.

The registration was in the name of K. Taber, 115 Elm Street, Philadelphia 10017, phone (212)448-4589.

J.J. looked at Kathy then at Bart.

"Pretty pathetic," said J.J., handing it to Bart. "I may not know zip codes, but I *do* do a lot of calling. Philadelphia's area code is 215. And this zip code looks a phony, too."

"Maybe *it's* real . . . maybe it's the *only* thing that's real. If you're registering and you're making things up on the fly, streets and cities are easy to fabricate. Zip and area codes are more difficult. Unless you've thought it through you use the first thing that comes to your mind, something you know off the top of your head. Everyone knows their own zip code and telephone number. I think these people are from New York."

"Well . . . that narrows it down to ten million people, then," said Bart.

J.J. laughed for the first time in a week. It might be a productive day, after all.

CHARLOTTE, NORTH CAROLINA

"Is it too late to get this in the afternoon mail?" asked the secretary.

"Who's it to?" asked the mail clerk.

"J.J. Carteret," came the reply.

"Elizabeth City? Too late. It'll have to go out tomorrow. He'll get it tomorrow morning," said the clerk as he took the tannish-yellow government folder and inserted it into an external mailer.

Mail to the Resident Agencies (ROs) was sent by courier once a day from the Regional Office. The URGENT URGENT URGENT across the top of the wire had been covered up with the fold of an envelope. Inside was a wire from René Chatillion.

NAGS HEAD

It had been a profitable day. Any day where the evil forces of the other world were thwarted, or even partially thwarted, was good. And today had been a partially good day.

Young Kathy at the Sheraton had given them a fairly good description of their two suspects, but not good enough to send out major alarm bells. J.J. needed names, places, statistics . . . the things computers could read, smell, gobble up, and spit out at a moment's notice. Instead, he had a handful of feathers. He'd grabbed at whoever they were and had come up with a shirt sleeve. Kathy did, however, confirm what Henry had thought. The woman and man were approximately the same height, about five-ten. The man was slender . . . not frail, but slender, not much to look at. The woman was tall and had more substance than a first glance would indicate. And, she was "pretty."

Henry Onslow was glad to be back doing work which he enjoyed, anything but the dreadful paperwork and telephoning. Still, until he was finished and unless Henry came up with a match of the man's partial prints they'd gotten in the Mustang, then all they had were suspects. They could have been two people just wanting to get away.

It was after five when things finally started to jell. First, the call from a patrolman who had been checking car dealers.

"Mr. Carteret, we've come up with something unusual. I think we've got a lead on Dijon."

J.J. sat up in his chair, his tired body now alert.

"We're down at the Chevy dealership on the Bypass. A man came here almost two weeks ago and bought a Chevy Suburban—in cash!"

"Cash? You mean dollar bills, cash money?" said J.J., incredulous.

"That's right, cash. And that's not all. The salesman thinks the Suburban was modified, but he's not sure where. Anyway, I've got a pretty good description of him. He's foreign, that's for sure. The salesman thinks the man is either European or an Arab."

J.J. found himself on his feet, excited. The rolled-up-shirt-sleeve work had paid off.

"Find how and when the Suburban was modified. Do you have the plate numbers? Descriptions?" J.J. rattled off his questions.

"Yes, I do. Both were delivered with 30-day temporary tags. I've got the numbers," said the patrolman.

J.J. listened while the policeman read him a list of the plate numbers, vehicle IDs, and vehicle descriptions.

"Good work. Very good work. Thank you," said J.J. earnestly.

Both Roy and J.J. watched as Bart's clerk entered the data into the NCIC Vehicle File.

EF.NC7789HAT.T2290D337.NC.88.TM.V445HCBD3320
TR449.88.CHEV.SUBR.LL.RED.021788.SUSPECT 0301
GEORGE DIJON WANTED FOR QUESTIONING USE
CAUTION SEE RECORD.HAT44491.NOAH

The first line indicated a felony entry (EF), the originating code, the temporary plate number, state, year, the type of plate, and the vehicle ID number. The second, third and fourth lines consisted of the make year, the manufacturer, model, vehicle style (LL=rugged trail pleasure vehicles), color, date of "theft," misc. description field and the case number. The clerk finished both entries in a matter of ten minutes. Both entries were cross-referenced to each other. There was no time for a warrant.

"Put in a temporary felony on Dijon. I'll get a warrant tomorrow," said J.J.

ET.HAT44492.DIJON, GEORGE.M.W.XXX.XXX.XXX.
XXX.XXX.XXX.OLV.NON.AA6318TTCIMI18154XI09.
XXX.0301.WANTED FOR QUESTIONING SEE RECORDS
HAT44491.NOAH

The vehicle was the key.

ST. LOUIS, MISSOURI

The only traffic crossing the I-70 bridge over the icy Mississippi River were long-distance trucks. The northwest wind was so strong that even the heavily laden Suburban, driven by Aziz al-As, shook as it crossed into the state of Missouri and the city of St. Louis. To their right, a mile up the river, was the historic Eads Bridge, and a quarter mile beyond it, the Martin Luther King bridge. Both bridges connected East St. Louis, Illinois with the downtown area of St. Louis, Missouri.

The entire area between the Eads and I-70 bridges was a rolling open field of concrete and frozen turf. But it wasn't empty. The Gateway Arch, an incredible feat of engineering and expressive architecture, twisted its way into the sky and dominated the skyline of the city. The plaza was bordered on the west by Interstate 70, which, after crossing the river, curved its way north through town and past the arch on its way to Kansas City. East of the plaza, running parallel to the Mississippi and the Arch was Wharf Street, renamed Leonor K. Sullivan Boulevard. People still called it Wharf Street.

Khan motioned for al-As to take the Memorial Drive exit off I-70. Going northbound on Memorial to their left was the modern skyline of downtown St. Louis—the circular Clarion Hotel, KMOX/KHTR, the local CBS affiliates, and the newly renovated Adams Mark Hotel. Behind the Clarion was Busch Stadium, guarded by a statue of Stan Musial. This February night Musial's left-handed stance had three inches of snow on the bill of his bronze cap. Between KMOX and the Adams Mark was an uncluttered grassy mall which led the eye west, away from the Arch to the historic Jefferson National Expansion Memorial—the iron-domed old courthouse and centerpiece of historic St. Louis. From the courthouse steps the Arch, a half mile away, was perfectly centered and unobstructed by the clutter of office buildings. The courthouse was perfectly centered in the middle of the arch a half mile away.

Lights splayed on the arch, which got more incredible the closer it was approached. The Gateway Plaza was empty, the benches covered with snow. The walkways which wound through the rolling tree-lined grounds were well maintained and cleared. Crunchy granules of salt had been sprinkled on the shovelled pathways.

A nearby digital temperature sign displayed 18°. Tiny flakes of powdery snow started to fall.

The Suburban made a slow pass around the Plaza, up Memorial to just before the Eads Bridge, then right on Washington Street downhill toward the river. To their left was the bridge's stone abutment, the first steel-truss bridge in the world. A two-layered bridge, the Eads had allowed the railroad to cross the Mississippi on its now-unused lower deck and had helped change the history of westward expansion in the United States. Cut through the abutment at one-block increments were four arched passages which allowed pedestrians and automobiles to enter the renovated waterfront area known as Laclede's Landing, a grouping of drinkeries, pubs, and entertainment houses.

At the bottom of the hill, Washington Street dead-ended at Wharf Street.

"Stop," said Khan.

Aziz stopped at the intersection. The white snow looked eerily beautiful when contrasted against the bridge's soot-stained blocks of stone. Khan's whole attention was on the underside of the stone belly of the Eads Bridge. Towering above the Wharf Street underpass were four sixty-foot-tall archways. Nearly directly above them was the manned toll booth where fifty cents was charged for a trip to East St. Louis. Running parallel with Wharf Street and the river, fifteen feet above ground level, were the remains of two narrow-gauge railway tracks that had been used in the mid-60s for hauling the triangular-shaped segments of double-walled steel wedges for the arch. The tracks passed under the Eads Bridge, over Washington Street, and into a tunnel that led to an underground storage area, now mostly unused. North of the bridge the railroad tracks ran above ground for several blocks and acted as the demarcation line for the still-unfinished Laclede's Landing.

"In there?" asked Rahman on the radio.

"Possibly. See what's on the other side," replied Khan.

Rahman and el-Rashid got out and walked under the bridge. The road was icy in patches. Piles of dirty snow were on both sides of the narrow street. East of the intersection the ramp leading down to the row of paddleboat restaurants, now mostly closed, was dangerous to navigate. On the other side Rahman looked, then shook his head and returned to Khan, who rolled his window down. The icy night swept into the warm cab.

"There is no concrete wall on the other side, only a wire gate which looks like it has been open for quite some time," said Rahman.

It was not an enclosed area. While it would have been difficult to scale the wall, it could have been done.

Khan got out. Together the three men walked back up Washington Street to a cobblestoned alley named Commercial Street and walked through the abutment archway and under the bridge. On the other side were abandoned warehouses of old red brick with every window broken, each looking as if it were the perfect home for the street-people of St. Louis. They walked down to Lucas Street, an equally cobblestoned lane that was one-way downhill to Wharf Street and the river.

Khan shook his head no, and walked back to Washington Street. His eyes had caught a potential hiding place, but he had to be sure there wasn't something better. If they went farther uphill they would be in the center of Leclede's Landing, which would be an unlikely place to hide the weapon.

In his mind's eye Khan could see the Plaza four months and one week from this evening. Almost exactly to the hour! Nine o'clock, Monday, July 4th! Two million people would line the banks of the Mississippi waiting for America's celebration of celebrations, Independence Day. The fireworks would be the last act in an almost orgasmic display of patriotism. West of I-70 were the tall, modern office buildings of St. Louis. Every window would be occupied with corporate party-goers waiting for the fantastic pyrotechnic demonstration.

At nine o'clock weapon #2 would detonate, killing nearly three million Americans as they innocently celebrated their birthright. The Gateway Arch, the museum and administration building, and two million people in the plaza would be vaporized. Gone. Ashes. The first line of office buildings across I-70 would be destroyed. Nearly three hundred thousand people would die in the buildings, another fifty thousand killed by the collapsing buildings. On the other side of the river, north of the Peabody Coal Company, the eastern banks of the Mississippi would be packed with Illinois residents who would have celebrated in their own right. The prevailing winds would dump most of the dirty radioactive debris into East St. Louis.

It would be a catastrophe of the highest order.

The plaza grounds were out. The ground was frozen solid. It would take a pneumatic jackhammer to get through the turf. The Plaza was nearly pristine. There were no obvious places to squirrel away his weapon. The Eads Bridge was going to be the place.

Khan walked across Washington Street toward the solid abutment of the bridge. At its base, underneath the railway tracks, was a boarded doorway into the abutment. Like most large bridges, the Eads was built with a maintenance room in its abutment. Long since discarded as a storage room, the hollowed-out abutment had acted as a haven for street people until the city had covered it up with two ten-foot-tall sections of sheet board, each three feet wide and an inch thick. It wouldn't take much effort to dislodge the boards, place the bomb, then cover the opening.

"Over here," Khan pointed to the dimly lit abutment. "We must hurry."

They all agreed wordlessly.

Rahman opened the Suburban's rear panel door downward. El-Rashid climbed inside. Together, the men lifted weapon #2 out from its compartment to a resting place on the door, where their hands were joined by those of Aziz al-As. In unison, the three men shuffled across the icy flat and set the bomb down beside the abutment.

"Good. Good!" said Khan, with enthusiasm.

Using the business end of one of the SVD rifles as a crowbar, Khan carefully loosened the plywood boards.

"Flashlight!" Khan ordered.

Aziz held the light while el-Rashid and Khalid carried the bomb into the Eads Bridge abutment. Shrill, squeaky noises of complaint filled the room as the rats reacted to the foreign light. It would take only a matter of moments for el-Rashid to arm the bomb.

"Over here," el-Rashid ordered the placement of the light.

Without asking, Khan helped el-Rashid lift the bomb out of the container and place it down on the cold, dirty concrete. The polished stainless steel gleamed in the eerie light. The firing arm protruded out at a 45° angle, giving the bomb an oddly askew appearance. Stabilized, el-Rashid carefully went to work. He hated to take off his gloves. He cursed to himself as he fumbled with the screwdriver.

For the next few minutes the only sounds came from the soft metallic clicking of el-Rashid's work and an occasional deep rumbling from a car leaving the toll both seventy feet above.

— • —

Alvin Dierdorf and Hap Wilson had what was commonly referred to as Bum Duty. Third shift cruising the waterfront was not only bum-crummy, but all they saw were bums, drunks, and dopers. They saw the human trash of the city, the Excess People. Fortunately, most of the time the slime did nothing but hurt themselves. Dierdorf and Wilson were there to see that they didn't go outside their own kind.

While the routine was fairly regular, every night brought something different. Every situation was potentially lethal. Even though most of the Excess People were identified, their patterns known, Bum Duty was dangerous duty. And, it was never boring. A shot-up junkie could do anything bizarre imaginable. Breaking up a fight between two sleazy drunks trying to knife each other for a dead man's pair of shoes was not fun.

They patrolled the heart of downtown, from Busch Stadium north to the Convention Center then east to the river and south to the rail yards.

"Slow down, Alvin," said Wilson.

Dierdorf stopped. Together they looked down Wharf Street from the darkness under the King Bridge. A vehicle of some kind was parked under the Eads Bridge.

"Parked?" asked Dierdorf.

"It's not moving," replied Hap Wilson.

There were no cars under the bridge when they'd made their last pass through the wharf area an hour ago. This area was no lover's lane. Parked cars meant one thing: drugs.

"I don't feel like doing this tonight, Hap. It's too damn cold outside," said Alvin Dierdorf.

"You'd better turn around. Go down 2nd to Lucas. We can probably get right on top of them," said his partner.

Wilson went to the radio.

"This is Two Baker Ten. We have some suspicious traffic under the Eads Bridge. We're going in."

"Do you wish backup, Two Baker Ten?" replied dispatch.

Wilson paused. Dierdorf shot him a yes glance.

"Affirmative," said Wilson.

The Eads Bridge was no more than a quarter-mile from their position. Dierdorf quickly backed up out of the possible line of sight of the parked car, turned around, made a left onto 2nd Street, passed under the King Bridge and then left again onto Lucas Avenue, which ran down-hill, parallel to the bridge's superstructure. Dierdorf slowly crept his cruiser underneath the train tracks and nosed out into Wharf Street. They were less than a half block away, still out of sight from the parked car, which now could be identified as some sort of van or truck.

"Ready?" asked Wilson.

"I guess," sighed Dierdorf.

Lights out, Dierdorf rounded the corner, went through the narrow, single-lane southbound arch.

The vehicle was parked at the corner of Washington and Wharf Streets. Hap Wilson got his first, and last, good look at it.

"It's empty," said Wilson.

"No! Look!" Dierdorf pointed at two men standing in the dark under the train tracks.

The two men on foot, both indistinguishable, began to shout words in a foreign language.

One of the men pointed at the police cruiser.

He was pointing with a gun.

— • —

Williams and Reynolds had been a half-mile in front of the Suburban when it had crossed the I-70 bridge into St. Louis and had been totally out of position when Khan turned off the Interstate onto Memorial Drive. North of the Eads Bridge, Memorial Drive turns into Third Avenue, which was the exit they took. The pair had parked, waiting for instructions. They had a reasonable view back toward the Eads Bridge, but that was about all. They had seen Dierdorf's police cruiser silently cross through the intersection on its way to Lucas Avenue.

"Police are in the area," warned Williams over the CB.

"Khan has stopped under the bridge," came Katrina's reply. "They're at the foot of Washington Street. They've stopped and gotten out. I can barely see them."

Rostov doubled back on Memorial and found the service road to Wharf Street south of the arch and the plaza. He and Katrina were a mile from Khan, but there were no obstructions along the waterfront.

"He's going to blow up that . . . thing," Rostov had no words to describe the arch.

"I'm picking up other voices," said Katrina, monitoring the COMEX. The CB squawked.

"The police have moved in . . . wait a minute! I . . . think, yes . . . there is gunfire," said the excited Williams.

All hell was breaking loose.

"They must not be caught," said a stone-faced Alexander Rostov to his partner.

"Move in! Do whatever is required to prevent their capture. Do you understand?" shouted Katrina as Rostov gunned the Caravan down Wharf street toward the intersection.

"Acknowledged," replied Reynolds.

Rostov reached behind him and brought out their loaded Berettas; they had no long-range weapons. Williams and Reynolds had come equipped with Ruger M-77s equipped with 4X Weaver scope. They had the only rifles in the group. Rostov was thankful that Korz had at least been able to supply them with the best; the M12S 9mm 32-round machine gun could devastate a small area within seconds.

Rostov covered the mile in less than a minute. The fight had already started.

— • —

Rahman stood above the kneeling el-Rashid, providing him with the light he needed. Aziz stood in the doorway. Khan remained in the darkness of the musty room. El-Rashid methodically took the weapon apart and armed it. Removing the glove from his right hand, he unscrewed the weapon's detonator arm. Carefully he loosened the plastic explosive and rolled it between the forefinger and thumb of his left hand. With his right hand he reached inside the pocket of his jacket and withdrew a four-inch, pencil-thin, detonator cap. He molded the plastic around the detonator then replaced the combination back inside. Patiently, el-Rashid rechecked the time and date of the clock. July 4th, 9:00 P.M. Carefully, he attached the black and red leads from the firing cap to the clock then slowly removed his fingers from the head of the weapon. Lastly, he depressed the ALARM button and firmly rethreaded the stainless steel cap onto the firing arm.

He stood up and smiled at his work. Dust kicked up from the wind that whipped around and through the Eads Bridge.

"Is it ready?" asked Khan.

"It is done," replied el-Rashid.

"We must go," Khan ordered.

The three men turned as one when they heard the shout of "the police!" in Farsi from Aziz al-As.

Khalid drew his gun and began firing at the police car. From the boarded archway Aziz al-As came toward the cruiser and also began firing.

"Up there!" shouted Khan, pointing up Washington Street.

A second police cruiser, its red and blue lights strobing, screeched to a sliding stop thirty feet behind the Suburban, just west of the overhead train tracks. They were blocked. Two policemen jumped out of the second car and began firing. Khan was more protected from the first pair of policemen than the second. It wouldn't take long before the second pair would have a shot at him from behind the Suburban. If the second car had time to report, it wouldn't be long before every policeman in St. Louis was on the spot.

Aziz al-As opened fire on the squad car, shattering the passenger window and injuring the patrolman.

"It is over!" he shouted in Farsi to Khan.

"We will not be captured!" ordered Khan.

Aziz fired again, then was stuck in the leg by the only shot Hap Wilson managed to get off. Pain shot through al-As's body, as he ran, staggered, back toward the abutment.

"Bafq el-Rashid—you are cursed!" Aziz shouted to his tormentor. "You will die and not be forgiven for what you have done to me! You have taken my manhood and now you will die!" Aziz shouted, oblivious to the barrage of fire from the policemen, and now from another source.

Bafq el-Rashid, ducking behind the meager protection of the abutment, turned and fired at Aziz. The shot hit him directly in the right temple and exploded his head. Bits and pieces of blood and brain splattered across the fifteen-foot distance between the dead Aziz and the now-kneeling Bafq el-Rashid. Aziz fell face forward into a grimy mixture of blackened snow and sidewalk. The top quarter of his head was nothing but goo. From across the street Khan watched in horror at what had happened. For two seconds the men locked eyes. Khan realized the hopes for his Ultimatum were dashed. He had chosen the wrong men.

Khalid Rahman was in no-man's land, and paid for it. He was the only target which could be seen by both sets of police cars. All four policemen fired at him. As he dove for protection, Khalid took a bullet in the back, one in the left arm and another in his right leg. He fell against the rear bumper of the Suburban, then slumped between the vehicles, his body torn. He was critically injured. Except for their handguns, Khan's arsenal was entirely in the storage compartment of the Suburban, which now was unreachable. Bullets smashed into the vehicle.

Ducking down, Khan wriggled his way toward his friend Khalid. In the same moment, he sensed movement up Washington Street behind the police cars. In a blur of motion a van squealed to a stop in front of the Suburban, leaving a trail of rubber, its two front doors opening before the vehicle seemed to stop. Out one side came a woman, a man from the right door. The two had automatic weapons of some kind and opened fire immediately, spraying death and destruction in a double arc.

The police quickly switched from their original targets, now obviously slowed and wounded, to their new aggressor. They had absolutely *no* idea what was going on. If, at the time, Dierdorf had been asked his impressions he would have said that they'd fallen into a Mafia shootout. Dierdorf and both of the policemen from the second cruiser switched their fire to the two cars which had come up from behind them.

Dierdorf reached into the back seat of his car and pulled out his riot shotgun. The distance was too great, but he fired his rounds anyway. He quickly reloaded and fired again. The other officers continued a rapid burst of support fire. Two men fell to the ground. But the pressure was too great. The frontal assault by the people in the van, a blistering attack of 9mm Beretta machine-guns, caused the police to take whatever shelter was available.

Reaching the bleeding and dazed Rahman, Khan looked at the scene in amazement. The woman ripped the right side of both cruisers back and forth. The passenger windows and front windshields splattered glass in every direction. The cars seemed to be exploding from within. From up Washington Street came fire from a hidden source. Whatever they were using was powerful. The slugs riddled the second cruiser and the the policemen kneeling behind them.

There was no glass left in the squad cars. There was no place to hide. The police had been caught in the most deadly of crossfires. The whole event took fifty seconds. Shots echoed against the underpass. The woman got back inside the van and restarted the engine.

"Who are you?" Khan shouted.

The man did not respond.

"Who are you?" Khan repeated, his voice echoing across the cold night.

"Get out of here!" returned the man.

Khan walked out into the intersection and could see a car a half block up Wharf Street on the other side of the bridge. A lump lay in the middle of the street. Another man, rifle in hand, bent over him. Reynolds was dead. Dead policemen were everywhere. The only sounds were that of the unanswered queries of the St. Louis police dispatch, loudly squawking over the cruiser's speaker.

Khan snapped back to reality.

"Board it up!" he shouted to el-Rashid.

There was no time to waste. He had no choice. El-Rashid had done something terrible to al-As. The angry words of the slain young man alluded to the abomination of abominations. Bafq el-Rashid would die, but not tonight. There was too much yet to do. Khan knelt down beside al-As, rolled the body over and rifled his pockets, finding loose change and his wallet, which he stuffed into the pocket of his coat. He then went back to Khalid, helped him to his feet and guided him toward the back seat of the Suburban.

"Hurry!" Khan shouted through the snow, his words punctuated by the white billows of his breath. Steam rose from the open death wound of Aziz al-As. Hearing Khan's words and sensing the immediate urgency, el-Rashid bent over the weapon again.

"What are you doing?" shouted Khan, angrily.

"No one is going to get *this* bomb," hissed el-Rashid in return.

Quickly taking several strands of thin wire out of his coat pocket, el-Rashid twisted and tied one end around the two-inch screw whose head was in the center of the faceplate. Dropping the wire through the screw hole, he turned the screw into its place. As his last step before putting the faceplate back on, el-Rashid looped the other end of the wire and wrapped it around the small ON/OFF toggle on the clock. Finishing, he slithered through the right side as Khan reinserted the heavy boards into place. There were no marks, no footprints. The two men ran for the truck, el-Rashid driving.

They carefully avoided the sprawled bodies of Wilson and Dierdorf, went under the Eads Bridge and sped up Wharf to Morgan Street where they turned left and wheeled two blocks up the hill to the eastbound entrance onto I-70. With Khan pointing, el-Rashid deftly exited onto southbound I-55, and again at the mixing bowl intersection took I-44 southwest. They were out of town in fifteen minutes.

Khan looked back. A half-mile behind them was the van. Pacing ahead of them was another car which he recognized as being the one who ambushed the second squad car.

Who were these people?

CHAPTER 4

From Sea to Shining Sea

ST. LOUIS

Police Chief Duffy O'Brien, a barrel-chested man of 56, walked back and forth beneath the towering archway of the Eads Bridge underpass. The cold wind whipped through his thinning salt-and-pepper hair, but although he might have felt the chill, he didn't care. In his thirty-four years of police service Duffy O'Brien had never seen four policemen murdered as these four men had been.

The area around the Eads Bridge was cordoned off a block in every direction, not that there was any traffic, anyway. There were no real people here, only the newspapers and TV. Ten police cars, blue and red lights flashing, blocked Wharf, Lucas, Washington Streets and Memorial Drive. Ambulances waited to take the covered bodies. Patrolmen and inspectors combed the area for clues.

O'Brien would have to make a statement pretty soon. To say what? Four fine men, three with families, had been killed . . . no, not killed. Assassinated. Murdered. What had these men gotten themselves into? Duffy reached down and picked up a handful of shell casings. Empty casings were everywhere. There must be hundreds. Nine mm military. The cruisers were ready for the junkyard. O'Brien ran his hand along the right side of Dierdorf's patrol car. Even the cars had been killed.

What happened here? How did this start?

Damn!

Dierdorf and Wilson! They'd worked together for eight years and were the toughest pair he had. They'd worked nights for the last three and had almost single-handedly made the Gateway Plaza area safe for normal people to use at night. In the summertime people could come downtown, come to the Arch, stroll along the waterfront and not worry that their cars would be busted or that they might get mugged.

Wilson had called but had no description of the vehicle. It was dark. Do you want help, asked dispatch. A pause. Yes. Two Baker Six was the closest, at Broadway and Olive. They were three minutes away, if that. Kelly and Gingrich were Two Baker Six. Murdered from behind by high-powered rifles.

O'Brien walked toward the the covered body of Aziz al-As. O'Brien knelt down and uncovered the head. It was an ugly sight. But at the same time, Duffy knew that one of his men had done the deed on this man and he was filled with a kind of odd satisfaction.

"Who is this son of a bitch?" Duffy asked.

Trailing O'Brien was his A.A., Lieutenant Paul Worley.

"There was nothing on him, Duffy. Nothing but some loose change," said the 40ish Worley.

With the prevalence of drugs in crime, it was hard for Duffy O'Brien and Paul Worley—for any policeman—to disassociate any crime from what in their minds had caused it. Drugs were at the bottom of everything evil in America, the rotten core . . . it would be the fall of society. It was easy to become jaded when confronted daily with the overwhelming evidence of where America had been and where she was going. Duffy O'Brien had a grotesque mental image of Miss Liberty not holding up the light of freedom but with one arm wrapped tightly, giving herself a heroin injection. It was an image he couldn't shake.

"Damn!" mumbled Duffy to himself. It didn't feel like drugs. These were foreigners, but not Latinos.

Thirty yards from the cruisers, down the middle of Wharf Street, was a pair of skid marks perhaps fifteen yards long. On either side of the tracks the street was littered with 9mm shell casings. It was fairly easy to picture what had happened, but not easy to picture the relationship of the people and the sequence of events.

Duffy walked up Washington Street to the second cruiser. The off-and-on snow showers which had been forecast for the night were on again. Snow trickled down through the railway tracks, more heavily on the unprotected cruiser. Kelly and Gingrich had taken automatic fire from the rear. The right side of the cruiser, facing downhill, was riddled with what probably was more of the 9mm shells from whatever had stopped in the intersection.

"Do we have pictures?" O'Brien asked.

"Yeah, we've got enough, Duffy," replied Worley.

O'Brien waved to the ambulance men, signalling that it was OK to remove the bodies.

"Jesus," Duffy muttered as he picked up the .270 shell casings. "These sons of bitches knew exactly how far away to be. These are shells from a hunting rifle."

Shoes crunching on the cindered pavement, O'Brien completed his tour of the battle by walking back under the bridge and up Wharf Street to where a lumpish body was lying in the middle of the street. This had to have been a lucky shot, most likely from Dierdorf.

"You got the son of a bitch, Alvin," said Duffy to the dead man.

Duffy O'Brien started back toward the waiting press. It was time to get it out of the way. On the way he gave Paul Worley his instructions.

"Get the prints on these men," pointing to the two unknowns. "I want the make on the skid marks. I want the area combed again. Everything! Understand? I want this area closed until we know exactly . . . exactly . . . what happened here. Notify the Illinois police, and our state police. I want roadblocks on the Interstates. I want every god-damned bullet hole in those cruisers marked for projectory and probable distance. I want to know who these sons of bitches are! Have the families been notified?"

"Not yet," answered Worley.

"Jesus," muttered Duffy O'Brien.

It was going to be a long night.

LEBANON, MISSOURI

The night air smelled of oil. A cold wind made Katrina's ears tingle with numbness and scattered her now-bleached hair in every direction. The roar of the trucks on I-44 caused her to hold up one hand over her right ear in order to hear Korz. The clatter-clatter of a car with chains, its driver unsure of the advancing weather, mixed with the squawks of a CB cranked up too high. The soft sounds of The Judds came from somebody's cab, making the truckstop a snapshot of America. The Soviets were oblivious.

"Reynolds was killed. One of their men as well, another seriously injured. I . . . we don't know how long we can protect them. They made a serious mistake tonight," said a very tired Katrina Tambov.

She was weary. She'd killed again tonight, almost as if she had been programmed. Point and fire. Hold the trigger in place, wide open . . . back off, slap in another magazine . . . it was rote. The policemen had been in the wrong place at the wrong time. But it was different tonight. These weren't little children.

Dimitri Korz talked to her like she was his daughter. Korz tried to project himself into her shoes. The police would be in a fury. The FBI would be called in. Khan was over his head.

"Yes, it is serious. But, you did the right thing. Now, Katrina, I want you to listen to me . . . you must not be captured. What has happened tonight has changed things. Is Rostov on the phone?" Korz asked.

"No. This is a pay phone. They have stopped for fuel. We have stopped for fuel. They know we are following them," replied Katrina. "We can see them and they can see us."

There was no pretension any longer. They all had gotten off I-44 near the town of Lebanon, fifty miles northeast of Springfield, one hundred thirty miles from St. Louis. Khan had gone to the Union 76 station, Katrina to the Shell. Both stations were truck centers open twenty-four hours a day.

"Good . . . no, no . . . I mean . . . " Korz's thoughts were moving too quickly for his mouth. "Katrina, you must not be captured. If it comes to it, you must kill Rostov . . . and the others. This plan will only work if the Americans believe Khan is the sole person responsible. There must not be a hint of our involvement. Do you understand, Katrina?"

Korz was sweating. He didn't like having someone else in charge of his destiny. One whiff of Soviet involvement in a plot to use atomic weapons inside the United States and . . . the thought was overpowering.

"Yes, I understand," came her reply.

"You must shoot Rostov, if necessary," emphasized Korz.

"Yes, I will," replied Katrina mechanically.

"Katrina . . . Katrina!"

He tried to slap the weary woman over the phone with his voice. It worked.

"Yes, Dimitri," was her more alert response.

"Get them off the main highway! The police will do everything they can tonight. Get them off, now!"

"But they have stopped—we haven't made contact."

Things were moving too quickly. Events were changing too dynamically for them to stop and regroup. If this was going to work, then his agents—Katrina and the others—would have to take command now.

"You must contact him now. You must make a deal with Khan," said Korz urgently. "Furthermore, you must learn how to detonate the weapons."

"What?" came her confused reply.

"A deal. Make a deal with him!" shouted Korz.

"No—no, I understand the 'deal.' What do you mean about detonating the bombs?" replied Katrina with concern in her voice.

"You must, Katrina. One, perhaps two, of these bombs will actually explode. And if Khan won't do it, then you must. Do you understand?"

There was a long pause before Katrina answered.

"Yes, I understand." The words almost came out in a hiss.

"Good! Say anything—offer him protection, sympathy, weapons—anything—just speed things up! Whatever it is he plans to do, he must do it quickly, before the Americans have time to catch up. They are slow, but they have advantage of territory. They will catch up. You must get Khan to execute his plan quickly," Korz urged.

"Then you must tell me what our plan is," said Katrina, not without a touch of sarcasm.

She was alert. She knew what Korz expected of her. Death before capture. It was Moscow's wish.

"Do you have a map with you?" Korz asked.

"Map . . . " Korz heard her ask someone, perhaps Rostov. "I have it."

"You do not concern yourself with why," Korz began sternly. "At some point Khan will issue his demands. You must make sure that he does it sooner than later. You will need several days to reach your destination. Since I will be unable to provide further assistance to you, you must make your deal with Khan such that he believes the targets are a good choice for his purposes. This will not be easy, but not impossible. They will appeal to him. You must do it, comrade! If he resists, kill him. It is vital the plan be executed quickly."

Korz could hear the voice of Alexander Rostov in the background, urgently telling her something.

"We've got to go . . . they're leaving . . . wait, no . . . they're going inside. I've got to go! The target, Dimitri!" Katrina implored.

"Arizona . . . the first is in the state of Arizona. Listen carefully . . ."

— • —

It had only taken minutes for Katrina to understand her mission. It was true, she did not have to know why. She—they—were to execute the plan. She hung up the cold phone and rapidly instructed Rostov. There was no time to let him make decisions.

"They've gone inside to eat. It will be a matter of minutes," said the irritated Rostov.

"Comrade, listen to me . . . there is no time. I will explain later. *You* must be the one to talk to Khan. He will never take suggestions from a woman," Katrina said, her breath cutting a white knife in the cold Missouri night. "He *must* get off this highway. We *must* make him . . . *you* must make him . . . the police. Say anything . . . promise him anything . . . I will explain later."

Rostov was professional enough to know that Katrina was right. This was no time for discussion. Khan would be gone within minutes.

Leaving the van, Rostov walked alone across the oily street to the Union 76 restaurant where he was almost overpowered by the smell of food and warm temperature. There was a certain jovial atmosphere, a clubish environment. To the left was a large area, mostly filled with bearded men in bulky parka-vests, marked Truckers Only. No explanation was required.

To the right were two horseshoe-shaped eating counters, a small area with perhaps six 4-person tables, and a row of red vinyl-covered booths which seated four . . . six uncomfortably. Each counter had a stack of pie slices and a large covered dish which hid the mystery cake. Cigarette smoke filled the diner-like restaurant.

Khan sat uncomfortably by himself at the U of the second counter. He should be uncomfortable, thought Rostov. Rahman was injured, his good young man al-As was dead, and he was left with a man whose skills were needed, but whose personal habits were disgusting. El-Rashid remained in the Suburban to watch Rahman, who had passed through various stages of lucidity. Khan had ordered food to go.

From the opposite side of the room, Rostov could feel Khan tense. Under Khan's parka was an automatic rifle, an Uzi or something similar. If things went wrong, it was possible that within seconds thirty people or more could be dead. Rostov and Khan exchanged eyes. No one paid attention to them. Everyone minded their own business, either talking good-old-boy road talk or burying their heads in the sports page. Rostov made a motion with his hands which said he was unarmed, raising both slightly above his waist, and walked directly toward Khan. The ill-fitting clothes, bought at the Ben Franklin in Kill Devil Hills by Rahman, looked as phony as they were.

"You must leave," said Rostov quietly, but with conviction.

Khan returned a face with an ironed-on expression of distrust. Rostov looked around. Nobody was listening to their conversation. Their ketchup-stained waitress, used to the verbal abuse of the help and the customers, was busy trying to carry a meal for six with only two hands. Plates were stacked on each arm. It was quite athletic.

"I will explain later. You must leave, and you must get off the main highway. The road out front goes south. Someplace along the way there will be a place to stop. You will be caught if you stay on the main highway," Rostov said almost under his breath.

Khan heard every word, his hand on the trigger of the gun under his coat. Khan sized Rostov up. The opponent, if that was what he was, was formidable.

"Who are you?" asked Khan.

"You must leave. We saved you back there. We're on the same side," said Rostov.

"Is there anything else?" interrupted the waitress, handing Khan two bags of food and another of drink.

Khan shook his head no, paid for the food, and headed for the door. Outside the two men faced each other, their words competing with the rumbly raucous noise of the interstate trucks.

"Use channel 14. We will talk, but we must go. Follow us."

Rostov turned around and walked past the Suburban, not giving el-Rashid even the slightest acknowledgement.

FAYETTEVILLE, ARKANSAS

The sophomore night manager at the Quality Inn hardly batted an eye when a woman walked in and asked for four rooms at four-thirty A.M. It was weird, but then in his two years at this part-time job he'd seen some weird stuff. The resident population of Fayetteville was nearly matched by the number of students at the University of Arkansas. It appeared as if at one point in time state leaders had decided to deliberately place the University as far away as possible from the populated sections of the state. Missouri had been the choice of some legislators, but Fayetteville was selected. Located in the rolling hills of northwestern Arkansas, students had access to every non-educational activity possible . . . except for the Big City. On most weekends the motel was packed with students. Nothing was out of the ordinary. With one eye on a chemistry book, the young man registered the rooms, taking cash as it was offered.

Adults weren't normally up at this time of the night. The sophomore went back to his studies.

—•—

"Did Korz say exactly what we were to do, afterwards?" Rostov asked cynically.

"Yes. I will explain it to you. But, we're on our own. We've been on our own, and you know that. I want to get back to New York and you . . . well, I assume you want to get back to wherever you were before you came here," replied Katrina strongly to his implied criticism.

The two had been on the edge of civility since the night of the murders in North Carolina and the act he'd forced her to perform. She involuntarily rolled her tongue around her mouth. She could still taste the bitterness of his semen, the demanding pressure of his erection on her lips, his hands on her head urging her back and forth, then the final explosion as he came with a hot rush into her mouth. He had not even gotten undressed while she had been kneeling naked, exposed before him.

Every time they'd exchanged glances in the last week she had thought that he was mentally undressing her. Why had she allowed herself to do it? Because she was weak. She needed affection but she craved abuse. He had brought out the weakness in her and it made her angry. She had used her body many times to get information from people, but it had been under her control. Katrina had had no idea that she enjoyed being subjugated.

It was a perversion of her image of her character.

Mentally shaking her head to clear her thoughts, Katrina outlined what needed to be done with the bombs.

"Can you handle it?" Rostov asked.

"I think so. Williams has some experience also. I don't believe they are using a complicated mechanism," she said.

Rostov grunted.

"That leaves the deal. Make a deal. Those were his words?" he asked.

"Yes. Bargain. You should be good at this—we should be good at this," Katrina answered.

"Yes, but so should they," he replied.

—•—

Khan was so tired. He'd been unable to sleep since St. Louis. In the back seat lay his good friend, seriously, perhaps fatally, wounded.

Driving was el-Rashid. They had exchanged not a word the entire night. Something had happened between el-Rashid and al-As, something terrible, although from Aziz's last anguished cry, Khan suspected what it was. The thought disgusted him. *I should kill him right now and be done with it*! thought Khan. But he needed el-Rashid, at least for another two or three days—at least until the Ultimatum was issued. Set one more bomb and it would be time.

Who were these people? They had come from nowhere to save them in St. Louis. More frightening was the look in the man's eyes. He knew. How could he know? How could they know?

With the probability of failure in St. Louis very real, it was imperative that the bomb in Dallas be set before issuing the Ultimatum. The Washington bomb was set for detonation at six P.M. the day after tomorrow—no, it was tomorrow! Tomorrow? How could it be? Khan shook his head. Khalid lay in the second of two double beds, his precious life-blood oozing out through make-shift bandages. In a few days, success of the operation, the Ultimatum, would be up to the pedantic negotiating skills of Abdul Waquidi.

At 5:15 A.M. there was a soft knock on the door. It was more of a tap than a knock. Khan cracked the door to the point where he could see only a sliver of his visitor's face illuminated by doorway lights outside. It was the intervener. He was smaller, no—thinner, more slight—than he thought. Khan let the stranger inside. The man said nothing as Khan checked him out. His eyes were black, the skin under them puffy with years of lack of sleep, but they were alert.

"We must talk," the man said softly, but with a resolve which would not be denied.

There was determination and even the threat of force behind the simple sentence.

"Why?" asked Khan, now standing.

They were only feet apart, their eyes never leaving one other's stare.

"We know your plans," Rostov replied calmly.

Khan held his facial and body position, but his eyes flickered and darted, revealing his surprise.

"Oh?" Khan replied, without emotion. Was he bluffing? Who was he? Red Brigade? The man was foreign. He spoke with a French accent. How could he know? He was bluffing.

"Who are you?" Khan asked.

Again the pause. Rostov debated, but then spoke.

"It is not important, but you're an intelligent man—also a brave man. You would probably guess, so I'll tell you anyway. It will clear and hopefully prove to you that we are your friends. But, it at first it will seem unlikely."

The man paused. Khan warily eyed him. The man looked over Khan's shoulder to the injured Khalid Rahman.

"I, too, lost a man last night. You have lost one—soon to be two. It is too bad, I thought the young man had promise."

Khan raised an eyebrow at the familiarity of the man.

"My name is Alexander Rostov. I am a KGB officer based out of the Soviet embassy to the Republic of France, in Paris. I run a network of agents throughout southern France, Italy, and Switzerland. We followed al-As. He illegally entered the United States, drove up the eastern coastline to the fishing village, hired a boat, met up with Bafq el-Rashid . . . "

Rostov decided to go for the throat.

"I assume you did not know about el-Rashid, that he buggered your young man several times. Do I need to go into the details?"

Without waiting for Khan's reply, Rostov continued. He was on a roll. He was going to punish Khan with details. Rostov's voice started to rise slightly, increase in intensity.

"Yes, we have used electronic surveillance the entire time. We have almost every word you and your men have spoken since you have entered the country inside a portable computer. It's all there. We know you have weapons . . . atomic weapons. You have planted one underneath the Willard Hotel in downtown Washington. The second—well, we all know about the second don't we? Personally, I don't give that one much of a chance. Six bodies in a hail of bullets—the police will be everywhere after you—after us. All of us."

Rostov went for the coup de grâce.

"I compliment you on your choices. You took some risk leaving the car—a blue Fairmont—in the hotel. I assume the tape you have talked about is in the automobile," he said with nonchalance.

"How . . . how can you know?" asked Khan, nearly devastated with facts.

"You—we, don't have much time. Let me see if I remember how you phrased it . . . "

Rostov paused.

"Five days will be sufficient—February 25th, 6:00 P.M. Then I think . . . "

"Don't say another word!" said Khan, angrily.

"The hotel wasn't easy, what being underground and all," Rostov drove a hot knife into Khan's ego.

Yes, the man named Rostov knows, Khan thought. They know. They know everything. The Soviets know. Khan had to concentrate. His heart was thumping. He was in mortal danger, as was his plan. This man, these people, stood in his way. But he had the weapons. They were protecting him. Why? The Soviets do nothing for free. *What do they want? So, I still have some leverage.* Khan thought, *not much, but some.* The Soviets weren't completely in control. What do they want? And why?

"What do you want?" asked Khan plainly.

"We want to help you," replied Rostov, turning and facing Khan again.

"I doubt it," said Khan. "The Soviet Union does nothing that is not in its own self-interest. No nation does. You are not acting as individuals but rather as members of the state. You are KGB. Your orders come from Moscow. *I* take orders from no one but Allah and my own conscience. The fact is, you are here . . . for whatever reason the Soviet government wants, you are here. We started as four, now we are three, perhaps two. I will not be captured. If I can't get home, I will detonate the last bomb in the middle of Los Angeles, or some city—then be with Allah. I suspect you will not see your home again, either. I would doubt if your controllers have ensured a safe passage out of this for you. It would be too risky. In any case, if your help meets my needs, I will allow you to help. When it does not, we part ways . . . one way or the other."

Khan had overcome his surprise and had absorbed the facts of the situation quickly. Ideology set aside, for whatever reason, Rostov . . . the Soviets . . . offered a layer of protection which was needed. *Remember the objective! Remember why you are here!* thought Khan. *We are here to make the United States bend, to break its foreign policy, to help restore the economy of Iran and punish the Israelis and the hated Iraqis. If Rostov can help, use him.*

"So . . . you understand where we are headed?" Khan asked, accepting the situation.

A truce had been made.

"Yes, we do. However, we have a suggestion for the placement of your fourth bomb."

Suggestion? His threat is thinly veiled, thought Khan.

"What is your suggestion?" Khan replied, knowing his position was weak.

Khan did not speak the entire ten minutes Rostov took to explain the plan.

"I will think on it," replied Khan, now very weary.

ST. LOUIS

Duffy O'Brien impatiently shifted from one foot to another as he stood watching over the shoulder of sergeant Wilkins, third-shift computer operator, Records Division. His feet were aching—no, screaming—at his brain for a rest. But Duffy's brain knew better. If it allowed Duffy's butt to perch in a chair, we were all going to go to sleep for a while. There was no time for sleep. Sleep would come when we allowed it to.

"Hurry up!" said the clearly ill-tempered, now slightly irrational chief of police.

The sergeant wished he could speed things up, but NCIC had been down during the night for maintenance.

"Sorry, Chief, I can't make it go any faster. These things just seem to get slower and slower. You'd think with all the money the FBI's got . . . "

O'Brien tuned the man out. He didn't want to talk or listen to him. The only thing he wanted to talk to were two cold beers and eight hours of sack.

No, that wasn't true. What he wanted to talk to were the two sons of bitches in the morgue at City Hospital; one with his gut hanging out, the other with half a hatrack. The one with a stomach problem was an average, good-looking, clean-cut young man of 28 or so. The other was—what? an Arab, a European?—a pretty-boy. But both had done some work in their time. Their hands were rough.

O'Brien shifted his weight from one aching foot to the other. Wilkins pointed to the display, his finger leaving another print on the already dirty surface. It hadn't been cleaned in who knew how long. Every inch was covered with grime, layers and layers of oily finger smudges. The green characters were barely legible. Wilkins entered the data on Reynolds, a John Doe.

NO NCIC WANT

Duffy O'Brien wanted to shake the damned thing. Give me a clue! Who is this son of a bitch? Why is he here? Why did he and his friends kill four of my men? What happened down there?

Wilkins went back to the main computer screen and requested another inquiry, then entered the data for Aziz al-As, also a John Doe.

QW.SL338904.NAM/DOE, JOHN.SEX/M.RAC/W.HGT/510.
WGT/155 HAI/BLK.EYE/BRW.SKN/OLV.SMT/NON.
FPC/TT1648POPICI1819AA06.EOT

The inquiry sequence was the same as data entry. If the querying office had data in a field, it indicated it by the standard field abbreviation..NAM, SEX, RAC, etc . . . followed by the known data. In that way they did not have to tell the computer the fields in which they did not have information. It made things faster, and more importantly, reduced the amount of keying errors.

In this case there weren't many good fields. There were a lot of men in the NCIC computer with olive skin, black hair, and brown eyes. It would be the fingerprint field which would trigger the right man.

SL338904
MKE/WANTED PERSON—CAUTION—WANTED ILLEGAL EN-
TRY 0301 ORI/MAN667431.NAM/RAMSEY, JOHN SMITHTON.
SEX/M.RAC/W.

HGT/509.WGT/150.HAI/BLK.FBI/COLD0002.SKN/OLV.SMT/NON.
FPC/TT1648POPICI1819AA06. REF/MAN666890 COLD0001 SUS-
PECT BOARDED FISHING TRAWLER BEDFORD CLIPPER NEW
BEDFORD MA ON 12 FEB NOAH.

"Bingo!" shouted Duffy O'Brien.
His aching feet were temporarily put on the back-burner.
"Print that out," O'Brien ordered.
Wilkins pressed his PF9 key and received a response of REQUEST SENT TO PRINTER. Duffy O'Brien tore the paper off the printer's platen. There was a lot of information there. It was a match, all right. Whoever COLD0002 was had guessed pretty closely on the man's height and weight. Olive complexion. The fingerprints matched.

But, wait . . . SUSPECT BOARDED FISHING TRAWLER BEDFORD CLIPPER NEW BEDFORD MA ON 12 FEB NOAH.

The guy was in the City Hospital morgue.

"Damn!" shouted Duffy.

Change of shift would be in another hour. Duffy O'Brien needed rest badly. Seven A.M. was one of the few times during an entire day when the station was relatively quiet. Normally it was chaos from first shift change through about four-thirty A.M. Even the animals of the night needed sleep sometime. Duffy sure needed his. Wearily, he turned to Worley, who was just as tired, perhaps more.

"Get me the FBI in New York."

Duffy sat down.

It was a mistake. His legs sent messages of thanks all the way up to his shoulders.

WASHINGTON

"You look like ... "

Special Agent Irwin Harding just waved, ignoring and not even hearing the rest of the joke on his condition.

"Why are you going into the office?" his wife had demanded.

It had been a reasonable demand. He felt terrible. Not bad enough to die, but not good enough to live. His temperature had broken yesterday around noon, but it was nearly ten in the evening when he'd been able to give his bathroom toilet a rest. He was drained. He needed at least two days recovery before even thinking about going back to work. Criminals don't take sick days, he thought. It was a professional habit to go to work. It was better to go to work—then leave—than not go to work at all.

"What the hell?" Harding mumbled in irritation at the stack of requests, memos, correspondence, forms, and miscellaneous internal junk—some marked URGENT, others FYI, still others ROUTE AND RETURN.

With a sigh, Harding began to sift through the stack, mentally separating the READ LATER from the JUNK from the DO NOW. He looked at the wire from the New York regional office, an agent named Scott Coldsmith. The wire was properly countersigned by the NY SAC, Murphy Monahan. It went into the DO NOW file along with the other eleven requests which had been allowed to pile up in his in-basket.

The process of going through his mail had been more than Irwin Harding had wanted to do, yet the fact that there was so much to do prevented him from doing what he should have done—go home.

NAGS HEAD

The telephone numbers the man and woman had called were easy to trace. J.J. didn't even need to call Cynthia, his contact at Carolina Telephone Co. in Elizabeth City. The 441 exchange was Nags Head, the 443 Manteo. J.J. recognized the 441 number as one on the list of motels, the Sea Oats, which had already been queried. The motel had had a pair of men who had registered together, arriving on the 15th and departing on the 20th. Each man paid in cash, in advance, and did not use a credit card.

While the names were surely false, the registration clerk at Sea Oats was able to give a description of the men. Both were white males, normal-looking, clean-cut Americans in their late 20s or early 30s.

J.J. was frustrated. He wasn't helping Bart get anything substantial. There weren't going to be many clues left. It had been three days—no, four. Four days! They could be anywhere. The only hard facts they had were the Suburban—that and some partial prints.

J.J. walked out onto the second floor porch of the beach patrol building. The cool wind was less biting today. The barrier island these people lived on had been spared the unmerciful development of other East Coast cities. The bankers had in most cases managed to keep development to a minimum. Nags Head hadn't changed much in the last ten years.

"J.J.!" said Roy, who opened the door and handed him a note.

It was from the FBI agent in Oklahoma City.

HERTZ RECORDS SHOW GEORGE DIJON RENTED A BLUE FORD FAIRMONT ON 8 FEB AT HARTSFIELD AIRPORT, AT-LANTA. HERTZ RECORDS DO NOT SHOW SUBJECT VEHICLE HAS BEEN RETURNED. THE CAR CARRIES GEORGIA LI-CENSE ADH-903. BEST WISHES.

What had he said before? The vehicles were the key. Hot *damn!*

216

NEW YORK

"Coldsmith!" shouted Murphy Monahan.

Scotty hadn't even had a chance to unlock his desk. Putting down his coat he walked back to Murphy's office, his scarf still hanging around his neck. Monahan's secretary rolled her eyes at Scotty. Trouble in River City.

"Where the hell have you been? Everybody in this god-damn office has been looking for you."

Good morning, Mr. Monahan, Scotty thought, his mouth ajar. He'd spent nearly all day yesterday standing and waiting, sitting and waiting, then waiting and waiting for the clerks at the Department of Motor Vehicles to come up with a simple list of the automobiles registered to the Mission of the Union of Soviet Socialist Republics. *Yes, it is a country,* he had patiently told the clerk.

Incredibly, the Soviets had thirty-four vehicles registered to them. Given that this was New York City, and that driving was absurd to begin with, and that the Soviets weren't allowed out of the city, then why did they need an assortment of thirty-four vehicles? And the mixture was rich. There was not one Soviet automobile in the bunch. Four Cadillac limos. Four more late model Mercedes and as many Saabs, three Volvos, three Dodge vans, and miscellaneous Fords and Chevys.

The sons of bitches should take the subway.

Monahan really wasn't interested in Scotty's traffic problems, so Scotty let the question slide.

"I've been on the phone with the St. Louis Chief of Police. They think they've found your sailor-boy," said Monahan, his gruffness losing its edge.

"Ramsey?"

"Yes."

"They've got him?"

"The Chief's name is Duffy O'Brien and he's madder than hell. He wants to know what your boy is doing in St. Louis and why he was involved in a shootout that killed four of his officers."

"Shootout? . . . four . . . what happened?" exclaimed Scotty.

"That's what he wants to know," replied Monahan.

"What about Ramsey?" asked Scotty.

"Dead."

Scotty's face showed his disappointment.

"I told O'Brien you'd be on the first plane to St. Louis. You'd better get going. I'll call the SAC in St. Louis and tell him you're coming.

Before you go see O'Brien, check in first. Goodbye, Coldsmith."

Monahan was giving Scotty a chance to follow through with the case. Just like that. No discussion. Murphy was giving Scotty as much rope as he wanted—plenty enough to hang himself or haul in a big one. It was the best approach to training. The practical was always preferable to the theoretical.

Scotty was in a daze as he packed his briefcase with the records and notes of cases COLD0001 and COLD0002. At eleven-thirty he arrived at LaGuardia Airport and bought a G-class ticket on TWA flight 129 leaving at 12:05. It would arrive in St. Louis at 1:45 CST.

WASHINGTON

"Documentation Office, Ensign Ripley speaking," came the crisp voice over the telephone. One could almost hear Ripley salute on the other end.

"Ripley, this is Lieutenant Bradshaw at Ft. Belvoir. We've had a request from the FBI. I need information on a fishing trawler called the *Bedford Clipper*. Whatever you've got. I've got to put out a bulletin on it right away," said Bradshaw.

Through luck, good timing, and western work ethic, Scotty's request had taken only slightly over twenty-four hours to actually get to the right person within the Coast Guard. Using National Bureau of Standards government measurements, this was considered to be the official speed of light. Given the incredible possibilities for delay, mis-routing, sloth and general application of Murphy's Law, the fact that Scotty's request was being acted upon within a day, was truly amazing. Scotty's request had gone from the ill Irwin Harding through the Domestic Liaison desk of CI-3 in the Intelligence Division. There, the special agent had not been sick, and had received the request directly—without intervention of multiple clerks. A local phone call had been made to the Office of the Secretary of the Department of Transportation in its headquarters building at L'Enfant Plaza, 7th & D Streets. Under Title 14 of the U.S. Code of Law, §1 *Establishment of Coast Guard*, as amended Oct. 18, 1976, the Department of Transportation was the "mother" organization for the Coast Guard. Once within the Coast Guard organization, the request quickly got to the right person . . . Lieutenant Bradshaw. His counterpart, Ensign Ripley, was in the Documentation Office in Norfolk, Virginia.

"Yes, sir. Do you have the registration number?"

"No, I do not. The FBI has given us the task of digging up the information. I'll wait," said Lieutenant Bradshaw, not allowing Ensign Ripley to put him off.

"Yes, sir. Just a moment, sir," replied Ripley.

It did take Ripley only a few minutes to come back with the registration number, description, location, weight/length, ownership history, and insurance data on the *Bedford Clipper*.

"Thank you, ensign," replied Bradshaw as he hung up.

At 4:00 P.M. a message was sent to every Division HQ within the service. Each of the Group HQs were to ensure that all of the operating Groups within their respective commands were notified.

FEBRUARY 24TH

J.J. was in a blue funk. He sat at his small, cluttered desk, and tapped his pencil on his worn notepad. In the dog-eared pages of the book were the leads, the semi-leads, and just plain hopeful leads—some crossed out, some with asterisks next to them, some with people's names. The pad was nearly full.

J.J. had given Roy the day off. They both had been averaging fifteen hours a day for the last week—sometimes twenty. Roy had entered the blue Fairmont into the vehicle file along with the obviously phony name of George Dijon, and tagged the entry with the FBI number of the NCIC entries for Marmande, Dijon, and the two purchased vehicles.

Dijon and Marmande. And a man and a woman. And at least two other strangers who could have been connected. Why here? J.J. sifted through his notes and made a new list.

partial prints on Marmande's windshield—male
partial prints in Sheraton—female, possible male
possible license plate 8644NTO,
description from hotel clerk—female, possible male
description of Dijon from automobile dealer
description of Dijon from construction company
possible prints Dijon in house

local telephone calls to Sea Oats motel
description of two men—"American"
matching tire tracks on abandoned car, Pamlico Sound
late model Dodge Caravan, skid marks
footprints, estimated height and weight of man/woman
Marmande following Dijon
Dijon drove blue Fairmont, no evidence Dijon involved
  in murder—license tag
were man and woman following Dijon? and not Marmande
everyone is gone
key: the Caravan, the Suburban, and the blue Fairmont
damn

J.J. reached over to the stack of mail. Inside were new wanted posters, updates on internal procedures, and—a wire. The wire jumped up at J.J.. It was tucked inside an internal mailer, but the poor dot matrix printing was easily read.

It was from INTERPOL!

The life of John James Carteret was about to change forever.

TO: JOHN JAMES CARTERET
         FBI—ELIZABETH CITY, NORTH CAROLINA USA

FROM: RENÉ CHATILLION
         INTERPOL—PARIS

SUB: YOUR WIRE 22 FEB

REGRET TO INFORM THAT FRENCH CITIZEN JACQUES MARMANDE IS EMPLOYEE OF THIS AGENCY. INSPECTOR MARMANDE LEFT PARIS ON 8 FEB. WHEREABOUTS HAVE BEEN UNKNOWN SINCE THAT DATE.

MARMANDE WAS FOLLOWING A MAN KNOWN AS GEORGE DIJON, ALSO ON SAME DELTA FLIGHT 8 FEB PARIS TO ATLANTA. DIJON AKA KHALID RAHMAN IS KNOWN TO BE SECOND IN COMMAND WITHIN ZAID ABU KHAN JIHAD TERRORIST GROUP.

MARMANDE WAS TO HAVE MADE CONTACT WITH YOUR ORGANIZATION UPON ARRIVAL. FRENCH CUSTOMS SHOW DIJON ENTERING FRANCE IN MARSEILLE ON 6 FEB. MARMANDE TRACKING DIJON/RAHMAN.

THERE ARE NO FINGERPRINTS ON FILE FOR KHALID RAHMAN. I HAVE TELECOPIED WITH THIS WIRE A RECENT PHOTO. HE IS 5'10", 175 POUNDS, 48 YEARS OLD, WITH SCARS ON RIGHT SHOULDER FROM MULTIPLE GUNSHOT WOUNDS IN 1972. IF RAHMAN CAPTURED WE WILL SEEK EXTRADITION TO FRANCE.

PLEASE PREPARE BODY OF JACQUES MARMANDE FOR SHIPMENT TO PARIS. WE WILL WIRE YOU WITH FURTHER DETAILS.

REGRETS IF THIS INCIDENT HAS CAUSED YOU CONCERN.

RENÉ CHATILLION

Regrets! Concern! God-damn INTERPOL has been bagging us all the time! Khalid Rahman—Zaid abu Khan! These were men in the International Terrorism Hall of Fame. What was Rahman doing in the United States?

J.J.'s mind raced ahead. Rahman was Dijon. An infamous Arab terrorist had been playing house, just like a regular tourist, on the Outer Banks of North Carolina. Not France, not Spain, not Italy—none of the places Arab terrorists were supposed to be. No—he had been on the serene white beaches of North Carolina. *Under my nose! God damn it!*

J.J.'s hand rested on the telephone. He hated to make the call. As soon as he raised the flag, it would be all over. What had been his case would now be their case. J.J. would be lost in the flurry of activity, absorbed and sent to the rear by the squadrons of young shiny faces from Charlotte and then by droves from Washington. Every young agent in the Bureau would want a crack at finding Khalid Rahman—how good it would look on their record. It didn't matter that he'd done all the leg work, got the facts. What management would remember was that an Arab terrorist came through J.J. Carteret's territory. There had been only scattered feeble attempts by world terrorist groups to infiltrate the United States. Until now, they all had been thwarted.

Rahman had gotten in through Atlanta, purposefully driven here, stayed for two weeks, then just as purposefully left, most likely after meeting someone.

The conclusion would be obvious to anyone listing the facts, as Washington would. Khalid Rahman was meeting up with an American underground force—either to commit an act of terrorism or to plan one.

The risk on Rahman's part was tremendous, so the payoff must be of equal value.

At least turn over complete records, J.J. thought. Once the alarm goes off, they'll be over you like locusts on a field of new wheat. Why doesn't this record show this? Why doesn't that record show that? Pick and pick and pick. No matter what good had been done, no matter what procedures had been followed, J.J. knew he wasn't going to come out in good shape.

He picked up the phone and dialed.

"Bart, I'm afraid I've got some bad news . . . "

FAYETTEVILLE, ARKANSAS

"We have made a truce of sorts with Khan. He has plans for all but one of the weapons. We will be in Dallas tonight. That means three of his bombs will be placed, leaving two. "Can he be persuaded?" said Korz in a firm voice.

Katrina paused, seeking the right answer.

"We aren't sure he can be turned. He is planning to notify the Americans tomorrow afternoon. Until then, we can't touch him. He wants to set the next bomb and be well away. It means a lot of driving. We're getting ready to leave now," she said.

"Katrina," Korz urged. "When? When is the Washington weapon to be detonated? Is it real?"

"Yes, we think it's real. The one in St. Louis is. We don't know the exact time. We're guessing sometime late tomorrow afternoon. We've heard bits and pieces of their conversations since they got off the boat, but we haven't been able to pinpoint the exact time. Rostov told Khan that we knew everything, but it was just a guess. Khan doesn't suspect. But, it is tomorrow."

"How long will it take you to get to the target?" Korz asked, anxiously.

Katrina hesitated.

"I don't know. It's over a thousand miles from Dallas to the target. Distances are great between places out here."

"Do you have any idea how he plans to implement his threat?"

"No," said Katrina. "We don't know what's on that tape. We haven't approached him with our plans. We've barely had time to sleep. We're leaving in a matter of minutes. Rostov doesn't think so, but I think we will have to fight Khan within the next two days. We are too open out here, Dimitri."

"But the timing . . . what about the timing?" anxiously asked Korz.

"Assuming we leave Dallas tonight and drive as far as we can, and assuming Khan buys the fact that our site is just as good as his, perhaps better—and that nothing else goes wrong—then we could be at the location by late in the day, the day after tomorrow," said Katrina.

"Sites, Katrina. Sites, plural," reminded Korz.

"Yes, I'm sorry. Sites. You're right. That, of course, absolutely means we must have an arrangement made either before we leave Dallas or shortly afterwards. Are my instructions the same?" she asked.

"They are. If you cannot persuade him, then kill him. If in the end he resists, kill him," said Korz intensely. "Now, most important of all . . . what about the timing?" asked Korz.

"Yes, the timing. Seven . . . no, six o'clock Friday the 26th, the day after tomorrow. They are on a different time schedule, an hour earlier. It will be eight o'clock New York time. What time will it be in Moscow— I can't think."

"They will not be paying attention to time in Moscow, my dear Katrina. Goodbye."

Korz disconnected. The time and date were set. Moscow would have two days to make final preparations. The seismic equipment in Moscow would tell them of the explosions, as would the satellite photography. It would be the signal for the Soviet takeover of the Middle East and the entrapment of Pakistan. The Soviet Union would at long last have access to the Persian Gulf and the Indian Ocean.

Glasnost would be dead. The years of careful window-dressing in world diplomacy would be dead. But the result would be worth the price. Mikhail Sergeyvich Gorbachev would live forever in Soviet history books as the leader that single-handedly brought Mother Russia to her rightful position of the worldwide dominance envisioned by Lenin.

ST. LOUIS

Duffy O'Brien's mood had not changed. It remained as sour as it had been for the previous eight hours—and with good reason. Duffy had been unable to get roadblocks on Interstates 55, 44, and 70. For one reason or another—the late hour, the weather, politics—he'd been unable to conduct a car-by-car search for his killers.

"OK, who is this son of a bitch?" Duffy asked with cigarette hoarseness and Irish bluntness.

"His name is John . . . "

"Jesus Christ! You didn't come all the way out here to give me that crap? I can read! What's his real name? Who is this son of a bitch?" Duffy shouted.

Scotty was glad there was a desk between the two of them. The local FBI office had been glad to have Scotty follow up on this case. But if there was one thing Scotty had discovered about himself in the last month it was that he didn't like to be pushed. Being pushed into the Acushnet River was enough. He wasn't going to be emotionally bullied when he didn't have to be. And this was not a case where he had to be.

"Chief O'Brien, I didn't kill your men. It was the Missouri State Police who missed the roadblocks, not me. As far as I knew, John Smithton Ramsey was at sea. It was only yesterday when I was allowed to put a tracer on the *Bedford Clipper*. I've told you everything I know, and that's a hell of a lot more than you'd get from most FBI agents. I've told you everything because I want to get those sons of bitches more than you do, and *maybe*, just maybe, you'll have a clue for me. I'm sorry for your four dead patrolmen. I'm sorry the state police didn't block the roads. I'm sorry it's snowing. But I can't help any of it. There's a Soviet spy—two of them, maybe more—who are involved. I don't know why. It has taken Ramsey—and I don't have another name for him—twelve days to get here, including time spent at sea. He's come from east to west and I bet that whomever he was with, or whoever killed him, has gone farther west."

"My men killed him," said the subdued Duffy O'Brien, sitting down.

"Where would you go?" Scotty asked.

"If I was going to escape? Easy. I'd go to Chicago and get lost in a southside hotel for a couple of weeks."

"Where else?"

The young agent had gotten the police chief to forget about Scotty's age.

"There's plenty of places—southwest to the Ozarks, southeast to the Kentucky Lakes or into Tennessee."

"Could I go out to the scene? Do you have someone who could take me?"

"Worley!" shouted O'Brien.

Paul Worley was much closer to Scotty in age, but he looked terrible—deep, dark bags under his eyes and red highways through his eyes. Worley was paying a price to someday get O'Brien's job. He was carrying a heavy load of mental baggage.

The two men introduced each other. Scotty thanked the chief and left as Worley made his way to the elevator.

"Do you want to see the body first?" Worley asked.

"Might as well get it over with," replied Scotty, trying to be cool. *He hated morgues.*

Twenty minutes later he was looking at what was left of John Smithton Ramsey's skull.

Ugh, thought Scotty, repulsed by the color and texture of death.

It was Ramsey. How long ago had it been? Was it only two weeks ago that he'd followed Ramsey down the cobblestones of Union Street in New Bedford? It seemed like months. Where had Ramsey gone? Scotty looked at the rusty brown fragments of skin and brain tissue and got angry. Where in hell did you go, you son of a bitch? How'd you get here?

"How was he killed?" asked Scotty.

"By one of our patrolmen," interjected Worley. "We're not sure who."

The coroner looked at Worley, then at Scotty.

"Not unless this came from a .38 police special," said the coroner, dropping a 7.62mm shell into a cold, stainless steel trey.

Both men knew the difference in the slugs. Worley was astonished. *Ramsey was killed by his own men?* Scotty's mind raced. *Why?*

"Are you saying that this man was not killed by the police?" Scotty asked confirmation.

"Yes," replied the coroner.

"Jesus," muttered Paul Worley.

"What else did you find?" Scotty asked the coroner.

"Not much. He's not one of us, that's for sure. He hasn't been immunized or circumcised," replied the coroner.

"What about his clothes?" Scotty asked.

"They're in the bag," the coroner answered while reaching under the gurney for the plastic envelope of clothes.

Scotty emptied the contents out on a nearby spotlessly clean stainless steel counter. The loose pocket change rattled on the hard surface. The clothes had been bought at a Ben Franklin store. They were fairly new. They looked like they were getting dirty for the first time. While it was possible that Ramsey could have bought the clothes in New Bedford after that night, he certainly didn't buy them between New York and New Bedford. It would be easy to check out if there was a Ben Franklin in the New Bedford area. If not, then Ramsey bought them after the *Bedford Clipper* was docked. The obvious deduction was that the clothes came from a Ben Franklin near the coast. While the obvious didn't always hold true, the obvious was easier to check out.

"Do you want to see the other one?"

Not particularly, Scotty thought.

"Sure, why not?" he answered.

Scotty didn't recognize the man.

"I'd like to see the scene," Scotty asked Worley, looking away from the dead man.

Ten minutes later they were in Worley's plain brown late-model Dodge on Memorial Drive northbound. The arch was off to the right. The mall area was covered with snow. Eighteen degrees seemed colder in St. Louis than it did in New York, thought Scotty. Maybe it was the wind blowing from Alberta down over nine hundred miles of flat, open land.

Worley turned right on Washington and dropped downhill to the corner of Wharf Street where he met up with two police cars who still blocked the intersection off from normal traffic—not that there was much in February, anyway. Still, Worley put on his portable bubble to let folks know that the police were here. The two men got out.

"We found the boy here," said Worley pointing to the dirty area under the tracks.

Scotty walked over to the position of where the second police car had come roaring down Washington hill the night before. The outline was marked in the middle of the street. Scotty walked over to it, looked back down the hill to the intersection and tried to picture two policemen arriving on a scene, then getting caught in a crossfire. Scotty walked down to the roped-off intersection. The skid marks were obvious.

"We've got samples for your boys in Washington."

The gnomes. The gnomes would figure it out.

"Have they gone out?" asked Scotty.

"This morning, as soon as we got them ready," replied Worley.

"I'm interested. I want to know the results, no matter what."

The look on Scotty's face belied his age. Worley could see the intensity in his face.

"Sure," he replied.

Scotty looked around.

"They used 9mm Berettas. Submachine guns. Dierdorf and Wilson never had a chance," informed Worley.

Somehow it wasn't a coincidence. Rostov had been here. Only now there were more of them. Was the woman here? How many were there?

"Come on, turkey—think!" he mumbled to himself, his breath caught in sharp darts of white smoke.

Scotty looked up Washington—then north under the Eads Bridge up Wharf Street. The second man had been killed north of the bridge. He'd come by car and left by ambulance. The cars were gone. There were at least two of them.

"What about any other shell casing or bullets you might have found?" Scotty asked.

"We've got them, but we can't come up with the type. It's something for the FBI."

There had been at least four of them. This was a full-scale Soviet operation. What the hell was going on? The Soviets had intervened and helped kill four St. Louis policemen.

"What did the patrolmen say, again?" Scotty asked.

"There was a vehicle parked under the bridge," said Worley.

Why was Ramsey here? Who was he with? Were they meeting someone here? Ramsey had gotten from someplace along the east coast—someplace with a Ben Franklin store—and had come to St. Louis, Missouri—in the dead of winter—to this god-forsaken place. How long does it take to drive from the East Coast? Two days was reasonable. That left ten days. Ramsey left New Bedford on the 12th—there were ten days left unaccounted for. Was he at sea all of that time? How fast do boats go? How far is it from New Bedford to Sable Island? Could he believe old Mrs. Triolo? It was hard to do the math in his head while standing under a cold bridge. Scotty came back to reality.

"What's the name of this bridge?" asked Scotty.

"The Eads Bridge." replied Worley, stamping around to keep warm.

Scotty walked back up underneath the train tracks, near the abutment of the Eads Bridge. His mind was racing in several directions. There were more people involved. More Soviets. More—more *Ramseys*. Scotty leaned back on the bridge and tried to envision what had happened. To his right was a boarded-up entrance way, probably to keep drifters out.

He couldn't see it. There was no vision.

The Soviets were protecting Ramsey. That was Scotty's gut reaction. Ramsey had come here—for whatever purpose—and had been surprised by the police. The Soviets came to his rescue by killing four policemen.

Where did they go?

WASHINGTON

"Sir, this has just come in. It's important."

William Sessions, Director of the Federal Bureau of Investigation, had one of the best views of the U.S. Capitol building in Washington. Unfortunately, he didn't get much of a chance to look out the window.

Sessions' aid, Craig Wainwright, had been the Special-Agent-in-Charge in Omaha and wanted one of the larger Regional Offices. He was spending his duty time in Washington, and it was his pleasure to be in the hot seat. Wainwright had the job that every agent who aspired to higher grade levels wanted—administrative assistant to the Director. It wasn't a job for the faint-hearted or thin-skinned. Wainwright was neither.

Wainwright summarized the note for Sessions as the director read it.

"The Charlotte regional office reports that there is evidence of Arab terrorist infiltration—specifically, by a man named Khalid Rahman. I have his folder. It's not much."

Wainwright placed a thin jacket in front of the director. Indeed, it wasn't much. Other than a name, a few bad photos, and sketchy personal information from INTERPOL, there wasn't much on the man.

"The SAC in Charlotte is Jim Bailey," Wainwright continued. Sessions couldn't mentally picture Bailey.

"When?" asked Sessions.

"Our agent in eastern North Carolina now thinks that Rahman has been staying along the coast for the past two weeks. He believes that Rahman stayed on the Outer Banks until the 20th, then left in a Chevy Suburban purchased for cash in North Carolina."

"Cash?"

"Yes, then Rahman linked up with an unknown group—we have no evidence one way or the other."

"How have we found out?"

"Our agent has been working with the local police on a murder investigation. A national Park Service ranger was shot and killed while on duty—several other people were killed as well."

"I think I remember it in one of my updates," said Sessions, handing the folder back to Wainwright.

"Yes, sir. There's more," Wainwright paused. "It appears that INTERPOL sent an agent to track Rahman, and didn't inform us."

Sessions let out a string of expletives. No matter how much each of the national agencies opened up, each country still thought that their sovereignty had no limits—whatever could be gotten away with, was OK.

"What does the Agency have?" he asked, referring to the CIA.

"There hasn't been time . . . " replied Wainwright.

It was the wrong answer. Administrative assistants were always supposed to have the answer. Not only that, they were to anticipate the problem and have the answer—just in case the question was asked. It was unfair, but that was the way The System worked.

"I'll find out right away, sir," said Wainwright, not allowing Sessions to smoke him.

"What's being done right now?" asked Sessions.

"CID's sending a team to North Carolina this afternoon. The agent *has* developed a lead on three automobiles. We've notified our regional offices and sent wires to the appropriate state highway patrols," replied Wainwright.

As they were speaking, a team from the Espionage section of the FBI's Criminal Investigation Division had deplaned from their short Piedmont flight from National airport to Norfolk. From there they would drive directly to Elizabeth City, then to Manteo.

"Does C1 know about this?" Sessions ranted angrily.

The C1 and C2 sections within the Intelligence Division were the interface between the FBI and all other intelligence agencies throughout the world. One group had responsibility strictly for "Activities of Foreign Intelligence."

"No, but they will. The damage has been done."

"I want those bastards reamed on this one," Sessions muttered.

It was an idle threat and Sessions knew it. Everybody did it. Occasionally things got out of hand. This might be one of those times. It was the threat which everyone feared, because terrorism was almost impossible to stop. Anybody could kill anybody if they had a mind to. With help, one Arab terrorist could hide for a long time in the United

States. How much damage could *one* Arab terrorist do? More psychological than anything else . . . probably.

"I want the son of a bitch found," said Sessions with finality. "What does Customs say? Why didn't they catch him? That's their job, isn't it?" Sessions said sarcastically.

If something really bad happened, the blame would fall on the FBI. Some of it could be fobbed off to Treasury, but that could be blamed on a lack of people—a lack of funding. Treasury hadn't had a real budget for a decade, what with the annual abortion amendment placed on it by the right-to-lifers. The agency had been living with the infamous Continuing Resolution for what seemed like forever. Their budget simply continued on from the previous fiscal year with a small addition for inflation. No, the real blame would fall back on the FBI.

"Damn!" Sessions said as Wainwright left the room.

He would have to make sure the White House was informed. Whether the president was actually told anything or not was irrelevant. That was the responsibility of his Chief of Staff and the people who reported to him. What was important to the FBI was that they alerted the White House—what the White House did was its business. Although the president couldn't fire him, the heat generated could blow away many a political career. As mandated by Congress, the director of the FBI had a ten-year term. The J. Edgar Hoover Bill had been enacted after the late director's death to prevent the coronation of a life-long agency head.

Sessions punched his telephone, buzzing his secretary.

"Get me the Chief of Staff at the White House."

MANTEO

The locusts had arrived.

Hoards of FBI agents were combing through every detailed account of every call made by J.J. and all the local Dare County police. J.J. had been right in his assessment. Not only wasn't he participating, he wasn't wanted. He was nothing more than a piece of evidence, a witness. Everything was "we'll take over from here" or "I bet you'll be glad to get back to your routine." Jim Bailey had done nothing to help him, to keep him involved. The locusts had come and had devoured his case.

The case jackets were photocopied a hundred times, as were his notes, observations, and personal contacts list. It was embarrassing to have some square-jawed law school grad from Bethesda call up his contacts at the telephone company, Hertz, and the airlines. By duplicating what had already been done—and done properly, timely, and accurately—they were ruining his contacts, and making J.J. look like a schmuck. They went back through every process, even down to Henry Onslow's fingerprint collection—which had already made its way to Washington. After two hours of being ignored, J.J. waved at Bart.

"I'm going out for a beer. See you tomorrow."

And that's exactly what J.J. did. J.J. was on the fringe of several conversations in which other agents speculated where Rahman would have gone. The consensus was north, up through Washington, Baltimore, Philadelphia, New York, Boston—as if that were where all good terrorists should go. By dinner time the beach patrol office had been turned into a mini-command center. Task forces were being devised and manned.

But J.J. knew they would soon tire of being in such an isolated place as the Outer Banks. The action would be up north—catch the terrorists!

This was a Headquarters operation now.

J.J. slid out of the office and slowly drove over to T.J. Mundy's. It would be dark before he would come out.

DALLAS, TEXAS

They stood and watched as the driverless two-car Airtrans train slowly made its automatic way into the darkened section of Terminal D on another of its twenty-four trips a day around the overwhelming circumference of the Dallas/Ft. Worth Airport, known to all who hated it as DFW—and the F didn't stand for Fort. The Department of Transportation had decided that because it was in Texas, the biggest god-damned airport in the world should be built there. When they finished, planners then realized that perhaps, just perhaps, people—real people—might want to actually change airlines from one flight to the next.

Seemingly this thought had never occurred to the Department of Transportation planners. Why would anyone want to transfer from Delta to American . . . or Continental to American . . . or even American to American? The four semicircular terminals were separated by distances of up to two miles. Getting a cab to leave his precious place in line to take a passenger from one terminal to another was impossible. Driving was out of the question. Instead, the passenger—laden with as much carry-on luggage as legally allowed—was forced to exit the terminal into baggage area, locate one of the few poorly placed signs—and under-stand what the acronym Airtrans meant in real language—then take an escalator down to the arrival area, negotiate the automatic doors and pay turnstiles, pay fifty cents, wait and eventually take a surface train from one terminal to another. Upon arrival at the correct terminal the pas-senger had the privilege of going through the lines at the security scanners again. A frequent flyer only had to do this once before learning the lesson—don't change airlines in Dallas.

Behind O'Hare, Hartsfield, and Los Angeles International, Dallas/Ft. Worth was the most-used airport in the United States. It was home for American Airlines and second in use for Delta. Like O'Hare and Harts-field, DFW was important because of its role as a switch in the cog of American transportation. ORD and DFW were critical links in the east-west air traffic flow across the United States.

There were three stops at each of the terminals, roughly one-third of the distance along the half-mile long terminals. Terminal D, stop 1, had at one time been used by Braniff, but now was mostly unused. Still, the trains stopped and the recorded messages played.

"I will stay and watch," said Khalid Rahman, sitting up, shifting to get into the driver's seat.

All day long Rahman had listened to the frank discussion of "what ifs" and had gradually forced himself to become more alert. By the end of the afternoon Khalid was actually sitting up, smiling, and talking with Khan. He was hurting badly. While the bleeding of his wounds had stopped, his system could not make up for the loss of blood. He was weak. The bullets had done terminal damage to his body. Khan looked at his friend. Life was fading out of his eyes.

"I am dying," said Khalid.

"Yes, my friend," replied Khan.

El-Rashid pulled the Suburban close to curb, the Caravan behind it, the car driven by Williams trailed. Casually, Bafq el-Rashid opened the back of the Suburban. People arriving at the airport didn't stop to look

232

at them. For the average passenger, the field of concentration is fairly narrow. Although cameras scan the parking lots and loading areas, there would be little to distinguish Khan, el-Rashid, and Katrina from any group of tourists who were struggling slightly with a heavy piece of luggage.

"I want you to come with me," Khan said to Rostov, who shrugged and waved for Katrina to accompany him. Rostov would have had it no other way.

The weapon was in a box, and airlines took boxes of all sorts and sizes and packaging. Williams and Rahman stayed in their vehicles. It would be an hour before they would be back to the same position. Each of the cars would have to be moved several times. The last thing they needed was to draw attention to themselves. Williams and Rahman would park the cars in short-term parking, then wait for the Airtrans to return.

Within minutes a two-car train came by. There were passengers inside—their eyes glassed over with the slowness of the transfer.

"Wait for the next one," said Khan.

In another five minutes came another car. Both of the heavily shaded cars were empty. From its underground position the Airtrans slowly made its way out from the enplaning ramp of Terminal D and headed out over the flat Texas countryside toward the first American terminal, terminal A. The cars had no cameras inside. There were bench seats on three sides of each car. Khan and el-Rashid immediately went to work on the bench seat to their left, el-Rashid producing an all-purpose tool kit with screwdrivers and wrenches of all sorts and sizes. The plastic-coated seat cushions covered an unused storage area underneath. In some systems the compartment was used for spare parts. In Airtrans it had been easier and more cost-effective to install this type of seat. Quickly the Phillips screws were removed and the seat cushion removed. There was plenty of room for the weapon.

"Careful," said Khan, as all four of them lifted the bulky weapon from the floor and into the empty compartment under the seat.

Rostov and Katrina concentrated on the simple movements made by el-Rashid. It took twelve minutes for the train to move from Terminal D to the third stop at American's Terminal A. It had taken them eight minutes of moderate work to place the weapon.

At 3:15 P.M. (CST) Sunday, April 19—Easter Sunday—an atomic bomb would be automatically detonated from Airtrans car number 3381. Because DFW was so large, only one of the terminals would be vaporized. The rest would be destroyed, but it was possible that people could survive. It all depended upon where car 3381 was at the time and what unlucky souls were nearby.

They spent an uneasy hour slowly circling the four terminals. At 9:12 they were back at terminal D. Williams was the only one waiting for them.

"He's gone," Williams said simply. "We parked the cars—one minute he was there, the next he wasn't."

Khan knew what Khalid had done. He'd gone off to die. When they located the Suburban, Rahman's wallet with identification was on the front seat. From Khan's standpoint, there was no need for an explanation. But Rostov was furious.

"Where is he? What happened?"

"We do not repay loyalty with murder. He is dying and he knows it. Allah rewards those who die in battle with paradise. Khalid Rahman will find paradise. It is not important that we return to our home. We have come here already knowing what fate Allah has prepared for us. By leaving, Khalid will save us the trouble of dealing with his death—but do not fear, he will not be taken alive. He has a gun."

We were better off if he'd been stuffed in a trash bin someplace, or down a sewer drain, thought Rostov. But, what was done, was done. The cold Dallas night smelled of jet exhaust. Rostov was tired.

"It's time to talk, Khan. We have gotten you this far. If you want to go any further, you will listen to me. You will ride with me. We will talk, you and I."

Khan stared at his counterpart for a long minute, then followed Rostov to the Caravan. They would talk.

ST. LOUIS

" . . . Jacksonville, Fort Pierce, Miami and Miami Beach, Sarasota, Tallahassee, Pensacola . . ."

The list of the Ben Franklin stores seemed endless—and depressing.

" . . . Lake Charles, Galveston and Corpus Christi. That seems to be about it, Mr. Coldsmith."

Scotty thanked the woman then looked at his list of 32 port or near-port cities along the east and gulf coasts. There was a real good chance the *Bedford Clipper* was near one of them. But so what? Ramsey had shown up in St. Louis with his head nearly blown off. He'd come with somebody, and that somebody had left him dead in the streets.

Scotty didn't know whom to call.

Who in Washington was responsible for sending the wire to the Coast Guard? What was the status? The thought of having to first find out where the Coast Guard station was, then calling each commander . . . there wasn't enough time!

Scotty felt paralyzed. There was so much to do but it was all in different directions. Pick something! Do something! he told himself. Should he start with Florida or Maine?

"*Jesus!*" he berated himself. "*Make a decision!*"

He looked at the map again. Start with Jacksonville and move north.

DALLAS

"Hey, buddy—it's the end of the road," said the Surtran driver as he shook the sleeping man. "Mister . . . ?"

For two hours after slipping out of the Suburban, Khalid Rahman had walked through the seemingly endless maze of underground parking at DFW searching for a car whose owner had forgotten to lock. At 11:30 P.M. he'd found a Plymouth Duster in the long-term parking area, crawled inside and bled all over the back seat. His life passed through his dreams during the night. Allah would reward him for being a foot soldier of the true faith, dying in battle against the supreme enemy.

At seven-thirty on the morning of the 25th, Khalid, his body racked with pain, struggled outside and started to walk as best he could away from the parking area. He had to give Khan as much distance as he could. The gunshot wounds ached and burned so much. It seemed to take him forever to first climb a concrete stairway up two levels, then find an elevator to the arrival area of Braniff Airlines. His coat covered his wounds, although blood ran down his arm. At 10:30 he boarded a Surtran bus bound for the downtown hotel area, with intermediate stops in Las Colinas. It was noon before the bus finally stopped at the Hyatt.

At 12:20 P.M. CST the Dallas police arrived, along with an ambulance sent from Parkland Hospital. Khalid Rahman was dead.

TUCUMCARI, NEW MEXICO

Tucumcari wasn't much more than a few scrubby trees midway between flat and not so flat. However, it did have a Denney's, and of course, it was always open. It also had a phone.

It was 4:00 P.M. in Washington and time to deliver the Ultimatum. Khan was oblivious to the cold wind slapping the right side of his face. This was it. In a few minutes the president would be groveling at his feet—furiously angry, but unable to do anything but comply with his wishes. Khan smiled as he dialed the number.

In Washington, D.C. the number of the White House is listed in the business section of the White Pages. There were four separate numbers; presidential inquiries (202-456-7639), the switchboard (202-456-1414), tours (202-456-7041), and a number for the U.S. Secret Service (202-395-2020).

"Please deposit three dollars and forty-five cents," came the digitized voice.

Khan deposited his quarters and dimes from a stack piled up near the base of the black phonebox.

"Thank you," came the automated reply.

Within five seconds Khan's countenance changed to black clouds. He'd gotten a circuits-busy signal, the fast busy tone indicating heavy traffic somewhere on the line—the same signal received by millions of Americans on Mother's Day, Christmas, and Easter—and on a day when twelve inches of wet snow had already fallen in Washington. There was no sign it was going to stop anytime soon.

Katrina looked on from the warm confines of the Caravan, Rostov stood outside with Khan. Rostov's face showed concern, but then he was concerned about everything. Khan became obviously upset. He pulled out his sheet of paper, page 352 of the Washington, D.C. white pages, business section. He dialed again, and again loaded in the change. Busy again.

It was 2:05–4:05 in Washington. The weapon was set to explode in less than two hours. Neither the Soviets nor the terrorists had any clue to what was actually happening back East with the weather. Neither had read an American newspaper, listened to American radio, or watched American television. The winter storm which had grazed St. Louis two nights before had dropped to the south, rushed into the warm waters off Georgia, reformed and started up the Carolina coastline where it slowly made its way north—angrily drawing in Atlantic Ocean moisture over the still-frozen land. The result was a meteorological disaster. Cities from Richmond to Philadelphia had been caught unprepared.

In Washington, the problem was made worse by the Office of Management and Budget's inability to decide if the government workers were required to come to work or not. A no-decision meant yes, the workers had to report on time. It wasn't until 10:00 that the director of OBM told everyone to go home. As a result the 200 badly worn-out snowplows in the District were unable to get to the streets and clear the snow. The snow evacuation routes out of the city quickly became parking lots. The METRO subway system closed down because snow covered the hot third-rail track on the above-ground sections. By midday, downtown Washington was virtually closed down. But Zaid abu Khan only knew that something was wrong with the telephone. It was 4:10 (EST) when Khan slammed the telephone down and muttered to himself

"What's wrong?" asked Rostov, stepping close to the angry Khan.

"The phone isn't working," said Khan, looking around for another. If there was another outdoor pay telephone in Tucumcari, New Mexico, its location wasn't obvious. The phones in America always worked. Rostov took the phone and repeated the process. Katrina got out of the car.

"What does this mean?" Rostov asked her.

Katrina listened. The signal was familiar to New Yorkers.

"The phone is not broken. The circuits are filled. You'll have to wait."

Wait? World War III was an hour and forty minutes away. The bomb would detonate without the Arab threat being delivered. Soviet seismologists would detect the detonation of a weapon, relay the signal to the army who would start the invasion of Iran. Regardless of what words were said by Gorbachev, the military government in the United States would blame the Soviets and launch a counter—there would be no evidence to the contrary.

This time Katrina tried the phone. Still busy.

"Is there a military base nearby?" asked Rostov.

The wind whipped Khan's map. There probably was, but it was difficult to see.

It was 4:28. The Americans would need every minute they could to get to the weapon and defuse it. Katrina grabbed the phone and dialed a number.

"Credit card call . . ." and she gave the operator the number.

NEW YORK

Today was the day the Americans would be warned. As a matter of fact, it was probably happening right this moment. Dimitri Korz smiled in satisfaction at the extreme discomfort the Americans would have. It was about time. Korz looked down onto 67th Street where the scene never changed—policemen, limos, joggers, tourists, demonstrators—and the CIA and FBI.

Korz was slightly startled as his desk phone rang. It was his private line. He tensed. Only a few people knew the connection—Moscow, Ambassador Kemeravo . . .

"Dimitri . . ." came the high pitched voice of Katrina Tambov through the encryption system.

Korz was relieved . . . yes, Katrina had the number. She was troubled. No, more than troubled. There was a problem and she was about to involve him. Korz listened as Katrina told him the situation.

"The bomb is set to explode at 6:00, Dimitri."

Korz involuntarily looked at his wristwatch. It was 4:35 EST.

"It is snowing in Washington, Katrina. A bad storm."

The first flakes of the storm's leading edge had crept up the coastline and had begun to dust the sidewalks of New York with a white residue.

"We cannot get through to warn them. You must make the call."

I must make the call? Korz thought. Ambassador Kemeravo, along with a handful of his top staff, had flown to Moscow from Dulles last night as a precaution. Unaware of what was happening, the rest of the embassy staff would have to take their chances.

"You must call, Dimitri!" implored Katrina, her voice anxious. "The number is area 202-456-1414. This is what you must say . . ."

It was 4:40 and snowing in New York City.

WASHINGTON

Adrian Graves had worked on the White House switchboard since 1968 and had in the last two years become second in seniority and was now the daytime supervisor, a job which meant she could live a relatively normal life. Although they were still very much underpaid

238

considering their responsibilities, the operators at the White House were paid higher than normal wages. And rightly so. Each operator had to sift through a maze of wrong numbers, prank calls, legitimate inquiries, normal business, urgent messages, angry wives . . . and occasionally, trouble.

Always alert, Adrian quickly picked up on a hand signal from one of her operators, a young girl from Pennsylvania who had joined the staff only last year. She was very quick. From her control panel Adrian tapped into the call. In the same moment she started the trace. AT&T had installed a special computer system which enabled any inbound call to be traced at the initiation of the White House. It was the supervisor's responsibility to start the process.

The tracer also activated the tape system which would record the conversation.

"I will say this once, and once only. I expect this is being recorded, however if it is not, I will speak as slowly and clearly as I can . . ."

Adrian scratched impressions on a notepad. The man was white. He had a European accent. The call was not local.

" . . . Two blocks from you there is an automobile parked in the third level under the Willard Hotel. It is blue Ford Fairmont, Georgia license ADH-903. The door is locked, the keys are on the floor of the driver's side . . ."

The man believes what he is saying—but then, most cranks do.

" . . . Inside the trunk is an atomic weapon. The timing mechanism is set for 6:00 P.M. today, roughly an hour from now . . ."

Adrian and her operator looked up at the clock at the same time. It was 4:56.

" . . . Under the passenger seat is a tape which has been sent to the President of the United States from Zaid abu Khan."

Click. The call was disconnected. The computer stopped tracing, the tape stopped recording. Atomic weapon. Zaid abu Khan. Atomic weapon.

Was it a crank? A looney?

Adrian pushed two buttons. The call had come from New York City, area 212. But the computer, as fast as it was, hadn't been able to reverse the path of the call to the exact phone. Somebody from New York had placed a long distance call, hadn't asked to speak with the president, hadn't threatened the president, but had passed on a warning. The man knew he was being traced.

With secretarial speed Adrian tapped out a number on her console. It was the control desk of the Secret Service, also located in the basement of the White House.

"Jenkins," was the stiff reply.

"This is Adrian Graves at the switchboard. I've received a threat which I think needs to be investigated . . . and quickly."

It was 5:02.

Jack Jenkins was a second-line Secret Service supervisor, currently detailed to the White House. This afternoon he was supervising himself. Before the phone rang, he had been watching the wet snow fall onto Pennsylvania Avenue, which by now was in a state of gridlock. *Where did the pigeons go in the winter?* he thought. Except for one man picketing for some cause that burned through his gut, no one walked the street. Jack had watched the snow pile up on the man's clothes all day long, until now all that was discernible was the red of his hat. It took guts to believe in something that hard.

In the thirty seconds it took Adrian Graves to tell him what had happened, Jack Jenkins had already analyzed the possible decisions. The man in the red hat was forgotten. Jenkins trusted the woman's intuition. This was so far off the wall that it could possibly be accurate.

An atomic bomb in the parking lot of the Willard Hotel! If 6:00 was accurate, it would take 20 minutes for Chopper 1 to clear the president and his family out of Washington—assuming the weather wouldn't be too bad for liftoff. The snow was heavy, lift was difficult. Dulles, National, and BWI airports had been closed for six hours.

It was 5:07.

Jack went to his command console. He could speak directly to any Secret Service agent covering the president. Every agent had two-way communications.

"I want Chopper 1 here in fifteen minutes to evacuate the president," Jenkins said calmly to the helipad.

He lightly touched the keypad of the touch-sensitive pad which put him inside the right ear of the agent standing outside the door of president's office. The president and the first lady were doing what many people in Washington were doing, they were sitting by the window watching the winter storm. It was quite beautiful.

"Yes," said Earl Hardy, chief of staff to the president, picking up the private phone on the first ring.

"Mr. Hardy, this is Jack Jenkins downstairs. We've received a threat against the president. The caller said that there is an atomic weapon nearby—under the Willard Hotel."

"Jesus," muttered Hardy.

The White House received threats all the time.

"Mrs. Graves heard the call. She thinks the caller thinks it's for real," added Jenkins.

Adrian Graves had a good reputation. Earl Hardy twisted the beige telephone cord. It was a nervous habit. He went through six or eight cords a year. Evacuate the president?

"Have you called the FBI?" asked Hardy.

"No, sir. You're the first one I've called," replied Jenkins.

"Thank you, Jack," said the president's chief of staff. "I'll call."

Evacuation was only for the president and his family. Hardy, his staff, the president's staff, the computer operators, the maintenance crew, the kitchen workers, the switchboard . . . all would remain.

The clock read 5:14.

Hardy's right leg bounced with anxious energy as he called the FBI.

"God damn it!" he shouted as he was first passed through the switchboard only to get a ringing, but unanswered, phone. The operator didn't come back on to get him. The FBI was no different from any other government agency on a snow day. Except for a skeleton crew—the gnomes in the lab, a few highly secretive task forces, and some agents who wisely figured it was better to stay in a warm office than fight the immobile traffic—nobody was in the Hoover Building.

Early Hardy paged through his list of private telephone numbers.

"See if he answers his own phone," he mumbled as he hurriedly dialed William Sessions' number.

It was 5:17.

"Yes?" said Sessions, picking the phone up on the first ring.

"Bill, this is Earl Hardy at the White House. Ten minutes ago the White House switchboard received a long distance call from someone warning that there was an atomic bomb planted under the Willard Hotel. It was in the trunk of a blue car—a Ford Fairmont . . ."

"Georgia license ADH-903!" interrupted Sessions, slamming his fist on his oak desk.

"Yes . . . how did you . . . ?" questioned Hardy. "Is this related . . . ?"

"You're god-damned right it is! Where is it?" shouted Sessions.

"Third floor, underground parking . . . under the Willard Hotel."

The hotel was almost exactly half-way between the White House and the Hoover Building.

"Wainwright!" shouted Sessions, still on the phone with Hardy.

Outside the snow continued to fall in a 2–3 inches per hour rate. "Earl . . . listen to me. Get the president out of there! This may be for real! Holy crap!"

Sessions hung up. Hardy called down to Jack Jenkins.

"Jack, we're going to evacuate the first family. Where's Chopper 1?" Hardy asked with urgency.

"It's just left Andrews. It'll be here in fifteen minutes."

It took seventeen minutes for the helicopter to fly from Andrews Air Force Base in suburban Prince George's County, Maryland, to the White House.

Jack's watch read 5:23. There was enough time—if nothing went wrong.

— • —

"Call bomb disposal!" shouted Craig Wainwright to his boss, as he took off on a dead run down the eighth floor hallway. There was no time to look up names in a telephone book. He flew past the cafeteria and slammed through the door leading to the stairwell, which he started taking three at a time. One misjudgment and he'd break a leg, or at least turn an ankle. Bursting through the third floor doors, he sprinted past the investigative labs, into and out of an administrative area to the Terrorist Section of the Criminal Investigative Division (CID). Within the section was a squad of agents that comprised section 174, Bombings, Terrorists and Other.

What a great name for a department. What was "Other?"

Two men were in the section—Hank Reading and Noah Pierce.

"There's an emergency—we need to defuse a bomb—now!" shouted Wainwright.

"In the building?" said Pierce, standing up.

"No—up at the Willard Hotel . . . hurry!"

"That's the job for Bomb Disposal. We just investigate after the thing's gone off . . . we don't defuse them," said Reading.

"The Director says you do—now!" ordered Wainwright. "If you've got a kit, bring it with you."

Pierce opened his bottom desk drawer and pulled out a lunchbox-sized kit that he used on investigations.

"God damn it! Hurry!" shouted Wainwright.

Pierce and Reading grabbed their coats and started down the hallway behind Wainwright, then were lost from sight as they tumbled down the steps toward the lobby level.

"We're on our way, sir," Wainwright shouted into his walkie-talkie. The clock on hallway wall said 5:36.

— • —

"Answer the phone!" Sessions shouted to an uncooperative telephone.

The District of Columbia government was closed. The local police department was six blocks away, up 14th Street.

"This is William Sessions of the FBI—let me talk to the chief!"

"Man, I don't care if you're the god-damned president himself—the chief is out in that traffic as is every man in the force," said the desk sergeant factually. "And nobody's movin' nowhere."

"I need a bomb disposal crew—*now!*"

"You want *what*? A BDU? Good luck. In this kind of weather?"

Sessions put down the phone and listened to Craig Wainwright on the walkie-talkie. He looked at his watch. It was 5:38.

— • —

The heavy snow was ten inches deep on the sidewalks. Pennsylvania Avenue was nothing more than four brown ruts in a sea of white. The wind whipped through the unusually-designed FBI building. The Hoover Building was constructed around a central courtyard, an amphitheater which let people sit outside at noontime on nice days. People sitting on the benches had the distinct feeling that someone was watching because the building towered above the courtyard on all sides. An access road, for FBI-only traffic, cut right through the building at ground level from 9th to 10th Street. The wind tunnel effect was tremendous. Add snow, and there were places where two-foot drifts had already accumulated.

Craig Wainwright, Hank Reading, and Noah Pierce were up to their knees in snow. Wainwright, out in the weather in nothing more than his dress wingtips and three-piece suit, was already soaked. Reading and Pierce at least had had the good sense to wear a coat. At 11th Street, opposite the Old Post Office building, Wainwright went out into Pennsylvania Avenue and into one of the four sets of brown ruts. It was easier than the sidewalk. The wind-driven snow gusted all around them as they slogged up the choked street.

The time was 5:39.

—   •   —

"Mr. President, it's Bill Sessions," said Earl Hardy.

"Bill?" said the president, his inflection asking all the questions which didn't need to be asked.

"Our men are almost there, Mr. President. The answer is, I don't know. It could very well be there. We've found evidence there is an Arab terrorist in the country. I informed . . ."

"Yes, I know. What about the people?" asked the president.

"Where are they going to go, sir? They don't have helicopters," replied the Director of the FBI.

"Mr. President, you've got to hurry," said Hardy.

It was 5:40 when the first family, including the second first dog, boarded Chopper 1. The Washington Monument couldn't be seen through the early darkness and the swirling snow.

—   •   —

The finely-dressed doorman barely had time to open the thick glass doors when three cold and wet FBI agents along with a cold blast of wintry air burst into the ornate lobby of the Willard Hotel.

"FBI! Where's the stairs to the parking garage?" shouted Wainwright, flashing his badge.

The interior of the Willard glowed with care and expensive refurbishing, its colors richly mixed in reds and golds.

"Down the steps to the ballroom, then look for the exit sign. You'll see it," replied the bellman. "No! Over there!" he pointed to his left as Wainwright had started in the wrong direction.

Their faces flushed with the cold and the extreme exercise of running through knee-deep snow, the three men dashed down the double set of thickly-carpeted steps directly to a sign marked Parking Garage. Through the doors they found themselves on P1.

"What floor?" shouted Reading.

"Third. Georgia tags . . . blue Fairmont," replied Wainwright.

They ran down the twisting, steeply-sloped concrete driveway through P2 and down to P3.

It was 5:47 when they reached P3.

"Where the hell is it?" Reading shouted.

"There!" replied Pierce, spotting the smaller car tucked up into the darkened corner. Georgia tags ADH-903. A Hertz rental out of

Hartsfield International Airport. Rented by one George Dijon, alias Khalid Rahman—the right-hand man of Zaid abu Khan.

Wainwright tried the door, without success.

"Damn!" he exclaimed.

The keys shined up at them from the floorboard under the steering wheel.

It was 5:49.

Wainwright felt like his body was moving in silly-putty.

"We've found the car, sir," he reported to Sessions.

Finding the car right where the caller said it would be added credence to the threat of a bomb in the trunk.

Pierce opened his kit and found a door pick. Reading closed the box and started to beat on the window, attempting to smash it in. The specially treated plastic-glass windows were designed not to shatter upon impact in an accident. Reading was trying to cause an accident.

"Wait a minute! I've got . . . got it!"

The door lock popped up, Pierce reached in, snatched the keys and handed them to Wainwright, who in turn struggled briefly with his cold hands inserting the key into the trunk lock. There was no time to think of the trunk lid being booby-trapped.

The trunk lid opened with a pop.

It was 5:51.

In the dimness of the P3 parking garage the bomb was imposing. A patch of yellow light obliquely reflected off the grey stainless steel ball. Pierce and Reading sucked in their breath. Wainwright shivered with the cold and wetness of his clothes.

"Mother Mary . . ." muttered Reading.

"There's a bomb here, sir," Wainwright radioed, the squawk echoing through the garage.

"I've never seen a bomb like this one," stated Pierce. "What the hell do you think it is?" he said, turning to Reading.

Reading didn't know.

"We've got five minutes," said Wainwright.

Pierce and Reading had never defused a bomb in the field before— plenty of times in the lab, in practice—but never in real life. They'd analyzed the terrible destruction of all kinds of amateur weapons. This one was professional.

"What do you make of this arm?" asked Reading, leaning into the trunk.

Pierce slowly ran his hands around the exterior of the three-foot long weapon. The ball was roughly as big as a pregnant basketball—more the size of a medicine ball—with an appendage of roughly two additional feet off to the right. It was all smooth stainless steel.

"This didn't come from somebody's garage," remarked Reading.

"No leads, nothing attached. It's self-contained," said Pierce, finishing his inspection. "The ball has been fused from two half-bowls. This side has been specially designed to insert the arm. It's well made. I don't see any way to get into it except through the arm. Do you?"

Craig Wainwright started to shiver uncontrollably. It was fear and hypothermia rolled into one. But he couldn't leave. Another few minutes wouldn't matter one way or the other.

The minute hand had crept up to 5:57.

"No, either do I. Do you want me to do it?" asked Reading.

Instead Pierce reached for the slender cylindrical arm. There was a metal screw in the middle of the cap. Reading handed Pierce a regular screwdriver.

"Left or right?"

"I'd try left first," replied Reading. "We've got two minutes. I don't know what other choice we've got."

It could have been a booby trap. A screw which didn't actually connect the cap with anything of substance other than the mechanism for triggering the weapon. Pierce slowly applied pressure to the screw, which after bearing down slightly, began to turn.

"You're going to have to hurry, Noah," said Wainwright.

It was a fact. He got the screw to finger-turn and carefully withdrew it. It was three inches long, and indeed had been secured into a socket within the weapon. Pierce turned the four-inch wide stainless steel cap, also to the left. The metallic sound was of steel on steel. The components were well made. With both hands, Noah Pierce slowly lifted the cap up. Hank Reading was on his hands and knees, shining a pencil light so see if there were any trigger wires attached to the cap itself.

"It's clear, Noah."

Pierce discarded the cap into the trunk. The red numbers of the bomb's small digital clock said 5:59. Reading's light filled the small opening. It appeared to be a simple clock attached to two sets of wires, which in turn were presumedly connected to detonator caps buried inside the plastic explosive which completely filled the visible portion of the bomb's arm.

"What do you think, Hank?" Pierce looked at his partner.

"Looks like an alarm clock to me. I'd go for the alarm button."

"Me too."

With that, Noah Pierce touched the SET ALARM button, first feeling it depress slightly, then rise to the OFF position. Nothing happened.

The clock turned to 6:00.

Still nothing happened.

Craig Wainwright fell to the oily concrete floor of the parking lot and was sick to his stomach.

"What the hell do you think it is?" asked Pierce to Hank Reading, as he went in to disconnect the embedded detonator caps.

"It's an atomic bomb," said Wainwright, coughing.

Reading dropped his screwdriver, which clanked once on the Ford's bumper then again to the concrete. He slumped against the wall.

DALLAS

Khalid Rahman had been taken to the morgue where it was discovered he had been killed by two .38 caliber shells in the chest. He was fingerprinted, logged in, and placed on a cold slab in the basement of Parkland Hospital. At 5:00 P.M. his prints were in the hands of detective Red Catchings of the Dallas police.

He watched as the clerk typed AA6318TTCIMI1814XI09 into the NCIC Wanted Persons file.

ET.HAT44492.RAHMAN, KHALID.M.W.IR.XXX.510.175.
BRW.BLK.OLV.SC R SHLD.AA6318TTCIMI18154XI09. XXX.01
03 ARAB TERRORIST ALIAS GEORGE DIJON WANTED FOR
ILLEGAL ENTRY ESPIONAGE INVOLVEMENT IN SIX MUR-
DERS NORTH CAROLINA SEE RECORD HAT44490 AND
HAT44491.NOAH.

The last ten digits of the fingerprint were identical.

"I'll be a son of a bitch."

"Pull up that other record! Damn!" encouraged Red.

EF.NC7789HAT.T2290D338.NC.88.TM.R443THVU3309
RE221.88.CHEV.SUBR.LL.RED/BLACK.021788.SUSPECT
0103 ARAB TERRORIST KHALID RAHMAN ALIAS GEORGE
DIJON ILLEGAL ENTRY SUSPECT ESPIONAGE CAUTION
ARMED AND DANGEROUS SEE RECORD HAT44491.NOAH.

Red Catchings' hands were moist. The dead man was an Arab terrorist—and he died a violent death in Texas.

ELIZABETH CITY

J.J. sat in front of the television set, watching but not seeing it. The noise was just company. The kitchen sink was littered with dirty dishes. J.J. felt old and incompetent, less sorry for himself than last night and this morning, but not much. A second manhattan was almost finished. Another one and it would be back to bed. Tomorrow he'd go back to work.

The phone rang but J.J. didn't hear it until the second ring, even though the phone was on the table next to him. For a second his mind confused the sound of the phone with whatever was happening on the television.

"Hello," J.J. said absentmindedly.

"Carteret?" came a voice with a flat midwestern accent. It was a man, and a man he'd never heard before. With as much of his life spent on the phone as it was, J.J. did remember voices.

"Yes."

"This is Detective Red Catchings from Dallas Police Department "

J.J. put his cocktail glass down, perking up.

"Yes?"

"I think I've got your man down here," said Catchings.

"Dijon . . . I mean—"

"Khalid Rahman."

Red Catchings butchered the pronunciation. What came out was something like cowlid raman.

"Where? You've got him? Is he with anyone? Is . . ." J.J. said animatedly.

"Whoa, partner. If he's with somebody, it's in the next world—the promised land, or whatever those folks call it. He's dead . . . killed by two .38 slugs in the chest," said Red.

Ugh.

"I called your local police department there in North Carolina and they gave me your home phone. Hope you don't mind."

"Mind! Damn!"

J.J. was up out of his chair, moving the telephone cord around the couch so he could get at a pencil and paper.

"Dallas, you say?"

"Yep, what's all this about a terrorist?" asked Catchings.

It was a lead. Of course, he would have to tell everyone—but maybe not right away. Where were the others? Where were the man and woman? They weren't in god-damned North Carolina, that's where they weren't!

"I'll be there tonight, Red," J.J. said, looking at his watch and flipping through his pocket copy of the Official Airline Guide. It was 7:30. Call Roy . . . better yet, leave a message—he could make a Delta connection to Dallas through Atlanta.

"I'll call you when I get there, Red."

Jim Bailey could wait a couple of hours.

THE WHITE HOUSE

By 6:20 the Willard Hotel parking garage was closed off, the lower level ballrooms off-limits. By 6:40 the bomb had been safely defused and taken inside the hotel, where it rested obscenely on top of a meeting room table under heavy security—including Charlotte SAC Jim Bailey and the rest of the terrorist task force, who had been inside the Hoover building, even while Craig Wainwright had been personally preventing the start of World War III. Given the weather conditions—which were getting worse, if possible—the hotel had not been evacuated. By 6:45 the president was back in the White House and had been given a personal update by William Sessions.

"There was a tape inside, sir—addressed to you," said Sessions.

"Have you seen it?" asked the president.

"No sir, there hasn't been time. I'll bring it over to you personally," replied Sessions.

"The bomb . . . ?" asked the president.

"Yes, sir, it was real. My people are analyzing it now. But, make no mistake . . . it is—was—an atomic weapon."

— • —

Seated around the large second floor conference table were the president, Earl Hardy and William Sessions. The vice president was in

249

Ohio. The director of the CIA lived in McLean and would be unable to get into the city. The secretary of state was in West Germany. The secretary of defense, James "Bulldog" Russell, had left his upper NW Washington home an hour ago.

It would be a miracle if he got there. Washington was closed. There were over 14 inches of snow on the ground and it was still snowing heavily. Although the visibility was slightly better, it was easy to see the snowflakes passing in front of the streetlamps. The Washington Monument was beautifully outlined across the Elipse. There were blizzard conditions outside. William Sessions had walked the last two blocks when his limo had stalled in front of the Treasury Building.

"Before we see this, I'd like to review exactly what we do know," said the president.

What was said in the room was taped, and everyone knew it. Sessions listed the facts and the times as they had been given to him by the participants.

"See that those men are properly thanked," said the president.

"Yes, sir. I will," replied a now-warming William Sessions, his feet soaked.

The president nodded to Earl Hardy, who inserted the three-quarters inch VHS tape into the wall-mounted VCR. The tape ran past the lead-in segment. Suddenly, there was the face of Zaid abu Khan. He wore Bedouin-style clothes. He looked trim and athletic, confident of what he was about to say. As he spoke, his face gradually turned from a smiling, benevolent father-figure image to the dangerously evil, arrogant terrorist he was.

"Congratulations, Mr. President. I assume your men have found and disarmed my little calling card—if not, you had better get busy. [laughs] Yes, it is an atomic weapon. Well made, I might add. I'm sure your men are analyzing the contents and construction by now, but in case you haven't, perhaps I can save you some time. All the materials are European with the exception of the batteries for the clocks—they were purchased locally since we have been here.

"Yes, I use the word 'we' precisely. I and a group of my men have been in the United States for some time now. I would rather not tell you how quite yet—we may wish to use the same method to leave.

"As to the construction—the processed uranium 235 was stolen from the French firm of Pinchot in April of last year. Through negotiations I have gained possession of half of the supply—not all of which I have brought to the United States with me. Yes, there is more. Yes, I have had it made into the same kind of weapons you have found. The other materials—polonium and lithium, in small quantities—were acquired by the same kind of methods. The stainless steel balls were forged in England and were originally designed to house nuclear waste. Somehow appropriate, don't you think?

"Enough of this small talk—let us get down to particulars, for you will be very busy in the next hours, perhaps days. Since I know you will spend every effort to find me, the next 48 hours are critical. Time is short and my requirements are very specific—and difficult to fulfill. But, they must be met!

"I have let you find one of my bombs. Here are the rest. [handheld camera pans to the right, backlighting reflects off stainless steel balls of five identical bombs]

"I'm sure you will have your staff quickly bring you everything your various spy agencies have on me. I will verify certain facts for you.

"The cause of Allah is right and just. You and your people are unclean infidels, made fat and gross by the luck of nature's weather patterns. You and other politicians have misled the American people into believing that it is your right to meddle into affairs which do not concern you. It is time for you to learn a lesson, to repent for your misdeeds, to pay for your sins against Allah. You see, Mr. President, I do not believe you will obey my orders. You have a chance to redeem yourself, but I know you won't. The detonation of these bombs will be on your shoulders, Mr. President. Yes, it will be your pride, the false pride of the American people, that will cause death, destruction, and chaos in the United States!

"You can see that I am a determined enemy. You will also see that I do not believe in sending men on futile missions of suicide. I never waste my resources, Mr. President. So, the fact that I have come to your country with five atomic weapons means that I fully expect to return to my homeland, without retribution.

"Before the Prophet Mohammed, our people lived by a simple code of law, a code written by the King of Babylon, Hammurabi. The essence of this law is an eye for an eye, a tooth for a tooth. I am Hammurabi's messenger, Mr. President. I have with me the tools for your destruction, the punishment for your evil-doing. You have one chance, the one I present to you now.

"I have five weapons, one of which has been located and discovered in Washington. By the time you are watching this, I and my men will have set three others in place. They are all in crowded cities, in impossible locations, in places where a minimum of a million people will die. The fifth bomb will stay with me until I and my men have safely returned.

"My requests . . . my demands, are not complicated. I have only two.

"Your first act of contrition will be to immediately force the withdrawal of Iraqi forces from Iranian soil and to establish a monitored zone of neutrality which will include a new southern boundary along the Tigris River to the village of Kut, which under the ancient tribal law, rightfully belongs to the Nation of Islam. As part of this demand—as a gesture of goodwill, you will provide the Waquidi government whatever aid is required to quickly rebuild both the government and the army. You will remove all American presence in the Middle East, including the shipping lanes of the Persian Gulf, and Air Force bases in Kuwait and Saudi Arabia. Before leaving, you will, of course, want to clear the Persian Gulf of all wrecked and abandoned ships and repair all Iranian facilities on Kharg Island and other coastal refinery areas.

"As a further goodwill gesture, the United States will be pleased to purchase 80% of Iranian oil at the fixed wellhead price of $35 per barrel. Naturally, you would want to repair any of our facilities that have been damaged or destroyed during our long war with Iraq. The computerization of the oil fields would be one of your first acts.

"My second demand is that you and your government immediately stop all economic and military assistance to the illegal Zionist government of Israel. The lands stolen in 1967 will be ceded to the proper occupants of Palestine. You will immediately provide mas-sive military and economic assistance so the nation may quickly become self-sufficient. You personally will lead the United Nations by formally recognizing the new government. You

"I realize that these demands are not easy to comply with—some parts of them will take time. However, they must be done! I am to be reckoned with, Mr. President! These are not idle threats!

"You are capable of removing your planes and warships from the Persian Gulf overnight. You are capable of sending your missionaries of good will to Teheran, on their bended hands and knees, on a moment's notice. You are able to contact the head of the UN General Assembly with a single phone call. Cargo ships of foodstuffs and supplies can leave eastern seaports within days. All of these things may be done quickly. And done quickly, they must be!

"Before providing me with safe passage to Teheran, I will tell you the locations of two of the bombs. But, you must have taken the following steps: remove your warships from the Persian Gulf; clear the Gulf of all debris; establish the zone of control along the Tigris River; recognize the state of Palestine and the exile government in Gaza; and send the first planeloads of computers and technicians to Teheran. Only after this has been done will I tell you the locations of two of the bombs.

"Yes, two! You heard me correctly. [camera pans again to bombs] You have found one. I will tell you the location of two. I will ensure my safety back to Teheran with the fourth. The fifth . . . yes, the location of the fifth will remain a secret. Only when all of my demands have been granted will I tell you the location of the fifth.

[leans into camera and smiles] "Perhaps there are more than five! [laughs] Imagine! Atomic weapons scattered across your country—yes, from sea to shining sea! No place is safe. Each of these weapons has a time mechanism like the one you have found. Look at it! These are modern marvels! [holds up clock timer] With these new electronic marvels I can pre-set the timer to activate now . . . next week . . . next month . . . next year . . . the next decade. Think of it! No place is safe! No time is safe!

"And, what if your people find out? Eh? Chaos! Mass hysteria. No sporting event, no rally, no airport . . . no city would be safe from destruction. And if you do not accede to my wishes, they will find out . . . and in a terrible way!

"And only I know the locations. Even Abdul Waquidi does not know. But what he does know is how to contact me, how to let me know that you have started negotiations—that you are dealing fairly—and, if you are not. Quite frankly, it is more important to me to know if you are not negotiating in good faith. Why? Because it will be up to me to teach you a lesson—a very painful lesson.

"President Waquidi is awaiting your call. After the negotiations have started, Waquidi will give you a coded message. It is the simplest of codes, words which are English, but words whose combination only make sense to me. We chose simple English words because we would not want to leave anything to the chance of a newspaper typesetter making a mistake. And that is how we will communicate. President Waquidi will give you a sentence or two of plain English words. You will place an advertisement in the classified section, situation wanted, of the top 150 newspapers in the United States. You may leave out Hawaii and Alaska. I am in the lower 48 as you refer to them.

"I expect the first session will take slightly longer than the others, since our nations have had no formal conversations in many years. You have 48 hours. I expect to see an advertisement in the final edition of your newspapers, the day after tomorrow. If the sen-tence is wrong . . . or missing, I will have one of the weapons detonated.

[waves book] "I have a code book with the sequential phrases. Abdul Waquidi has a similar book. At the end of your first session, when he can verify that you have started down the right path, only then will he give you your first phrase. You will have the phrase printed, I will read it, and I will not detonate one of the bombs. Hopefully, I will not have to set any of them off, Mr. President. [leans into camera again] You will not catch me, Mr. President. Do not try to catch me! I have the weapons! I will not fail to use them! I will not be taken alive!

"Remember, if I die, all weapons will detonate on their proper schedule. Waquidi does not know their location. You must deal with Abdul Waquidi, Mr. President. You must deal with me! Fail to bargain, fail to bend, and you will have death and destruction from sea to shining sea! Yes, from sea to shining sea!"

[tape goes black]

CHAPTER 5

Goodbye, California

WANCHESE, NORTH CAROLINA

SS1 Jason Swanquarter, 25, slowly maneuvered his forty-two foot UTB (utility boat), serial 42881, from the Roanoke Sound Channel into the lateral offshoot that led into the port of Wanchese. The Army Corps of Engineers was still having difficulty keeping up with the dredging of all the fishing and traffic lanes in the shallow sounds and channels on the Outer Banks. But, since they'd had the same problems for the last thirty years, it was unlikely things would change.

Swanquarter and his crew of three, including one of the two women stationed at the Coast Guard's Oregon Inlet facility, were out on normal patrol of the waters and harbors in the area. Most of the time patrol was boring and routine, but there was just enough excitement on an irregular basis to make it interesting. They'd rescued people, caught drug runners, broken up fights, settled disputes, and given citations.

One morning last summer they'd quietly motored past a docked fishing boat only to find a young couple busy making imaginative and enthusiastic love on deck. Unaware of the four voyeurs, the good-looking pair lay naked on a large towel and were locked in a passionate head-to-toe body hug, each giving the other intensive oral gratification. Quietly stopping the boat's engines, they'd been able to hear the personal moans of pleasure and see the naked bodies writhe to the short strokes of lips and tongues. The girl, not more than nineteen, had been on top and was facing away from the channel—her firm, tanned breasts swayed with the action. Her blond head was all motion as she moved back and forth, up and down—sucking his erection. At the same time, her hips moved urgently as his tongue flicked her toward climax. The morning sun glistened off her smooth back—now evenly covered with a mixture of suntan lotion and perspiration. Her legs were spread wide as his hands cupped her buttocks, his mouth absorbed in her young sweetness. Their grunts of pleasure increased in urgency as each came closer to what each one needed. His body tensed. He tried to hold back his explosion—but she was relentless. Her breasts rubbed against his stomach as she slowly brought him to climax. She moved her tongue over his wet, demanding erection—massaging every inch. Starting from the tip, she slowly but firmly moved her lips down over him one last time, sliding his entire organ into her mouth.

It was enough to make them all break out in a sweat. Jason restarted the engines and moved on, leaving the couple in their passion, unaware that they'd made a lasting impression.

However, this cold February night Jason and his crew were looking for something specific. His group commander, Lieutenant Hap Reynolds, had gotten a wire from Washington and had passed it on to the OICs in Hatteras, Oregon Inlet, and Coinjock. Watch for a trawler called the *Bedford Clipper*. A man was aboard who was wanted by the FBI for illegal entry.

As the 42881 entered the Wanchese harbor it was easy to tell that it was wintertime. The harbor was crowded with different boats, boats which had come down from the frozen waters up north to fish the warm Gulf Stream.

"Over there," said one of the crew, in a hushed tone.

It was the *Bedford Clipper*. Without lights the finely-trimmed trawler was moored to the right channel wall.

"Oregon, this is patrol 42881. We've found the boat. What are our instructions?"

"Maintain position, patrol, we will notify the Dare County police," came the reply.

WASHINGTON

Frances Harvey, Fran to her friends, was an unlikely candidate for gnomehood. The attractive thirty-six-year-old chemical engineer had worked for the FBI's Laboratory Division for the last eight years, and had worked her way up to star status. While the computers were helpful, it had been Fran's brain and ability to sift quickly through mountains of facts and rubble to piece together related bits of information that impressed her colleagues.

The only windows in the lab were the the ones which the tour used. Sometimes she wondered who were the monkeys and who were the keepers—us or the tourists. Once inside the lab there was no evidence there was an outside world. Once she'd heard there was a terrible snowstorm outside, Fran simply resigned herself to another all-nighter. She'd work straight through, then take the next available workday off.

There was no obvious difference between night and day in the lab, so she'd just work until she was too tired, then sleep in one of the crash rooms.

She had in front of her scrapings of a skid sample from St. Louis. Along with the samples was a fairly good photo, as well as accurate measurements of the mark, including the mark-to-mark distance, the width of each mark, and the length of the skid itself. The other pieces of evidence—bullet shell casings, photos, etc.—had been sent to other analysts.

Hand on head, she closed her eyes and tried to activate her normally reliable personal computer—her brain. You must be tired, Frannie. She thought. This narrow tire track is from a van—a Dodge van.

The Goodyear tread in the picture was familiar, as were the measurements—even the skid. Fran got up, went to the third row of four-drawer filing cabinets, and started sifting. Where was it? She knew it was in the computer, but Fran only used the things as a last resort. She knew she could go in, qualify on Dodge Caravans and come back with a recent list. Impatiently, she sifted through the folders. Finding one, she pulled it out, looked at the photos and case data, then just as impatiently stuffed the folder back into the drawer and went on.

She pulled up another.

There it was.

The tread was the same. The length of the skid the same, the direction similar. It was possible the driver had been the same. This one was from a murder investigation in North Carolina. Fran was convinced the vans were the same. She pulled the North Carolina folder and compared the photos. It was the same.

Frances Harvey flashed a pretty and very satisfied smile. Another victory for the synapses.

THE WHITE HOUSE

The president stood in front of the window and watched as nature laid a huge white blanket over the city. Although the storm was starting to taper off, the latest reports from the Weather Service in Silver Spring was that another four inches would accumulate by morning. What had been predicted as three to six inches would turn out to be eighteen to twenty-four inches. Without quick melting, Washington would be paralyzed for three days, minimum. The airports would be closed for at least twenty-four hours, perhaps thirty-six.

"Damn!" he shook his head.

How could a country so small, so backward, have such control over our society? the president thought. *How is it possible? Are they more intelligent? What is it? In the past ten years the United States has twisted and turned to the slow knives of the Iranian government. We don't even need their damn oil! Here we are again, the great and powerful—humbled before a handful of fanatics.*

"They could be anywhere, Mr. President," said Sessions.

It was a doleful Director of the FBI who reluctantly admitted that they had virtually no lead on the location of Zaid abu Khan, Khalid Rahman, and others in his gang. Furthermore, the task force which had been assembled—top agents from east coast offices—were all stuck in Washington in the Hoover Building. Alerts for the two vehicles had gone out nationwide, but the northeast corridor had been especially targeted as a probable target area. Additional resources, in the form of special agents, had been immediately drawn in from West Coast and midwestern cities as early as yesterday afternoon. Logically, the areas to be hit by terrorists would be the heritage cities of Washington, Philadelphia, New York, and Boston. It would be in these cities where the greatest physical and psychological damage could be inflicted on the American public.

The snow would have one side benefit, however. It would keep the media at bay. The snow would be a blessed buffer between the presshounds and the president. The president had a thought of Sam Donaldson standing outside in two feet of snow waiting for him to appear—the thought was brief, but reassuring.

It had taken Bulldog Russell nearly three hours to get to the White House. By mutual agreement, all U.S. military bases worldwide were on alert. It took nearly an hour to get secretary of state Oden Bennett in Jerusalem. It was 5:00 in the morning when the president had finally reached him.

"Do you want me to go to Teheran?" he'd asked.

"Not yet, Oden. I've got to find out what the man really wants. These people have declared war on us. I can't send you into that kind of situation. You'd just be taken hostage. But, stay where you are. I don't want the Israelis to know anything. They can't keep their damn mouths shut for ten minutes. It'll be all over the *Washington Post* tomorrow morning," the president had said. "Get some coffee, Oden. We're going to keep the line open."

By long distance, Oden Bennett was a part of the meeting.

"We have to make contact with the Waquidi government. What do we know about the man?"

Bennett's response came back after a half-second propagation delay from the satellite connection to Jerusalem.

"I hate to say it, but we don't know much. He seems to be a moderate, but then he has no track record. He was a functionary, a faceless bureaucrat in the Khomeini government," replied Bennett.

"He couldn't have been too faceless," added the president.

"Yes, but he had to be faceless in that environment. Anybody who showed initiative was subject to be purged because they were a threat to Khomeini's rule."

"Options—I want options," said the president plainly, his anger now barely controlled.

"Leak it to the press," said Earl Hardy.

The others turned to him, questioningly—"are you daft?"

"I'm serious. If Sessions' troops are caught by this storm, and we've got less than thirty-six hours . . . then we need more eyes. Call the networks and tell them yourself. Go on the air. Describe the problem, tell the public what to look for, and why."

It was a radical idea, especially for someone as conservative as the president's chief of staff.

"Jesus, Earl . . . where'd you come up with that one?" asked Russell.

The president gave his long-time political ally and friend a doubtful look, one which wordlessly asked if he was joking.

"It's an option, Mr. President," shrugged Hardy.

"Well, we'd be lucky to find these people with just the FBI. Am I right, Bill?" asked Bulldog Russell.

"Yes," replied the William Sessions. "We've got to have more arms and legs. We have to let the state and local police know . . . something. We have a description of the cars they're using—they should be conspicuous enough."

"Right now we and a handful of Bill's agents are the only people who know how bad this thing is . . . am I right?" asked Hardy. He got nods of yes. "This is very, very tricky. The more people who know, the more opportunities there are to screw up."

"Earl, the man has atomic weapons and he's not going to just turn them over. He's a fanatic. For all we know he'll drive into downtown

Los Angeles, ask for a TV interview, and blow the god-damn things up!" the president said angrily.

The thought of buried atomic weapons ticking away toward a random future detonation was chilling. The president continued.

"As I see it, we have two solutions that we need to be working on concurrently. We do need more eyes and ears. Bill, we need to get the description of Khan's vehicles down to the street level . . . but not that Zaid Khan is one of the men. Is there a way you can do a 'locate but do not apprehend?' Bill, I want your men to capture him. Can you do that?"

Sessions thought, then responded with the only answer which was correct.

"Yes, Mr. President."

"Good. With what kind of range can this be done?" asked the president.

"Do you mean, can it be done nationwide?" questioned Sessions.

"Yes."

"That's almost impossible. I'll need to concentrate my . . . our . . . resources to get the most out of the local departments. And this snowstorm isn't helping."

"While I agree with your assessment of where we think Khan may be, my gut tells me his phrase "from sea to shining sea" was more than just a jibe at one of our national songs. What if he's not in the Northeast?"

It wasn't that he hadn't thought of the idea, but voicing it was another story. Bill Sessions was pained.

"We're going to be pretty thin out there, Mr. President. If we concentrate on the Northeast, then it'll be several days before I can start to spread the search out to other states. We can't just put out a broadcast message . . . Jesus! Every radio and TV station from here to Portland will have it. Then all we need is for the word to get out that this nut is carrying atomic weapons. Do you know how many people have guns, Mr. President?"

The question was rhetorical.

"Neither do I."

The thought of having ad hoc vigilante groups out looking for one of the world's most wanted criminals was terrifying. The president spoke.

"Well, you'll have to go with what we've got. But the second piece of this is that Khan waved a small notebook. It contains the codes he's using to monitor our talks with Waquidi. There's no way he knows what we are saying to Waquidi, if anything. Hell, the words could be anything. The more random the better—at least that's what I'd do, if I were them. If we can't catch Khan, we've got to somehow say the right words to him through the newspapers. Do you realize how difficult that is? We've got to somehow get ads into the papers without anyone knowing. Even if we do talk to that son of a bitch, putting an ad in 150 newspapers is no trivial task," said the president, with a tone of futility.

"Without them knowing that the White House is doing it," added Earl Hardy.

Bill Sessions interjected.

"My men will have to do it. It'll be up to my organization to make sure the local editor understands the importance. The FBI's the only organization you've got to do that, Mr. President."

Bulldog Russell stepped into the conversation.

"Mr. President, you've got to make contact with Waquidi, and soon. This is the simplest of coding mechanisms. Only two people know the key. You are right, it could be anything. The sentence could be 'the moon is green' and the key word could be moon or green, or the structure of the sentence. That phrase could mean affirmative. Yet a negative might be 'I'll have peas tonight,' something completely different and random . . . not 'the moon is red.' Do you understand?"

Russell paused.

"This whole conversation is leading up to a question. You're going to ask me if it's possible to get Waquidi's copy of the book," said Russell.

That was exactly what everyone was leading up to.

"Yes," said Hardy.

"We don't exactly have a track record of success in this area," Bulldog Russell replied, looking at the president.

"But those were covert operations we tried before, Jim. This is different. These people have declared war on us!"

No one within the top echelons of government had to be reminded how the nation of Iran had repeatedly played the Americans for fools. In one sense, the Americans were so easily led astray because of the nature of their government and the people who ran it—their leaders were from the general populace, albeit normally from the upper economic stratum. Still, American leaders reflected the general good nature, positive attitude, and friendly and outgoing nature that the American people had. While duplicity was never tolerated in leadership, naiveté was. The American political naiveté was a perfect foil for the Iranian government leaders. The Americans wanted so much to have the Iranians like them.

The secretary of defense sighed. Plans for an Iranian invasion had been played in Pentagon war games for ten years. While not a no-win game, there weren't many win-only solutions. If anything, the logistics had gotten worse since 1979-80. Syria had gotten much stronger, with the quiet nod of approval from the Israelis. Neither Syria nor Israel would put up with an expansion of the bloodshed in Beirut. The boundaries of Iraq and Iran changed daily. Tens of thousands of young men, some as young as twelve, had been drawn into the battle. There had been so many "Final Battles" that the Khomeini government had stopped announcing them. The hospitals from Teheran to Baghdad were filled with torn and dying men—all while the arms merchants made obscene amounts of money peddling weapons made in Leningrad, Peking, Havana, and American cities like Detroit, Los Angeles, and St. Louis.

The river valleys of the Tigris and Euphrates, from which organized mankind spread to the four corners of the earth, was now a black hole of despair and disgust.

"Yes, we can do it," said Bulldog Russell. "This time there is a difference. This time the men are expendable. In the past we've been worried about not losing any men—did the end justify the means? Carter couldn't lose a hundred troops in order to rescue four hundred hostages—the political price was too high. This is more like Vietnam. It's a mission. The political reality says that you have much more to lose by not trying, by not doing anything, than by losing every last man on a mission."

"Or several missions—or a full scale attack . . ." said the president.

"Yes," replied Russell.

"Can you do it, Jim?" asked the president.

"We can assume Waquidi is in Teheran, in the presidential palace. But if he's not, you're going to have to try and locate him for us, Mr. President."

"Do we have anybody on the staff who speaks Farsi?" asked the president.

"You mean, in the building right now?" replied Hardy.

The question was obvious. It was doubtful that Waquidi spoke English. Certainly none of the Americans spoke Farsi. Establishing telephone connections to Teheran was going to require the combined linguistic skills of several people.

"I have people who speak Farsi," said Oden Bennett over the speakerphone.

— • —

"Graham Atkinson?" said the official-sounding voice.

"Yes?"

"Mr. Atkinson, this is Earl Hardy at the White House. The secretary of state has recommended you for an assignment. We're sending someone over to pick you up right now."

"Now?"

"Yes."

"But the city is closed . . . the snow . . ." came Atkinson's confused response.

Atkinson and his wife rented a three-story townhouse on C Street SE in a section of the District called Capitol Hill. As Graham put the phone down he looked out in amazement at a three-vehicle caravan which slowly moved up C Street—two District of Columbia snowplows followed by a sleek, black limo. Atkinson barely had time to kiss his wife goodbye, then jump through the fifteen inches of snow on his stoop to the warmth of the limo.

"Mr. Atkinson is on the way," said the driver over the radio.

WANCHESE

"What the hell's going on here, Hap?" asked Bart Claiborne. "What the hell am I supposed to do with this boat?"

Hap Reynolds, commander of the Coast Guard Group Cape Hatteras, laughed. Although only forty miles away in Buxton on Hatteras Island, the conversation sounded like it was taking place with two tin cans on a piece of string.

"I don't know. There was a wire from Washington on it. Just find it and notify, it said. We found it. You report back. I'll tell Portsmouth that we've found it, and they'll clear it back through Washington. Since this was a FBI request, you might want to give J.J. Carteret a call. Maybe he can tell you what's up."

Bart knew J.J. was bent out of shape on this Rahman business, about the case being taken away from him. Yet, they both knew there was a large grey cloud of unknown information which they hadn't even come close to finding. Bart and two of his men climbed aboard the *Bedford Clipper* and gave the boat a quick search.

"Bart!" came a shout from one of the men.

Bart climbed up the steel ladder into the pilothouse. Bloodstains. Dried redish-brown blobs of blood were everywhere in the cabin.

"Nothing down here!" came the shout from below.

Bart's gut feeling was that the *Bedford Clipper* was somehow tied into The Case. This was the missing link. This was how that terrorist got into the country.

— • —

"Aye, he said it was research," said the old harbormaster, not a bit reluctant to express his displeasure at being rousted out of bed. "He wasn't a seaman, that's for sure. I don't think he'd been at sea a day in his life, mind you."

Bart showed old Mr. Winsloe a series of pictures, including the one of Khalid Rahman received from INTERPOL.

"That's him. That's him, all right," Winsloe tapped at the picture. "Who is he?"

Bart ignored the harbormaster's question.

"I think you'll need to open up the office, Mr. Winsloe. I need to look at your records."

While Winsloe got dressed, Bart called dispatch from the squad car.

"Put a message out to J.J. Carteret—tell him it's urgent."

ST. LOUIS

"Thank you," Scotty said as he hung up for the umteenth time. There were only two more Coast Guard locations to try. One was in Portsmouth, Virginia, the other in Buxton, North Carolina. There was a Ben Franklin store in the general area of both—Chesapeake and Nags Head.

What was satisfying was that most of the Coast Guard locations had received the wire, and had put the *Bedford Clipper* on their hit lists. Scotty was determined to finish before calling it a night.

But he was more than a little bit nervous about what to do next. He had talked briefly with the St. Louis SAC, but had left his office without a direct offer of support. The 9mm Beretta shells were part of the evidence which the St. Louis police had sent on to Washington. Scotty fingered Paul Worley's report absentmindedly. He saw the image of Alexander Rostov taking dead aim at him on the cobblestones of Union Street in New Bedford. That son of a bitch used a 9mm Beretta then, and he used it here in St. Louis. Rostov had somehow followed Ramsey, wherever he'd landed. Ramsey . . . ? The thoughts ran into questions. How did Ramsey get here? Who was with him? Why was he in St. Louis? Why in that part of St. Louis?

Scotty looked down the nearly empty bullpen. There were two agents and a rotor clerk on the night shift. The FBI never closed its doors. Scotty dialed the area 919 number in Buxton and could hear the connection get degraded with every switch. Scotty had found out today that the Coast Guard never closed, either.

"Coast Guard, SS1 Ridley," came the crisp reply.

Scotty identified himself and the reason for the call.

"One moment, Mr. Coldsmith," as Scotty was politely, but firmly put on hold.

Two minutes went by.

"Mr. Coldsmith, this is Hap Reynolds. I'm the commander of Group Cape Hatteras. Where are you calling from?"

"The FBI Regional office in St. Louis. I'm the agent who put in the request on the *Bedford Clipper*?"

Reynolds would have to verify Scotty's telephone and location. Scotty hung up and waited.

Three minutes later a call came, was answered by the night switchboard operator, who then transferred the call to Scotty's line.

"Yes, Mr. Coldsmith. We have found the *Bedford Clipper*. What do you want us to do with it? It appears to be abandoned. I've notified the local Dare County police, so whatever you need, you'd better deal with them. We found it this evening, not more than two hours ago."

Reynolds gave Scotty the name of Bart Claiborne and the telephone number in Manteo.

North Carolina!

As Scotty was thanking the Coast Guard commander, the switchboard operator gave Scotty the high sign, indicating he had another call on hold.

"Thank you, commander," Scotty said as he punched the other line.

"Coldsmith," Scotty said, becoming excited.

"Paul Worley. You're working late," was Worley's good-natured, but sarcastic reply.

"Thanks."

"We just got a wire from Washington—from your laboratory people.

They identified the skid marks as a Dodge Caravan, probably recent model ..."

Dodge Caravan? Where did he have a Dodge ... ?

"... and they also think it matches a similar tread sent to them from the police in North Carolina a couple of weeks ago. Manteo, North Carolina, she said. She thought we'd be interested," said Worley.

Interested? Dodge Caravan? North Carolina?

"The requesting agency is the Dare County police ... a sheriff named Bart Claiborne. An FBI agent named J.J. Carteret was involved. I don't have much else. Sounds like our boy might have come through North Carolina," said Worley.

Scotty wanted to blurt out his other news, the combination of news ... but managed to contain himself. He had to talk to the North Carolina people.

Dodge Caravan?

THE WHITE HOUSE

As the snow began to taper off to a fine mist, Graham Atkinson was starting the adventure of his lifetime. Nothing before or after would compare with the thrill of Doing Something Important.

His first task was to help the White House switchboard establish a link with the Iranian telephone system. Wearing a headset he listened as the call was routed through a cacophony of myriad voices. In the old days—pre-Ayatollah—Iran was an emerging modern nation, with only the crudest telecommunications. Talking via satellites was part of joining the world community. With the deliberate cultural withdrawal from other national civilizations, Iran had not only politically distanced itself, but had also cut off the way to communicate to other nations. Iran was a microchipless society. Those few people who had telephones, like much of the iron curtain nations, were completely under government control and censorship. The state ran the telephone system. As a result, telephone communications relied on the same twisted-pair-with-repeaters technology which hadn't changed much since Alexander Graham Bell.

Ankara, Turkey was the last stop for communications using modern equipment. Atkinson could hear every link as it was opened between

Ankara and the small eastern border villages. At each stop the burden seemed to get greater, the static louder. Finally, at the village of Urmia the telephone system came to the border of Iran.

"This is the office of the president of the United States. We wish to establish a circuit to Teheran and talk with the president of Iran, Abdul Waquidi. I believe he is in the presidential palace. Can you find out, please?" Atkinson, spoke in Farsi to the Kurdian operator.

He mentally crossed his fingers. For all he knew he could be talking to someone in occupied territory and the call could end up being patched to Baghdad. To say the least, the fragile connection was the worst possible from a security standpoint. Anyone could tap it—anyplace.

Surprisingly, the operator came back in only a few minutes.

"Your call to the presidential palace is ready now," said the operator.

"Thank you. Please relay to Mr. Waquidi that we will be back on the line in ten minutes," said an elated Graham Atkinson, giving the high sign to the watching Howard Hardy.

While Adrian Graves patched the connection to the president, Hardy and Atkinson made their way on a run through the White House to the oval office.

"Mr. President, we think Waquidi is in the presidential palace in Teheran," said Hardy.

"Well done! Jim?" the president nodded to Bulldog Russell.

After all, what other assumption could they make? How many men would it take? How much supply? Will the telephone line stay open? What about killing Waquidi? Hostages? How much resistance will there be? Should there be a diversion? If so, what will the Soviets think? Should we tell the Soviets? What about the Israelis? There were more variables, but it didn't do much good thinking about them.

It was five in the morning in Teheran. Soon it would be daylight. A nighttime attack would be the best—assuming there was no sandstorm. The aircraft carriers *Nimitz* and *Kennedy* were in the Mediterranean. The mean son of a bitch Strike Force marines were aboard the *Nimitz*. Each ship had Apache helicopters. Several C-130s could be launched almost on a moment's notice from Düsseldorf to provide whatever logistics were required, including mobile armor. In short, a small army could be quickly sequestered behind an enemy line. It made a big difference that stealth was secondary to success. Prevention of the detonation of atomic weapons in major U.S. cities was worth whatever price had to be paid.

"Yes, we can do it, Mr. President. I would recommend launching the attack when it is dark in Teheran tomorrow night. That should be about ten o'clock tomorrow morning, our time. You might want to wait until later that evening, say ten o'clock—two o'clock tomorrow afternoon. The later the better," said Russell.

"That will be too late for Khan. We'll need to do something. The papers . . . the demand," replied the president, not confused, but instead aware of the possibilities—unsure of how things would unfold.

"You're going to have to negotiate like you've never done before. Tough—and long. I doubt if they will give in on any point, or at least not much."

"I have no intention of giving in," replied the president, angrily.

Sessions and Hardy exchanged glances. William Sessions continued.

"Mr. President, we will have to say we will do some of the things. We need to keep Waquidi occupied for the next twenty-four hours. We need that book if we're going to be able to negotiate with Zaid Khan. The only way Khan will know what is happening is through the system they've set up—through the newspapers," persuaded Sessions. "At least until we catch him. We need to get past the first forty-eight hours. My teams are locked here in Washington. The whole East Coast is the same. It may take a week to get a handle on Khan. We need that book to get Khan to communicate with us directly."

The president nodded sternly. He did not like to negotiate. Nor did he like to be told what he had to do. The Carter and Reagan administrations had been burned severely by the Iranians, and here it was happening again. He hated it. Yet Sessions and the others were right. He had to give in, to do whatever was required to keep Abdul Waquidi on or near the phone for eighteen hours.

"Damn!" the president muttered to himself. "All right, let's get on with it. Damn!"

Clearing his throat, Graham Atkinson pushed the talk button on the speakerphone.

"My name is Graham Atkinson, and I am the translator for the president of the United States . . ."

DALLAS

The airline gods had, for an evening, suspended the normal rules of business travel and spared J.J. from a case of the Frequent Flyer blues.

He made it to Dallas before the industry mercifully went to sleep for another night, releasing its tired and haggard passengers to whatever place of rest each might find. Something good must be going to happen, J.J. thought. In real life this doesn't happen.

"Catchings, this is J.J. Carteret," J.J. had called.

"Jesus, Carteret! The whole damn world's been looking for you!" was Catching's reply. "You've gotten two calls from your clerk, a fella named Roy—and I've gotten three calls from a special agent named Coldsmith in St. Louis, and another call from Bart Claiborne—a sheriff back where you come from. I'm not sure you've got time to see this Rahman character tonight. He's not going anywhere—he'll be here tomorrow morning. You've gotten to be some popular fella."

J.J. took down the numbers as Red gave them.

"Where did you find Rahman?"

"At the Hyatt Regency downtown—he was aboard one of the airport buses. Is this Rahman the same one I've heard of?" asked Catchings.

"I'm afraid so," replied J.J.

"What the hell's going on?" Catchings asked.

J.J. paused.

"I really can't go into it, Red. I'm sorry. Yes, I would like to see Rahman. Is the medical report in yet?" said J.J., patiently. "Look, I've got to get some answers. I'll call you back tomorrow morning early."

Using his credit card J.J. called the Dare County police in Manteo.

"He's out on a call, Mr. Carteret. In Wanchese. I'll put you through," replied the dispatcher.

Bart Claiborne was out on a call in the middle of the night? It was past midnight in North Carolina. It took two full minutes before the connection was made. Bart wasted no time.

"J.J.? Where are you, boy?" asked Bart, somewhat peeved.

"Dallas," replied J.J.

"Well, all hell's broken loose tonight. They came in on a boat, J.J. There was some blood and I've got Henry working, but you're going to have to get your IDENT boys down here. This thing's been here all along—named the *Bedford Clipper*. It came in on the 20th, last week. We got it because of a NCIC want put in by an FBI agent named Scott Coldsmith out of your New York office. Not only that, there are two more wants. Get this—one is for a Soviet agent and the other is for some guy named Ramsey who is wanted for illegal entry. I couldn't reach you, so I called your office in New York where this Coldsmith works."

New York?

"They gave me a number in St. Louis to call. I don't know why he's in St. Louis, but that's pretty close to where you are. I didn't get three words out when this guy Coldsmith just about jumps through the phone at me. You'd better call him before he has a fit. He's called back a couple of times since then to see if you've called in for messages. Roy's called once as well."

J.J. tried to get a quick mental priority list together. He had to let Jim Bailey know where he was and what had happened—but after he talked with Coldsmith. Bart needed help from the gnomes. The special task force would be very interested in the *Bedford Clipper*.

Soviet agent?

"Get what you can, Bart. I'll contact Bailey. I think he's in Washington with the rest of them. I'll talk to you later."

ST. LOUIS

"Mr. Coldsmith? Mr. Coldsmith? Wake up . . ."

It had taken some shaking to wake Scotty up out of what was the start of a very solid night's sleep. He had fallen into one of the cots in the crash room and had gone instantly to sleep.

"Telephone call. It's an agent named Carteret. He says it's urgent. I think it's the call you were expecting," said the young agent.

Young agent? Since when did I start thinking about someone else as a young agent? That's me, thought Scotty. It was too complicated to think about. Scotty sat up, shook his head, and ran his hands through his hair. He took a deep breath. *Wake up! Wake up!* He had just started his descent into deep sleep. It would take a few minutes for him to get his senses back together. Scotty walked back into the bullpen and over to the desk he was using. A single light on the six-button telephone flashed impatiently. In the semi-darkened room, the light seemed to transmit the urgency of the caller.

"This is Scott Coldsmith," Scotty answered firmly.

Later in life Scotty would remember details of the five seconds between his answer and J.J.'s return, the time when his whole personality seemed to flow down the telephone wires and assault J.J.'s instinct. Something more than just words had been exchanged between the two men—trust, exuberance, experience, pain, frustration . . . a bond was created. Later, neither would be able to express it, but the root lay in the five seconds when Scotty's tired greeting reached out over the six hundred miles between the dark, empty St. Louis FBI office and the busy Delta Crown Room in the Dallas/Ft. Worth airport.

The acceptance of one to the other was instantaneous.

"Coldsmith, my name is John Carteret. I'm a special agent out of the Elizabeth City, North Carolina Resident Office. I understand we might have some cases that are linked."

J.J. paused. He knew nothing of the voice on the other end. A man, another agent, had independently investigated a case that was linked to his. Without knowing anything more, J.J. had immediate empathy and admiration.

"I've been on a plane for the last several hours. I'm in Dallas now and I haven't seen your NCIC records," J.J. continued. "But, I've got a local police chief back home who's been jumping up and down waiting for me to call. What's up?"

Scotty's whole body jumped. His hand nearly knocked the telephone off the desk. He nearly fell out of his chair. *Finally!* He was *finally* getting someplace. Gaining his composure somewhat, Scotty sat on the edge of his chair, leaning into the telephone as if it would somehow make it easier to pull the information out of the Carolina agent. Carteret had a definite southern accent. He spoke quietly and slowly. Scotty wanted to hurry the man's words on. The words spilled out in a disorganized spew.

"I know! I know! The Coast Guard found my boat tonight! The sheriff down there wanted me to talk to you. He didn't want to tell me anything over the phone—not until we talked. What's going on? Is there . . . ?"

J.J. looked around the Crown Room. A few tired businessmen lapped up the last of the night's free booze and slumped into easy chairs, waiting for delayed flights. Some would have to spend the night. J.J. smiled. Coldsmith was a youngster.

"Whoa!" J.J. ordered. "One thing at a time. Let me start. You jump in when something ties. Yes, they found your boat. A boat named the *Bedford Clipper* docked in Wanchese harbor on the 20th. It . . . ," J.J. delayed, ". . . appears as if the boat was used to smuggle Arab terrorists into the United States," said J.J. finally, taking and admitting the guilt for the first time. *Why not?* he thought. *The god-damned Arabs came right by me! Face up to it. Carteret!* he silently berated himself.

"Terrorists? Arab terrorists!" Scotty replied, incredulous. Involuntarily, Scotty lowered his voice and looked around the darkened room, mentally checking to see if anyone had overheard him. The night dispatcher had gone back to the phones. *What have you gotten yourself into?* Scotty thought. J.J. continued.

"INTERPOL has confirmed that one of the terrorists is a man named Khalid Rahman. Rahman is the right hand man of . . . ," J.J. delayed briefly, ". . . Zaid abu Khan. Rahman's photo has been confirmed by three sources on the Outer Banks."

"Son of a . . ." came Scotty's involuntary interruption.

"Rahman entered the country on February 8th through Atlanta via a Delta flight from Paris. He drove directly to the North Carolina Outer Banks, where he rented an ocean front home on the 9th," said J.J. slowly. He could feel Scotty's excitement rising on the other end. J.J. could feel that he was in a special place in a special moment in time. The noise of the room, the ebb and flow of the businessmen, the TV in the background—his mind cut right through them, ignoring anything that got in the way. Confidence and an almost omniscient feeling of his destiny surged through him. He was right! Damn it, he was right! J.J. wanted to pump his arms in victory. He just *knew* Scotty was going to provide the missing links!

On the other end Scotty jumped in, dumping the details of his part of the case in a tumble of words. It was almost as if the speed of his words insured their verification.

"On the 8th I was asked to follow a Soviet courier named Alexander Rostov, a man who came in on an Air France flight from Paris. On the 9th, he left the Soviet mission and began to trail a man who, I would find out later, was called John Smithton Ramsey. Ramsey entered the country illegally on the same Air France flight. I lost Rostov but followed Ramsey to New Bedford, Massachusetts. Apparently Rostov was following both of us, because on the night of the 10th he tried to put me away. He and a woman . . ."

"A woman?" interrupted J.J.

"Yes, a woman. Why?" asked Scotty, reversing the roles.

"I'll tell you in a few minutes. Go ahead!" said J.J., excitedly. The two men were equal in youthful enthusiasm. Scotty continued.

"Rostov had a woman with him. I heard her footsteps and got a description from some motel clerks. Anyway, we had a shootout. I was mugged and nearly killed by some locals and woke up in a Boston hospital three days later. Sometime in between, Ramsey had hired a local fishing boat named the *Bedford Clipper*. He and another man got aboard."

"He met up with somebody?" asked J.J.

"Yes, the harbormaster in New Bedford remembered. I got prints and descriptions of Ramsey and Rostov. INTERPOL came back with a known on Rostov, but was unable to verify Ramsey's British passport. Ramsey had apparently come through Marseille a few days earlier before leaving for the United States on the 8th. With no valid passport, I put an illegal entry want into NCIC, then got my SAC to agree to asking the Coast Guard to put a want on the *Bedford Clipper.*"

"Why are you in St. Louis, Scott?" asked J.J., trying to slow Scotty down.

"Ramsey's dead. So are four St. Louis policemen. So's another guy we can't identify. I wouldn't be surprised if he's with Rostov. But, listen . . . I called you before I knew the *Bedford Clipper* was in North Carolina."

"Before? You mean earlier tonight?"

"Yeah! I got a call from Washington—I mean, I got a call from the St. Louis police who had gotten a call from Washington. Somebody in IDENT matched up the skid treads from the murder spot here in St. Louis with some marks you'd sent in from some trouble in North Carolina. It's the same damn vehicle! A Dodge Caravan."

J.J. flashed back to the night in the Hatteras Seashore—his pants wet from kneeling on the wet macadam, the cold rain dripping off his face, and the blood of two innocent children and a faithful companion named Charlie. *The sons of bitches were going to pay!*

Scotty continued.

"So, the Caravan was a match in North Carolina and there was a Ben Franklin store in Nags Head . . ."

"A Ben Franklin store?" interrupted J.J.

"Ramsey's clothes were bought from a Ben Franklin store and I was guessing it was after he'd brought the *Clipper* back to port. I've been spending the last day and a half trying to get a match on Coast Guard locations and Ben Franklin stores. Damn! I've got so much loose evidence . . . 9mm military-type Beretta shells . . ."

"Time out—time out, kid!" exclaimed J.J.

This had to be a kid he was dealing with. And the voice on the other end didn't seem to mind.

"How long have you been in the Bureau, Scott?" J.J. asked.

"Six months," replied Scotty, coming down a bit.

Six months!

And he probably wouldn't get a bigger case in his entire career. He was temporarily sad for the voice known as Scott Coldsmith.

"All right, all right . . . you've done well! You've gotten far. Farther than I have. Our cases are tied together. There's too much evidence. I've got 9mm Beretta shells and a mass murder, too—six dead people, including two kids, a Park Ranger, and an INTERPOL inspector following Khalid Rahman. My killers are a man and a woman. I've got their footprints and partial fingerprints. They got down to North Carolina on the 13th and left on the 20th. That's the same day the *Bedford Clipper* showed up in Wanchese—the same day Khalid Rahman met up with Zaid abu Khan—and probably with your Ramsey. Damn!" cursed J.J., deep in thought.

"What's wrong?" sensing trouble on the other end.

"My case was taken away from me, Scott. You'll find that it happens in real life. Washington thinks the Arabs are on the East Coast. We— the Bureau—are concentrating our search from Washington north to Boston. But those sons of bitches aren't on the East Coast. They're out here someplace. When did this thing happen in St. Louis?" J.J. rushed his question to Scotty.

"Two nights ago, the 23rd," replied Scotty.

"They drove from the Outer Banks to St. Louis in three days, then south or west," muttered J.J., still deep in thought.

"How do you know?" asked Scotty.

"Khalid Rahman was found dead this afternoon on an airport bus in Dallas. I'm calling from the airport, now," J.J. said. "After Rahman came to the Banks he bought a Chevy Suburban and modified it with a special interior for the storage area," J.J. said, his words flowing quickly and with intensity.

Scotty jumped back into J.J.'s thoughts.

"Before the St. Louis police were killed they reported a truck-like vehicle parked under one of the downtown bridges—at an intersection. The police came in and got themselves into a firefight. Even the backup crew was killed."

"Damn!" muttered J.J. "What the hell are the Russians doing in this? They killed Marmande when they found he was following Rahman. They killed the St. Louis police when they were about to be caught."

The enormity of what was happening struck J.J. across the face. The ends of his fingers went momentarily numb, the left side of his face and his scalp went tingly with a near-electrical surge of adrenalin.

"Those sons of bitches are protecting Khan! They did the same to you—or thought they'd done the same. You were too close!" J.J. nearly shouted.

Fumbling with his briefcase, J.J. fingered through his OAG pocket flight guide. There were no more flights from St. Louis that evening.

"Listen, Coldsmith, can you get NCIC updated from there?"

Scotty shrugged.

"Sure," said Scotty, now confident of his ability to do most any-

J.J. gave Scotty his case numbers.

"Somehow, I'm going to have to raise the flag. There's a 7:30 A.M. TWA flight tomorrow—today, to Dallas. I'll meet you at the gate. Got it?" asked J.J. in a rush.

"I think so. Where will you be if something goes wrong?" replied Scotty.

"I'll be in Delta's Crown Room. And Coldsmith . . ."

The delay was a full five seconds.

"Yes?"

"Good work. We wouldn't have made the link without you. I'm looking forward to meeting you. See you tomorrow," J.J. hung up.

Scotty sat at the empty desk in the empty bullpen, then let out a yahoo shout of joy, loud enough to distract the night clerk in the adjacent office. The clerk was was about to become very busy.

THE WHITE HOUSE

An aide shook the shoulder of FBI Director William Sessions. Outside, the last flakes of winter's worst snow storm fell to the ground. What had been predicted as a four-inch accumulation had turned into an eighteen-inch disaster. Most of the northern Maryland suburbs had over twenty inches of snow. Telephone lines were down everywhere. Electricity was out in a fifteen-county area around the nation's capital. Only places with their own power supply, like the White House, had electricity.

"Mr. Sessions, there's an urgent call from the Bureau. From a Mr. Bailey."

Bailey was the SAC in Charlotte—and he was on the special task force. Had they found Khan? Sessions went to the phone.

"Yes?" he demanded.

"Mr. Sessions, I'm afraid I have bad news."

Jim Bailey hated to be the messenger. The FBI was an agency where the bearer of bad news was indeed shot.

"I just got a call from one of my agents named John Carteret. He and another agent from New York believe they are on the track of Zaid abu Khan."

"Excellent!" said Sessions.

"Yes, sir . . . but they believe Khan is west of the Mississippi, perhaps far west of the Mississippi."

Sessions let out a string of obscenities. Bailey could do nothing but wait. Both the Director and the task force had banked on Khan going for what were the logical targets for their brand of terrorism.

"How do they know, Mr. Bailey?"

Jim Bailey told everything he'd gotten from J.J.

"I want to talk to Carteret . . . now! Damn! Where is he?"

"At a Delta Crown Room in the Dallas/Ft. Worth airport. He's commandeered it for the night. He and the agent from New York—the one who pieced the Soviet angle to this—are meeting this morning in Dallas."

"What does the task force think?" demanded Sessions.

Bailey stuttered his response.

"We . . . uh . . . tend to agree with agent Carteret. After listening to the tape several times, and after inspecting the weapon . . . we think Khan has not gone into the populated eastern corridor after all, but instead has gone west," said a reluctant Bailey.

"From sea to shining sea . . ." muttered Sessions.

"Yes, sir. I'm afraid so."

"How do I reach Carteret? Somehow, he's seen what we haven't been able to. Whatever help we can give him from here, we'll do it. Understand?"

"Yes, sir," Bailey replied. "John Carteret has always been a good agent," replied Bailey, knowing instantly that he was being terribly transparent, and regretted it.

"Yes, I'm sure he has," replied Sessions sarcastically, hanging up.

DALLAS

The Delta agent shook J.J.'s arm.

"Mr. Carteret, there's a call for you. Over there," the woman pointed to a bank of private phone booths.

"Carteret," was J.J.'s tired response.

"Carteret, this is Bill Sessions. Tell me what you know and why you know it," the Director ordered.

Without hesitation, J.J. spent the next ten minutes updating the Director. The conversation concluded with an offer of help from his Ultimate Boss.

"What help can I give you?"

"I could use a few hours sleep. If you could just let me have three or four hours sleep, then I'll take all the help you can provide. The one thing you can do, is to get a priority-one on that red and black Chevy Suburban. Coldsmith seems to think it's been in a firefight, maybe bullet-damaged. The record is in the system. Rahman was in St. Louis on the 23rd. He was found dead this afternoon in Dallas. It doesn't take two days to drive from St. Louis to Dallas. I would guess they headed straight south into Arkansas or southwest into Oklahoma. My guess is Khan and whoever is with him—at least the Soviet agent Rostov—are heading west someplace. Texas, New Mexico . . . hell, they could be in California by now. If you could get the state agencies moving, it would be a great help," said J.J.

"I'll have the Dallas SAC call you immediately," said Sessions.

"Thank you, sir. We'll need some planes, helicopters . . . if you don't mind, I'm going to catch a little shuteye."

"Before you nod off, Carteret, there's one thing you need to know . . ."

"Yes, sir" replied J.J., with some resignation.

"Khan has atomic weapons."

Static.

"Sir? Atomic bombs? Khan has atomic bombs?"

J.J. was astonished, but not so badly that he couldn't begin to feel the terrible enormity of the weight of responsibility being transferred to his shoulders. Whatever would happen would be his responsibility. There would be no help from Washington. There was no time for help from headquarters.

J.J. hung up. He had griped about the unfairness of his treatment, of his case being taken away from him. It was time to step up and into the real world. This was his case now—his case to make or break, to win or lose. He would be a star or a bum. There would be no middle ground.

The telephone monitor mindlessly asked him if he wanted to place another call. J.J. had stepped through his own personal twilight zone. He was on a one-way journey to an unknown place. No matter what happened from here on out, he wouldn't be able to return—he wouldn't be able to put back the comfortable pieces of his life again. This was what he'd dreamed of as a young man, the case—the opportunity—of a lifetime! But did he really want it? Did he really want to risk his life? Did he want to push his emotions up to the razor's edge needed? Once up there, once up in the rarified emotional atmosphere, there would be no return to the casual day-to-day-going-through-the-motions of life.

J.J. knew that once he tasted the addiction of what-could-be, he'd never want to go back to what-was.

THE WHITE HOUSE

The president was very tired. There were four, sometimes six, people on the line at once. The constant listening to every man's voice, determining who the voice was, then feeling for the inflection of the words, was very difficult—especially under the deep layer of stress. The stress was heavy on both sides. Waquidi needed to have the president accede to his demands. This was the single most important moment in the history of the 2500 years of the Persian Empire. On the other side, the president needed to be firm, while yielding slowly to the demands. He needed to be sharp, learning to twist and turn words as the Iranians could do so well. As they talked, the president had to be alert enough to silently read the handwritten notes passed to him from Hardy, Bulldog Russell, and the transcription of Oden Bennett's suggestions.

The adrenalin of the first hours' talk was gone. What was left was the drone of Waquidi's invective and his boring rhetoric. The president had been quick to agree to the clearing of the Persian Gulf, but balked at providing fully automated facilities from wellhead to tanker. The request to buy the new Iranian oil at $35 a barrel had been ignored. Waquidi hadn't returned to the subject yet.

Perspiring, and just as tired, Graham Atkinson continued his soft-spoken translation of Waquidi's words. A concerned Earl Hardy passed a roughly scratched note across the president's desk. It was from Bill Sessions.

> MY AGENTS HAVE LOCATED TWO OF KHAN'S MEN; ONE IN ST. LOUIS, ANOTHER IN DALLAS. BOTH DEAD. KHAN APPEARS TO BE HEADED WEST. UNABLE TO SEND EXISTING TASK FORCE BECAUSE OF SNOW. NEW STRIKE TEAM TO BE

ASSEMBLED IN DALLAS THIS MORNING. DISTURBING INDI-
CATIONS THAT SOVIET AGENTS ARE HELPING KHAN IN HIS
MISSION.

The president hit the OFF button on the speakerphone to prevent his
voice from being heard.

"The Soviets! Gorbachev's helping this madman? What the hell does
he think he's doing? If one of those damn bombs goes off . . . I'm going to call that son of a bitch . . . get me . . ."

The president was so angry, so passionate, that his thoughts came in
phrases. Sessions appeared at the door.

"Bill! What . . . ?"

Sessions raised his hands in a calming motion.

"We can't prove it, Mr. President. One of my agents, a trainee named
Coldsmith, from Manhattan, followed a Soviet courier and an illegal
entry named Ramsey from February 8th to the 10th, where he lost
them. We believe Ramsey was a member of Khan's army and that the
Soviet was following him—for what purpose, we don't know. Ramsey
hired a fishing trawler—and now we're even more fuzzy—and, we
think, met up with abu Khan at sea. On the 23rd, Ramsey was found
dead under a bridge in St. Louis, shot by police. Four policemen were
killed. Just this evening, the Coast Guard located the fishing trawler in
North Carolina. Another of my agents, a man named J.J. Carteret,
along with the local North Carolina police, have pinpointed the arrival
of the trawler as the 20th—which makes sense, considering how long it
would take to get there from Massachusetts. The man we had originally
identified, Khalid Rahman, has been killed in Dallas from gunshot
wounds. We're working on identifying the bullets, but it's highly
probable they came from one of the slain policemen in St. Louis. The
cars, the men, the prints—all match. Independent of our operation,
Coldsmith and Carteret have linked the evidence together. Khan entered
the country on the 20th in Wanchese, North Carolina. The same day,
they drove to Washington and planted the bomb in the Willard Hotel.
Hotel parking records indicate they entered the garage at approximately
4:45 in the afternoon. Between the evening of the 20th and the evening
of the 23rd, Khan and an unknown number of terrorists—at least two
others, Ramsey and Khalid Rahman—drove from Washington to St.
Louis. We suspect the number is a handful, no more than what would
fit in a Suburban. We have the identification of the vehicle. Given what
we know from Khan's message, we can only presume that he has
planted a weapon or weapons between here and St. Louis . . ."

Sessions was almost out of breath, the words came so quickly.

"You said one of them was killed in a police shootout in St. Louis?" asked the president.

"Yes, sir. Four policemen were killed on the night of the 23rd, along with this man Ramsey," answered Sessions.

"No weapon was found . . . no bomb?"

Sessions was stuck with the obvious. If Coldsmith had no idea who Ramsey was, then why would he be looking for a weapon? "Damn," William Sessions said under his breath.

Ramsey was killed in the darkness underneath an old bridge. The bridge was near the Gateway Arch, an obvious target.

"Damn," Sessions repeated. "Excuse me, Mr. President, I need to . . ."

"Yes, you do, Bill—but, finish what you've got," ordered the president.

Everyone in the room knew the United States was in peck of trouble. William Sessions continued.

"From the shell casings found in New Bedford, again in North Carolina, and in St. Louis, it appears as if the Soviet courier—named Alexander Rostov—has been following and protecting Khan. We think it was Rostov who killed the policemen in St. Louis. Rostov and a companion also killed six people in North Carolina, including an INTERPOL inspector. While the Soviets aren't doing the planting, they are up to their eye teeth in this by protecting Khan. I've got to go, sir. I'm convinced there's a bomb under the Eads Bridge in St. Louis."

Sessions hurried out of the president's office.

"Damn," said the president.

ST. LOUIS

Scotty didn't need the Rotor Clerk to shake his shoulder. Instead, his eyes opened with the sense of the other man in the room.

"Mr. Coldsmith, it's for you. It's important. I'm sorry."

"This is Scott Coldsmith," Scotty said wearily.

"Coldsmith, this is William Sessions," the voice on the telephone said.

The William Sessions?

"Yes, sir?"

"You've done some fine work, Coldsmith."

"Thank you, sir."

"Coldsmith, have you searched the area where you found this Ramsey character?"

"Yes, sir. I went back with the St. Louis police—twice. There was no evidence . . ."

"Do you know what these people are doing?" asked Sessions.

Scotty was slightly perplexed.

"You mean about the bombs? Mr. Carteret . . ."

Scotty could have kicked himself for using the word "mister."

". . . agent Carteret said these people are . . ."

Holy mother! Scotty's voice trailed off as his mind's eye saw the intersection of Washington and Wharf Streets and the darkness under the Eads Street Bridge. There were hiding places there for a weapon. He looked at his watch. In two and a half hours he was to board a plane to Dallas to meet Carteret. Had Khan hidden one of his bombs under the bridge?

"There are places to hide a weapon," Scotty said, somewhat unsure.

"Coldsmith—if there's one there—if there's a place you haven't looked, find it," said Sessions.

Scotty could almost see the director's white knuckles gripping the phone. He could feel the urgency and tightness in his voice as the director described the weapon and what had been done to disarm it.

"Help will be on the way, Coldsmith. Find it!"

— • —

"Paul, this is Scott Coldsmith. I just got a call from Bill Sessions. We have some evidence that the people who killed your men were Arab terrorists. We also think they've hidden some kind of bomb near the Eads Bridge. That's why the two cars were there. I need to keep this low profile, but I need to get it done right now. Can you get a bomb squad together?"

"At this time of the morning?" replied Worley.

It was 4:00 A.M.

"Paul, it's vital," said Scotty.

Vital was more important than urgent or needed.

"Damn!" muttered Worley.

"Paul . . . no radio contact. We can't have the newspapers on this. Understand? It's that important."

"Ok, ok," agreed Paul Worley, now half dressed.

— • —

St. Louis was as cold as a city could be—its buildings seemed to be tightly wrapped, huddled against the north wind. Spring seemed more than six weeks away. It would be another hour before the newspaper boxes along Tucker Boulevard and Market Street would be filled with fresh copies of the *Globe Democrat*. The only people awake were the night clerks in the downtown hotels, a few cabbies, and the short-order cooks who made their livelihood dishing breakfast to lonely people trying to keep warm. The traffic signals all flashed yellow. A single street cleaner slowly moved north on Seventh Street past the Marriott Hotel and headed toward St. Louis Centre.

Scotty knew his way to the Eads Bridge.

The arch was magnificent. From a distance it looked like granite, but instead it was polished steel—two layers of steel sandwiching a maze of thick steel rods and poured concrete. Scotty quickly turned off Market onto Memorial, then right onto Washington and found himself at the bottom of the hill facing the rolling Mississippi River.

In a few minutes Paul Worley drove up in his sedan.

"Might as well get started. The bomb boys don't look for them, they just remove them," he said.

"Bomb boys?" asked Scotty.

"Yes, I called the BDU," replied Worley.

"Paul! I told . . . I asked you not to involve anyone else! We're here to find the damn thing, not disarm it!"

Scotty's mind was spinning. He was trying to make decisions on things which might happen in the next few minutes. More people! More people meant more potential for leaks. Scotty hadn't even wanted to tell Worley.

The old abutment was rich with hiding places. Scotty walked up Wharf Street under the bridge and looked at the unrenovated sections of Laclede's Landing. The bomb could be in one of ten or so five-story buildings. The thought was depressing. Overhead he could hear the thump-thump of an occasional truck hitting the expansion gaps on the roadway's cement surface.

"What kind of bomb are we looking for, Scott?" shouted Worley, as he poked his light into the dark recesses of the cinder pit under the low-hanging train tracks. The protective chain-link fence had long since been ripped.

Worley poked around with his shoe, getting the obvious results—a shoe covered with grime. He grimaced at the thought of having to dig through the hardened muck. Scotty ignored Worley's question and walked back under the bridge, shining his light up and through the now-unused, narrow-gauge track. The track disappeared into the ground under the gateway arch. Up there? He questioned. The director said the bomb weighed over eighty pounds, was bulky, and was nearly four feet long. Khan would need a ladder to get up to the tracks—probably two ladders. It might have been a good place, but unlikely.

Lights flashing, a truck pulled up. The white and gold lettering of BDU identified it as the St. Louis bomb disposal unit—three men who did a job which paid them only marginally more than other policemen, certainly nothing in comparison to the risk. The three men got out and without introduction started to gear up for bomb disposal. Volume set on high, the words of the police dispatcher echoed through the crisp morning air.

Everybody in St. Louis would know there was a bomb under the Eads Bridge. Worley came back, shoes grimy, and waved to the men. The leader started walking toward Paul and Scotty.

"Damn it, Paul! I didn't want . . ." stuttered Scotty, now very concerned.

"You find it yet?" said the squad leader, a barrel-chested man named Owens, fiftyish.

"Not yet," replied Worley.

Scotty walked over to the spot where the head of Aziz al-As had been drilled with two 7.62mm slugs, knelt down on the cold pavement, then looked up. In front of him was a boarded entrance to what had been a maintenance shed. The damned bomb was inside the abutment—on the other side of the boards. Scotty knew it. It was the only other logical place.

Scotty walked over to the boards and shined his penlight along the edge of the boards. There had been tampering, but who knows when? This *had* to be it.

"Paul, I think the bomb may be in here," said Scotty.

"Excuse me, gentlemen. This is our job," said Owens, now wearing his lead-lined suit. It wouldn't do much against a one-megaton atomic bomb.

A gust of cold wind whipped down the river and drove up a cloud of cinderdust in their faces. Owens quickly inspected the outside of the boards for booby trapping. Finding none, he and his men used crowbars to pry the plywood sections down.

"If there's a bomb in here, you're only to secure it," said Scotty. "I've got orders from the . . ."

"Sure, sure," replied Owens, with practiced sarcasm. "Don't worry, we'll take care of it," ignoring Scotty completely.

The room was disgusting—littered with rat droppings, mostly-decayed birds, and the bones of eaten mice. Using a light attached to his belt Owens shone a powerful beam into the room.

"Looks like we found us a bomb, boys," said the red-cheeked Owens. "Time to get to work. You boys need to stand clear."

"Wait a minute! Your instructions are not to try and defuse the weapon, just secure it," said Scotty, now very agitated.

The light reflected off the surface of the steely grey surface, making it seem as sinister as it was. Owens paid no attention to Scotty's instruction and bent down next to the weapon.

"What do you think this is?" Owens asked another of his men, referring to the appendage.

"I've never seen anything like it," was the reply.

"Looks like it's been molded . . . ."

Scotty was in mental quicksand. His feet seemed stuck to the bare floor. His mouth was full of cotton.

". . . yeah, I don't see any way in except through this plate."

"Me either."

"What is this, Scotty?" asked Worley.

He had to tell them.

"Don't touch it!" Scotty shouted.

The men ignored him.

"Through the top?" asked one man.

"Yeah," replied his partner.

No! Mr. Sessions said help is on the way. Why isn't Worley doing anything? There was enough firepower in that bomb to vaporize everything within a half-mile. There was no telephone. No place to call.

Make a god-damned decision, Coldsmith!

"You two will have to get back now. We're going to disarm it," said Owens.

Scotty pulled out his service revolver.

"You're not touching this weapon," Scotty replied, finally with assertion, pointing the gun at Owens' chest.

"What the hell are you doing, Scotty?" shouted Worley, reaching for his gun.

"Don't, Paul!" answered Scotty, now pointing his gun at the St. Louis policeman.

"Are you out of your mind?" asked Worley.

Out of the corner of his eye, Scotty could see that Owens was nearly on the verge of deciding to jump him.

"Back off!" Scotty shouted.

"What's going on?" asked Worley.

"It's an atomic bomb, Paul." Scotty finally said. "You and this crew will have to be detained. By orders of the president."

Scotty stepped back into the doorway. He could hear the unmistakable deep thumpa-thumpa sounds that large helicopters made. Soon the air around the Eads Bridge was thick with dust and debris as the choppers negotiated their landing on Wharf Street. Two squads of Marines quickly took positions, sealing off the roads in the area.

"Mr. Coldsmith?" said the captain in an authoritative voice.

"Yes . . . it's in there. These men must be detained."

The Marines were from Scott Air Force Base located thirty miles southeast of St. Louis, in Illinois.

"I'm sorry, Paul," were Scotty's last words to a man he'd gotten to like in a short period of time.

Scotty turned to the captain.

"I need to contact the White House."

ABOARD THE AIRCRAFT CARRIER *NIMITZ*, MEDITERRANEAN SEA

"Briefing at 1600 hours," said Captain Emil Silverek. "I want everyone there, on time, ready to roll."

His orders were crisp and clear. Unmistakable. Emil Silverek was going into battle again and he loved it. He had been briefed by a direct telephone call from the White House. It was up to him to come up with the strategy for success. This time it wasn't a rescue. This time they weren't the ones waiting, not like Beirut—no, this time they could take no prisoners. The objective of the mission was a notebook, a book of codes. Why? Who cares?

It isn't for me to know or be concerned about, Emil thought.

The White House, the American government, thought the mission was so important that it would risk starting a war with the Iranians. From Mr. Russell's voice it sounded like we might already be at war with Iran.

The assault would begin at 2200 hours this evening. The probability of failure was greater than 60%. They would leave the *Nimitz* at 1700 hours, four squads totaling eighty men. Mr. Russell had told him to make his plans assuming that the Israeli government of Yitzhak Shamir would approve the flyover of Navy jets into Saudi Arabia. The Saudis had indicated they would allow the fully-loaded C-130, already in the air from West Germany, to land at an airfield off the coastal oil port of Dhahran on the Persian Gulf. Inside the belly of the C-130 were four fully armed Boeing Vertol Chinook CH-47D attack helicopters, ten French-manufactured Panhard ULTRAV M11 armored vehicles equipped with laser-sighted gun turrets, handguns, ammunition, food, and six racks of General Dynamics surface-to-air Stinger POST (passive optical seeker techinque) missles. The hand-held missles could lock onto infared and ultraviolet energy, and had been thoroughly tested by the Afghan rebels in their guerrilla war against the Soviets. Backed with six *Nimitz*-based F14s, the four squads of tough Marines would be the best-equipped men ever to have gone into battle.

Getting in was easy.

Getting out was a bitch.

The multi-million-dollar C-130 was considered disposable to the mission. It would land on the Teheran-Kashmar highway east of the capital, offload its cargo, and be left for the Iranians. Each of the Chinooks was equiped with extra fuel tanks. Two would be used to provide close air cover for the ULTRAVs during the attack, two would be held in reserve for backup and escape. It was theoretically possible for the Chinooks to fly from Teheran to a haven in Turkey.

Emil Silverek didn't believe in theories.

GALLUP, NEW MEXICO

To the north were the Navajo villages of Tohatchi, Coyote Canyon, and Yah-Tah-Hey. To the south were Black Rock, Pescado, and Ojo Caliente in the Zuni Reservation. In between the two ancient civilizations was the manmade town of Gallup—nothing more than a string of cheap bars, motels, liquor stores, and pawn shops set between I-40 and the twin tracks of the Atchison, Topeka, and Santa Fe railroad. The land was barren. The town was a hopeless and depressing example of what the American government had done to the Indian tribes.

The oblique light of the morning's first rays made the surrounding snowcapped mountains seem closer than they were. The day would be clear. To Alexander Rostov, a man who did not believe in luck, the good weather was simply noted—it was a factor which wouldn't have to be planned for.

Today was the day.

Khan would die, as would el-Rashid.

Williams and Katrina had seen the inside of the bombs, and they weren't that tough to arm.

"I believe I can handle it," Katrina had said, on edge.

The bombs were heavy to carry, but easy to arm. Today, this afternoon, both bombs would be placed and detonated. The mission would be over. Rostov had no idea what Katrina had planned, but he knew her plans did not include saving him. Once completed, it was everybody for himself. Tambov could find her way back to New York and more than likely find the haven of the Soviet mission. Rostov was on his own, trapped in a country seven thousand miles from his home territory. He knew how to get out of situations in Marseille—but not in Arizona. Mexico seemed the logical choice. Once the target was destroyed it would take all his skills to make his way south, hopefully crossing the border west of Nogales. From what Korz had said, the Americans would be confused immediately. He would need to negotiate the distance in the dark of night. Tomorrow morning he would need to be watching the sun rise over the Arroyo el Coyote or else risk certain capture—no, death.

There could be no capture.

"We should be finished today," said Khan, smiling.

"Yes, finished," replied Rostov, folding his map. "Have you decided who will go to the primary target and who to the secondary?" Rostov questioned, instantly regretting his choice of words.

Khan raised his eyebrow. El-Rashid's senses were alerted to his leader's vibrations. Rostov had made a mistake. He had been caught up in the execution and had not paid attention to the deception.

"Primary target? Secondary target?" asked Khan, now openly suspicious. "I have said nothing about a primary target," Khan said coldly, backing up slightly, his hands softly working toward a better position to reach for his handgun. He had never trusted the Russian.

Rostov knew his mistake. He needed Khan only if something went wrong—only if Khan was needed to talk to the Americans. At 6 P.M. this afternoon Khan's usefulness would be over.

El-Rashid lay on the second of two double beds, and was now alert. Khan stood near the bathroom door, his image endlessly reflected between the vanity and dressing mirrors. Rostov, map still in hand, stood by the triple-locked door. Under his breath, Rostov cursed to himself in Russian. Rostov looked at Katrina, who sat tensely in a red vinyl armchair near the circular lounge table.

I have a gun, her eyes said.

Rostov did not want to fight it out with Khan in a Ramada Inn hotel room—at least not until after the target was set. They had three hundred miles to go. There were too many things that could go wrong. At this moment Rostov needed Katrina. Unarmed, he needed her Beretta.

"Yes, primary," said Rostov. "We're going to split up today."

"No, I don't think so," said Khan. "We never agreed on what you call the secondary target. I have no intention of giving up my last weapon. If the American government refuses to act, then I must act. I will know tomorrow, when the newspapers are out. He will have had time. No, we do not split up today. What are you trying to do? You were right about the Americans and you helped us in St. Louis, but I have no intention of changing my plan," Khan said angrily.

Bafq el-Rashid now sat up on the edge of the bed, warily watching Rostov. He paid no attention to Katrina. He glanced up at Khan, who had moved slightly toward the opened bedroom closet door.

Khan's mind raced. Primary target? Since the night in St. Louis it had been easy to ignore the possibility that the Soviets wanted to do more than be insurance agents for Khan and his plan. Rostov had followed him from France.

They'd known all along—of course, they'd known—Rostov had admitted it. The Soviets had not wanted his plan to work in the first place. They had used him.

"You plan to detonate one of these, don't you?" asked Khan.

"Yes . . . both," replied Rostov, telling the truth.

Shifting in her chair, Katrina's hand touched the calf of her right leg and felt the steel of the six-shot .25 caliber Beretta single-action model 950. The four-inch handgun was snugly strapped to a holster wrapped around her calf. Gently she nudged the cuff of her pants and inched the fingers of her right hand up toward the small barrel.

"No! Everything will be destroyed . . . I will . . ." Khan's words were lost in his mouth.

Khan faced the realization that he and Abdul Waquidi would be blamed.

"Yes—you will be blamed," said Rostov, now facing Khan. "But it is irrelevant who is blamed. I have a job to do and I'm going to do it. You are disposable, Khan," Rostov said coldly.

Attention drawn to Rostov, Khan let the well of anger rise from his chest to his lips. At the same time Katrina's fingers found the .25 Beretta and withdrew it from under her pants.

"Khan!" warned el-Rashid, lunging—diving—across the sixty-inch bed which lay between him and the Soviet woman.

Aiming at Khan, three soft pops burped from the .25 caliber handgun. All were intercepted by el-Rashid—one in the face, one in the chest, and the third in the shoulder. Khan scrambled toward the closet and his revolver. Rostov dove for his legs, missed, and slammed into the wall, one leg hitting against the bathroom door, which in turn ricocheted against the bathtub.

Bafq el-Rashid hit Katrina with a flying body block, hitting her hard with his stony 170-pound body. At 135 pounds, Katrina was overmatched. The red chair toppled backwards into the corner of the room, the table and floor lamp crashing in opposite directions. El-Rashid's bloody wounds spilled in all directions, splattering in rough drops against the worn wallboard.

She'd hit him with all three shots!

Yet he was pummelling her with blows to the head. The right side of el-Rashid's face was bleeding out of control. The bullet had gone through his mouth from cheek to cheek, destroying the man's teeth, but not killing him.

On the other side of the room, Rostov and Khan—both approximately the same in age and size—were wrestling in the confined closet-bathroom area. Khan had a hand on his gun but Rostov had his arm. Rostov could easily see that Khan was the stronger of them. Unless he could gain control quickly, Khan would wear him down.

El-Rashid was on adrenalin overdrive. Grunting with every blow to her head and chest, he slowly began to realize that he was critically injured. He would have to finish the woman and then help Khan. Flattened under his bulk, Katrina felt Bafq's hands around her throat. She would be dead in less than a minute, her neck broken, strangled. His knee pinned her right arm to the unvacuumed carpet. She still held the Beretta 950. Meaty hands on her neck, with a last reservoir of energy she twisted and turned against his body—kicking and kneeing whatever she could feel. She couldn't breathe. Spots dotted her eyes as she started down the tunnel to blackness and death.

Was her arm free?

Did she still have the gun?

It was hard to tell. Feeling had left her.

Please let the gun be there.

Katrina slapped her right hand up to Akbar's face, the metal of the four-inch gun hitting him on the temple. It made no difference. She turned the gun in what she hoped was the right direction and fired once. Then she blacked out.

On the other side of the room Rostov was in a losing position. With his superior strength, Khan had maneuvered the Soviet agent into a balled position in the corner. While Rostov still had both hands on Khan's arm, Khan's determination had enabled him to slowly inch the gun to an angle where he would very soon have a shot at Rostov's shoulder, neck, or head. All it would take would be one or two bullets to shatter Rostov's grip, and it would be all over.

The men grunted with the exertion, both drenched with sweat. Khan smiled as he could see Rostov's eyes widen. The Soviet was losing his grip! Then, he saw Katrina stagger toward them!

"Shoot! Kill him!" Rostov spit out with exertion.

Khan then sensed the presence of a body behind him. It was the woman!

Katrina, blacked out for fifteen seconds, had come to with el-Rashid's body sprawled across her. She was drenched with sweat and blood. After sensing that he was dead, her mind then allowed her ears to hear the scuffling of the two men across the room. In a great deal of pain, Katrina squirmed out from under him. The last shot had gone through the man's left cheek, but this time directly into his brain. Balancing herself on the edge of the bed, she could see the tangle of men in a death struggle on the other side of the room. Woozy, she stumbled across the two beds until she was behind Khan.

"Shoot him!" urged Rostov again.

Not releasing his grip, Khan's attention was drawn to the figure behind him. He turned his head, only to see the tiny barrel of the .25 Beretta not more than four inches from his face.

"Breathe—and you're dead," said Katrina with an icy voice.

Her blouse was torn and bloody, her pants were soaked with el-Rashid's blood. Khan's attention was totally on the barrel of her pistol. He glanced up to her eyes. Hair disheveled, her eyes were black pits of hatred.

"Shoot him!" said Rostov again.

"No. This isn't over yet. We'll keep him until the target is gone. Things can still go wrong, Alex," Katrina replied in a voice which assumed control. "Drop the gun, Khan, or I'll blow your brains out."

No ifs, ands, or maybes.

Khan released his grip on the weapon, which in turn was quickly controlled by Rostov. In a matter of minutes Khan was trussed and gagged. Outside in his car, Williams had been unaware of the struggle. Inside, the room was destroyed. The beds were askew. Lamps, tables and chairs were overturned. Bed linen was bloodied, as were the carpets and walls. The pictures on the walls hung oddly as a result of the thrashing. Chests heaving, Katrina and Rostov sat back and tried to get their breath. Neither could talk from the exertion. They had done it again. Murder and mayhem.

After five minutes the two exchanged glances.

"Can you really handle the weapon?" replied Rostov.

"Does it matter? We have no one else. We must leave, quickly," she replied, without answering his question.

"Can you handle the weapon?" he asked urgently, taking her arm firmly.

"Yes!" she snapped, pulling her arm back, and getting up.

The two spent a few minutes cleaning their appearance. Both changed shirts. Khan followed them with his eyes. Clothes changed, Katrina stepped outside into the crisp morning air. The clear, cloudless sky made the sunshine brilliant, the colors of nature true. They had to leave quickly. The Indian housecleaning crew wouldn't arrive until nearly noon for their short shift. There was no way to hide what had happened. The authorities would be all over the area. They only needed a few hours lead. Although they had not talked of escape, Katrina had resigned herself to a one-way trip. She would not see New York again. She walked over to Williams.

"Leave your car. I will drive the Caravan, you will take the Suburban and go with Rostov," she ordered. Williams obeyed her without question or response.

Katrina looked around at the nearly empty motel. The office was out of view. She knocked on the motel room door.

"All right," she said.

Rostov quickly shoved the tied-up Khan into the back of the Suburban, then got into the passenger seat. Within two minutes they were back on I-40.

The sign said Flagstaff, 180 miles.

THE WHITE HOUSE

"They're off, sir," said Bulldog Russell.

The president looked and felt old. At 2:00 A.M. Waquidi had agreed to a six-hour hiatus in the talks.

"It's your time, Mr. President," said Waquidi.

The Arab leader had not given the president the code which would have to be inserted in the major newspapers across the country by tomorrow morning. And every one of the newspapers would have to be contacted directly by the White House because there was always a one-to-three-day delay in getting ads into a paper. Negotiations were moving slowly because the president had no intention of giving in to a single point. But this morning he would have to ask Waquidi for the code.

The raid might not work.

The attack on Teheran wouldn't start until two this afternoon (EST). The Marines were optimistically thinking on a two-hour operation, in and out. The president was much more skeptical. Murphy's Law had already been generously applied. He looked outside across the huge expanse of white. The temperature hovered near freezing, although the sun had come out. Washington was paralyzed. National Airport was still closed. Dulles was scheduled to open one runway at eleven, but only for diversion of foreign flights which couldn't get into Kennedy or Logan. The 12-mile Dulles access highway was closed, as was all but one rutted lane of the Washington beltway. Philadelphia had been spared the worst part of the storm by no more than twenty miles. The worst of the heavy snow lay along the coastline.

"Is there anything new on this Soviet involvement?" asked the president. "No, sir," was the reply on all sides.

"I've got to have something hard to go to Gorbachev. I've got to have evidence, proof—I need one of those agents. You give me something and I'll ram it down his throat. Nuclear blackmail . . ." the president's thought trailed off. "Son of a bitch!" he mumbled.

"We're ready to go back, sir," said Graham Atkinson. "He wants to talk about computers."

"Computers!"

The president was visibly upset at dealing with a third-rate bureaucrat from a nation whose political and religious background were more than foreign to him. Across the room Jim Russell and Earl Hardy exchanged glances. The president's jaw was locking in determination.

"Mr. President . . ." said Hardy, realizing the president was on the verge of going his own way.

"Is the line open?" he asked Atkinson.

"Yes, sir," came the young teacher's reply.

"Then tell that son of a bitch there'll be no more talk until I get the code. No computers. No oil. No nothing . . . not until he gives me the code."

Russell and Hardy silently groaned.

The line was open on the other end as well—fast and furious discussions in Farsi. Atkinson relayed what he could.

"Back and forth . . . Waquidi doesn't . . . somebody else is in the room . . . several people . . . I can't get all the details. Something about the book. No, more words . . . I don't understand it all. I think they're split on what to do. You've rattled them, Mr. President," said Graham Atkinson, smiling.

"We will get back to you shortly," came the terse reply.

An unshaven William Sessions came back into the room and gave a report to the president.

"It's the same bomb as the one in the hotel, sir. One-and-a-half megatons. It was set to go off at 9:00 on the night of July 4th. There would have been more than two million people down on the waterfront," said Sessions.

The president looked at the piece of paper. His real concern wasn't Waquidi, nor the raid. Where was Zaid abu Khan? And how many bombs did he really have?

DALLAS

At 9:15 A.M. TWA #247 arrived at DFW, surprisingly on time. J.J. stood impatiently in the Gate 6 waiting area along with a planeload of people ready to board the return flight to St. Louis. Everybody was bundled up. J.J. hadn't been outside since leaving Norfolk and hadn't really considered where he was going, or that he'd be outside much. Dallas was colder in winter than most people thought. All J.J. brought with him was his kit, a single change of clothes, and a lightweight jacket with gloves. Taking up the prime parking spaces directly outside were three government automobiles, their engines running, waiting for their temporary leader to appear. Waiting with J.J. was the Dallas Regional SAC, Columbus Whitehall, appropriately nicknamed Columbo for his casual, if not sloppy, manner of dressing. Whitehall had been directly notified by William Sessions that J.J. was to be officially in charge of this case and that he, Columbus Whitehall, was to provide whatever support, manpower and equipment Mr. Carteret needed. Sessions had told Whitehall that he was to consider the North Carolina agent as a personal representative of the president of the United States.

There wasn't much idle chitchat between Whitehall and J.J. After all, what was there to say to a genuine Personal Representative?

J.J. mentally shook his head. The few hours of sleep had done him some good, but he had come out of the sleep terribly disoriented. With Columbus Whitehall and four of his top agents hovering above him, waiting for his direction, John James Carteret fully realized how heavy the weight of responsibility was going to be.

"The plane will be down in a few minutes. I'm Columbus Whitehall, SAC in Dallas. I've talked with Mr. Sessions. You're in charge of this operation. What can I do for you?" had been Whitehall's greeting.

"We'll need a situation room and bodies—agents—to handle the phones. We've got to find these people—today," had been J.J.'s first words.

Without thinking or asking, J.J. assumed command. He thanked the Delta people and headed to the gate. Scotty was the first one off the plane and J.J. immediately put the voice to the face.

He *was* a kid.

"Coldsmith?" asked J.J., stretching his hand over the railing for a friendly greeting.

"Yes. You're Mr. Carteret?" replied Scotty.

When will I ever stop calling older people mister? thought Scotty, instantly blushing.

"Call me J.J.—meet you over there," J.J. pointed to the group of tall men in white shirts, dark suits, and tan overcoats. They were either IBM salesmen or FBI agents.

"I'm Scott—but everyone calls me Scotty. I guess I'm stuck with it. I'll be 25 forever," Scotty returned the greeting with a smile.

J.J. looked at Scotty and laughed. Taking Whitehall's direction, the group walked quickly toward the illegally parked automobiles.

"So, has anything happened since three o'clock?" asked J.J. with a half-laugh.

Scotty waited until they ducked inside the back seat of the middle car.

"Oh, not much," Scotty started with concealed irony and excitement that he could barely contain. "I found one of Khan's bombs under a bridge in St. Louis. It was set to explode on July 4th, but it had been booby trapped and could have exploded not more than three hours ago, vaporizing me and all of downtown St. Louis, except that Mr. Sessions called for the Army to help and they came in on helicopters—which was good because I didn't know what to do with my prisoners," Scotty blurted in a rush.

J.J. looked at his young companion in amazement.

"Other than that, you've had a pretty boring morning?"

— • —

By 10:15 J.J. found himself speaking to a packed room in the CritSit Room of the Dallas regional office. Columbus Whitehall waved for the group's attention. J.J. stood in front of the room.

The speakerphone crackled. The room was quiet.

"This is J.J. Carteret."

More crackling.

"J.J., this is Bill Sessions. The weapon found in St. Louis was an exact replica of what Khan left as his calling card here in Washington. Is Coldsmith there?"

"Yes, sir," replied Scotty, clearing his throat.

"Good work, Coldsmith!" said Sessions.

Scotty blushed again. Sessions switched intensities.

"You must find Zaid abu Khan—and he must be captured alive. We've found two weapons and we know he has at least three more. One or more of them may have already been planted. The president has asked me to personally convey to you the need to find Khan . . . and the Soviet agents whom we believe are helping him. It is in the security interest of the United States that these Soviet agents be captured alive. Do you understand? Alive!"

J.J. looked around the room of silenced agents, mostly fresh squared faces with blond hair.

"Alive—yes, sir. We'll bring them back alive."

The line from Washington went dead.

J.J. Carteret was in charge. He was in charge because the Director of the FBI said he was. He was in charge because he had earned the right to be in charge, and had assumed it.

He was a long way from Elizabeth City, North Carolina.

"This is not a simple case and we're behind the eight ball. From what I've pieced together from agent Coldsmith, and what's happened to me, the net of the story is that we've got an unknown number of terrorists out there," J.J. pointed to a map of the Western United States, snapping the rubber-tipped wooden pointer to the southwest U.S.

"And, they're getting help from the Soviets. We also have an unknown number of Soviet spies—at least two, possibly four or more—who are protecting them—who have protected them. These people are ruthless murderers. We know of at least ten people who have died at their hand."

Spellbound, the packed roomful of agents listened for ten minutes as J.J. reviewed what was known.

"They have atomic weapons with them. They've planted them across the country, and it's reasonable to assume they have at least one with them now. The one they found in Washington yesterday was the same design as Scott found in St. Louis," J.J. nodded to Scotty, ". . . simple, but effective. It's a weapon that will work and, properly placed, can kill millions of people. These people must be captured alive because we've got to know where they've put the other bombs. And that's what makes it so god-damned tough."

"What about the state offices?" asked one agent.

"Right now, we're considered a national command center. I need one or two men for each of the western states. Not only do we have to contact our offices, but we have to have the state highway patrols brought in—immediately, and without telling them the whole story. No one outside this office knows about atomic weapons. We've quarantined the police in St. Louis, and we'll do it here if necessary. The press can't know!"

They had the description of the Chevy Suburban, Alexander Rostov, and Zaid abu Khan. California and Arizona had inspection stations at their borders. Other states would have to use roadblocks. Interstate travel would have to be shut down by the state highway patrols in conjunction with the regional FBI offices. J.J.'s gut feeling was that Khan was headed through the Southwest. Every border crossing in Texas, New Mexico, Arizona, California, Nevada, Utah, and Colorado would have to be monitored. The task was staggering. In Arizona there were fourteen highways to New Mexico, six into Utah, two to Nevada, and five into California. In order to make the process easier to implement, the different state patrols would have to work together—a task not easily done. The FBI regional offices in Salt Lake City, Las Vegas, Phoenix, Albuquerque, Denver, and El Paso would have to invest every available agent and lead the effort. Recalcitrant officials or politicians would receive a direct call from the president of the United States.

By 10:00 MST the FBI's Dallas regional office became headquarters for the largest manhunt in history.

FLAGSTAFF, ARIZONA

They had driven quickly along I-40, through the brightly lit painted desert of eastern Arizona. Ten miles east of the snowy truckstop of Flagstaff, U.S. 89 intersected I-40. In a Denney's parking lot the three Soviet spies discussed their plans for the last time. They waited for Katrina to finish with Dimitri Korz on the telephone. Katrina wrote in shorthand as Korz gave her his last instructions.

"We have both weapons, Dimitri," she said, without emotion. Her bleached blond hair now looked dirty and stringy, emphasizing her haggard and drawn look.

"The first is already armed for 6:00. We will program the second, when needed. We are splitting up to ensure that one or the other will succeed. We have Khan, but we no longer have need for him. He will be killed as soon as we are in position. Everything is on schedule. You may tell Moscow."

"Good work, my Katrina," replied Korz, sad that such a woman would be lost. "You know what you must do if you are caught."

The statement was rhetorical. Yes, she knew. She could not be taken alive . . . and she could not return to New York. Her experience with Rostov had been more than she'd been prepared for. She would have to escape with Rostov or find her own way in the darkness of the night. Somehow, her fate would ride with whatever happened to Alexander Rostov. As much as she detested the man, their destiny seemed to be in tandem. Their fate was out of their control.

"Yes, Dimitri, I know what to do," she replied.

The thought of the death pill was constantly on her mind. She had too many things she wanted to do in life to dwell on the pill.

"Goodbye, Dimitri," said Katrina.

Korz hung up without answering.

Katrina replaced the handset. It was time to split up.

Katrina would go to the alternate site, with the last of the weapons. Rostov remained silent as Katrina gave the final instructions.

"If you fail, or if you are unable to find a helicopter, I will do the best I can to destroy the alternate target. If you are able to get a helicopter, I will wait as long as I can, but I don't want to die—neither of us does. I will know if you have succeeded by the light in the eastern sky at six o'clock," said Katrina, grimly. "I will wait here," she said, pointing to a spot on the map. There are mountains on both sides. Dimitri says that on the eastern side there are a cluster of maintenance sheds near the crest of the mountain, up a dirt road to a level spot with a view of the entire area. The sheds are unattended and contain the snow removal equipment and other supplies. We will park there and wait. I will leave my headlights on so you can spot me."

Rostov understood. Williams could handle a helicopter, assuming they could find one. The last weapon had been transferred to the Caravan. There were no other questions and no farewells.

GALLUP

Consuela Joseph pushed her supply cart from room 118 to 120. The task was menial, the pay minimum. Only a few people tipped her a dollar, sometimes two, as a courtesy for the underpaid who clean motel rooms. But not many. Even bad service in a restaurant got ten percent, but very few people tipped maids—especially in Gallup, New Mexico. People only stayed there because they had no choice—they were too tired to make Albuquerque or Flagstaff, depending on their route.

When she opened the door, Consuela's first impression was not again—not another disaster, a trashed room. She first saw the torn beds and scattered furniture. Then her mind let her eyes see the second layer of impressions. There was blood on the wall, on the sheets. As she walked into the room she seemed to be drawn into what had happened, and she was chilled. There was a body here, she just knew it. Still, she moved through the room toward the bathroom. She pushed the door. It wouldn't budge. Something was holding . . . a pool of blood, drying at the edges, oozed across the smooth bathroom floor.

— • —

When it rained it poured, thought Sheriff Tom Naschiti. An hour ago he'd been asked by the New Mexico Highway Patrol to help with a roadblock and search being set up ten miles west of Gallup, near the Arizona border. The Arizona state police were involved as well, which was unusual. Whatever it was, it was important. Kevin Blaine of the FBI's regional office in Albuquerque, was here as well. Kevin and Tom had worked several cases together, mostly dealing with crimes on In dian reservations and drug running. This was different. There was a manhunt on. The descriptions of the men were in everybody's hands. The names were John Doe. They were driving at least one Chevy Suburban and possibly a Dodge Caravan.

"Sheriff Tom," came the dispatch call. "There's been a murder at the Ramada."

"Damn!" cursed Tom, under his breath. "I'll be there in ten minutes."

He would be there in seven minutes. He had the supercharged Dodge up to eighty-five in no time. Already there was a quarter-mile backup on I-40 as cars were carefully inspected. Tom's deputy was waiting.

"It's incredible, no one heard a thing, Tom."

No, it wasn't incredible. Unless forced to, people did not want to get involved with other people's problems. It didn't matter if a woman was being beaten or raped in the next room or if there was a fight going on—the best thing was to stay out of the way.

"They came in a group," said the hotel manager.

"They?" asked Tom.

"Yes, they stayed in three rooms. There was at least one woman."

There is always at least one woman, thought Tom.

"What time did they leave?" asked Tom.

"They paid for their room in cash—I don't know. It was early," replied the manager.

Tom walked inside the room, still a disaster. The body was still crumpled up in the bathroom. Dark, olive complexion—European, no . . . he was an Arab.

They were looking for at least one Arab. This wasn't him, but the wire from the FBI had said that this John Doe could have one or more men with him. In fact, it was probable that there was a group. It didn't take much to leap to an assumption.

"What were they driving?"

The manager sheepishly looked at his registry. The vehicles hadn't been entered.

"I don't know. I think one of them might have been a ORV or a van, I can't remember. We were over half-filled last night."

Sheriff Tom Naschiti pressed the talk button on his always-open radio.

"Patch a call to Kevin Blaine. He's at the border roadblock."

— • —

Out in the open stretch of road west of Gallup, traffic was quickly backing up. Methodically, Kevin Blaine and the New Mexico and Arizona highway patrol teams went from car to car, carefully inspecting the faces of the occupants—paying close attention to the vans and trucks.

"You've got a call, Mr. Blaine. It's important," said one of the state troopers.

DALLAS

Every telephone in the office was humming. Sessions had called again, not more than an hour ago, to check on the progress. The runways at Andrews were almost cleared. Air Force One would be used to bring the Washington task force to Dallas. J.J.'s hours as case leader were limited, and he knew it. So did the young man he hadn't had much time to spend with, Scott Coldsmith.

Although his adrenalin was still pumping, Scotty was starting to fade. The scene under the Eads Bridge, the bomb, the army, the rush to the airport—he hadn't been able to sleep more than fifteen minutes on the flight. It wasn't that he minded being part of a larger team—no, that wasn't true. He did mind. Scotty looked around at the room. *They were getting in on his case!* He could see the same reaction in J.J.'s eyes. He was losing the case again, just as he did in North Carolina. *They* would take it away. Yet the job was more than one or two men could handle. It demanded more arms and legs.

One of the men waved at Scotty.

"Line 2—"

"This is Coldsmith," Scotty answered.

"This is Kevin Blaine. I'm covering the roadblock on I-40 at the New Mexico-Arizona border. Right now I'm at a Ramada Inn outside Gallup, New Mexico. I think I've found one of your men. He's an Arab, and he's dead. Violently dead. There's been a struggle and a shootout. There was only one body—I can't tell if there were more. There was a group of them, three cars. The motel manager thinks at least one of them was a van or covered truck."

Scotty ran across the room to J.J. with the information.

"We're closing in on them, J.J.," Scotty said, his eyes excited but anxious.

He didn't want to miss out on the finale. He hated to give up the capture. Scotty wasn't a good poker player. His emotions were close to the surface, and it didn't take much for J.J. to pick them up. J.J. felt the same way.

"I'll be damned if I'm going to let somebody else get that son of a bitch!" said J.J., with near anger.

J.J. thought of Marmande, the dead children, and the humiliation of having the case abruptly taken from him. Scotty's eyes showed the same determination—the tailing through New York, the shootout in New Bedford, the cold water of the Acushnet River, the terror under the Eads Bridge.

Scotty's eyes begged.

J.J. looked at the large map of the United States that occupied the entire wall of the conference room. J.J.'s finger touched Gallup, New Mexico. He looked up at the clock. HQ would be here in a matter of hours.

"Damn!" said J.J.

If Khan left Gallup this morning, then he was either in Arizona or California—most likely still in Arizona. The nearest FBI regional office was in Las Vegas. J.J. picked up the phone and dialed the White House.

"This is J.J. Carteret, let me talk to Bill Sessions, please," J.J. said firmly.

The director was on the line almost instantaneously.

"We've found one of them—in a motel in Gallup, New Mexico. It appears as if they had a falling out. There were signs of a struggle, but no other bodies. I think they're headed to California. There's no need for us to stay here, sir. Coldsmith and I have been on this from the start—and we're going to be there at the end. I'd appreciate it if you'd notify the Las Vegas office that we're coming."

"But—what . . . ?"

"Mr. Sessions, I'm not a chief, a manager, or a supervisor. I'm an agent. *I'm not going to have this case taken out from under me again.* I—*we*—are leaving. Can you call for us, sir?"

There was silence.

"I'll notify Las Vegas," was Bill Sessions' response.

J.J. couldn't see it, but Bill Sessions was smiling. He liked the style of John James Carteret.

TEHERAN, IRAN

They'd had only a mild case of Murphy's Law. They were only an hour late in arriving, but considering the snafus, Emil Silverek was glad they were landing at all. The lumbering C-130 had been late getting to Dhahran. And the Saudis had at the last moment come up with objections to the Americans leading a strike across the Persian Gulf to a country with which it had neutral relations.

If there was money in the deal, they wouldn't have any problems, thought Emil. There wasn't anything in the pot, so no gain, no pain—to paraphrase an ad slogan.

The force had skimmed the littered Persian Gulf at fifty feet. The bodies of dead tankers, uncleared since 1978, were strewn from Abadan to the Strait of Hormuz. Shippers were lucky a channel was open at all. One bump, one thermal, and they'd waterski across. The F-14s, pulling back to sub-cruise speed, accompanied the oversized, heavily laden cargo plane. They crossed the border in the darkness of night at eight-thirty, apparently unseen.

They crossed the Gulf in a matter of minutes and were quickly over the unpopulated wastelands of southern Iran, the Dasht-e Lut Desert. The night was clear. No sandstorms this time. Emil walked up and down the line of troops, quietly but firmly reminding each man that this was not a rescue mission.

They were at war with Iran.

They were going to attack the presidential palace and capture the president of Iran. It would be reasonable to expect heavy resistance, although not until they got closer to the city.

They'd relied on reports that most every able-bodied man was on the Iraqi front lines. The eastern suburbs of Teheran should be fairly clear of troops.

Once into the badlands, the C-130 looped out toward Afghanistan and came northwest toward Teheran over the seemingly endless Dasht-e Kavir Desert.

"Coming down, gentlemen," relayed the pilot.

Lights out, the pilot made a nice landing on the four lane highway. However, there was no chance the C-130 would ever leave the landing spot except by being towed. It's huge wheels were too wide for the pavement and simply sank into the soft desert sand. Built during the rule of the Shah and designed to link the rich valleys along the Caspian Sea, the road was now used not by automobiles but by oxen-driven carts.

"Secure positions," instructed Silverek as the four squads scrambled out of the tail section of the huge plane, anxious to get out of the way of the logistics crew.

Emptying a C-130 of its cargo wasn't something done in a matter of a few minutes, yet it was done with surprising skill and speed. Two of the four Chinooks were offloaded in matter of twenty minutes, as were the ULTRAV M11s. Emil led squad #1. Squads #2-4 were led by Delgato, Smith, and Bradley.

"This highway goes straight through the eastern section of the city, right to the market area," said Emil.

Rule number one: nothing in Iran ever runs straight.

"Do you know where you're going?" shouted Emil to the pilot of Chinook #1 as he warmed up the powerful attack helicopter.

It was a question which should have been asked. By law and simple economics, the city was completely dark. One building looked like another. Emil couldn't risk putting his men in helicopters which possibly couldn't land near the target. Half of Smith's squad were into Chinook #s 1 and 2, although it was the firepower of the helicopters which Emil Silverek knew he would need. No, they would have to rely on ground attack to make their way through the city—the conventional way war was fought.

At 11:15—3:15 EST, 1:15 MST—Emil Silverek's armored attack force rumbled through the eastern outskirts of Teheran toward the presidential palace of Abdul Waquidi.

PAGE, ARIZONA

Alexander Rostov kept a close eye on his rearview mirror. El-Rashid would have been found by now. The Americans were far from stupid. The FBI had to be close at hand. A close encounter with an Arizona highway patrol car would mean the death of them both. There was no way Rostov could or would be taken. Capture meant the bitter pill and death. If he refused, Rostov was sure that Williams had orders to kill him, then take the pill himself. At worst, there would be no live evidence of Soviet government involvement. No bomb, no attack.

Of course, Khan wouldn't be alive either. The thought gave Rostov some slight amusement. No Khan, no Rostov—nobody left to tell where the bombs were hidden. Maybe he did have some negotiation chits left in his pocket. Maybe they weren't worth much, but they were better than nothing. The Americans would do anything to know where those bombs were hidden.

Leaving Flagstaff behind, Rostov eschewed taking U.S. 89. Instead, with the view of snowcapped Humphrey's Peak in his mirror, he took off on a circuitous route through the Navajo and Hopi Indian reservations via Indian highways 2 and 15, then state highway 264. His whole purpose was to avoid the Arizona inspection station north of the bridge over the Little Colorado River at the turnoff to the Grand Canyon. The group had passed a similar station on I-40 shortly after crossing the New Mexico border.

Rostov was taking no chances—not so close to the objective. The route had cost him nearly an hour and a half, but had avoided the inspection station. Finding himself back on U.S. 89, Rostov's route steadily climbed up through the Navajo lands toward the high plateau of the Colorado River. At Bitter Springs the road turned east and climbed up over a ridge. To his left Rostov could see the narrow but deep canyon of the Colorado off in the distance. Beyond were the crimson rocks of the Vermillion Cliffs, the border of Arizona and Utah. A half-hour later Rostov, followed by Williams, slowly passed through the town of Page.

Perched on top of a hill at the northernmost point in the Kaibito Plateau, Page was a city built by the U.S. government in 1959. Taking the business route, the two vehicles slowly climbed into the city, passing Page High School, then turned left and passed through the town proper. A twelve-store shopping mall was on the left, enough to support the two subdivisions of lower-middle-income tract homes which occupied the terraced north side of town. East of 89 were several newer subdivisions of more expensive rental homes. These homes had a better view.

And what a view it was.

Rostov pulled into the nearly empty parking lot of the Holiday Inn. Past the Inn the road dropped sharply. Below lay the beautiful expanse of Lake Powell, a manmade lake created by the completion of the Glen Canyon Dam in 1964. It had taken seventeen years for the waters of the Colorado River to be fully impounded behind the dam.

At six o'clock MST, February 26th, twenty days after killing Arab terrorist Ysed Bandar in a Marseille jail, Alexander Rostov would destroy the Glen Canyon Dam. The destruction of the dam's power plant and the nearby Navajo steam generator would cause a massive, cascading blackout throughout most of the Western United States. Not only would Glen Canyon dam be permanently destroyed, but so would Hoover, Davis, and Parker dams further down the Colorado. Nearly five million kilowatts of electricity would be instantly, and forever, lost to the power system of the western states.

Waiting at Hoover Dam, with the last of Khan's bombs, was Katrina Tambov. If anything went wrong at Glen Canyon, it would be her responsibility to take out Hoover.

The nuclear silo sites in Idaho, Montana, western North Dakota, and eastern Washington would be dark. The B-1 bomber bases at Fairchild (Spokane, WA), Minot (Minot, ND), Ellsworth (Rapid City, SD), March (Riverside, CA), Castle (Merced, CA), and Mather (Sacramento, CA) would be dark. The ICBM bases at Malmstrom (Great Falls, MT), Minot, Ellsworth, Warren (Cheyenne, WY), and Monthan (Tucson, AR) would be dark. The Interceptor bases at the Great Falls Airport (Great Falls, MT), Minot, Monthan, George (Victorville, CA), the Fresno Air Terminal (Fresno, CA) and Kingsley Field (Klamath Falls, OR) would be dark. The Nuclear Storage and Logistics operations at Hill (Ogden, UT), Kirtland (Albuquerque, NM), Nellis (Las Vegas, NV), Seal Beach (Seal Beach, CA), Concord Weapons Station (Concord, CA) and the Sierra Army Depot (Susanville, CA) would be dark. The Naval Air Stations at Alameda (Oakland, CA), Lemoore (Lemoore, CA), Long Beach (Long Beach, CA) and San Diego (San Diego, CA) would be dark.

With all or most of these bases temporarily without electricity, the defense of the United States would be subject to immediate counterattack by the Soviet Union. A limited defense would be the only action possible. Offense would be out of the question.

Mikhail Sergeyvich Gorbachev would be free to seek his place in history.

— • —

For the first time in nearly a month, Alexander Rostov paused to consider his place in history. He was the man on the point—the loner whose job it was to find the enemy. On the opposite side of the world thousands of Soviet troops lined the Iranian border and hundreds of pilots checked their planes for the last time. And it would be Alexander Rostov who would lead the charge.

Rostov smiled. You're getting old, he thought. This was as close to being sentimental as he'd ever remembered. He was not a patriotic man.

He did a job, and he did it well. Cynics suppress emotions. *Back inside!* he thought. Inside they went. Rostov stopped smiling and walked back to the Suburban.

"Are you ready to die, Khan?" were Rostov's words to the terrorist leader.

Two miles to Rostov's right were the triple stacks of the Navajo Power Plant. At night, powerful strobes danced on the three-hundred-foot-tall smokestacks and could be seen for fifty miles in all directions, a clear warning to any low-flying airplane. Although the "smoke" rising through the stacks was actually steam, the plant was one of the largest coal-burning facilities in the world and had been a controversial project from the days of its first design. Environmentalists had fought the project from day one, but in the end had failed to overcome the tremendous political and practical realities. What they had ensured, however, was the cleanest sub-bituminous generating plant in the world. The smoke rising from Navajo's three units would not produce acid rain in Colorado forests or destroy wheat fields in Kansas.

In less than three and a half hours, the Navajo Power Plant, with its running capacity of 2,225 megavolts (MV), would be destroyed.

At the bottom of the hill below him was the two-lane, steel-arch Glen Canyon Bridge crossing over the 700-feet-deep gorge of the Colorado River. An engineering feat of the highest magnitude, the bridge had been a prerequisite for the construction and completion of the Glen Canyon Dam and the town of Page itself. Behind the dam were 180 miles of impounded river water that formed Lake Powell.

In less than three and a half hours the bridge and dam would be destroyed by atomic blast. Lake Powell would begin to move toward the Gulf of California. At 110 miles an hour, the first wave would cross the border at San Luis Rio Colorado in Mexico at approximately eleven tonight. Much of eastern California and western Arizona would be flooded, cities destroyed, people killed.

Crossing the bridge, Rostov turned right and into the nearly empty parking lot of the visitor's center. Both he and Williams got out and went inside. The center was named for Carl Hayden, a long-time U.S. Senator from Arizona who had befriended the construction of the bridge, dam, and city.

"Stay here, Rostov instructed. He didn't like Williams. He didn't like *any* of the men selected by the American Soviets.

Rostov walked into the circular building and was immediately struck by the incredible sight of the dam in the forefront and the massive Lake Powell behind it, it's cold, blue waters in stark contrast to the reds and yellows of the surrounding barren land. Near the main entrance was a twenty-by-fifteen foot relief of the entire Glen Canyon area. To the left was a Park Service gift shop and a corridor which led to the administrative offices and an elevator to the self-guided tour of the dam.

Perched high above the dam, Rostov looked through the floor-to-ceiling windows, sizing not only the scope of effort but more importantly for a place to put Khan and his bomb. It had to be in a place that could do maximum damage. The bomb had to take out the Navajo Power Plant as well as the dam, its powerplant, and the transmission lines—although the dam was the primary target.

There was enough water behind the dam to cover the entire state of Pennsylvania to the depth of one foot. The lake stretched 186 miles up the Colorado and was named for army Major John Wesley Powell, who first mapped the area. The air was crystal clear, making mountains seventy-five miles away appear close at hand. There were no trees to clutter the view. Vegetation needed rainwater, not standing water, and it only rained four inches a year in Page.

Before any part of the dam proper was constructed, the Colorado was diverted from its normal flow. Diversion tunnels forty feet in diameter were dug into both canyon walls at riverbed level for a distance of three thousand feet. At the same time, two spillway tunnels were being built. Starting at a point on each canyon wall, almost five hundred feet above the riverbed, each forty-foot-diameter spillway was cut through and down into the canyon wall to meet up with the diversion tunnels at riverbed level. The spillways were designed for potential overflow conditions when Lake Powell was fully impounded. From start to finish, it took eight years to build the dam.

And a microsecond to destroy it, thought Rostov.

The dam had been constructed to conserve the scarce water resources and to generate electricity as a by-product. There were eight generators in the riverbed power plant, each capable of being driven at 150 revolutions per minute. The generators were spun by turbines which in turn were turned by water passing by them at high speeds. Water from the lake passed into one of eight penstocks. Each penstock was a fifteen-foot-diameter pipe built into the dam on a diagonal, starting at elevation 3470 feet at the lake and falling through the dam to the power plant at elevation 3140 feet. Water flowing through the penstocks was controlled by opening or closing of a 300,000-pound steel gate. At the head end of each intake penstock were a series of mesh trashracks which protected the generators from lake debris.

With all turbines going full blast, all penstocks open, the dam could pass 18-19 million acre-feet per year, or 24,000 cubic feet of water per second, no more. If Lake Powell had more than 18 million acre-feet of intake, the lake would rise and the dam would overflow. It was that simple. One level foot of water equaled 165,000 acre-feet.

Rostov took the elevator down three floors to the dam's crest, following the signs to the self-guided tour. Slightly wider than a two-lane highway with sidewalks, the top of the dam was twenty-five feet above the surface of the lake. On the river side, the dam's power plant and the Colorado River were seven hundred feet below. There was nothing but deep canyon to the west. To the east lay the expanse of Lake Powell. Running along the dam were roads leading to the spillway tunnels. How did the cars get down to the dam? Above him there was a road which paralleled the north shore of the lake. From a visitor's viewing area, a dirt path connected the road to the dam's crest through a chainlink fence.

It looked promising. There was no chance the bomb could be placed on the dam itself. Rostov looked around for guards. There were none. The dam was massive. It would take an atomic bomb to blow it up. Rostov smiled. From the top of the dam, Rostov stood alone in a large elevator that went down 70 stories through the center of the dam to riverbed level, then walked down two narrow hallways to an exit into a large courtyard. Up close he could see the design of the huge blocks of concrete. Small rivulets of water ran down to a concrete drainage ditch which eventually ran to the Colorado. Dams leak—either through or around the intake penstocks, the abutment joints, or through the concrete itself.

From the grassy courtyard it was a short walk to Generator Alley. At the time only three of the eight generators were humming. The generators were large enough to require a three-story working area just for the placement of the equipment and another three stories for the two 300-ton cranes to be able to slide back and forth to do the heavy work of replacing either a turbine or a generator when required. In the unseen "basement" was the draft tube which fed the water into the Colorado River after it had done its job with the turbines. At level one was the penstock gallery, a service walkway for the penstocks and the lower section of the turbine. Level two contained the main body of the turbine, its stainless steel engine firmly buried in concrete. Sitting above the turbine on level three was the thirty-three-foot-diameter generator, painted yellow with a head painted bright red.

With the exception of two or three maintenance men on the other side of the huge area, Rostov was alone in the room. Rostov looked at his

309

watch. It was 3:15. It was time to get into position. Retracing his path back to the parking lot, he wordlessly got back inside the Suburban. Williams sat passively in the Caravan.

With deliberation, Rostov drove along the shoreline of Lake Powell, toward the small marina and recreation center called Wahweap, which consisted of a moderately priced, three-story motel and restaurant, houseboat and motorboat marina with five hundred slips, two camp-grounds, and a small series of shops and various outdoor activities. Rostov pulled into the parking lot. Ahead of him on the opposite side of the lake, perfectly framed between the two motel buildings, were the imposing sheer cliffs of Castle Rock, the place where on November 4, 1776 a party of Spanish explorers led by Fray Francisco Atanasio Dominguez and Fray Silvestre Velez de Escalante crossed the Colorado river, discovering the area.

Rostov saw what he wanted to see.

Next to the motel was a small office with bright red oversized letter-ing—*Will Gregory's Canyon Tours*. Gregory, a former helicopter pilot in Vietnam, now ferried tourists up and down the canyons on hour-long tours of the backcountry in his sleek Rockwell International six-passen-ger corporate helicopter. Rostov walked inside. It was evident this was the slow season for Will Gregory.

"Are you available for hire, Mr. Gregory?"

Gregory laughed ruefully.

"Any time you're ready, pardner."

"How about in an hour? There are two of us. We'd like to see the sunset on the canyon. You can get to the canyon from here?"

"No problem. Hell, we could go to Las Vegas and back if you wanted," Gregory laughed. "As a matter of fact, your timing should be pretty good. Just let me get your champagne on ice and my bird warm," replied Gregory, smiling. "That'll be $185 each," Gregory looked up to see if Rostov would back off or try to negotiate.

Rostov did neither. He pulled out his wallet and laid four one hun-dred dollar bills on the table.

Walking back to the Suburban, he scanned the marina area. *Where do I put the bomb?* he thought. The dam was nearly three miles away, as was the Navajo plant. He could leave the Suburban right where it was. While the Navajo plant wouldn't be vaporized, it would be de-stroyed, its smokestacks toppled, crushed by the blast. But would the dam be destroyed? Rostov was no engineer, and it would take someone who knew physics to tell if the direct force onto the top 25 feet of the dam, plus the violent concussion of the water, plus the overtopping of the dam due to the wave action would collapse the structure. Leaving the vehicle in the lot with other cars meant low risk. The only safe option was to stay with the weapon until detonation. Alexander Rostov wasn't keen on suicide. It was the option not considered. Khan will go up with the bomb, he thought. But the Wahweap marina wasn't the place to do it. He had to get closer.

In a back compartment, Khan was squashed into one of the empty bomb compartments. He struggled futilely with his ropes. He was going nowhere. Rostov slowly drove back toward the dam, the calm waters of Lake Powell down a fifty-foot embankment to his left. The sun was low in the horizon and it was only four o'clock. They didn't have long. Halfway back to the dam, Rostov pulled into a small gravel and dirt parking area above the north spillway a quarter-mile from the crest of the dam. The explosion would vaporize everything.

Rostov parked the Suburban, then crawled back into the storage area, already smelly from the sweat of the Arab. It would get worse as six o'clock approached.

"Do you hear me, Khan?" asked Rostov over his shoulder, a cruel smile on his lips.

Khan muffled what surely was an Iranian curse.

"I thought so. You're going to get your wish, Khan. You're about to blow up one of the largest dams in the world," Rostov said coldly.

The pupils in Khan's eyes were fully dilated.

"You will be blamed, Khan. You and your lackey, Waquidi. You both will be blamed. Yes, I've followed you! I've followed you because my government can't believe how stupid you are! You handed us the perfect opportunity to dupe the Americans and capture your country. The Middle East solution is at hand. And you have provided it—not for your Arab friends, but for the Soviet Union," Rostov cried triumphantly.

Khan squirmed and grunted in anger, the circulation in his hands and feet were nearly cut off by the ropes.

"I've got to go, Khan. Don't worry, I'm sure the Americans will kill your friend Qaddafi immediately. You won't be the only one to die."

Rostov looked at his watch. It was 4:15.

"You've got an hour and forty-five minutes. One of the good things about this is that I don't think you'll know it when it happens. One second you'll be here—the next you won't. But I'll be alive, Khan—I'm not going to die, not for any cause. The difference between you and me is that I'm doing a job. You've let all this emotion and idealism get in the way—it's all clutter, it gets in the way. Well, say your prayers—or whatever you people do."

Rostov closed the door on the compartment to the bomb, and did the same on that of Khan. The terrorist leader was locked in a three-by-three box. The extra heavy tinting, installed by Khalid Rahman, prevented anyone from seeing inside. Rostov closed and locked each door, slamming the last with a degree of satisfaction that bordered on cruelty. The job was almost done. There was plenty of time to meet Katrina.

With Williams driving, the two men left the Chevy Suburban parked in the gravel lot and drove the short distance to Will Gregory's Canyon Tours, where Gregory's helicopter was already warmed and waiting.

"Fasten your seat belts," said Gregory. "Put your headsets on. I'll be talking to you through the headsets. You won't be able to hear anything else!" Will Gregory shouted over the thumpa-thumpa of the helicopter's blades. "Ready?"

Without an acknowledgement, Will Gregory let the engine go. In a single smooth motion the helicopter lifted up and backwards from the small landing pad. In what seemed like an instant, they were 500 feet over Lake Powell. Gregory guided the sleek helicopter directly over the Dam. The 700-foot dropoff to the Colorado River was just as impressive from the air as it was up close. Ahead, the Colorado snaked its way down narrow Marble Canyon. In the distance to the right were the Vermillion Cliffs, to the left the high plateau and the city of Page. Seen from the air the city seemed even more lonesome than it was. There was not a tree to be seen for 70 miles in any direction, not a single one.

Rostov allowed himself the luxury of listening to the Vivaldi playing in his earphones. It would be another 45 minutes before his adrenalin would need another kick.

TEHERAN, IRAN

Emil Silverek surveyed the situation. There had been no misunderstanding the purpose, the importance of the mission. Gain the objective at all costs. Retreat was not an option. Take no prisoners, and expect no quarter from the enemy. If captured, expect to die.

It had taken longer than expected to offload the C-130, which shouldn't have been a surprise. Nothing ever worked like it did on paper. All of the equipment was expendable, including the state-of-the-art ULTRAVs, the C-130, the Chinooks—and the soldiers.

At 12:45 A.M., with Emil Silverek in the lead vehicle, the U.S. Marines started their assault on the capital of Iran. Each of the ULTRAVs had satellite microwave transmission capability, with backup. Communications between the four units was from ULTRAV to satellite to ULTRAV. There would be no need to try to pinpoint the location of the other units and send directional signals. There was also no attempt to keep the communications secret. Anybody tapping the signal would get an earful.

Emil got final confirmation of each squad's readiness.

"You all know what is at stake. If you get stuck, get in trouble, get stopped—you are free to fire at will. Let's go!"

From different directions the four groups of Marines launched their assault on the city of Teheran. Considering the ruggadized engine and frame, the ULTRAV M11s made less noise than one would expect, hardly more than a Jeep. Lights out, the M11s rumbled through the outskirts of Teheran at 45 miles per hour. There was no traffic. There were no lights. There were no people. They were, however, very conspicuous. Other than the normal olive green, black, and brown camouflage there were no other markings on the M11s.

It wouldn't be long before all hell would break loose.

THE WHITE HOUSE

The President cupped his hand over the receiver and banged his fist on the table.

"Tell that son of a bitch I'm going to level his country to a pile of rocks."

"Sir? I can't tell him that!" said the young interpreter.

Mollified, as he knew he would have to be, the President smiled. He had to have a vent for his anger. The bile he felt for the pipsqueak bureaucrat was overwhelming. They were going to bomb St. Louis, kill millions of people. What other cities did they have lined up? What did the Soviets have to do with this? The Iranians and the Russians were enemies and had been so for decades. The Iranians were devoted to their religious beliefs, completely different and opposite from the president's, but nevertheless diametrically opposed to the godless rule of the Soviets. The evidence of Soviet involvement was undeniable. Yet he needed proof. He wouldn't put anything past Gorbachev.

The president spoke into the telephone.

"What agreement do you have with Khan, Mr. Waquidi?"

"We have no agreement, Mr. President," came the response. "It is growing late. We . . . you . . . have little time. Khan will expect to hear something positive by tomorrow morning," said Abdul Waquidi.

"Or what?"

"Or you may have to be shown how sincere we are in our beliefs."

"Meaning?" asked the president.

"I think it is best you and I try to negotiate. It is getting late here in Teheran. It is the middle of the afternoon in America, but near the middle of the night in Teheran. I have heard nothing from the Iraqis regarding a cessation of the war, nor a rollback of the present line. I have heard nothing! My generals tell me the war rages as before! Your ships are still in the Gulf! You have done nothing, Mr. President! You deserve what you shall receive!" shouted Waquidi.

Waquidi was obviously upset with the lack of progress and surprised with the determination of the American president, faced as he was with massive destruction of several of his major cities and the loss of life which would accompany it. Khan had not prepared him for this stubbornness. The American president was playing a close game.

"Is there an interim message you can send?" asked the president. "Is there a message which will tell Khan that negotiations have started?"

"Negotiations haven't started, Mr. President. I see no evidence you have any intention of satisfying our demands. I will not give you the code Khan needs to see. The blood of your countrymen is on *your* head, Mr. President."

"You listen to me, you two-bit paper-pusher! If one single American dies from one of these weapons, you won't see the morning! You'd better pray to Allah, because I've got B-1 bombers ready to annihilate your country. There won't be anything but sand and ashes for five hundred miles around Teheran. Do you hear me, you little son of a bitch?" shouted the president.

"Mr. President!" said Earl Hardy.

Jim "Bulldog" Russell leaned over and touched Hardy on the arm.

"I'd do the same thing. Leave him alone. He needs to get the anger out."

TEHERAN, IRAN

Eugene Branch, Unit 3, was the first to run into difficulty. Almost lost in the maze of inner-city streets, none of which had recognizable names or identifications, Branch had run smack into a police patrol consisting of three ageless Citrons and a battered 1975 Chevy. Branch's men had hardly waited for his signal to fire. The men were more than ready. They were eager to fight the bastards. This was revenge a long time coming, a dozen years since the hostage humiliation.

Initially the police were no match for the laser-guided automatic weapons. But the police knew the terrain and had managed to radio for help while scattering from the old cars into nearby buildings. Branch and his men spread out as best they could on the debris-littered streets and started to fire heavy weapons into the first floor of buildings in direct line. The shells, armor-piercing, ripped through the adobe-like structures. Cries of death were heard everywhere. No prisoners were being taken.

"Forward! We're losing time! Unit 1, this is Unit 3. We've encountered local police. Limited resistance, but I'm sure they're on to us. I don't exactly know where I'm at, but I think I can see what might be the old Holiday Inn up ahead. Over," shouted Branch.

"Unit 3, I can hear you. Forge ahead. Leave them if you can. We're just north of the square. I think I can see it ahead. Wait a minute. I see troops . . . over," returned Emil Silverek.

And troops there were. And they were firing at Unit 1. The shells bounced off the M11s, pinging and ricocheting into the sidewalk. The men returned fire. Shots came at the ULTRAVs from all directions. Tracers flew down the narrow alleys, explosions lit the night. It would get down to hand-to-hand combat very soon.

"Unit 2! Unit 2! Where are you? Over!" said Silverek from inside the protection of his armored vehicle.

An explosion rocked his M11 as someone had tossed a grenade down the street, missing the ULTRAV but destroying the corner of an old building. Stay here and they'd be buried in rubble.

"Forward! Fire at will!"

The sound of rapid automatic-weapon fire ripped through the night as the ULTRAVs made their slow way toward the great open square where years before happy Iranians had celebrated the wealth and status of their oil kingdom. Iranian palace guards and what few Army troops still remained in Teheran had pulled back and concentrated their positions in front of the presidential palace. Their return of fire was considerable. It was a matter of time . . . Emil heard the death of a nearby ULTRAV as it received a direct hit from several rockets.

"Spray the area! I need wider coverage! Unit 2, where are you? Goddamn it, Sam, where are you? I need air coverage! Where's my goddamned air cover?" Emil shouted.

Where where the Chinooks? Where was Unit 2?

There was no "over" any longer. Emil's Unit 1 was getting stiff resistance.

"Unit 1, Unit 1, this is 2. Lieutenant Delgato has been killed. This is Waters, Jimmy Waters."

The voice was young.

"Waters, this is Unit 1. Where are you? Over," said Emil.

"Unit 1 this is Unit 2. I don't know, sir."

Jesus and Mother Mary.

"Listen Jimmy—listen Waters, you're in charge. Identify what is directly ahead of you. Fire at will. Come on, boy, you've got enough firepower in these babies to knock out a squadron. I need your help, Waters! We don't have much time! Hurry!"

DZERZHINSKY SQUARE

Bodnof looked at the printout. It couldn't be true! How could it be true? Moscow and Teheran were in the same time zone. Lights were on all over Red Square. Reports had come in from various monitors along the Iranian-Soviet border. Bodnof ran for the door, then down the hallway to Viktor Chebrikov's office.

He arrived breathless.

"The Americans are attacking Teheran!"

"What?" was the general's astonished response. "How do you know?" he demanded.

"Radio transmissions. They are using open signals, clear channels. The Americans have a force inside Iran and they are attacking the governmental palace! If they take over . . ."

"Enough! I heard you! Have you verified this? You will rot in a Siberian hell if you are wrong, my friend," Chebrikov waved his index finger at Major Bodnof.

"I am not wrong, general. The Americans are attacking Iran."

"We have no evidence of this. There are no . . ."

"General, it is happening as we speak. If you want to hear the transmission, I can have it sent."

Bodnof reached for a phone. With a look Chebrikov made him hang it up.

"Damn!" said the chairman of the KGB.

Chebrikov reached for his private telephone.

"The Americans have launched an attack on Teheran," he said.

"How?" said Shevardnadze.

"I don't know, they just have."

"I want to know how!" demanded the foreign minister.

"Why don't you ask your army friends?" Chebrikov replied.

"You are supposed to know, my friend," said Shevardnadze.

"What about the plan?" Chebrikov asked.

"I don't know. Mikhail must make the decision. I will tell him," Shevardnadze replied.

Fifteen minutes later Eduard Shevardnadze was in the office of Mikhail Gorbachev.

"What are our alternatives?" asked Gorbachev, seemingly unperturbed, his career, perhaps his life, in the balance.

"We have no evidence the Americans are attacking in full force. Their submarines haven't done anything unusual. Their fail-safe positions haven't changed. There has been no movement of NATO troops. As far as we are concerned they don't even suspect our operation," said Shevardnadze.

"And if we cancel?" Gorbachev asked.

Shevardnadze was disheartened, nearly appalled.

"We can't cancel. This is our opportunity. We won't have another chance to strike at the heart of the American defense. We won't have another chance to gain positions on the Arabian Sea and Persian Gulf. Please!" begged Shevardnadze.

"Yes . . . yes, I know," replied Gorbachev.

Glasnost was still in effect. To the all-important Western journalists he was still "Gorby," *Time*'s Man of the Year, the powerful man with the attractive wife.

"What are their positions?" asked Gorbachev. "Why are they there?"

"We don't know," was Shevardnadze's simple reply.

"Do we launch?" Gorbachev asked.

"Ahead of schedule? We aren't scheduled for another half-hour. The bomb won't go off for another half-hour," said Shevardnadze, now beginning to worry about spending the last half of his life in a Siberian hole. "We must! Ahead of schedule? I don't know. Yes, we must."

Mikhail Gorbachev looked at his hand-picked subordinate. If they failed, their political careers were over, their lives were over. It was clear, either start it now or don't launch at all. The Americans were starting a preemptive strike of some sort. A limited strike. Why? Did they know? Would they find the bomb? In less than an hour the American defenses would be helpless. If the Soviet government wanted to launch a missile attack, they could. It was only a half-hour. Why not get a head start?

Mikhail Gorbachev had had enough time to think of the possibilities. He had already decided. He was shooting for the history books.

"Strike!" said Gorbachev, giving permission for the combined Soviet forces along the Iranian border to cross over and launch an attack on the oil-rich, defense-poor country.

Shevardnadze reached for a phone.

"Start the operation," were his only words.

GRAND CANYON NATIONAL PARK, ARIZONA

Will Gregory gave a tremendous tour. To normal people it would have been the thrill of a lifetime. After passing the Glen Canyon Dam, he flew down into Marble Canyon and followed the narrow passage for fifty miles. At one point he even went under the Navajo Bridge where Alt. U.S. 89 crosses the canyon. Off to their right was the Kaibab National Forest and the Kaibab Plateau of the North Rim. The road to the North Rim was still closed due to snow accumulation, and would remain closed for another month. They came around Point Imperial at the point where the Little Colorado River meets the Colorado and there it was! The whole of the Grand Canyon opened up to them. It was an incredible sight.

"Time for some champagne!" said Will Gregory to his passengers.

Each of the helicopter tours included a 15-minute stop someplace along the way for a couple of glasses of champagne. It was part of the memory—sipping champagne while the sun set over the Grand Canyon. It was an excellent marketing tool. In a move which would surprise most passengers, Gregory brought his helicopter into a semidive, quickly coming below canyon-rim level, then further down until he skimmed over the Colorado River, then just as quickly brought the helicopter up to rim level and hovered over a small patch of land just east of Desert View. It was an area which the Park Service allowed the helicopter tours to use for their champagne stops.

"Coming down!" shouted Gregory into the headphones.

With the noise of the rotors and his attention taken by landing his helicopter, Will Gregory did not notice what was happening in his passenger compartment. Rostov gave Williams the eye. They sat behind Gregory, splitting the space of the five-passenger compartment. Williams was directly behind the pilot. Closer—closer, touchdown. Stabilized, Will Gregory paid more attention to shutting his craft down than he did to his passengers. It was his last mistake.

From behind him, Williams, in bear-hug fashion, wrapped his thick arms around the pilot's seat and Will Gregory's neck, then pulled backward with everything he had. Will Gregory had only a moment before he was dead. He had no comprehension as Rostov fired his revolver at close range into his right ear. The bullet passed through the helicopter's Plexiglass window and out, without shattering it.

Rostov quickly scrambled into the co-pilot's seat, reached over and opened the pilot's hatch, disconnected Gregory's harness, then dumped the pilot unceremoniously onto the frozen turf.

The sunset was indeed beautiful.

Within minutes Williams was in the pilot's seat, Rostov in the co-pilot's. Williams had command of the helicopter.

"Go!" said Rostov.

Williams went.

WAHWEAP, ARIZONA

Elected as a young man in 1968, sheriff John Kiley had been the only sheriff Page and the surrounding villages had ever had. Earlier in the afternoon Kiley had gotten a request by the Arizona highway patrol to assist in setting up a roadblock on U.S. 89—but the request was rescinded when it was agreed that the sheriff of Kanab would take care of it. It was just as well. It was seventy miles to the border. However, Kiley had received instructions to watch out for any suspicious vans or 4-wheeled vehicles.

Who were they kidding? Everybody and his brother owned a 4-

wheel in Page, some families had more than one. Nevertheless, Kiley made his rounds with one extra eye open for something out of the ordinary. He didn't know why he was looking for some suspicious van, just that he was to notify the FBI if he found one.

Part of Kiley's rounds included a pass through the Wahweap campgrounds and marina. Very seldom was there any trouble, but nevertheless he kept to his schedule. It was important for people on vacation to remember that they weren't supposed to do things in Page that they wouldn't do at home. It was the vacation, screw-it mentality which got a lot of normal-behaving people into trouble when they got out of their routines.

The sun had just set, the sky filled with a spectacular sunset—an array of reds and yellows. Kiley turned off 89, past the closed visitor's center, and onto the road to Wahweap. His stomach was telling his mind to pay attention to dinnertime. The lake's color changed with the deepening of the sky, but the tops of the stark mountains in the background were lit with the last rays of the day.

Kiley's heart went into his throat when he saw the Suburban parked in the small lot above the dam. Gut instincts are rarely wrong. This was what they were looking for. This car meant trouble. Kiley had one part-time and one full-time deputy. He radioed the office.

"Henry, this is John. Put me through to the state police."

"Something wrong, sheriff?" asked the deputy.

"Just put me through, Henry," Kiley said with irritation.

The boy was a bit slow. The call was patched.

"Yes, sheriff?" came the static-ridden patch to Flagstaff.

"Can you check something out for me? I'm responding to your request about an unusual van or 4-wheel-drive vehicle. I've got one. It's a Chevy Suburban, North Carolina temporary tags. Red with black roof. Kind of beaten up. Could be bullet holes. It looks empty. I'm going in."

"Wait a minute, sheriff!"

Kiley could hear the dispatcher frantically talking with someone, probably a supervisor.

"Where are you, sheriff?"

"I'm north of the Glen Canyon dam, on the road to the Wahweap marina."

More frantic talking.

"We have instructions, sheriff. Don't touch anything. Can you see if there's anything inside?"

"Sure, hang on," said Kiley.

John Kiley carefully drove down into the parking lot and pulled up beside the Suburban. The doors were locked, the windows heavily tinted. Kiley could make out shapes in the back compartment, but that was all—nothing definite.

"There's something in there, but I can't make it out," reported Kiley.

"Just a minute, sheriff."

The line went to static for the better part of two minutes. A different dispatcher came back on, more authoritative.

"Sheriff Kiley, help is on the way. Please do not touch anything. Keep the area clear, please."

It was 5:38.

GALLUP

It took a little over two hours for the military helicopter to cover the distance from Dallas to Gallup. They were met by Special Agent Kevin Blaine. Before they could inspect the motel, Blaine received a call. It was for J.J. The call had been patched through from Dallas.

"Mr. Carteret, this is Bill Stone of the Arizona State Police in Flagstaff. We've found the Suburban," said Stone.

"What!" J.J. exclaimed. "Where?"

"In the town of Page. It's in the northern part of the state. It's parked near the Glen Canyon dam. The local sheriff is watching it."

J.J. turned to Kevin Blaine.

"Where's Page?"

Blaine pointed to the map.

"These people are in Flagstaff. How far away are they from Page?" he asked the agent.

"One hundred thirteen miles. An hour and a half even if they drove like a bat out of hell, forty-five minutes by helicopter," replied Blaine.

"How far are we?" asked Scotty.

"As the helicopter flies, about two hundred miles," Blaine replied.

J.J. returned to the phone.

"Is there a military base nearby?"

"Nellis is outside Las Vegas, but it's probably a toss up between it and Luke AFB near Phoenix," replied the agent.

"We've got to get there," J.J. replied, with urgency in his voice. "Tell the sheriff to not touch a thing! Help is on the way." J.J. hung up the phone and turned to Scotty. "I want to leave in five minutes. Kevin, can you get me the commander at Nellis?"

In less than 90 seconds J.J. was talking to the base commander of Nellis Air Force Base, outside Las Vegas.

"Commander, this is John Carteret of the FBI. I'm going to need a weapons disposal crew sent to Page, Arizona. Nuclear," added J.J.

The commander's attention had been grabbed.

"I'm leaving now. We believe an atomic bomb has been planted by Arab terrorists near the Glen Canyon Dam. We need to get it out of there, ASAP!"

J.J. could feel the reluctance of the commander to accept the information.

"Stay on the line, commander!"

Mumbling curses to himself, J.J. ran inside the devastated motel room and direct-dialed the hot line number inside the White House.

"This is Carteret! I need to talk to the president. Now!"

Thirty more seconds went by. It was 5:42.

"Yes?" came the familiar voice of the president.

"Mr. President, I have the commander of Nellis Air Force Base on the radiophone We need a nuclear bomb crew sent to Page, Arizona immediately. We've found the Suburban and just know one of those bombs is in it. The base commander is reluctant to help me."

"The Glen Canyon Dam?"

"Yes, sir,"

"Good God!" exclaimed the president. The news took the president's breath away. He was very familiar with the water problems of the western states and the battles with environmentalists. He also knew what a disaster it would be if the dam were blown up.

"I'll take care of it, Mr. Carteret," replied the president, firmly.

J.J. ran back to Blaine's car.

"Commander, in the next few moments you will receive a call from the president. I'm leaving for Page within the next two minutes. I expect that bomb squad to leave within five minutes," ordered J.J., his emotions now pipelined for action.

J.J. thanked Kevin Blaine and ran for the helicopter. Scotty was already inside. Ducking down, J.J. jumped in and buckled. He hadn't finished when the helicopter took off, swooping out past the motel and out over the barren desert of eastern Arizona.

It was 5:50.

TEHERAN, IRAN

For being cold, hungry, and ill-equipped, the Iranian palace guard was putting up one hell of a fight. For the better part of the last fifteen minutes Emil Silverek had found himself pinned down in a one-square-block area just to the north of the square. Roadblocks had been set, grenades and firebombs prepared and thrown. Two of the M11s had been taken out, with the loss of life inside. Emil's squad had been halved.

Other than the one conversation with Unit 2, he'd heard nothing from them. They must be lost in the city. It was easy to do unless you could read the markings on the maps supplied by army intelligence. Unit 3 was on the south side of the plaza pretty much in the same condition. The were pinned down at the edge of the plaza.

"Can you see how they've got the plaza covered?" Emil asked Eugene Branch.

"No, I can't. They've got us covered pretty well. You put your head outside in the street and you can pick it up later."

"Look—god-damn it, Eugene—these M11s should be able to get through most anything. We don't have much time. They've got to have ordered backup. If they come from our rear, we're cooked. We've got to go for the palace! Now!"

"Roger. I hear you, Emil. When?"

They had to make a rush. The Iranians would soon see they had the Americans covered and bring in air cover or bring snipers onto the rooftops to pick them off one at a time. It was nearly two in the morning. This operation should have been over an hour ago.

"Two minutes, Eugene! Drive right into the god-damned palace! Where's Unit 2?"

"I don't know."

"Listen! Base! Where's my god-damned air cover?"

THE WHITE HOUSE

"Sir, satellite recon is picking up what appears to be troop movement along the Iranian border. It looks like the Soviets have moved inside Iran. In force, sir. We can't tell yet, but it looks like they're doing the same from Afghanistan," said an aide, handing the president the infrared photos.

Just at that moment William Sessions chose to make an entrance into the Situation Room.

"We've got a team from Nellis on the way. They'll be there in minutes. We've closed Arizona down at every border. We're going to get them, sir."

The president looked at Bulldog Russell.

"Go to Yellow, Jim. I want all the planes up."

Then he instructed another aid.

"Get me Gorbachev."

"It will take a few minutes, sir."

"Do it."

It was 5:52.

TEHERAN, IRAN

The two Chinooks appeared out of the darkness, evil and monstrous, their snaggled look giving the appearance of a monster dipping for a clawed kill. Without touching ground, the two hovered, disgorging their cargo of fresh troops into the plaza.

"Go! Go! Go!" shouted Emil Silverek.

It was an all-or-nothing run for the roses. Silverek swung his four remaining M11s out into the alleyway and headed straight for the plaza. Both the front and rear turrets were pointing directly ahead of them. The forward gun spit 7.62mm bullets at the rate of 300 per minute. The rear gun launched hand-grenade-sized rockets at 10 per minute. They had enough ammunition to sustain a continuous rally of three minutes.

"Go! Go! To your right! Watch out! Up ahead. There it is! Got the son of a bitch."

They could see the plaza. Emil had no idea of what to expect when he got there. For all he knew there could be eight thousand troops up there, all waiting to pounce on him. The roadblocks were set in place.

"We're through!" came Eugene's voice on the radio.

"What does the plaza look like?"

"They're moving back! Not as many as we thought!"

Emil's lead M11 smashed through the roadblock, quickly surveyed the situation and gave the forward turret enough time to spray a semi-circle of death. The place guard had moved back. There were many dead. Fires had started all around the plaza. A section of houses where Unit 3 had broken through was raging uncontrolled. There was no fire department.

"We don't have much time! Go for the palace! They're inside!"

The M11's bumped over the cobblestone plaza, its solid hard rubber tires chewing up whatever got in its way. Over bodies, debris, fire, then onto steps. There were a hundred and fifteen steps in three tiers to the top of the palace. It was fruitless to try to make it on foot. There wasn't enough time.

The sight of the heavily armored M11s motoring up the ancient steps was terrifying to the Iranian troops. Each vehicle spit streams of fire in a constantly moving arc. Bodies were everywhere. Unit 1 met Unit 3 at the top of the steps. There were five M11s left, twenty-two men. Unit 2 was still nowhere to be seen or heard.

They crashed through the hastily constructed barricade and found themselves inside a huge antichamber.

"Out!"

It was time for hand-to-hand. Each Marine was equipped with a Colt 9mm submachine gun, a very light and versatile version of the M16 rifle. The sub was designed especially for fast-moving attack troops or SWAT operations. Each carried a long-handle, double-edged Swiss knife and each was fully trained in use of the garrote. These troopers took no prisoners.

"We've got to go room by room. They're probably in the room up-stairs. Take it one room at a time!"

The room suddenly was filled with smoke from what appeared to be a tear-gas canister. Then a shout.

"Grenade, right!"

On instinct the men dove to the left. The grenade detonated, shattering part of the front wall and killing two Marines.

"Squad 1, up the steps! Now! Go! Now! Squad 3, to the rear!" shouted Emil Silverek.

Shielded by a blistering shower of bullets, Unit 1 attacked the front stairs. Squad 3 ran from room to room on the main floor, meeting some resistance. They had no idea how many palace guards there were or even if Waquidi was in the building. Near the rear of the building, on the second floor, Emil's Raiders met stiff resistance along the length of a hallway which connected various living areas with more business sections. The tapestries on the walls had long since been taken and used for wraps to keep warm. There was very little furniture except for the bare essentials.

These people are hanging on by the thinnest of threads, thought Emil. The guards would have run at such an attack, so this must be the place. Waquidi must be in the back room.

"Eugene! Back of the building! Second floor. They're right in front of me! Is there any way up?" shouted Silverek.

They had forgotten to bring their walkie-talkies and were forced to shout. It was a very dangerous situation. Split in two, they were subject to an attack from the rear. Things had to be finished quickly.

"Sergeant Branch, can you hear me?" Emil shouted.

Eugene Branch's acknowledgement was a blast from his submachine gun through the ceiling of the first floor. The 7.62mm shells ripped through the ceiling tiles, up through the floorboards of the second floor and lodged themselves into the ceiling of the ornate roof. It had to be enough to scare the wits out of anyone not suspecting it.

There was no sense asking Waquidi to surrender. These people would rather die. Allah would praise them for dying in combat against their enemies. It didn't make the job any easier.

"Gas," said Emil. "In there," he pointed to what appeared to be an occupied room.

"Masks," instructed Silverek.

He didn't need to bother. The men were well aware of what was going to happen. The launcher belched the shell through the empty space of the open second floor and into the far room, which quickly filled with cries of panic when the shell exploded and the gas spread.

"Wait . . . wait," said Emil. "Sergeant Branch, fire to the left. Now!"

The second-story wooden floorboard erupted with exit wounds, the fragments and splinters thrown everywhere. There were more cries, this time of death and injury.

"Go!"

The men of Unit 1 ran down the wide hallway and flung themselves into the room. There were bursts of fire, then grappling and scuffling, and still more cries of death. It was over in a matter of minutes. The palace guard was defeated. Emil Silverek walked through the smoke.

"Get that thing out of here," he instructed to a Marine to dispose of the still smoking tear gas canister.

He walked into a room which at one point had been a library. There were two men sitting at a table, arms over their face. Neither man was armed. Silverek pulled out a picture of Waquidi, then looked at the man in the chair. It was him. The other man must be the translator.

"President Waquidi, my name is Emil Silverek, Captain, United States Marines. I've come for your code book, sir."

Waquidi was in amazement at the sights and sounds. With the window now open the cold February air quickly cleared the acrid smoke from the room. Waquidi shivered. He couldn't understand what Silverek was saying.

"Are you his translator?" Emil asked the other man.

When there wasn't an immediate response, Emil walked across the room and shook the man by his lapels.

"Are you the translator?"

"Yes," came the frightened response.

"Then translate!"

Emil turned to Waquidi.

"You know which book I'm referring to, sir. If necessary I will have you tied down on this table. I am trained to give you an injection of sodium pentathol. One way or the other you will give me what I'm looking for. I must have the answers now."

While the translator translated, Emil shouted to one of the men in the next room.

"Bring the kit," he shouted.

In an instant the small kit was laid open on the table in front of Waquidi. Emil snapped open the crisp paper envelope of the needle, then the syringe. Two vacuum-sealed vials of pentathol came with the kit. Any more than that would be a waste, for the subject would be dead. He inserted the needle into the vial, then quickly let the forces of nature draw the liquid into the syringe.

"Tie him down," said Emil, in his best stage voice.

Three burly surly Marines grabbed Waquidi and roughly picked him up and threw him down on the table. Papers flew everywhere. Emil looked at the translator.

"Last chance, translator. He dies, you die. What is it?"

Waquidi started to babble, the translator talked.

"He . . . he . . . the president wishes to . . ."

"Where?" demanded Emil Silverek.

"In the desk drawer," said the translator.

Emil found the book and opened it. It was half in English, half in Arabic. He could read both entries. It was what he had been told to get. He didn't understand what the messages meant, just that he was to get them. Emil reached for the phone. The line was still open to Washington.

"Mr. President, this is Emil Silverek, U.S. Marines. Sir, I have what you asked me to get."

PAGE

Why had he come over here this afternoon? He should have let well enough alone. He looked at his watch. A few minutes before six. When was anybody coming?

Kiley paced outside his cruiser—door open, radio on loud. It was going to be a long night. These guys—whoever they were—would be hungry. And the local sheriff would get the hind tit. He'd end up driving over to the McDonald's to get ten large bags of carryout, probably taking every last French fry in the place.

What was that?

A sound. It wasn't the wind.

Again the same sound.

Damn.

Things don't make sounds. People do.

Kiley's steps crunched on the cold gravel as he walked back to the dirty red Suburban. Why hadn't he heard these sounds before?

Muffled sounds.

Damn!

Someone was inside that truck! Kiley peered through the dark glass. With the high beams of his cruiser on the Suburban, it was impossible to see inside.

Somebody was inside!

Kiley tried the door again, but no luck. The noise increased. Somebody was trapped inside!

John Kiley's instinct told him that someone was in trouble, needed help. What was one window? Kiley smashed the driver's window with the business end of his revolver. One window wouldn't hurt. He reached inside and opened the door. The door opened and spilled the odor of impending death out into the night.

"Damn!" recoiled Kiley.

The smell was of sweat and urine and . . . who knows what.

It was 5:59 P.M. MST.

The sounds came from the rear compartment of the Suburban. With

328

the dim inside light on, Kiley crawled into the back seat toward the noise. Fumbling with the cover, he pushed the wooden latch back and uncovered the terrified body of Zaid abu Khan. Kiley recognized this man. But who was he? He was gagged and tied, and clearly hurt.

Kiley undid the knot in the man's mouth.

Khan spoke in rapid Farsi—then quickly corrected to English when he realized that Kiley had no earthly idea what he was saying.

"Bomb! Please! Bomb! Hurry! Over there! Next compartment. It's set to go off at six o'clock! Hurry, please! Hurry! Bomb!" stuttered Khan, his mouth sore from nearly twelve hours of gag in his mouth.

Bomb? Jesus! thought Kiley.

Kiley had no idea what was happening, but he followed the head motion of the man to the next compartment. Kiley opened the compartment and saw the gray sphere.

It was six o'clock P.M. Mountain Standard Time.

The alarm buzzed for an instant. It also sent a jolt of electricity down a short wire to the firing pin of the detonator, which itself was buried in a tomb of plastic explosive. The detonator and plastic did indeed explode, but instead of blowing outward, the stainless steel shell forced the eight pounds of processed uranium down its two-foot path. The lithium-tipped missile smashed into the larger cavity of the bomb, which contained fifty-eight pounds of U-235. Directly in the path of the missile's lithium tip was an equal amount of the alpha-emitting polonium element. Instantly the combination of the two started a process where neutrons were stripped off, making the uranium process completely unstable. The uranium then started to tear itself apart, one atom at a time, but very quickly.

Within one second the explosion vaporized the parking lot, the Suburban, sheriff John Kiley and his squad car, Zaid abu Khan, the road, the side of the hill, the path to the dam, the glassy Carl Hayden visitor's center, the electrical switchyard, and the top of the Glen Canyon Dam.

Chaos was coming to America.

At the epicenter, the explosion dug into the sandstone, hungrily eating the earth to a depth of one hundred feet. The crater radius went out a quarter-mile in all directions. To the south the crater extended into Lake Powell and encompassed the north half of the Glen Canyon Dam. The red sandstone canyon walls were disintegrated and expelled upwards at great speed, initially engulfed into the fireball, but eventually finding space as particles in the mushroom cloud which would rise above the desert floor to an altitude of 15,000 feet.

The disintegration of matter from solid/liquid to its lowest atomic structure included the vaporization of a great deal of Lake Powell in the semicircle area around what had been the Glen Canyon Dam's north spillway area. Closest to the shoreline, lake water was turned instantly into vapor as the force of the explosion acted as a giant hand pushing the mass of the lake in the opposite direction, east, south, west. From the surface of the lake down to the lake bed the water was vaporized. Further out into the lake the effect was lessened. One hundred yards into the lake, as the lake bed steepened, the effect started to level out at a depth of fifty feet. At the perimeter of the half-mile the depth of the vaporization was almost back to the surface.

In the matter of two—perhaps three—seconds, the dam was gone. The above-surface shock wave reached the dam in a fraction of a second. The top twenty-five feet of the dam, consisting of large blocks of meshed concrete, were turned from solid matter to dust. Below the surface, the dam presented a convex surface to the force of the explosion. At the same time the explosion's force vaporized the water nearest the shoreline it sent a shock wave under the water, which was magnified into billions of agitated water particles. As the shock wave approached the dam, there was no place for the water to go. Since air molecules are much less dense than water, much of the physical damage above surface was due to the wind and heat of the shock wave. Much more powerful was the hydraulic hammering of the water against the entire 1400'-x-710' exposure of the inside of the dam. The dam's underwater surface was instantly struck with a billion jackhammers, all trying to force the water through solid matter. Above the surface, the explosion ripped a hole in the solid sandstone, vaporizing the Carl Hayden visitor's center perched high above the north spillway. The abutment where the dam met the north canyon wall was destroyed at the top, weakened to the point of failure all the way down to riverbed level—like a seam unravelling.

One of the effects of the explosion was the generation of tremendous heat as matter changed form. Temperatures approaching one million degrees were registered at the point which had been the Chevy Suburban. Temperatures in the 300-degree range could be measured a mile away. Three hundred degrees will not melt concrete, however it will melt grout. The grout between the twenty-foot cubes of concrete was a standard mixture of Portland cement, plastic resins, asphalt emulsion, clay, sodium silicate, and a catalyzer. Its melting temperature was between 165 and 175 degrees Fahrenheit. On the south side of the dam, all along the exposed upper twenty-five feet, the grout between the blocks of concrete melted to a depth of six feet. Exposed to such searing heat the concrete melted to a depth of six feet. Exposed to such searing heat the concrete did what every other substance would do, it expanded.

In combination with the heat, the instantaneous pressure differential and resulting shock wave sheared off the exposed twin twenty-foot-square elevator shafts, and weakened, then toppled the gantry crane, which fell into the lake. The automobiles parked on the dam's access road were incinerated, then thrown like so many matchbooks over the far side and down the 700-foot drop to the courtyard between the dam's foundation and the power plant.

The dam didn't collapse in a single motion, but in stages. Cracks in the dam were immediate throughout its entire surface. It took a few moments for the lake water to seep through the cracks formed from the powerful shock wave. Leaks formed along almost every grout point on the dam, including the vulnerable abutments on both canyon walls. The abutment along the north canyon wall was severed, water poured through the opening and into narrow Marble Canyon. The bomb caused a huge displacement of a large area of Lake Powell, much the same as if a large landslide had fallen into the lake.

A volume one-half-mile wide by one-mile long by fifty-feet deep was displaced, nearly twenty-six million cubic yards of water. Each cubic yard of water weighed approximately one ton. One-third of the water was displaced east, up the Colorado River away from the dam. One-third was displaced south directly across the mile-and-a-half width of the lake. One-third was displaced to the west, downstream toward the dam. Almost nine million cubic yards of water weighing almost nine million tons was thrown downstream toward a concrete structure forty feet in depth at the top.

The explosion created a solitary wave in all directions, a wave with a single crest riding over the flat plain of Lake Powell. In a solitary wave the water actually moves with the crest of the wave, as opposed to an oscillatory wave where the water stays in one position while the wave passes.

The solitary wave created by the Glen Canyon explosion had an initial height of seventy-eight feet. As the water moved toward the dam it found resistance under the water, there was no place for the water to pile up. So, instead of remaining in a bell-shaped configuration the wave flattened out, becoming elongated on the side nearest the explosion, steep on the outbound side. This bore wave became the lethal weapon which killed the dam. The force of the nine-million-ton wave struck what was left of the south half of the dam and overtopped it. At the moment of impact large cracks appeared, both front to back across the 40-foot width and up and down the interior wall. Between penstocks three and five, a great chunk of concrete, 120' long x 40' wide x 30' deep, was ripped off the dam's surface.

In one terrible moment the huge wave smashed into the dam then overtopped it. Once over the dam, water fell 710 feet to the riverbed level of the Colorado River after first crushing the power plant. The steel-beamed structure had no chance to survive the tremendous weight and force of the falling water.

When the first bore wave passed over and through the dam, it was followed by several other waves, much smaller. These waves were caused by rebound action of the original wave against other sections of the canyon walls. At first the water sprayed through the gaping, two-hundred-foot hole in the north abutment. Then more concrete was ripped off the dam's superstructure, the water spouted, then gushed. Finally, a large section of concrete along the canyon wall, perhaps 80' x 200', fell.

Lake Powell was on the move.

The blast not only took out the dam, it destroyed the 1,271-foot, single-arch bridge a quarter-mile downstream. The searing heat popped rivets from the girders. The pressure and force twisted the structure to such a point that the arch was unable to hold the weight of the bridge. As it collapsed from the center both the left and right abutments were torn out from their respective canyon walls. The bridge fell to the canyon floor almost in a single piece.

On the hill above the dam, the switchyard containing the 345kv and 230kv transformers were turned to twisted rubble. The transmission tie-line towers were destroyed. South of the dam, the blast incinerated every home along the hillside in the city of Page. Homes were blown apart, then the rubble set afire. The only homes saved were those on the south side of the hill, on the far side of the town.

Two miles south of the dam the Navajo Power Plant, its triple stacks shooting thirty stories into the sky, was destroyed. Two of the stacks were collapsed by the force of the blast, and all of the transmission ties for the 2200MW plant were destroyed.

It was 6:00:30. Page was dead and burning. Lake Powell was roaring down the Colorado, and the power system of the western United States had instantly lost 3000MW of electrical capacity.

The chaos was just beginning.

ABOVE EASTERN ARIZONA

The helicopter was at five thousand feet. They were high enough to see the flash of light in the eastern sky, although they were nearly a hundred miles away. The night was clear and cold, not a cloud in the sky.

"Holy Mother of God," said J.J., dazed.

The flash lit the sky to the west. There was no mistaking it. It was Khan's bomb. They were too late. The pilot continued in the direction of Page, but all aboard knew there was no town left. Silently each man thanked God that they had left Gallup earlier.

J.J. spoke into his headset.

"Patch me through to Sessions. How far are we?"

"Page? A hundred miles, maybe a half-hour."

"What are the prevailing winds?"

"Coming right at us, I'm afraid, Mr. Carteret. East to northeast," said the pilot, Jim Nichols.

It took two minutes for J.J.'s call to get patched through to William Sessions' office.

"Mr. Sessions, the bomb has gone off. There is a fireball in the sky to the east, where Page should be. We're going to swing south to get out of the path of the radiation," J.J. said.

There was a full thirty-second delay. All J.J. could hear was Sessions talking to someone else in his office.

"I don't know what to tell you, Carteret. We'll notify the army . . ."

Sessions' voice trailed off. J.J. disconnected.

"I don't think we want to fly this thing too close, do you?" asked J.J.

Nichols' wide eyes said yes. Scotty was speechless, his mouth dry.

PHOENIX, ARIZONA

"Dewey!" shouted Jim Green.

"What the hell's going on?" returned the calm Dewey Humboldt.

"The Flagstaff tie is out," said Green.

"Damn, we're ramping," replied Dewey.

In less than fifteen seconds every light on her 40-button phone directory would be lit with incoming calls. Dewey Humboldt was in for the experience of a lifetime. It was something the old-timers had told her about, something which could never happen with modern computers and backup systems.

Green and Humboldt were in the first hour of their eight-hour shift at the Power Control Center of the Western Area Power Administration (WAPA) on 43rd Street in suburban Phoenix. Dewey was Load Man, Jim was System Man. Load and System. They both sat at identical L-shaped consoles in swivel chairs which could be propelled across the slick computer-room floor from one station to the other on whim or need. Normally there was no whim and no need. They both were professionals. In case of emergencies both consoles could call up the same images. Under the floor the consoles were connected to a dedicated computer system in the next room, a mixture of fault-tolerant, fully redundant, SEL 32/35 Boeing Electronics, Prime and Gould specially designed power monitors.

Dewey and Jim had worked as a team for the last five years.

"The steamer's off line!" said Jim.

Green went to his direct line to the Navajo Power Plant in Page. It was dead. No answer, no tone—dead. Punching a button he went to the Glen Canyon line. Same thing.

Neither Dewey nor Jim paid attention to the irritating alarm bell ringing in the room.

"I've lost capacity out of Moenkopi and Palo Verde! Flagstaff's gone!" shouted Dewey.

While not in panic mode, Dewey Humboldt was scared. This was the emergency which had been only whispered about during her training and four-year apprenticeship. Moenkopi was a 500kv substation on U.S. 160 east of the Grand Canyon. The needle on the Moenkopi/Palo Verde tie-line was stopped. In one instant 325,000 volts of electricity had been surging down the huge transmission lines, the next moment, nothing. The plotter paper moved past the stylus, the plotter drawing a straight line at +0. Right beside it the Navajo/Palo Verde tie-line, also 500kv, was equally as dead. The Navajo steamer was off line. The Flagstaff/Glen Canyon tie-line, a 345kv line was also gone. A disaster had happened in northern Arizona.

Dewey picked up Line 1.

"What the hell's happening, Phoenix?" shouted Jack Clemente of Southern California Edison.

"I don't know, Jack. We've lost Glen Canyon," she turned to Jim.

"Jim, what's up?", she asked.

"This is a contract, for Christ's sake!" shouted Clemente, highly agitated.

Programmed sales of electricity always took place from five minutes before the hour to five minutes after the hour. Power was distributed between systems on one of three arrangements: "Firm," that is A will promise to deliver x amount of electricity at y dollars to B and come hell or high water will deliver the power; "Non-Firm," A agrees to sell to B as there is line space available; and "Available," if additional capacity is made available, A agrees to sell to B.

Jim Green was deep into his console screens. The computer's software enabled the Systems Man to pull up at any time the configuration of any of the substations and within the substation any block within any city to see the condition of lines. Lines north of Flagstaff were green, which meant they were disabled. Automatic circuit breakers had been thrown the instant the line sensed a failure. The three hundred miles between the Palo Verde substation near Phoenix and the Navajo Power Plant was green. So was the Moenkopi/Palo Verde and the Glen Canyon/Flagstaff.

When electricity is being sent from A to B to fill load requirements, it is like B is sucking on a giant straw. When there is no capacity on the line, somehow B has to have a way to disengage. Circuit breakers on the transmission ties sense that there is a load requirement which isn't being fulfilled, so instead of burning or blowing up, they simply cut the connection.

Of course, that really doesn't solve the problem. Circuit breakers save the hardware of the system from exploding. The lines are carried between transmission towers, normally five lines at a time. The top two lines are for static protection from lightening, the bottom three are the actual hot lines carrying the electricity. At each of the towers, at the point where the four-inch-thick cables are connected, are a series of bell-shaped porcelain insulators, the kind kids like to shoot at with their first gun. Up to 19 of the insulators will be strung together for a 345kv line, less numbers for a 230kv or 115kv line, and more for a 500kv line.

Circuit breakers are installed at each of the transmission towers. When a fault occurs at a power source, each of the transmission towers will go off line, one at a time. This process will continue until a circuit is reached which has enough electricity to meet the load. In the case of the Navajo/Palo Verde and Glen Canyon/Flagstaff lines, the transmission towers were turning themselves off one at at time.

It was the job of the Power Control Center in Phoenix to find capacity to meet the load. As Load Man, it was Dewey's job to find power. She punched Line 8.

"This is Phoenix, I need two hundred, now. Something's happened in . . ."

"I can't give you 200, Phoenix. We're going down. I'm pulling Four Corners off line."

"Jesus, you can't do that, Montrose! We've got a programmed buy! This . . ."

"Listen, Phoenix, I'm shedding already! Something's happened to Glen Canyon, and I'm shutting down! I've got to save what I can!"

The frenzied reply to Dewey's request came from Hayden Meeker, power dispatcher at the Montrose, Colorado Power Control Center for WAPA-Upper Colorado. Navajo and Glen Canyon were directly in their territory. Lights were already going out in the Four Corners area of Colorado, New Mexico, Arizona, and Utah. Without capacity, Montvale would have to shed load until it reached the point where capacity equalled load.

The situation was actually worse than Jim Green or Dewey Humboldt could imagine. The circuit breakers on the huge transmission ties weren't just breaking and dropping the line. They were burning and snapping. Like a series of Chinese firecrackers the ten-story steel towers blew up, one after another. Circuit breakers which had been installed for a theoretical limit of power differential had been blown to cinders by the scorching blast of a circuit waiting for 300,000 volts of electricity. One at at time, every fifteen seconds, the towers went . . . BAM, POP . . . the explosions went on, one after another as the fingers of blackout went toward the major metropolitan centers of the Southwest.

It was 6:05 P.M. (Mountain Standard Time).

Dewey's next call was to Dolan Yarnell, Southern California Edison manager at Hoover. Of Hoover's sixteen generators, the output of twelve were directly under the control of SoCal Ed. Three of the other four went to LA Water and Power, and the sixteenth went to Nevada Power. While the dam itself was run by the Bureau of Reclamation, the power plant was run by Southern California Edison.

"Something's wrong at Glen Canyon, Dolan. We've lost every line. I need whatever you can give me. I need it quickly, otherwise we're going down."

From the Systems desk Dewey heard Jim Green shout.

"We're down to 59.85! You've got to shed, Dewey!"

"Dolan, I don't know what's happened, but I need . . ." stuttered Dewey.

"It's Nevada Power! I've got to put you on hold!" interjected Green. "Flagstaff's gone," he added.

Dewey had to make a quick choice. Unfortunately, rural towns got the ax before the large cities.

"Jim, kill the Prescott-Cholla lines. Leave me Davis. Kill Westwing 1."

In the seconds Dolan Yarnell had her on hold, Dewey switched lines and talked to Jack Clemente at SoCal Edison in Los Angeles.

"I'm going to have to close down the Palo Verde lines, Jack . . ."

"Jesus, you can't do that Dewey! This is a contract buy. I can't get power . . ."

"Look, God damn it, Jack, in about ten minutes my pumps are going to kick in and we're going to be dark! Call Bonneville! I'll ramp what I can. I'll bring Davis through Mead. I can only split Parker with you," she yelled back.

Screen by screen Jim Green started to kill lines. From his console he instructed lines to be disabled, blocks at a time. Meanwhile, Dewey brought up her display of Parker Dam. Only one of the four generators was running. She punched three buttons and typed two commands into the system. The penstock gates were automatically opened.

"Dewey, Nevada Power says their Navajo line is dead! They want me to ramp from Parker," said Yarnell.

"I can't do it, Dolan. Parker's already going to L.A.," responded Dewey Humboldt.

"It'll take me an hour to get more generators on line, Dewey," said Yarnell.

"I know. It'll be too late."

HOOVER DAM

It was 6:08. Power lines in all directions from the Glen Canyon Dam and the Navajo steamer were exploding tower by tower. In eight minutes power was out in all of northern Arizona, southern Utah, southeastern Colorado, and northwestern New Mexico. In one minute Las Vegas would suck out the last of the electricity from the 500kv Navajo line and the city would go dark.

The synchronous power system in the Western United States was quickly degenerating to the islands of power it actually was. Reality dictated that the power distribution in the Western United States revolved around one city—Los Angeles. Its needs, its demands, altered and influenced the way electricity was generated and distributed throughout the entire region. While government leaders nominally paid lip service to the coordinated power system, the entire power grid in the eleven states west of the Rocky Mountains was set up to serve the power demands of Southern California, specifically the city of Los Angeles.

The Sump was sucking the system dry.

THE WHITE HOUSE

"The line is ready to Moscow, sir," said an aide.

The secretary of defense came back inside, his face even more ashen than normal.

"The bomb's been detonated sir," he said.

"What about the dam?" asked the president, rising out of his chair.

"We don't know, sir. We're checking."

"What about reports of the Russians? Is Sessions right? Turning to an aide he waved for the second interpreter to come in."

"Shall we keep the line open to Teheran, sir?" Graham Atkinson asked.

"Yes . . . if Gorbachev's up to this . . . can we defend Iran from what we've got in the 6th Fleet?"

"Air only. It depends on what the Iranians do. It depends where the Soviets have attacked. We aren't in the best position to defend a country we'd just as soon see defeated. We've put our eggs into supporting Iraq."

The president turned to the aide who in turn gave him the oddly connected line to the presidential palace in Teheran.

"Captain Silverek, this is the president."

"Yes, sir."

"Do you have the code book?" asked the president.

"Yes, sir. I do. It's written in Farsi. I'm not sure if I'm going to have time to read it to you. Things are going to get pretty hectic around there. We haven't heard from Unit 2 since we started. I think they're lost. This city is pretty tough to get around in. What do you want us to do with Waquidi and the translator?"

"Let me talk to Waquidi."

The president could hear Emil Silverek talking to someone, then he heard the shaky voice of the interpreter.

"This is the president of the United States. Can you both hear me?"

There were two acknowledgements.

"One of your weapons has been detonated inside my country, ten minutes ago. We are at a state of war, President Waquidi. But I must tell you, the Soviets at this moment are advancing toward Teheran. As far as I feel now, I could best repay you for this cowardly act by doing nothing, let the Soviet Union take over your miserable country. If I interpret the relationship between your two countries correctly, many of your people will be killed. It would serve you right."

Both translators were busy. Atkinson was drenched with perspiration as he translated the president's words to the Iranians. The president continued.

"President Waquidi, you will go with Captain Silverek. He is authorized to kill you if you get out of hand. Let me talk with Captain Silverek."

"Yes, sir," said Emil Silverek.

"Captain, I want you to get the hell out of there. Bring the book. We can have it translated quickly enough. Good luck, captain. And captain
. . ."

"Yes, sir?"

"Thank you," said the president.

The line went dead. The president turned around and looked at his war cabinet.

"What kind of force can we put in Teheran?" the president asked Bulldog Russell.

"Limited. Very limited. Not many troops. I can give him reasonable air cover, but not against the Soviet Army."

"What can we do with Qaddafi?" asked the president.

"Almost anything," replied Russell.

"Take him out. Make it painful and obvious," said the president.

"Sir, the . . ." started Russell.

"I don't care. This is the right thing to do. We should have done it a long time ago. Qaddafi is behind Khan."

The president changed subjects.

"What about the dam?" he asked an aide.

"No word, sir."

"Then get me Gorbachev," said the president.

It was 6:10.

BOULDER CITY, NEVADA

"And I'm telling you, Jack—Nevada Power is that close to a blackout. Something's happened up at Glen Canyon. I don't know what. What I do know is that ever god-damned line coming out of there is dead or dying. The only thing computerized at Hoover was the distribution of electricity. Since the dam had been built in the '30s, everything else was a manual operation, including the addition of capacity. Someone had to go down underneath the generators and open the lines to the penstocks to allow the water to rush through. Then each of the generators would have to be started. I've got to run down eight flights of stairs and manually open up every god-damned penstock gate to get anything working. I've got men doing just that right now, but it's going to take an hour."

"I can't wait an hour, for Christ's sake!" shouted Clemente.

"Jack, shed load! There's no way Hoover is going to be able to help. We're running our normal February shift right now, eight generators. Hell, we're not even running half-capacity. If Navajo's down, you've only got minutes before you're out of luck. I'm telling you, get somebody else!"

Dolan Yarnell had been manager of Southern California Edison's Hoover Dam operations for the last eight years. Other than the mild scare in the winter months of 1983-1984, when the Colorado and related streams had gotten so much snowmelt and Hoover had almost been forced to spill, there had never been one single critical point of near-failure. Sure, generators had blown, gone down, but they'd al ways been able to get a replacement up and running without any loss of service. This was different. Something was wrong, really wrong up there. His line to Glen Canyon was out. Not down, but out. There wasn't even a dial tone or busy signal, just nothing.

SoCal Edison's Control Room was on the eighth floor of Hoover Dam, with floor-one being down at the riverbed level. Two floors below, also built into the structure of the dam, were the operations offices for the Bureau of Reclamation, headed by Winsloe Holbrook. Holbrook had already gone for the evening. Dolan had one foot out the door himself.

"Get Holbrook on the phone. If you can't get him at home get him on his pager, or his car! *Now!*"

No one seemed to know anything. Dolan sat at his ancient computer, two banks of early-1960s equipment painted GSA grey-green which could only be described as clunky. All the computer could do for him was measure the intake valves and the power generation. It couldn't *do* any of the work which needed to be done.

Dolan called his counterpart for LA Water and Power.

"Jim, you're aware of the problem?" Dolan asked.

"What the hell's going on?" came the reply.

"I don't know. Can you get your other generators working?"

"No faster than you, my friend."

Dolan hung up, then went to the public address system which would broadcast within the huge dam.

"Maintenance to generators 2, 3, 7, 8, 11, 12, 15, and 16. On the double! Open all lines! Start up all generators!"

The phone rang. It was Winsloe Holbrook.

"Winny, there's an emergency . . ."

"I know, Dolan. I just heard it on the radio. There's been a nuclear explosion at Glen Canyon."

"That can't be true!" shouted Dolan Yarnell.

"Turn your radio on, Dolan. I'm coming back. We're going to close the dam down," said Winsloe Holbrook.

"But, we can't . . ." protested Dolan.

"I'm the manager, Dolan. You know what's happening right now, don't you? They're calling for a general evacuation of the Las Vegas area."

Indeed, Dolan knew what was happening. Lake Powell was crashing through the Grand Canyon on a one-way trip down the Colorado River. The thought was terrifying.

OVER THE GRAND CANYON

"Jesus and Mother Mary. Look at that!" said J.J., amazed.

The light from the full moon cast a spotlight into the Grand Canyon, making the various hues of red and orange seem washed out and milky, but nevertheless shining enough light to see well inside the canyon.

J.J. was spellbound. He was too far away to see what had happened to the poor city of Page. If he had been closer he would have seen that it lay wasted and burning. The Colorado River was free. Only 20% of the Glen Canyon dam remained intact, mainly the area around the south abutment where the dam met the canyon wall. Once free from the constraints of the dam, Lake Powell quickly returned to being the Colorado River. A seven-hundred-foot wall of water moving at 110 miles an hour was falling downhill from Page. In the first 14 minutes the lead body of water, churning and destructive, ate a twenty-six-mile path through the steep section of Marble Canyon. As it fell the water level flattened out, matching the height of the canyon's walls. Fifteen miles south of Page the old road, Alternate U.S. 89, crossed the River at the Navaho Bridge. The bridge was wiped out, destroyed, as the whole canyon was filled with rushing Colorado River water. Huge boulders, some the size of small houses, were picked up and became part of the dangerous debris.

The noise from the water could be heard above the din of the helicopters. They were witnessing an event of a lifetime.

"Mr. Director, the dam is gone. There's a disaster taking place down there," said J.J.

BOULDER CITY, NEVADA

"This station has been turned over to the emergency broadcast system. The sirens you hear are not, repeat *not*, a drill. There has been a failure of the Glen Canyon dam in northern Arizona. It is expected that within two hours water from Lake Powell will reach Lake Mead and overflow into the Las Vegas basin. All inhabitants of the Las Vegas area are urged to move to higher ground."

To describe the evacuation of a city like Las Vegas as being anything other than a Chinese fire drill would not do justice to the mass confusion and chaos which was started at 6:16 P.M. Casinos, hotels, McCarren Field, and local businesses had to be closed. Since most visitors didn't have automobiles, many people decided to stick it out in the top floors of some hotels. Casino and hotel owners were concerned with the protection of their assets. There was no place to go except to the mountains outside of town, either to the Muddy Mountains to the east, the Sheep Range to the north, or to the Clark Range on the California border. And as people left they had to make sure they had blankets and warm clothes, since the temperature in Las Vegas in February was in the 30s. It was dark and cold and a lot of people decided not to leave the warmth and safety of home.

By beeper Winsloe Holbrook told his staff to remove any and all records in the administrative staff.

"It might be a long time before we're back," said Holbrook. "*If ever,*" he said under his breath.

Indeed, if the dam managed to hold up under the tremendous pressure of the rushing Lake Powell, including the rocks and boulders it was striping clean from the canyon walls along Grand Canyon, then it still would take years for the water to pass. Years! The water would rush down the canyon at 110 miles an hour, thrashing and gushing into Lake Mead, then finding Black Canyon was the way out, overtop Hoover Dam. Once overtopping Hoover the water would have nothing to stop it on its way to the Gulf of California. In addition to being a national catastrophe, the loss of Lake Powell would mean one of the nation's most valuable resources was lost forever, the water itself.

The basin in which Lake Mead resides is separated from the populated areas of Las Vegas by a small range of low mountains, hills actually. The low point in the hills surrounding the lake is at a place called Las Vegas Bay, the place where Lake Mead is the closest to the city of Las Vegas. The elevation at the water's edge is 1162 feet above sea level. The lowest point in the River Mountain range was 1800 feet, where the Las Vegas Wash cuts through the mountains. The accumulation of Lake Powell's water into Lake Mead would overflow the gap. Once overtopped, the water would have an easy downhill run for twenty miles, through Henderson, through East Las Vegas, to the city itself, which sat in the bottom of a bowel-shaped basin.

— • —

With one foot out the door and his staff running around gathering all the company's records, Dolan talked first to Jack Clemente.

"Jack, we're pulling the plug. You've got maybe twenty-five minutes left before we kill the generators. I've got to go. I'm sorry."

There were three 500kv lines and two 230kv lines which connected Hoover's power, first to the Lugo and Victorville substations in the desert northeast of the Los Angeles basin, then to the huge Vincent substation north of the city in Lancaster. The Vincent substation also received the power from Pacific Gas and Electric in San Francisco, power transferred from the snowmelt of the high Sierras.

Dolan then picked up the line and talked with Dewey Humboldt in Phoenix.

"Do you know about it, Dewey?"

"No."

"Glen Canyon's gone. We're closing down. I'm going off line in twenty to twenty-five minutes. I've got to run. Good luck."

Without waiting for a response from his good friend, Dolan hung up. While the civil defense sirens started to wail in Las Vegas, Dolan Yarnell ran for the Hoover elevators, yelling at his compatriots in the LA Water and Power Control Center to follow him. The generators had to be shut down. Without a logical shutdown there would be *no* chance at a smooth recovery. It was procedure. Do what you can. Don't think of the fact that 186 miles of Lake Powell are crashing down the Grand Canyon. Don't think about it. Do your job.

It was 6:20.

PHOENIX, ARIZONA

"Dewey! We can't hold it!" shouted Jim Green.

HERTZ was down to 59.10 and falling. Green could visualize the lines exploding as he watched his monitor.

Dewey punched line 1.

"I'm dropping you, Jack. Hoover's closing down. I've got to save Phoenix. I'm re-routing Davis and Parker back this way. Sorry," said Dewey.

"Don't do it, Dewey! Please!" shouted Jack Clemente.

"Goodbye, Jack," Dewey said as she hung up the phone. "Goodbye, California," she muttered to herself.

"Westwing's down!" said Green.

Westwing was the point where power was diverted to the huge Phoenix area through a series of 345kv and 230kv lines from Glen Canyon. There was no power to buy. The load was too high. The HERTZ meter crashed through 59.00 . . . 58.90, then 58.85. Like lit fuses laid out all over the state, the lines burned their way back to the controlling source. In great chunks, lights went out in the northern and eastern suburbs—then through downtown, and the south. Finally it reached the 43rd Street switchyard of WAPA's control area. With the last explosion of a circuit, the lights went out inside the Power Dispatch Center.

Dewey and Jim Green sat in silence.

The room was pitch dark.

Arizona was blacked out. Within minutes control rooms in Montrose (Colorado), The Dalles (Oregon), San Francisco, Boise, Salt Lake City, and Jack Clemente in Los Angeles would be black as well. The power grid in the Western United States was closed down.

"Shit," said Dewey in disgust.

It was 6:22.

CHAPTER 6

Scotty's Last Climb

THE WHITE HOUSE

A grim-faced, haggard president sat at the head of the Situation Room's huge conference table. Bulldog Russell, Earl Hardy, a handful of Pentagon aides, William Sessions, and Oden Bennett (via telephone) were all there. A Russian translator named Carl Josel stood with Graham Atkinson. A dour secretary of defense spoke.

"Mr. President, we have satellite confirmation of a massive Soviet attack against Iran on two fronts; from the border east of the Caspian and from Afghanistan. There's no evidence of movement into Pakistan."

Before the president could speak, the open satellite transmission from Emil Silverek squawked. The noise startled everyone.

"Jesus Christ! What the hell? I can't tell who or what . . . take cover! Fall back, men! Unit 2, come in unit 2! Henry, we've got to take a position out of the city! Back to the helicopters! Sir, we need backup! Waters, get these sons of bitches out of here!" shouted Silverek.

"Captain Silverek, this is Defense Secretary Russell. Get out of the city! Do you understand? Get out of the city!"

The conversation was one way. Emil Silverek couldn't hear Russell, nor did he want to.

"The line to Moscow is ready, sir," said an aide.

The 25-inch television suddenly came on. In mid-thought and mid-step, everyone in the room was frozen as their eyes were riveted to the screen.

"Unbelievable," said Sessions.

"God in heaven," said the president, awe-struck.

As Emil Silverek's voice echoed through his 8,000 mile connection, the voice of J.J. Carteret filled the background behind an incredible infrared picture of a disgorged Lake Powell.

"Are you picking up these pictures?" shouted J.J.

"Sir, I have Moscow on the line! Chairman Gorbachev is ready to talk to you. He has other members of the Politboro with him. Sir, they're waiting!" said the aide, somewhat in a panic.

The Situation Room was chaos in a three-ring circus.

"The Glen Canyon dam has been destroyed! There must be a

hundred miles of water down there!" J.J. struggled to be heard over the roar of the helicopter and the noise from the rushing water.

At that moment another harried aide came rushing into the room, handing Earl Hardy a note.

"There's been a blackout," said Hardy.

"Blackout?" questioned the president.

"Yes, sir. Whatever is happening out there has triggered a massive power outage. I've got reports from . . ."

Hardy's comments were interrupted by an aide to Defense Secretary Russell, whose demeanor changed to shock.

"Sir, we've lost electricity from San Diego to Minot. Except for parts of Washington and Oregon, I've lost everything. Damn!"

Russell turned to his aide.

"I want to know when they reach emergency status! Now! Damn! Get me Omaha! Now!" he drilled another aide, who went hustling to get the connection to Omaha.

In less than thirty seconds came the image of an Air Force Colonel on screen 2. Screen 1 showed the terrible effect of Khan's atomic weapon.

"Status!" instructed Russell.

"Sir! Maimstrom and Minot are down and out. The telephone lines are jammed. I don't know what the problem is," said the Colonel from Omaha.

"Probably everybody on base trying to call home," mumbled the president.

"Sir, the Chairman!" said the hotline aide.

J.J. shouted over the noise.

"The water must be seven hundred feet high. I can't believe it! It's incredible! Sir, we're sure this is Soviet responsibility! They're behind this!"

The White House was near the point of information overload.

"Carteret, this is Sessions. I need proof! What do you have for proof?"

"You've got everything, sir! They're behind it! The agent's name is Rostov! He's around here someplace," the relayed telephone connection crackled with the poor connection. "My God! The city of Page is gone, the dam is gone! The town is glowing, fires everywhere! You've got to do something. There's enough water here to flood everything from here to California! You've got to do something quickly!" shouted J.J.

Back in the Situation Room each man looked at the other and received a blank face in return.

"Sir, I have reports from Las Vegas that a general evacuation has

"Sir, I have reports from Las Vegas that a general evacuation has started. Hoover Dam is being shut down and evacuated as well," said Earl Hardy.

The president didn't need to be told what would happen. Water troubles were at the heart of the development of the West. Control of the Colorado River had been enough to almost drive states into border wars over the years. If Hoover Dam failed, not only would there be the most massive flooding in the history of the world, but a tremendous national resource, the impounded water of Lake Mead and Lake Powell, would be lost forever. The force of the flood waters would destroy the dams along the Colorado and more than likely actually divert the river's path to the Gulf of California. The rich Imperial Valley of Southern California would be completely flooded. A lake would form in the Salton Sea area east of San Diego which would be five or six times as large as the current lake. If Hoover Dam was permanently damaged or destroyed the Los Angeles area would be without power for a long, long time. There would be chaos in Southern California. Whatever had to be done to save Hoover Dam, had to be done.

"This is Carteret. Do you copy?"

"We hear you, Carteret," said Sessions.

They heard J.J. very well. They could hear the helicopter's thrashing.

"It seems to me that the only thing that's going to stop this is another nuclear explosion. This wall of water is incredible. It's ripping through the Grand Canyon right now! It's dumping out of the narrow canyon— my pilot says Marble Canyon—right now, and into the wide eastern section of the Grand Canyon. It must be moving at a hundred miles an hour! Sir, you don't have long! I think you've got to throw a couple of bombs in there and create a dam somehow!"

Nuke the canyon.

The president put his hands on his head. An aide to Russell broke in.

"Sir, there's no evidence the Soviets have gone to war status. Their bombers are within normal boundaries. They aren't striking anyplace but on the Iranian border."

"What about the water?" asked Hardy. "You throw nuclear bombs in there and you'll poison the water for the next three centuries," he cautioned.

"You don't know that, Earl," said Russell.

"What other options does the president have?" Hardy returned to Russell.

"Sir, the Chairman is ready, now."

it, and do it!" the president instructed Bulldog Russell. "I'll talk to the Chairman now," he said turning to Hardy's aide.

The president walked to the opposite end of the Situation Room and nodded to the translator attending the speakerphone. The phone was activated. Aides turned down the volumes on J.J.'s transmission and that from Emil Silverek.

"This is the president of the United States."

There was a momentary pause, a half-second propagation delay for the voice signal to be transmitted to the 22,000-mile-high satellite and back down to the Soviet receiver.

"Good evening, Mr. President, this is Mikhail Gorbachev. It is very late here—rather, it is very early here."

Indeed it was, four-thirty in the morning.

The president got directly to the point.

"Mr. Chairman, we have clear indications you are moving masses of troops into Iranian soil. You are bombing the city of Teheran as we speak. Why? I cannot allow this to continue," said the president.

Gorbachev's voice came back in hurt indignation.

"Mr. President, we are only coming to the aid of your country in its time of need. I thought you would appreciate our effort, especially in light of the terrible thing which the Iranian hoodlums have done to your country," replied Gorbachev.

"How is it you know of this?" asked the President.

"We have seismologists, too, Mr. President. These terrorists must be punished, I'm sure you will agree."

"We cannot, we will not, allow you to take over Iran, Chairman. We are opposed to the regime there, but the country serves us both very well, a buffer between us. I must do whatever is necessary to preserve our interests there. If this means we will fight, so be it."

"Please don't misunderstand our purpose, Mr. President. We are on a mercy mission, to punish the Iranian terrorists for this terrible act against your country. Your people know we have not armed or readied our missiles. We have no intention of going to war against the United States. Our satellites indicate many of your missile locations are dark, without power. I'm not sure you are in position to tell us what you will do and what you won't do. We have submarines and carriers in the Arabian Sea. We have ships in the Mediterranean. What do you have? Nothing. We do this action as a favor to you. We do not want conflict."

"Mr. Chairman, we have evidence which links the atomic explosion in Arizona to Soviet agents, your agents. We believe *you* are behind this action, not the Iranians," said the president.

"What agents, Mr. President?" Gorbachev said with scorn. "There are no agents but in your mind. Pure fabrication. I expected you to thank us in your time of need and what do we get for our effort but the back of your hand. I fully expected a congratulatory call, one of thanks. I thought you would be telling me your plans to terminate Qaddafi. Together we would rid the world of terrorism. What do I get instead? The same vituperation your country has unloaded on the Soviet Union for the last fifty years. Your rhetoric is stale, Mr. President. I have no intention of recalling my troops. This is a good-faith effort. If we had the mind to do so, we could have launched an attack against you while your defenses are down. We can see your power blackout. But we are a peaceful nation. I suggest you look at the placement of your forces and the condition of your defenses before you threaten us. I am sorry this accident has occurred. We will deal with Waquidi while you find his henchman Khan."

The president was fit to be tied. His face was red with anger. There was nothing more he could say which would do any good. Gorbachev had the cards. There was no mistaking the Soviet intention. The speakerphone went dead. The president turned to his cabinet. It was not a good time to be in the same room with him.

"Whatever we can do to stop the invasion, do it. Whatever needs to be done to protect Hoover Dam, do it. Whatever needs to be done to find these Soviet agents, do it. Now! And I want the damn power back on!"

Every man in the room jumped at the president's angry words. It was time to go do "it," whatever "it" was.

Without proof, without a body—a live body of a Russian agent—there was no way to prove Soviet duplicity. A string of circumstantial evidence would take too long to explain to world leaders. It would be too easily denied. Gorbachev would back down only when the public was presented with the shameful truth of Mother Russia's complicity. The invasion depended upon the capture of Alexander Rostov.

It was 6:35 P.M. Alexander Rostov had to be found quickly or it wouldn't matter.

OVER THE GRAND CANYON

"I don't care what you do, Carteret! Get the hell out of the area! Find the god-damned Soviets!" shouted the president.

Nuke the canyon.

Like the droll T-shirts of the '70s.

Save the Whales. Nuke the Canyon.

J.J. could hardly believe the Pentagon was going to follow his wild-ass suggestion. Giving a hand signal to the pilot, the helicopter shot ahead of the angry water. Clearing Marble Canyon—spilling out of the narrow sluice—the water fanned out in every direction. The seven-hundred-foot wall of water smashed from wall to wall, then once entering the wide expanse of the canyon, like everything of time and distance, started to flatten out. The seven-hundred-foot wall of water now became a three-hundred-foot wall of water—only now it was a mile wide.

Rostov had done his job well. In twenty-eight minutes the water had moved nearly fifty miles. All of Marble Canyon from the Vermillion Cliffs outside Page to Point Imperial at the east end of the Grand Canyon was filled with frothy Lake Powell water. In ten minutes the water would rush past the point where helicopter pilot Will Gregory lay dead in the bushes. By seven o'clock the water would be approaching the first of several goosenecks the Colorado made to the west of the visitors' center.

"How long?" J.J. shouted in return.

"How long?" he could hear Bill Sessions ask an aide on the White House side. Then the answer. "Less than an hour. Forty-five minutes—maybe less."

J.J. switched Sessions off.

"Do you have a fast-forward in this thing?" he asked the pilot.

"Yes, sir. Two-fifty, maybe three-hundred miles an hour. Is that fast enough?"

"I hope so, son," mumbled J.J.

"Where to, sir?" the pilot asked.

J.J. mused. *Which direction, indeed? Where would you go if you knew the entire western civilization was after you? He's probably not driving. It's too slow, too risky. By now the highway patrol must be going through hell—what with a power outage and a nuclear explosion. People are going batty. Their status quo is being severely upset. I wouldn't go north. I would go east, into Colorado. Except it would be downwind of the explosion. But if they are in a plane, or a helicopter, they'll be long gone, well out of range. I'd still go east into Colorado.*

"Where would you go, Scotty?" asked J.J.

"Mexico or a big city—probably a big city first. The borders will be tight. Rostov is a big city kind of guy," replied the younger man.

"You're probably right—I wouldn't, but then I feel more comfortable where there aren't many people. Rostov would feel more comfortable in a big place."

J.J. leaned over to the pilot, the agent named Nichols.

"Back toward Las Vegas, Nichols—and step on it."

J.J. barely had time to focus his eyes before Nichols dove and accelerated at the same time. The noise from the rushing Colorado was drowned out by the thump of the engines and soon it faded as they left the raging river behind. But it was coming, no mistake about it. A rolling disaster out of hell.

MARCH AIR FORCE BASE, RIVERSIDE, CALIFORNIA

"This is James Russell, secretary of defense. Whom am I speaking to?"

Major Arlin Buckhorn's first thought was *Why me? Why did I have to pick up the phone? Why was I Officer of the Day on the night of the Great Blackout? Why did I have to pick up the phone when the secretary of defense decided to call?* It wasn't right. It was guaranteed that no matter what happened his butt was either going to be trouble or he had more work ahead of him than three people could do. It was just the way things happen when the brass call.

"Major Buckhorn, sir."

"Do you have electrical power, Buckhorn?"

"Yes, sir, we're just starting to get emergency power back. We've been out for 45 minutes now. We're not sure what has happened."

"There's been a nuclear explosion at the Glen Canyon Dam in Arizona. The dam has been destroyed. There's enough water coming down the Colorado River to flood Nevada, Arizona, and Southern California long enough that it could be permanent. If Hoover Dam and the others along the Colorado are destroyed, this country will be severely damaged. Our economy will be dealt a blow which could be irreparable. This bomb, this attack, is an act of war . . ."

Bulldog Russell stopped in mid-sentence. He was getting carried away with the implications.

"Major Buckhorn . . ."

Buckhorn looked around the empty room. How did this call get to this phone? Why is the secretary of defense explaining that the economy of the United States was in jeopardy? And why is he explaining it to me? The punchline was coming. Arlin Buckhorn braced himself. Somehow he was going to be tied into saving the United States from irreparable harm.

"Yes, sir?" replied Buckhorn.

"Major Buckhorn, March Air Force Base is the closest bomber site to the Grand Canyon, closer than Davis Monthan. You have 45 minutes to scramble a bomber above the Colorado River and drop enough nuclear weaponry to block the river."

There would be no Environmental Impact Statements filed with the Department of Interior, no Assessment Reports, no Snail Darter form 171s typed in quadruplicate.

Bomb the canyon.

"Yes, sir," was Buckhorn's reply. "Where would you like them?"

Arlin Buckhorn could hardly believe he'd said the words.

"You'll need map coordinates. I'll leave the line open. You'll talk with General Whitney. Five minutes, Major."

"Yes, sir!"

Jesus Jumping Jehoshaphat!

Buckhorn punched line #2.

"Sergeant, scramble Iron Leader."

"Sir?"

"Now! You heard me, sergeant."

"Yes, sir!"

Buckhorn's guts were rocking and rolling but his voice was true and firm.

"And get Haley in here. I'm going up with them. And get me topo maps of northern Arizona and Nevada. Quickly!"

Whatever was going to happen would be the highlight of his military career and Arlin Buckhorn wasn't going to miss it, not for anything in the world. He would fly co-pilot in Iron Leader. Haley walked in the room just as Buckhorn went back to the phone.

"We're scrambling now, sir. I'll have the maps in a second. You'll be dealing with Captain Haley. I'm going up."

The sergeant brought detail layouts of the Grand Canyon and northern Arizona, southern Nevada. With one swipe of his giant arm Buckhorn swept everything off the desk onto the floor, then spread out the maps. He positioned the maps, Lake Mead to his right. The maps came in sections, from longitude west 112 to west 113, latitude north

36 to north 37. This sector covered Grand Canyon village to the south to the Utah border, then west to the Havasupai Indian Reservation. There were two additional maps for the sectors 113 to 114 and 114 to 115, ending at Las Vegas and Lake Mead.

"Buckhorn, we have reports that the water is past the south rim of the canyon. By the time you can get there it will almost have reached Lake Mead. Do you see a place called Pierce Ferry?"

Buckhorn moved his hand along the map's surface, up the Colorado in section 114. There it was!

"Yes, sir. I have it."

"Do you see a spot called Wheeler Ridge?"

"Yes, sir."

Wheeler Ridge was the the last truly narrow passage of the Colorado through its gorge, located just inside the Arizona border. At that point the distance across the shore was no more than a few hundred yards.

"There, sir?"

"That's your secondary target, Buckhorn. Eight miles to the east is a section of canyon where the walls on both side are steep."

"I see it. There's an Indian Reservation above the south canyon wall."

Buckhorn's observation was ignored.

"Yes. Wheeler Ridge is your backup. Buckhorn, we have no idea how much it will take to block the Colorado River. You're only going to have one pass through there. Four twenties should do it. Space them out, two in the middle, one each on the opposite canyon walls."

Eighty megatons of hydrogen bombs in one place?

"What about the Indians?"

Russell was not insensitive to the question. He did not want to vaporize innocent Americans. But if he delayed, the resultant flood would be disastrous.

"I'll see what I can do."

"Yes, sir. We're on our way."

HOOVER DAM

" . . . and I'm telling you, Jack. I'm not turning those generators back on—no way, no how," shouted Dolan Yarnell.

Generators 6, 8, and 10 were still humming. Yarnell took the call from deep inside Hoover's guts at a service bay on the Nevada side.

Arizona would be down in a matter of minutes. They didn't have much time. It would take another 45 minutes to shut Nevada down. The dam itself was the only place in the southwestern United States which at that moment had electricity, except for a small circuit established by Dewey Humboldt and Jim Green in Phoenix as they started to rebuild the system.

Soon the dam would be dark and Dolan would have to make a terrifying ascent through the dam in the pitchest of pitch dark. Only occasional shafts of starlight, windows down long hallways, windows which had dim areas of less darkness than the maze of tunnels he would have to negotiate. Fortunately, he had remembered to bring a small flashlight with him. But the elevators would be out and he'd have to hike up the 700-foot face of the dam through the musty stairwells. Dolan was not a man who would be considered in good shape.

Dolan hung up and headed down generator alley to #6. Would she hold? The wave would be incredible, almost difficult to picture. But by modern dam standards Hoover was 80% overbuilt. Glen Canyon's widest base width was 300 feet. Hoover Dam had a massive 660 feet of concrete which tapered thickly to the roadbed of U.S. 93 crossing its brow. The geometry of the added concrete came up to almost double what was required to impound the lake. Spillway construction at Hoover was relatively similar to Glen Canyon's. Tunnels, fifty feet in diameter, were constructed into the canyon walls on both the Nevada and Arizona sides. Slightly above riverbed the spillway tunnels met the diversion tunnels which had been used in the original construction to bypass the flow of the Colorado during building phases. Glen Canyon passed water directly through the dam via penstocks built into the dam proper. Hoover, however, used syphoned water via four 395' tall intake towers, two on either side of the dam. Water fell from the intake towers into thirty-foot-wide penstock tunnels at the base. Each of the penstocks provided water for two generating units which, unlike Glen Canyon, were built eight to a side and were lined up perpendicular to the base at riverbed level. Rather than passing down and directly through the dam, the water went through the penstock tunnels built into the canyon walls. Once passing the dam proper, the penstocks entered the generating rooms at right angles through smaller eighteen-foot-diameter tunnels.

The generating units at Hoover were similar to Dante's circles of hell. The power plant consisted of three main floors and a subterranean dungeon where only river rats went. On the highest floor were the generators, clean and green. The walkway was grated around each so that maintenance could be performed on any section between floors. The eight units were spaced sixty-two-and-a-half feet apart. The lighting gave the fifteen-foot ceilings a somewhat antiseptic, almost nuclear, feeling.

One floor below were the main bodies of the turbines, each fifteen feet in diameter with a five-foot stainless steel shaft. However, the walls of the turbine room were of rough concrete, giving the twenty-foot-tall ceiling a feeling of depth. Around each turbine was a guardrailed maintenance pit, where presumedly one could maintain his way all the way to the first floor. The penstock level was the least artistic, poorest lit, most creepy area within the dam. Here the eighteen-foot penstocks fed a constant stream of water through the turbines. After passing through, the water exited at river level and flowed down the Colorado toward the Gulf of California. Down the dark penstock runway were the hulks of the other penstocks. Because Hoover was finished in 1935, in order to shut one of the turbines down it took the considerable effort of one or two men to manually close the penstock gate within the eighteen-foot tunnel. The steel gates were very heavy and required a great deal of work.

Just as generator #10 shut down, Dolan passed a ringing telephone. It was Winsloe Holbrook, BuRec operations manager. Hoover was his dam.

"Is that it?" asked Holbrook.

Holbrook had been around almost as long as Dolan. He could feel when there were no generators working. The vibration of the concrete stopped. It was such an unusual occurrence that for Holbrook it was easy to sense.

"All down," said Dolan.

"Can you make it all the way up, Dolan?" razzed Holbrook.

"Stick it in your ear, Winny," replied Dolan, smiling.

He didn't like it down in the bowels of the dam, at night. Even though he'd done it lots of times in different parts of the dam, it was still pretty spooky walking through the damp, raw stone corridors. Dolan didn't waste any time.

"Is everybody out?" Dolan asked.

Too late. Winsloe Holbrook had hung up. Holbrook had enough to do to make sure all the plant's administrative records were evacuated along with the people. The dam was closed down. There was nothing else they could do except wait and hope. Dolan had to do the same for SoCal.

Even though he knew every nook and cranny inside the dam, the light from his flashlight ended in a black hole ten feet in front of him. The darkness seemed to suck the flashlight's pitiful attempt at illumination.

Dolan stopped.

He cocked his ears. He was better on his right side. It was something. He turned around and walked back a few paces, bumping into the cold, damp canyon wall. He cocked his head again. Again he heard something. A voice? Dolan was on floor two, turbine alley. Above him were the generators, below were the penstocks.

"*Help!*"

The single cry for help froze him in his tracks. It was faint.

Jesus, Mother Mary.

One of the men was hurt.

"Hello! Where are you?"

Dolan's shouts echoed past the eight Nevada turbines. The huge room had a twenty-foot ceiling and was four hundred feet long.

"This is Yarnell! Where are you? Help me! I'm at the head of turbine alley!"

No response.

There had been a voice. It wasn't one of those things which he could ignore. There was a person down here.

"Damn!" Dolan muttered.

Dolan found his way to another telephone, picked it up. The signal immediately went to an unmanned switchboard. Dolan dialed his number. Nothing. He dialed Winsloe Holbrook's. Nothing. He dialed the visitor's center. Nothing. He dialed the administrative offices up the hill on the Nevada side. Nothing. *Come on!* Winny wouldn't leave until everyone was out and accounted for. It was the-captain-and-the-ship routine. Besides, Holbrook was a professional.

Dolan tried another number. It was the phone at the top of the elevator shaft where public tours started. It was also the top of the stairway where eventually he would have to climb the seven hundred feet from river level to the top of the dam. To climb seven hundred feet it took nearly nine hundred steps.

"Holbrook," came the terse reply on the other end of the phone.

"Winny! Someone's down here! He's hurt. Who hasn't checked out? Probably one of my men, although I don't know, did you have any people on the generators?"

"No, Dolan. Things have been a little chaotic. I've made a pass through the sixth and seventh floors and there's nobody there. Your area is clean. So is L.A. Water. I don't know about the maintenance crew."

"How long do we have?" asked Dolan. "It's mighty dark down here. I've got to stay. I can't leave someone down here."

There was only a slight pause.

"I'm the only one here, Dolan. I'll be down. Where are you?" replied Winsloe Holbrook.

"I'm at N-1, turbine."

The designation N-1 referred to the first generator on the Nevada side of the river, turbine level.

"I'll be right down," said Holbrook.

It would take him the better part of twenty minutes to be "right down." Going down nine hundred steps was much more tough on the legs than going up.

"How long do we have?" repeated Dolan.

Winsloe Holbrook looked at his watch. It was dark, there was no electricity and his watch wasn't luminescent. It was force of habit.

"I don't know, Dolan. I guess it doesn't matter. I'll be down, we'll find him, and we'll get out before whatever happens, happens."

"Bring a flashlight."

Dolan hung up. Holbrook looked at his phone. What was going to happen? All Winsloe Holbrook could think about was his good friend Brent Parsons up at Glen Canyon, that and the seven-hundred-foot wall of water cascading down the Grand Canyon toward them. Holbrook turned his flashlight toward the darkened OSHA-approved EXIT sign and headed down the pit-dark stairwell.

— • —

The Colorado River runs in a westerly direction all the way through northern Arizona. At the head of Black Canyon the river makes a dramatic left turn and heads almost straight for the Gulf of California. Four miles down the canyon is Hoover Dam. The crest of the dam is at elevation 1232 feet above mean sea level. After flowing through the intake towers and the penstocks, the water exits riverbed level at 506 feet. On the crest of the dam is an improved two-lane highway, U.S. 93, which makes an eighty-two-mile beeline from Kingman, Arizona through the high desert to the canyon area. Two miles south of the dam, at a point where 93 crosses over Sugarloaf Mountain, a small dirt road bears off to the right. The road was blocked by a single thread of chain link. In the summer it was a popular embarkment point for bikers and off-road vehicles to reach some rough country along the southern, unpopulated bank of Lake Mead. Within a few feet the road went up Sugarloaf, around a bend and was out of sight from U.S. 93. It went on for two miles, crossing the mountain to Kingman Wash, a low area on Lake Mead north of Black Canyon. One mile from 93, at the top of treeless Sugarloaf, an unmarked path bore off to the left, dead-ending on the edge of Black Canyon.

There, in a black Buick, patiently sat Alex Rostov, Katrina Tambov and Williams, the American-born Soviet agent. Fifty feet away, on a relatively flat and unrocky spot, was the late Will Gregory's Canyon Tours helicopter.

Katrina and Rostov sat in the back seat. Every ten or fifteen minutes Williams would run the engine and heat the car for a few minutes. Outside, the temperature hovered in the middle thirties, but the wind blowing through the canyons dropped the wind chill into the high teens. It had been a long winter.

"How long will it take?" asked Katrina.

She was tired. The day's pace had been incredible. The emotion and rush of adrenalin had kept her alert and awake. Now, with a lull with perhaps only one more act to perform, she felt tired. Every muscle ached. This was more than she'd bargained for, even though she'd performed her part of the job flawlessly.

"Not long, perhaps another hour. Maybe longer if the dam doesn't collapse. We'll have to wait and see."

Rostov pointed down below to the black outline of the unlit dam. From their vantage point they could barely make out the turrets of Hoover's intake towers. On either side the sheer walls of Black Canyon rose eight hundred feet.

Rostov mused. He was tired as well. The helicopter may or may not take them far enough. Regardless, it would be easier than trying to escape by car.

"For once, things may actually go as planned. The water should not only flood the area around this lake but it should also should overflow and destroy this dam. If it does, our job is done. The Americans will be without electricity, and we will have accomplished our mission."

"And if something has gone wrong?" asked Katrina.

"Then we have one more task to perform," said Rostov.

Rostov became deadly serious. It would be difficult.

"Hoover Dam must be destroyed."

"Why don't we do it now?" asked Katrina. "Nobody's down there. Do it now, and get out of here!"

Rostov had been mesmerized by The Plan.

Katrina looked out into the dim black of the night. The wind rocked the car.

"Rostov—I want to go home again." she said firmly. "Let's get this over with."

In the front seat Williams silently agreed.

They had two choices. They could leave the car parked in the lot, like they did at Glen Canyon—but they'd have to walk back up the two miles to the top of Sugarloaf Mountain to get to the helicopter. Given the timing, an impossible choice. The other choice was to use the helicopter to get the weapon wherever was close enough.

"We might be able to set it right on the dam," said Katrina.

"And get away," Rostov added.

Rostov mulled. Williams was a good pilot.

"All right, let's transfer the weapon."

Her idea made more sense.

— • —

Down-canyon and two miles away, power operations manager Winsloe Holbrook flicked his flashlight to the right, then to the left. The cold passageway led through a tunnel of unfinished raw stone. His light made every rock seem much larger. The wall appeared much more ragged than it was.

"It's about time!" shouted Dolan Yarnell.

It was a friendly, albeit sarcastic, jibe.

"What's all this commotion about, Dolan?"

Holbrook finally made it to the Nevada turbine row.

"I heard it, Winny. Somebody's here. I heard it," he repeated.

"OK, OK, you heard it. Where?" asked Holbrook.

Holbrook flashed his light onto Dolan Yarnell's face. Doubt and concern were there, so was a touch of fear. The odd lighting of the flashlight didn't do much for his appearance.

"I only heard it once. It was soft and it was in pain. He's down there someplace. I don't know if he was shouting from below and I just barely heard him, or whether he was close and just too weak. In any case, I only heard him once," said Dolan.

"OK, let's go. You take the left side, I'll take the right," replied Winsloe.

The task was formidable. They had over five hundred feet of turbine area to check. Each of the eight turbines, N-1 through N-8, looked like an island set in concrete. Each turbine was in a bay which occupied the entire width of the room. In the center was the huge five-foot-diameter stainless steel shaft which ran from the penstock area below, up and through the floor of the turbine area, through the turbine, then up another twenty-five feet, through the ceiling of the second floor to the generator on the third floor. The deck on the turbine was circular in design. To get from N-1 to N-2 one had to walk up three steps, walk forward eight feet, then navigate N-1's turbine either to the left or right, then exit back down three steps to the other side of N-1. The distance between each turbine was sixty-two-and-a-half feet.

The railing protected people from falling into the maintenance pit, a service area for the turbine itself. Also circular, it enabled anyone to crawl down into the hidey-holes of the turbine, even through the floor into the dark pit of the penstock. It was the penstock gate on the first floor, the basement, which had to be closed so that water rushing through the intake towers would be stopped. No water, no spinning power. Without water the generators could be shut down properly, without harm.

The two senior managers quietly made their way down turbine alley toward the concrete wall at the south end of the power facilities.

"Help!"

"Did you hear that, Dolan?" asked Winsloe Holbrook.

"I think it's downstairs," Dolan replied.

"I hope not," said Holbrook.

Me too, thought Dolan. *Please let him be easy to get to.*

"I think it came from N-6," shouted Holbrook.

"Go for it."

The two men made their way up, over, and around each of the huge turbines until they came to number 6, nearly 380 feet away from the main tunnel, which in turn was nearly 300 feet from the stairwell, which in turn was 700 feet up to the crest of the dam.

And it was dark.

And they were just a bit out of shape.

They were near N-6. Without a word Dolan took the right side, Winny the left. An injured man in all probability would be down in the service bay between floors. Each made a pass around his semicircle area of coverage. In between them was the turbine shaft which extended from floor to ceiling, twenty-five feet.

Nothing.

"I don't see anything, Dolan," said Holbrook.

"Me neith . . . wait . . . yes, I . . . come over here!" stammered Dolan Yarnell.

The weak flashlight almost lost its illumination eight feet down into the pit.

Almost.

There, at the end of the light from a weak series of AA batteries was a man's hand.

"There he is!" shouted Winny.

The drop from the platform around the turbine was nearly fifteen feet. At the bottom, maintenance could be performed on the internals of the turbine. Below the grated floor was a small, very small, area where someone could crawl from the turbine floor to the top of the penstock tunnels below. The eighteen-foot-diameter penstocks ran diagonally underneath the turbines, which led from the forty-foot-wide tunnels. Between the floors was a small crawlspace, nothing more than an airspace between the sheer rock and the concrete penstock.

Dolan Yarnell's light shined on the outstretched fingers of someone who had slipped down between the two floors. The only things visible were a hand and arm. The rest of the person was wrapped in the crawl-space around the penstock. His face must have been touching the wall in front of him.

Hardly looking, Dolan scrambled through the guardrail and down into the pit. From the pit he could see that the grated floor was missing several sections. *How could this happen?* he thought.

It didn't matter. It happened. Don't waste time on the history of the problem. Fix it.

"He's alive, Winny!" said Dolan. "It's Ted Dillon."

"Can we get him out?" asked Holbrook.

As he asked the question Holbrook ducked through the railing and dropped down into the pit next to his friend.

"How on earth did he get here?" Holbrook exclaimed.

"How much time do we have?" asked Dolan.

"Not more than an hour."

The two of them reached down and strained to pull the dead weight of the stuck maintenance man. They could only reach one hand. They managed to move him a few inches, but nothing more.

"One of us is going to have to go downstairs and try to either pull him through or push him up." said Dolan.

"I'll go," replied Winsloe Holbrook.

Dillon groaned, then opened his eyes, which were immediately blinded by the direct glow of the flashlight.

"Sorry," said Dolan. "What hurts? Can you talk?"

"My . . . my leg. I can't feel anything. I know it's broken. My arm . . . my left arm . . . is twisted. I can't move . . ."

"We'll get you out."

Dolan watched Holbrook climb up and out of the maintenance bay and then he was gone into the darkness.

"You'll be OK, just relax. We're going to try to get you out from below," Dolan said with some reassurance.

Holbrook made his way to the stairwell which led from the turbine room up to the generator or down to the penstock. At each generator unit there was a stairwell; a clammy, moist hall which was just wide enough for two men but not tall enough for Winsloe Holbrook's six-foot-four-inch frame. The stairwell went down thirty feet in three stages. Half way down, Holbrook's flashlight started to flicker.

Holbrook's heart jumped. He'd worked in dams for the better part of his career with BuRec, first in maintenance, then power operations. He'd worked O & M at Trinity, the same at Shasta, then through the Region for paperwork training, back out to Shasta as power operations manager. Hoover had been the culmination of his career. All these years at Hoover he'd been able to disregard the fact that his offices were inside the body of the dam, below water level. Mentally he'd been able to tell himself it was nothing different from working in an office building.

Winsloe Holbrook was a claustrophobic.

It was nighttime. The dam was cold and pitch-black. He was moving toward the very bottom of the dam, down where the natural seepage of water through the rock of the canyon and the grout lines of the concrete made the walking slippery in places. And his flashlight was going out.

THE KREMLIN

The Kremlin War Room wasn't as state-of-the-art as the White House's, but it was close. A blowup map of the Middle East was electronically displayed on one wall. On the opposite wall was a similar electronic map showing the current Soviet forces in red, the Americans in blue and the British in green.

Mikhail Gorbachev sat at the head of the oversized table, Eduard Shevardnadze to his right. No one else was seated. To their left, standing unobtrusively, were two translators. Messages were brought in by various staff clerks and military liaisons.

"Three of our planes have been shot down, sir," said one clerk.

"The Americans are still without power," said another.

Shevardnadze pointed to the map of the Middle East. Things were going well. The sweep across the Iranian southern desert from Afghanistan was doing well. By midday tomorrow they would be on the Persian Gulf and would link up with the fleet poised off the Arabian Sea. The other half of the Afghanistan forces were rapidly moving armor toward Teheran. Meanwhile, the two divisions based along the Georgia/Iran border had crossed the Elbrutz Range and were within shouting distance of Teheran already.

"Shot down?" questioned Gorbachev. "By whom?"

"We don't know, sir. We presume by the Iranians. Who else could it be?" replied the army liaison.

"The Americans could be attacking from their aircraft carriers in the Gulf. Meanwhile, the electricity supply is vanishing from their western states, one by one," said Shevardnadze smiling.

The plan was working well.

"Open the line," said Gorbachev. "I want to talk to the president."

The Soviet translator spoke to the State Department functionary in English, then nodded to Gorbachev that the connection was made.

"Mr. President, I presume you know that my satellites are telling me that the electricity supply in your western states is diminishing rapidly to zero. You are virtually defenseless from attack."

There was no response from the president. Gorbachev continued.

"I can also see that planes from your carriers in the Gulf are threatening our borders. I demand that they be recalled. You are in no position to negotiate. We are not attacking the United States. However, if you persist, I will have no choice but to agree with my generals. I have been protecting you, Mr. President. My people have insisted that this is the opportunity to win our struggle against the forces of imperialism and strike a blow for freedom. But I have resisted. You must instruct your planes to return to their bases. Your ships must be instructed to move away from the Middle Eastern area. We will liberate Iran. You must do this now, Mr. President."

Both Gorbachev and the Soviet translator could hear the American translator busily conveying Gorbachev's words and tone of voice to the president.

"Stick it in your ear," came the response from an incensed American president.

The line went dead. The Americans had hung up.

The Soviet translator was nonplussed. While he understood the president's tone of voice, inflection, and sense of anger the words made no sense. The translator couldn't put the right Russian phrase to match the American's words.

Gorbachev looked up and shook his head. There was no need to translate.

HUALAPAI INDIAN RESERVATION, GRAND CANYON NATIONAL PARK

The roar of the cascading water could be heard for thirty miles. Moving at 110 miles an hour, it rushed past the visitor's center area at Grand Canyon then smashed into the first of three goosenecks, rock formations created by the river as it eroded what it could. The river always took the easy path. The water negotiated the canyon like a racer moves on a sloped racetrack, only not at all as smoothly. A three-hundred-foot wave a half-mile wide does not move gracefully. However, it does move wherever it wants to. The canyon first turned north, then looped in a semicircle, then two sharp turns, north then south. The water was incredibly angry, smashing into one canyon wall, rebounding across and slapping the opposite side with equal force. Boulders were carved out of canyon walls and picked up from the river bottom. This agitation made the scouring action of the flood the same as running coarse grade sandpaper over soft wood.

As early as 7:10 the first group of Hualapai Indians began gathering near the rim of the canyon. The vibration of the earth had told them something terrible was going to happen. By 7:25 the Glen Canyon water had moved 170 miles down the Colorado River. Behind the initial wave was a destroyed lake.

The water shook the earth as the river turned southbound for its last major half loop, a 180-degree turn made over seventy miles, right past the Hualapai Reservation.

All of a sudden the water was in the canyon directly beneath them. The noise was deafening, so loud that the Indians did not hear the noise of a fleet of Huey helicopters advancing from the south at 130 miles an hour. They had little time.

— • —

"Are the helicopters clear, Major?"

"No, sir."

From twenty-eight thousand feet above the Grand Canyon, Major Arlin Buckhorn could see the white foam of the water in the darkness of the night. The sight was unbelievable. Each plane carried two twenty-megaton hydrogen bombs. This would be the first above-ground "test" in twenty years. It would be hundreds of years before the Indians could return. The fallout would be roughly that of Chernobyl. There would be a few direct deaths due to the blasts—Indians who couldn't be evacuated—but it would be fifty years before the worst of the radiation passed through the food chain enough times to affect human and animal reproduction.

It was a price which had to be paid. The destruction of Lake Powell and subsequent flooding of Lake Mead, the loss of electrical power to southern California and Arizona, the flooding of the Colorado River and the rich farmland of the Imperial Valley would cause chaos to the economy and harm the actual safety of all Americans. Although American leaders had no idea how, somehow the Colorado River could be used again—diverted, dammed—who knew? There was no choice. The Grand Canyon would become a great irradiated lake.

"Are the helicopters out of the area, major?" came the voice of a worried Bulldog Russell.

"Do you copy, Indian One?"

Although they were out of his vision, Arlin knew the fleet of helicopters from Nellis Air Force Base in Las Vegas was directly below him.

"Copy," came the terse reply from the squadron leader. "We're almost finished. Another thirty seconds."

The water rushed toward an unnamed canyon three miles from Pierce Ferry. On either side the canyon walls rose to elevation 4850 while the water was rushing past at elevation 1680. It was a perfect place to try and dam the water. Once past the canyon the surface elevation dropped to 1800 feet very quickly. It would be doubtful if Wheeler Ridge could be dammed. Once past the narrow canyon the angry water would enter the eastern edge of Lake Mead and the state of Nevada.

"Release your weapons, Major Buckhorn. Now!"

"Indian One! Indian One! Indian One! Get the hell out of Dodge, boy. I'm dropping my load!" shouted Buckhorn to the helicopter pilots below.

The water was past the canyon.

"Release your weapons, major."

"This is Indian One. We're gone! Give us thirty seconds! Please!"

Down below, at treetop level, the Hueys sped to the south. They needed to be at least fifteen miles away to have a chance at escaping the force of the hydrogen bombs.

The two aircraft were in tight formation.

"Over target! Fire!"

The four hydrogen bombs were released simultaneously. The two F-111s made a sharp bank to the north and accelerated while climbing. The bombs would take approximately ninety seconds to drop and were programmed to explode at one thousand feet above the surface.

At 7:38:35 (MST) eighty megatons of nuclear weaponry was exploded one thousand feet above the surface of the Colorado River, three thousand feet below the level of the surrounding mountains. The four weapons detonated as one explosion.

The air in the canyon went from a cold 34 degrees to over a million degrees Fahrenheit in a less than one-millionth of a second. In that same instant two miles of Colorado River were vaporized, as were the river bottom and canyon walls. The explosions had the effect of placing a giant hand temporarily halting the movement of the water. In fact, the explosions caused an instant energy barrier, a virtual dam.

At impact-plus-eight-tenths-of-a-second, as the massive mushroom cloud illuminated the desert sky, six-hundred-mile-an-hour winds swept out in every direction. Rock had been melted. Like a huge pile driver the canyon walls were excavated, crumbled, collapsed, destroyed. What rock hadn't been vaporized was pulverized, turned to powder and thrown into the air like the explosion of a giant volcano.

At impact-plus-twenty-seconds, the energy of the explosion had been thrown out into the atmosphere in all directions. A shock wave was rushing up and down the canyon in both directions. Once displaced, the temporary vacuum at impact had to be replaced. Canyon walls fell at the same time the force of the rushing Colorado overcame the energy thrown at it from the explosions.

The hydrogen bombs had crumbled a two-mile section of the Grand Canyon. The river was plugged. It would be many years before the new Lake Powell could be used for any purposes. It would take the best of

American technology and ingenuity to figure out how to get the river moving again.

But, because of the evacuation of the Hualapai Indians, almost ten miles of raging Colorado River had passed the impact point and had already entered Lake Mead. A wall of water, three-hundred-feet deep by one-half-mile wide angrily rushed over the calm lake toward its opposite side, Black Canyon and Hoover Dam.

OVER LAKE MEAD, NEVADA

The helicopter lazily drifted back and forth across the area between Las Vegas and Lake Mead. There was no sense landing in Las Vegas. What was there to do?

Damn! J.J. felt angry and frustrated. Rostov was out there someplace.

"Look at that, J.J.!"

The sky off to the east flashed brilliantly as the hydrogen bombs were detonated inside the Grand Canyon.

"Did they . . ." questioned Scotty.

"They must have. Damn!"

Below them, Las Vegas was down and out. It was time for the insane people of the night, the looters, thugs, rapists, and murderers to do what they do best; skulk in the night and hurt people, destroy things. There was very little the authorities could do at this point. The city was in chaos. The tourists had long gotten in their cars only to discover that in their rush to get to the city they'd forgotten to fill up their tanks. Gas got into a gas tank via electric pumps. Many people would head south on I-15 toward Los Angeles only to discover that none of the little burgs on the highway would have power or gas either. I-15 would be littered with cars which had run out of gas. With the temperature in the low 30s there would be people hurt and killed from exposure.

Those who stayed would do so at their own risk, both from the standpoint of the disaster about to strike and from the crazies out on the street. The National Guard and Air Force personnel from Nellis had their hands full just trying to maintain the massive exodus of people to higher ground in the Spring Mountains to the west and north or the McCullough Range to the south. The local police had more problems than trying to catch three foreign agents.

370

J.J. wasn't depressed, but his lack of sleep and the emotional drain of the last ten hours forced him into deep reality. He looked down at the dark city and grimly acknowledged the situation.

"They've got the advantage, Scotty. Rostov, Khan—they're like the night people who are out there right now. You and I, we're day people."

Scotty looked at his leader with concern. J.J. sounded older. He looked like he was at the end of his rope. Had he only known the man for a day?

"Scotty, I'm tired and I'm hungry. I really don't know where those sons of bitches might be."

Scotty was speechless.

They hovered over a closed McDonalds. All J.J. could think of was a Big Mac and an order of fries. When had he eaten last? Today? When did today start? In North Carolina? Really? He'd been in North Carolina, Virginia, Georgia, Missouri, Colorado, Nevada, and Arizona in one day. And the frustrating thing was, he'd been just one step behind Rostov all the way.

"God damn it, Scotty—I know we're close. He—they—can't be far."

Come on, use your brain. Think! I know you're tired. You're frustrated. But you're not thinking straight. Where is he? J.J. thought.

"Come on, let's go. We aren't going to find them down there, not until it clears out. Besides, if they're down there we aren't going to find them until the lights come on anyway."

J.J. pointed to a map section of Lake Mead.

"Let's see if that blast did any good," he shouted to Nichols.

Nichols motioned for the two of them to put on their headsets.

"Lake Mead," J.J. repeated.

"Yes, sir."

"They're out there, Scotty," J.J. said, but not convincingly.

HOOVER DAM

All they had seen was a bright flash in the sky, someplace on the other side of the Black Mountains. Sugarloaf Mountain, Fortification Hill, and Wilson Ridge all prevented Katrina and Rostov from seeing the direct effect of the nuclear holocaust on the Colorado River.

But Rostov sensed what had happened. The Americans had made some kind of effort to stop the flood. It had to have been nuclear. Nothing would light the sky like that.

Katrina looked at Rostov.

"What do you think they've done?"

"I don't know. We've got to go. We've got to be sure, Katrina," Rostov replied. "Go," he said to Williams.

Rostov let the cold desert air blow right through his body. This was it. This was the ultimate act of sabotage. The Americans had somehow countered their first move, but not this one. Williams took off into the wind, dipped slightly, then in an instant they were over land's end and the edge of a two-thousand-foot cliff.

"Slowly. Careful," cautioned Rostov.

Williams was not about to be anything but careful. The night winds blowing up-canyon buffeted the chopper. At fifty knots Williams took the helicopter out to the middle of the narrow canyon, eighty feet above Lake Mead. The water below them was 433 feet deep. The 1983 high-water mark appeared in white contrast, as if someone had drawn a line around the canyon walls with a giant marker.

"We don't have much time," said Rostov to Katrina. "We have to find a place and get it done, quickly."

The intake towers were visible. The turrets had been armed with nests of machine guns during World War II as protection against the godless Oriental hoards. There were no cars parked in the Arizona lots. U.S. 93 made a double turn as it made its way to the crest of the dam, allowing BuRec to build car and bus lots for the tourists.

On the Nevada side there were few places to park. The highway made a steep turn directly along the edge of the canyon wall, then a series of hairpin turns immediately away from the canyon up to Boulder City. One of them, however, was reasonably concealed. To the right of the small visitors' center was a reserved DON'T EVEN THINK OF PARKING HERE sign which threatened people with bodily harm if they even thought of stopping to take a picture. Dolan Yarnell and Winsloe Holbrook parked there, as did the Chief of Visitor Services. The two cars went unseen by the Soviets.

There had been no way to effectively place the bomb at the base of Glen Canyon. There the objective had been to knock out power and destroy the dam. Cutting off electricity had been the primary objective. Dictated from the bowels of the Kremlin, the objective had always been the destruction of Hoover Dam. In this case "making sure" meant putting the bomb near or inside the dam, certainly on the downside of the dam where the seven-hundred-foot wall of concrete would feel the direct force of the blast.

Williams brought the helicopter to a hover position over the dam. The feeling of vertigo was heightened as the edge of the dam came into view. Rostov activated two searchlights which immediately seemed brighter than normal as the dual switchyard 700 feet below was illuminated. At riverbed level the two power plants, each with eight turbines, faced each other 200 feet across the Colorado River.

"Down there," said Rostov, pointing to the power plant area.

Williams guided the helicopter down into the narrow canyon. It was very tricky flying. The dam's buildings, power plants, and transmission ties made the downriver canyon much more narrow than upriver. The helicopter bobbed in the wind.

The service road was too narrow to land on. Rostov calmly passed the searchlights from the dam itself back to the diversion outlets.

"Bring it back up a little," Rostov commanded.

At the downstream end of the power plant, on both sides, was an open working area which was designed to be used in conjunction with the 150-ton-capacity cableway which stretched across the canyon 800 feet above riverbed level. The cableway was used to move, lower, or raise the very heavy pieces of equipment down into or up out of the power plant area. The open area on both the Nevada and Arizona sides was used as a landing or staging area for the equipment to be moved. Williams was not excited about landing the helicopter in either of the small patches of concrete, especially with the GSA-green trucks parked near the entrance.

"What about the roof of the building?" asked Katrina, pointing to the roof of the four-story maintenance building, which connected the Nevada and Arizona power plants and was at the base of the dam.

"Yes! Good! Can you land there?" Rostov asked Williams.

The pilot was so relieved that instead of answering verbally, he flew the 400 feet, hovered for a few seconds, then easily placed the helicopter down on the roof. Katrina and Rostov got out in an instant. Katrina looked up. The dam was overwhelming. It extended peripheral vision from both eyes. Above them was over 600 feet of concrete, set in gigantic blocks 25 feet tall by 30 feet deep. Near the top on the lake side the blocks were twice that size, three-million-plus cubic yards of concrete with pressure grouting between each joint.

Williams' helicopter never came to dead still. He was out to help the two agents as soon as his bird stopped thrashing.

"Move—we don't have much time!" shouted Rostov.

There was no argument.

"We'll set it up over here!" he said, pointing to where the maintenance building was flush against the dam.

The blast would vaporize the entire dam.

It was 7:42 P.M. (MST)

— • —

It had been seventeen minutes since the flash of light disintegrated the rocks of Lower Granite Gorge, collapsing the canyon and forcing the Colorado to once again be artificially dammed.

But ten miles of angry discharge flooded the Colorado River, smashing whatever got in its way, falling through the canyon. The marina and picnic area at Pierce Ferry was destroyed. Coming to the rocky narrows between Paiute Point and Grand Wash Canyon, the Colorado was less than a quarter-mile wide. The water forced itself through the opening but not before creating a huge angry wave. Regaining momentum and form, the wave was aided by the deeper water of a straight section of Iceburg Canyon. Iceburg Canyon was only a quarter-mile wide but it allowed the wave to pile back up to nearly 250 high, after having lost some of its height at the lowlands around Pierce Ferry.

At the end of Iceburg Canyon the tsunami-like wall of water was 46 miles from the intake towers of Hoover dam. It would reach the dam in 28 minutes.

— • —

"I thought the explosion was supposed to stop the water!" said an obviously scared Scotty Coldsmith.

The terrible rumble of the water echoed upward to the helicopter as the bore wave smashed down the canyon. The wave displaced the water in front of it as it fell heavily across the lake.

"I don't know what happened," replied J.J.

"Will it flood Las Vegas?"

Who knew? The power of what was happening made J.J. feel as insignificant as he was. There was nothing he could do about anything.

"I don't know. Some of it might crest the western end of the lake. But that dam is going to go for sure. No way it can stand up" said J.J. with resignation.

Rostov had won. The Soviets had won. Southern California would be a wasteland. What wouldn't be flooded would be evacuated. Los Angeles without air conditioning. The spoilage of food supplies. J.J. shook his head at the possibilities. The defense industry lived in Los Angeles; Rockwell, TRW, Hughes, and all the thousands of subcontractors. What about the U.S. Navy in Long Beach and San Diego?

"We might as well get a ringside seat. Head down to the dam," said J.J. to the pilot.

J.J. looked at his map and pointed. The pilot banked to the left, hovered over the rushing wave, accelerated up and over the White Hills and the Black Mountain peninsula. J.J. looked down at the map and was momentarily heartened. Some of the water would be diverted when it met the Overton Arm of Lake Mead, the narrow body which stretches out to the north.

In minutes they swooped down over Sugarloaf Mountain and into Black Canyon. Hoover was an impressive dam. Massive.

"Maybe it won't go, J.J.! You know, that dam's pretty big. Maybe it'll wash over," Scotty said with enthusiasm.

Maybe so.

Nichols passed over the dam.

There were lights down there!

"What's that?" asked Scotty, excited, pointing to the twin searchlights on the maintenance building below.

"Rostov! They're down there!" J.J. said to Nichols. "Hurry!"

J.J. turned to Scotty.

"That has to be him! I'd be there, if it was my job to do. I wouldn't leave anything up to chance."

It was 7:43.

— • —

"Pull, Dolan, pull!" shouted a very tired Winsloe Holbrook.

Blood dripped down from an unseen wound on Ted Dillon onto Holbrook's hands, then his face. He was directly underneath Dillon, who had somehow managed to slip through into the tightest airspace possible. Holbrook couldn't see Dolan but could feel his effort. Dillon was moving!

"Pull!" he shouted again.

Holbrook himself was contorted around the crawlspace surrounding the turbine. He'd been in the desk job too long. He'd been a lot more lean in his days of O&M when he'd been the one to close the gates. Management was so structured that it seemed as if all he did was prepare budgets and estimate expenses. He missed the day-to-day operations, the people-to-people contact which management was all about. It was true he had one of the few offices with a window, a window actually built into the dam itself with a view of the downstream Colorado, but even so he'd rather be back on the line. The job didn't pay as much as his current GS-15 schedule, but it was more fun, although this wasn't his idea of a good time.

Ted Dillon's legs moved upward. Dolan had a good grip. In a minute Dillon was out of sight.

"I've got him, Winny!" came Dolan's response.

"Need help?"

"Yeah, he's heavy. He's unconscious."

"I'll be up."

Holbrook picked up his flashlight. It flickered twice then went out.

He could hear himself sweat. Was that the water piping through the penstocks? No, it couldn't be. They were closed. No water. It was his heart. *Calm down, Winny, calm down. There's a stairwell over there. Watch your head . . .*

"Ouch!"

Holbrook banged his head on the shutoff wheel.

"Come on, you jerk!" he berated himself. "Move! You know where things are. Now move."

The wall came approximately the number of steps he thought it would. He felt the moisture which was always in the rock. Move to the left? Yes, to the left. There was no vibration in the dam. It was deathly quiet. In his ten years at Hoover he couldn't remember a time when there was *no* water moving through, not even for maintenance. It wouldn't be long before the spillways would kick in.

"Come on, Holbrook," Winny encouraged himself.

The stairwell! He found the stairwell. Ducking down and feeling slightly more confident, Holbrook made his way up the stairs to the turbine galley.

"I don't like the dark, you know," Holbrook said to Dolan as the two men were reunited. "My flashlight went out."

"Give me an arm. Dillon's heavy," replied Dolan.

The only sounds which could be heard were their labored breathing and an occasional groan from Dillon. No sounds from the outside world ever reached inside Hoover. Getting through turbine galley was an extremely difficult process lugging the injured Ted Dillon. They had turbine areas to cross through, each of which meant steps up, go around the turbine, steps back down. But with persistence they made it to the point where the Nevada power plant met the base of the dam. There they met a stairwell which led them up to the primary lateral passageway across the middle of the dam.

"Wait a minute, Dolan. I've got to rest," said Holbrook.

They were at a point roughly one-third of the way through the dam and were walking along a moist rocky corridor in the direction of Arizona. Every two hundred feet or so there was a side corridor which led out to the dam itself, corridors purposely cut in the dam during its construction to enable the poured concrete to cool. At the end of the narrow side-walkway was a viewing port.

Both Holbrook and Dolan, perspiring and breathing heavily, saw the flash at the same time.

"What the hell's that?" said Dolan.

"Somebody or something's out there," replied Holbrook, equally surprised.

"Out where?"

They were three floors above the roof of the maintenance building, roughly ninety feet.

"Hold him," said Holbrook as he ran down the darkened walkway to the viewing portal.

"What the hell . . . ?" said Holbrook.

Immediately behind him was Dolan Yarnell. Fifty feet behind them in the dark lay poor Dillon, slumped on the cold passageway floor.

"Unbelievable!" said Dolan as he and Winsloe Holbrook peered through the window.

It was 7:44 P.M. (MST)

— • —

"Look out for the wire!" shouted Scotty.

Nichols barely saw the unlit twin four-inch cables. They were nothing more than dark threads in a starlit sky. He saw them just in time and swerved downward to the right at a severe angle. In an instant both Scotty and J.J. looked out their windows straight down to Colorado River, nine hundred feet below. It was a good time for seatbelts and a closed cockpit.

"Hang on!" shouted Nichols.

Diving through the canyon's natural turbulence, Nichols righted the helicopter and hovered at a point three hundred feet above the river and approximately directly under the cableway, near the end of the generating plants.

There, perched on the roof of the concrete maintenance building, was another helicopter, its blades still moving in a slow idle. Scotty turned a searchlight onto the roof which illuminated three people, one of whom was firing a weapon at them!

Slugs ripped into the helicopter. Nichols went into close-quarter evade mode as Scotty and J.J. watched two people run for the stationary helicopter.

"It's Rostov," said Scotty.

"And the woman. I know it's her!" replied J.J. "You've got to keep them down!" J.J. turned to Nichols.

"I don't know if I can, sir," answered Nichols.

The third figure threw off several more rounds then ran toward the helicopter.

"Unidentified helicopter—this is the FBI. Hold your position. You are under arrest. Make no attempt to leave. Come out of the helicopter with your hands above your head. This is an order!" shouted J.J. through the electric bullhorn.

Even if the order had been heard, it certainly was going to be ignored. Rostov's craft started to rise. Nichols, without instruction from J.J., advanced toward the opposing craft.

"What kind of weapons do we have aboard?" asked J.J.

It was a good question. Other than their standard sidearm, J.J. had brought nothing with him. Nichols turned and flashed a smile.

"Sir, this is a modified standard. I have dual machine guns. There are two .308 M1As behind the passenger seat."

The M1As were modified M-14s.

J.J. opened the co-pilot window. The craft was filled with the shocking cold of the February canyon air. Scotty did the same to the window behind Nichols. Both tried to take aim and found it too difficult to even try to get a reasonable shot.

"They can't get away! Understand? We can't let them get away. Nichols, do you hear me?"

"Yes, sir."

"We have to get them alive. That's *alive*, Nichols. Understand?"

"Yes, sir."

This time Nichols' "yes, sir" was a bit restrained.

"Can you keep them down?" asked J.J.

"I'll try, sir."

Nichols came about and raked the roof of the maintenance building with 7.62mm shells. Each shell hit the concrete surface and exploded what it hit into small chips. The bullet then ricocheted obliquely into the face of the dam where its badly mashed form was still a deadly missile. Some of the shells hit the Soviet helicopter after the first or second bounce.

"Don't let them go, Nichols!"

— • —

With the direct light from the helicopter's underbelly shining across them, Rostov's every hand motion was exaggerated in maniacal shadows strewn at odd angles on the dam's surface. Katrina stood to his side, not blocking the light but giving him silent encouragement. Williams stood anxiously near the helicopter. He was very nervous. He was close enough to the dam to touch it. It was awesome.

Rostov looked at his watch. It was 7:45 P.M. (MST) Twenty-five minutes should be enough. The digital timer sped through the hours and minutes. No . . . no, P.M. not A.M. Rostov gave a rueful smile. He wasn't coming all this way to set the thing for the wrong time.

"Hurry, Alex!"

Rostov went back to work as the FBI helicopter came over the top of the dam at a quick speed, its searchlights trailing in crisscross patterns throughout lower Black Canyon. Then the lights were trained on them! Each of them had two images projected onto the dam's wall, one from above and one from their helicopter's lights.

"Fire! Shoot them!" shouted Katrina to Williams.

Williams did what he was told. And he had the best weapon available, a Heckler and Koch PSG1, a modified military assault rifle. The rifle, imported from Germany, cost nearly six thousand dollars, but its light weight and supreme accuracy were world-renowned. Williams started firing at the hovering helicopter.

With deliberate speed Rostov finished arming the bomb, completing the job by screwing the four-inch stainless steel cap onto the detonator's odd-shaped arm. He gave it a last firmness test then followed Katrina toward the helicopter.

"Come on, hurry up!" he shouted to Williams.

The pilot had watched his counterpart rise, then abort, fall, and avoid a spin. It was nice flying. Too nice. Williams ran for the helicopter just as a barrage of high-caliber machine gun fire deliberately missed them.

Williams knew it was a deliberate miss by the fact that the police helicopter had plenty of range and enough time to fire. A couple of the bullets pinged into the side of his helicopter but did no damage.

"Now!" shouted Katrina from her right side rear passenger seat. Death was close.

Williams had only one way he could go and that was downstream. A helicopter isn't like a Harrier jet which can actually rise or fall in a direct vertical line, a helicopter needs to move backward or forward when it takes off. Backward was out of the question with seven hundred feet of concrete blocking the way. Situated as they were on the Arizona side of the maintenance building, Williams could move to the west, toward Nevada then up. Or, as he wanted to do, rise and head downstream.

The craft hovered and slowly moved forward. The wind buffeted the light craft. He had to do something. The searchlights from both craft splayed wildly across dam, canyon, and riverbed as Rostov traded high-powered rifle shots. Since only one side of the FBI plane could fire at any one time, they were really mano-a-mano. Muzzle flash and shell tracers lit the night. The American pilot jockied and got the better position, above and slightly downstream.

"Get up! Higher!" ordered Rostov.

"I can't—they're blocking our . . ." replied Williams.

"Look out!" screamed Katrina as one of the FBI's shots ripped through the helicopter's body.

Another shot smashed the Plexiglas side window, took a nip out of Rostov's shoulder and embedded itself into the seat. Rostov did not take notice.

Williams was in a bad position. They had to get out quickly. The helicopter couldn't hover and bob forever. It took considerable skill to keep the craft away from trouble. Williams had been able to advance only fifty or so feet downstream away from the maintenance building. He was dangerously close to the row of dead 230kv transformers which hung from the top of the Arizona power plant and connected to the 115kv transformers on ground level. Transmission tie-lines then connected the power plant transformers to the 500kv step-up transformers at the top of the canyon. The side of each canyon wall was a web of four-inch transmission lines. Get close to either canyon wall and they'd be picking up pieces of themselves in the river.

"We're going!" Williams shouted.

As Williams slowly forced his way downstream and higher, Rostov got off eight perfect hits on the other craft. From his position below, the four-inch 7.62mm shells ripped through the heart of his enemy's engine, one after another.

"Look!" yelled Katrina.

The FBI helicopter was in terminal condition. Positioned two hundred feet up and ahead of Williams' craft, smoke and oil instantly poured through the holes. There was no way it could be patched, no way the craft could remain aloft. It had no place to go but down. With the engine coming to a terrible death the pilot would quickly feel his controls stiffen and become unmanageable. The American pilot had only a few seconds to make up his mind to try and keep it up or get down to safety—if he could. Rostov watched as the pilot decided to try landing the helicopter. Williams' engine had been damaged as well, but not nearly to the fatal point as the other was. It coughed slightly, but resumed power when it headed downstream.

"Watch out!" screamed Katrina. "The wire . . ."

Her warning was cut off in mid-scream as the craft's blades barely touched the cableway stretching across the canyon at rim level. Seven hundred feet below them was the Colorado. One of the two huge blades had been clipped on one side. But one was enough.

While it wasn't like running into a canyon wall, it certainly did slow momentum. The engine couldn't understand what was happening, it was putting out RPMs but there was no response. With one blade out of control, out of whack, Williams had little or no control over the direction of the craft. All rules of logical motion were thrown out, simple gut reaction took over.

The helicopter started to fall. Katrina screamed. Rostov hung on. The copter slowly fell down and in reverse, like it was falling off a cliff. After a 200 fall, its blades still trying gallantly to gain control, Williams managed to straighten the craft out. But it was spinning. Only the blades were supposed to be turning not the body of the helicopter. Williams' arms were clutches of steel. Out of the corner of his eye he saw the open area at the end of the Arizona power plant, the staging area for the overhead cableway. He went for it.

A hundred feet, then fifty, then twenty-five. Too fast. Too heavy. The helicopter continued to spin as it fell.

"We're going to crash! Brace yourselves!" Williams shouted.

The dead helicopter smashed into the concrete staging area, but not hard enough to break the craft apart. It landed smack on its wheels, but hard enough to collapse them and impale the body. The broken blade snapped and fell. The Plexiglas pilot's bubble shattered. The fall was a chin-snapper. Rostov banged his head against the passenger side of the craft. Williams was cut from the debris. Katrina was unhurt.

They were down.

"Are you all right?" asked Rostov.

"I think so," replied Katrina.

Rostov looked at Williams, and for the first time in a long while, acknowledged the skill of someone other than himself. It had been a fine job of instinctive flying.

But they were all going to die. There was no way out of the canyon before either the tidal wave hit or the bomb was detonated. The three of them would die for their country, a situation which none of them would have wagered would have ever happened. If they were to die, so would the Americans.

"Get the weapons," said Rostov.

The three Soviet spies shakily got out of the broken helicopter to survey their situation. What had happened to the American craft?

"There it is!" pointed Katrina.

Indeed, there it was. Separated by two hundred feet of cold Colorado River was the American helicopter. It had managed to land on staging area downstream from the Nevada power plant. The Americans were just starting to groggily come out of their craft. Then they spotted the Soviets. For a long moment the three Americans looked across the river at the three Soviets, guns in hand. It was time for a more personal battle.

It was 7:47 P.M. (MST)

— • —

"Remember, we've got to take them alive," said J.J. as they stood looking at the three Soviets.

"Where's Khan?" asked Scotty.

"Good question. Is that Rostov?" returned J.J.

"Yes—and I know that woman! She works for the Soviet mission in New York!" exclaimed Scotty, seeing his attackers for the first time in a month.

The two agents hadn't moved. The wind tugged at their jackets, tossled their hair.

"How many rounds do you have?" asked Scotty.

"Not many. Nichols? What do you have?" asked J.J.

"Full round and ten," the pilot replied.

"I've got the same," said Scotty.

"What's in the helicopter?" asked J.J.

"Grenades, smoke, tear gas, another rifle," said Nichols.

"I think we'd better pack up. They're going to make a run for it in about two seconds," said Scotty.

"Where?" asked Nichols.

"Beats me. I have no idea how to get out of here," said J.J. as he looked up at the sheer canyon wall behind him and the awesome seven hundred feet of dam to his left and the cold Colorado River in front of him flowing to his right.

"There they go!" exclaimed Scotty.

The three Soviets went to their helicopter to get what firepower they had available. Scotty, J.J., and Nichols did the same. There was no sense in carrying too much. Somehow there had to be a way to get into the dam then up and out.

"Look, we've got to get them alive and get that bomb. Right now the bomb is more important. It's more important than any one of us, more important than catching them," said J.J.

Nichols was clearly nervous. Catching spies was part of the job description. Finding and disarming nuclear weapons wasn't.

"It's got to be on top of that building, J.J.," Scotty returned.

As the men hurriedly stuffed grenades, tear gas canisters, and extra rounds into their pockets, Scotty's hands fell on the helicopter's fifty feet of rescue ladder—lightweight nylon with plastic rungs. Whatever happened, it was going to be up to him to disarm the bomb. J.J. couldn't do it. *Had it only been this morning that he'd been in St. Louis, under the Eads Bridge?* He had to assume it was the same kind of construction as the one in St. Louis. Somehow he was going to have to get on the roof of the four-story maintenance building. He had no idea how.

"They're on the run!" shouted J.J.

The three Soviets sprinted up the service lane toward the maintenance building.

With the priority being the weapon, Scotty grabbed the collapsed ladder and slung his arm through it, then headed after Nichols and J.J. in a crouched run along the Nevada retaining wall toward the dam. The Soviets were almost there on the Arizona side.

Where were they going to go?

It was 7:50 P.M. (MST)

— • —

"What the hell's going on, Winny? Who are those guys?" asked Dolan.

Holbrook had a moment of dread, one of those rare times when a cold wave shakes through the body tingling every extremity. Nuclear weapons at Glen Canyon. The dam shaking a half hour ago from something powerful. It could only have been a nuclear explosion or an earthquake. Now the incredible sight of dueling helicopters over their dam.

"They're trying to blow us up, Dolan. They're trying to blow our dam up."

Dolan and Holbrook felt like they had ownership of Hoover. Dolan managed the power, Holbrook the facilities. Hoover was their dam and they both acknowledged the other's proprietary feelings.

"We don't have much time. Who are the good guys?" asked Dolan.

"I'm not sure, but it looks like the second helicopter was trying to stop the first. My gut tells me the guys on Nevada are the police," replied Winsloe.

If it had been daytime or the dam's floodlights had been on, they would have clearly seen the FBI markings on both sides of the helicopter. They would have seen *Will Gregory's Canyon Tours* on the other.

"Have you ever been on top of the shed?"

Holbrook shook his head.

"Never had a need to. Not once," Holbrook replied. "Do you think that's it?" he asked, pointing downward to the object on the roof, sixty feet below.

"What do you think?" Dolan answered with a question.

The two professionals looked at each other from very close range. Their eyes transmitted their fear and anger through the dim of the night. They turned around and looked at the figures of men running toward the dam from both sides.

Dolan looked back at the injured Ted Dillon. There was no time to drag him up the stairwell to the surface and try to help the police.

"We're not going to make it out of here, Dolan."

"We've got to try to save the dam," Dolan replied in agreement.

The two men took off running leaving Ted Dillon slumped in the passageway.

— • —

Rostov had a gut feel for what he was going to find at the head of the service road. The road had three tracks of rail gauge extending from beyond the helicopter crash site back to the dam to a heavy 12' x 14' corrugated steel door at the maintenance building. The rails extended into the building where the very heavy pieces of equipment could be put onto fitting lathes for finishing or repairs.

The door opened electrically from the outside via a red button on a panel. It could be opened manually, but only from the inside. Rostov looked up at the dam. He saw the four turrets. Intuition told him the turrets represented stairwells or elevator shafts. His intuition was right. The only way they were going to get out alive was to get into the building, find a stairwell, climb to the top, and . . . and what? Rostov looked at his watch. It was 7:50.

There was no way. They would have to go down with the dam. It was too bad, but it was necessary.

"Take cover. Pin them down."

The floodlights from Will Gregory's crashed helicopter indirectly lit the area. The lights on the FBI helicopter were dead.

Williams took refuge behind a twenty-foot-tall orange crane, Rostov behind the retaining wall, and Katrina near one of the transformers. In unison they began firing at the advancing FBI. The enemy was two hundred feet away, near the head of the Nevada power plant. One shot looked like it hit. One of the agents fell, then got up for cover behind a row of parked maintenance trucks.

"This is the FBI. Put down your guns. You are under arrest. Give it up, Rostov! We know who you are! Throw down your weapons! Come out with your hands behind your head! Now!" came the bullhorn shout from the other side.

"They know you?" asked Williams.

"How can they know?" asked Katrina. "Wait a minute . . . ! Isn't that . . ."

It was the young agent from New York. He hadn't been killed! Rostov could hardly believe his eyes. He'd seen the thugs take the man—how could he be alive?

"You are too late! If we cannot get out, then you will not get out! It does not matter. This dam will be gone soon. We will all be gone!" shouted Rostov in return.

Rostov punctuated his statement with a blistering round of automatic fire. The shells ripped through the parked trucks and off the grey twenty-foot-tall steel transformers behind them.

— • —

"They're in for the duration. We've got to move them out," said J.J.

"I can't see a way to the roof," replied Scotty.

"Are you all right, Nichols?" asked J.J., turning around and trying to locate the pilot's position.

Nichols was behind one of the transformers.

"I don't use that arm much anyway," was his reply.

J.J. turned back to Scotty.

"If only you can get up to . . ."

J.J.'s voice trailed off because at that moment he saw a light! A light inside the dam—inside the maintenance building. It wasn't much of a light, but nevertheless, light. Someone was in the dam!

The maintenance building was at the bottom of the U-shaped configuration, the power plants on either side, extending into the canyon walls. Someone had turned on an emergency generator.

Suddenly, the staging area was partially lit. J.J. could see that behind Rostov there was a large tunnel which led into the Arizona canyon wall. Where it went was anybody's guess. A string of naked bulbs—emergency lights—spaced out every one hundred feet or so, hung from the rock approximately twenty feet above the sloped surface, and had come on.

The emergency lights came on inside the maintenance building. That meant that they would be able to get around inside the dam. It also meant that Rostov might make a run for it.

"J.J., if they've set a bomb on top of that building, then we've got to get up there. If they get away, so what? We can't let this dam go."

Scotty was intense. He was also right. J.J. agreed.

"All right. We're going through that door."

J.J. pointed to a yellow-painted corrugated steel door on their Nevada side, no more than fifty feet from their position. Rostov had them pinned down well. He had at least one high-powered rifle. Whoever was using it, knew how.

"Scotty, we've come a long way to get this scum. We'll get you inside that building, but I'm not going to let them even think they're going to get away."

J.J. reached into his bulky parka and came out with a grenade.

"That door's coming down."

From their position there were two trucks and a car parked against the three-foot-tall concrete retaining wall, then a space of twenty feet with only the wall, finally an open area across the service road which ran along the front of the maintenance building. The dam's configuration was symmetrical. What it had on the Arizona side was matched on the Nevada side.

They would have to take their chances with the shrapnel.

"Get under the truck!"

Nichols dove from his cover behind a transformer to the last truck in line. His effort was rewarded with three bullets crashing around him.

"Feet first!"

Both Scotty and Nichols were under the truck, feet toward the door. The retaining wall protected them from shots across the river.

"Heads down!"

J.J. jerked the pin. He'd never touched a grenade before, much less thrown one. It was heavier than he'd imagined. In a half crouch J.J. rolled the grenade like he was flipping pennies against a curb. Closest to the curb wins. He had to get the grenade close enough to the door to do some real damage, enough to give Scotty a chance to get inside.

The only sounds which could be heard were the slow gurgling of the Colorado as its reduced flow came through the outlets, the cold wind blowing up the canyon, and the metallic tap-tap-thunk of the grenade as it rolled toward the door. J.J. dropped for cover.

The grenade came to a stop three feet from the yellow door and exploded. The sound from the explosion was louder than anyone imagined. J.J. felt a sting in his left leg. He'd been hit. The three men quickly came out from their positions to assess what had happened. The door was nothing but a jagged gash of twisted steel with tiny fingers of sharp fragments.

"I can get through," said Scotty.

Without being asked, Nichols started a barrage of cover fire. On hands and knees Scotty wormed his way down to the end of the protective wall. Only twenty feet of service road to negotiate. Helping him was a crane which stood at attention outside what remained of the door. The crane had been damaged as well. It would lift no more generators.

"Go!" shouted J.J.

Scotty went. J.J. and Nichols fired at Rostov and the man with the rifle and got the same in return. Scotty dashed for the relative safety of the crane. Shots pinged on the concrete beside him. He made it!

With only a few emergency lights on, everything appeared to be in hues of green and yellow. Trashbins were yellow. Huge bottles of compressed air stood at attention, seemingly all bundled up against the February cold. The middle floorspace of the entire building was a machine room. Huge lathes, presses and metal fabricators were positioned near access from a forty-foot-tall moving crane system. With its arms the crane could put a heavy piece of equipment anyplace on the shop floor. Scotty wasn't surprised. It made good sense to have a machine tool room. It wasn't like they could send out for a repairman. The people at Hoover had to fix anything which could break.

How in hell am I going to get on the roof? Scotty surveyed the situation, trying to make a judgment call on which way to go. Whichever way he went it had to be the right one the first time. There were no direct stairwells from inside the huge room to anything on or near the ceiling, at least none which he could see.

It was 7:58.

A noise from behind! Scotty wheeled around, gun in hand, to see J.J. roll into the room, accompanied by the sound of bullets from high-powered guns smashing into metal sections of the outside crane. Hardly slowing down, J.J. took off for the Arizona side of the room.

"Get the bomb, Scotty!" shouted J.J.

Where? With the feeling of not knowing what to do but that doing something was better than nothing, Scotty took off at a trot for the entrance on the Nevada side. Up a short series of steps and all of a sudden he was into the Twilight Zone. Outside the maintenance building he was now into the guts of the dam. Where to go?

It was 8:00. *Where's a stairwell? Damn*! He was jumping with energy and the anxious feeling of major failure. From his peripheral vision he saw a form! Turning and diving to the damp floor he arched his gun into firing position.

"Don't move. I have a gun," came the voice.

Scotty couldn't make out exactly where the form was.

"Who are you?" came the voice again. "Why are you trying to blow up my dam?"

The voice was filled with anger and determination.

"I'm with the FBI! My name is Coldsmith. The Soviets have planted a bomb on top of that building and I don't know how to get to it. I need your help."

Dolan Yarnell came out from behind the shadows of the dimly lit corridor. On agreement he and Winny had split up, Holbrook taking the Arizona side, Dolan the Nevada side. Holbrook knew how to get to the roof, after all he was the plant manager. He knew everything about everything, all the hidey-holes and places where the sun didn't shine. Dolan didn't. Dolan ran the generators. He was the Power Operations Manager. He didn't know beans about maintenance of the facility other than his turbines and generators.

Yarnell stood in front of Scotty, then lowered his gun.

"My name is Dolan Yarnell and I work for Southern California Edison. I don't have the slightest idea how to get to the roof."

It was 8:01 P.M. (MST)

— • —

The ten miles of angry Colorado River had spread out as it now smashed through Virgin Canyon and emptied into the Virgin Basin of Lake Mead. Some of it was dispersed northward up the Overton Arm toward a series of dry washes. The water was eighteen miles from the mouth of Black Canyon. It was a bore wave 200 high by 3/4-mile wide by 10 miles long. Carried by the incredible force were rocks, boulders, and heavy debris from the scouring of the canyon walls.

— • —

J.J. was in position. He was armed and protected. He reached up and pressed the red button on the inside switch of the huge door. The door made a noise! The emergency power was connected to the gates and doors! Slowly, and with noisy attention, the door slid upwards. The moment the door was three feet above ground J.J. began to fire shots at whatever he could see. Snapping the top off another grenade he rolled it through the door. He could hear it bounce against some machinery.

"It's a grenade! Get it!" someone shouted.

It was the woman. Shots rang from the other side of the river. Nichols was putting on the pressure. J.J. protected himself. He'd already taken a piece of steel in his leg. His pantleg was torn and stained with a stream of blood from his knee down to his shoe.

The grenade exploded just as the heavy door rolled up onto its tracks and out of the way. Shrapnel pinged and zinged everywhere. The sound from outside was that of something being destroyed.

J.J. darted from his cover to the inside wall next to the twenty-foot-wide doorway. A body lay on the service road, bloodied face down on one of the rails. An arm was missing. Nearby the rifle lay smashed and twisted. J.J. carefully peered around the side. Down at the end of the service road he could see their broken helicopter. Rostov hadn't tried to make an escape that way. The run was almost five hundred feet and he certainly couldn't have escaped the fire from J.J. or Nichols.

Where did they go?

"Mr. Carteret!" shouted Nichols.

"I'm OK, Nichols! Where are they?" J.J. shouted.

"They went down the tunnel!" came Nichols' reply.

"Are you all right?" J.J. shouted.

Nichols had gone from his position near the destroyed Nevada doorway and down the middle connecting service road, advancing one crane at a time until he was now just outside the Arizona doorway where J.J. was protected.

"I'm . . . I'm . . ." stuttered Nichols.

J.J. ran to meet the agent. He'd taken another shot in the exchange.

"Nichols—listen to me! Nichols!" J.J. shook the man.

Nichols' eyes responded yes.

"I've got to go after them. Go into the dam and try to find Scotty. If you can't—protect yourself as best you can. I've got to go after Rostov! Now go!" J.J. shoved Nichols toward the opened maintenance door.

J.J. turned around and looked down the large, dark service ramp. There was no sight of Rostov or Katrina. Then he heard shots and voices from deep in the bowels of the tunnel. What was going on down there?

— • —

"Down the tunnel. Get out of here!" instructed Rostov, half pushing Katrina from her spot behind a bright yellow forklift, a place which she'd barely been able to jump to avoid the same fate as Williams. It was three against two. Not good odds, especially when they had grenades and, more importantly, were willing to use them.

There was only one direction to go and that was down. The tunnel was huge, nearly sixty feet in diameter, and led down into the canyon wall on the Arizona side paralleling the dam. Nearly half of the width of the tunnel was taken up by various generating support equipment. The tunnel was a construction adit, a horizontal access to an underground workplace. It was originally used by construction crews to build the cofferdams and to provide access to the penstocks and Arizona spillway deep within the canyon's walls. Given the slope of the adit, by the time

Rostov and Katrina reached the darkness of the bottom, they were at or slightly below riverbed level some four hundred feet away from Williams' body and the gathering FBI men.

They were slightly out of breath when they reached the safety of the bottom. Only three miserable naked lights illuminated the shaft, none at the bottom. To someone looking into the tunnel, it appeared to be an endless dark hole.

Temporarily safe, they stopped to see that no one was following them. Behind them was the lower penstock, a huge steel and concrete pipe fifty feet in diameter. The penstock rested on large reinforced steel braces every thirty feet on its two-thousand-foot journey from the intake towers of Lake Mead, through the canyon walls to the outlet works downstream from the dam. Every sixty-two feet, an eighteen-foot-wide vertical shaft exited into the power plant, where the rushing water turned the turbines for the Arizona generators.

"With all this equipment, there's got to be a way out of here," said Rostov.

"Which way?" Katrina asked.

"Who are you people? Identify yourselves. I've got a gun."

Although the voice certainly startled him, Rostov dove for the anonymous safety of the darkened hallway at the same time readying his revolver for firing. When he hit the ground he rolled and snapped off three shots in the direction of the voice. There were two sharp pings and a thud, followed by a groan.

"Do you see him?" Rostov asked.

"No . . . wait a minute . . . I'm not sure. I think he's by that tall piece of equipment, by the ladder," she replied.

"You son of a bitch! I'm not going to let you blow up my dam!" came the shout from Winsloe Holbrook.

Holbrook threw off two wild shots which didn't even come close to Rostov.

"We don't have much time," said Rostov.

It was after eight o'clock. The bomb was ready to go off at 8:12.

"We aren't going to make it, Alex," said Katrina. "There's no time to get to the top."

In a calm, almost soft, voice Rostov talked to the plant manager.

"Listen to me, whoever you are. It's too late for your dam. In eleven minutes a bomb is going to detonate which will destroy it. But it's not too late to save yourself. This is just politics. We are doing a job. You're doing a job. Blocks of concrete are nothing to die for."

Rostov and Katrina listened to the heavy breathing of the obviously wounded man.

"No way, scum! If this dam goes, you go with it," angrily replied Winsloe Holbrook.

Rostov looked around him. A 40-watt bulb hung above an open two-tiered stairwell and dimly illuminated a catwalk which ran alongside the penstock tunnel. The wooden stairwell was approximately thirty feet high. Catching Katrina's attention, Rostov pointed to the stairwell. Getting to it unharmed meant risking that whoever had the gun would soon be out of bullets. They had to hurry.

"This is the FBI! Rostov, come out with your hands above your head! You're under arrest," came a shout from up the adit.

"Hello! My name is Winsloe Holbrook—I'm the plant manager. There are two of them down here, and they're going to blow up the dam!" echoed Holbrook up toward the voice.

"Run!" instructed Rostov.

Holbrook's attention was diverted as he responded to J.J.'s appearance. Katrina hit the stairwell on the run, followed closely by Rostov. Holbrook saw them and fired one shot which tore into the wooden frame of the first landing then his gun clicked empty.

"Damn!"

Holbrook threw down the gun and came out from behind the equipment. He had been the one who had turned on the emergency generator. He was wounded. Rostov's wild shot had torn through his side, right through the fleshy part of his waist. The bullet had hit no vital organ although it was messy.

J.J. came running down the adit just as Rostov and Katrina made it to the top of the stairwell. Both Rostov and J.J. fired rounds. The noise from the guns and the lightning flashes from their muzzles seemed as ferocious as it was. The Soviets turned right and ran down the catwalk out of view.

"My name is Carteret, FBI. Are you all right?"

"Yes, I am. They're going . . ."

"I know. We're trying to stop the bomb. There's another problem, though," said J.J. "There's a wall of water coming down the river through the lake."

"From Glen Canyon . . ."

"Yes. Where does that walkway go?"

Holbrook ignored J.J.'s question.

"Listen, you stop the bomb and this dam will hold up against anything the river can throw at it," replied Holbrook.

Even in the darkness Holbrook could see J.J.'s skepticism.

"There's no way this dam's going to collapse," Holbrook said with confidence.

It was 8:05 P.M. (MST)

— • —

"I've got an idea. Follow me!" said Dolan.

Scotty did what Dolan told him to do. He followed. Dolan took off through the darkness of the interior of the dam, down a short corridor, up two quick series of short steps, two left turns and into a oddly lit stairwell. Above them a yellow light barely filtered down to their level. The yellow light on the GSA-green walls made for a truly ugly combination.

Scotty gave the older man his due. He seemed to be driven with purpose. There was no time for formalities as the two men took the steps two and three at a time. There seemed to be an abnormal distance between each floor, Scotty thought. At the fourth level Scotty followed Dolan out into yet another dim hallway. From one end to another it seemed like it was at least a quarter-mile. *Where am I?* thought Scotty.

"It's here! In here!" Dolan exclaimed.

Here where?

"Wait a minute," asked Scotty.

"There's no time, hurry," waved Dolan as he went down a four-foot-by-seven-foot arched passageway through the cold rock. At the end of the narrow walkway was a window. A small window.

"It was your equipment that gave me the idea," pointed Dolan, excitedly.

"The ladder?" Scotty replied, somewhat puzzled.

"It's down there," pointed Dolan.

"The entrance to the roof?" asked Scotty, edging toward the small window.

"Not exactly."

Scotty peered out the window. Down below he could see the two helicopters. Rostov's craft still had its lights shining on the canyon wall. They were sixty feet above the roof of the maintenance building. Down below, Scotty could just make out a black form near the base of the dam on the roof.

You've got to be kidding me.

As soon as he thought the words, he heard the sound and felt the vibration. Scotty looked in Dolan's eyes, which reflected fear and concern. The dam made a trembly noise, not the same as when the generators were moving full speed. This was different. The water was coming.

"It doesn't matter," said Scotty. "We're going to get blown away, anyway."

"It matters!" shouted Dolan.

His voice echoed in the small chamber.

"It matters very much. This dam has a good chance to withstand any kind of flood. It has no chance to stand up to an atomic bomb. You've got to do it. I can't. I just can't. I'm not an athlete. I don't know how. You've got to help."

Before Scotty could answer, Dolan took off his jacket and wrapped his right hand and arm, then smashed the tiny window. Immediately the air pressure differential outside versus inside was altered. Air rushed through the opening and down the hallway. A wind tunnel effect had been created. The hallways whistled with a variety of moans and cries as the wind whipped through the narrow passageways.

Dolan grabbed Scotty's rope ladder, fastened the tie chains to the steel windowcase and threw the remaining sections out the window and down over the face of the dam. The light nylon ladder didn't fall straight down. The wind pushed it to the right, twisting it. Scotty would have to fight trying to straighten it out as he went down.

"There's no time. Either you go, or I'll have to. One of us has to go down that ladder. There's no other way," said Dolan Yarnell with a stone face.

"There's got to be an entrance to the roof," objected Scotty.

Scotty didn't want to go. He was afraid of heights.

"There may be, but I don't know where it is. Holbrook would know, but I don't."

There was no time to ask who Holbrook was or where he'd gone.

The window was at waist level. Chipping the last pieces of glass from around the pane, Scotty slowly put one leg out into the cold winter night, and maneuvered so that he was partially outside. His leg found the ladder.

Come on, where's the rung?

There.

One leg out and one leg in.

Twisting his tall but slender frame, Scotty snaked and torqued his back out the window, then his shoulders, arms, and finally his head. He still had one leg inside but most of him was outside. His right leg was firmly on one of the rope's rungs. The concrete was much rougher than he imagined. From a distance the dam seemed like a monolith, but up close its blocks of concrete were hardly smooth. The rope, now with some weight at the top, straightened out a bit, but the bottom still dangled and turned in the wind.

There was no way Scotty would be able to descend the ladder in normal fashion. The rungs were too close to the dam. He wouldn't be able to get a foothold with the ladder snug up against the dam's surface. The lightweight ladder's rungs were only an inch thick, one-foot wide.

He would have to go down with his back to the dam and the ladder out in front of him.

"Hurry!" shouted Dolan.

It was 8:05.

While it wasn't the most encouraging thing to say it did get Scotty's attention. Scotty was now completely outside, his life depending upon how securely a stranger had tied the rope to the inside of the window. He started down. The dam's rough concrete slid over the back of his parka, quickly wearing the material. His buttocks and the back of his legs rubbed directly onto the concrete, quickly forming brushburns.

He looked up to see the stars shining above the curvature of the remaining five hundred feet of the dam. Below, the water of the Colorado silently flowed downstream. Hand over hand he moved down. Each rung down was a step which required the attention of his whole body; right leg, left leg, move the butt, brace with the back, lower the right hand, lower the left hand. Repeat the steps.

"You'd better get a move on it, boy," Scotty said to himself.

— • —

At 8:06 P.M. (MST) the Glen Canyon discharge was 10.8 miles from the mouth of Black Canyon and Hoover Dam—at the point where Arch Mountain protects the Boulder Basin from the larger Virgin Basin. The water moved through the narrow gap like an angry rapist attacking a helpless victim. With elevations of up to 3500 feet on either side, there was little room for the water to disperse and spread out. However, once the water did get through the canyon it would enter the large expanse of Boulder Basin and begin to attack the more flat northern shoreline. Along the southern shoreline the water would move against the Black Mountains, mountains which would keep the bore wave intact. The Glen Canyon rush would have no choice but to spread out, but its main force would continue toward Boulder Beach and the adjoining Black Canyon.

The force of the falling water was tremendous. At close quarters the water stripped and polished the canyon walls as it ripped through. Beacon Island would be overwashed. The end was in sight. With seemingly malicious intent the water would smash into Hoover, certainly overwashing it, erode the canyon walls on either side, destroy the top of the dam and violate its integrity. The pressure of the agitated Lake Mead would further weaken the understructure and the dam would collapse.

— • —

Halfway down the ladder Scotty's arms were killing him. His legs were strained, his back hurt. He looked down at the roof, which fortunately was a lot closer and looked less terrifying than it did a few minutes ago. He could make out the markings of the crate. They'd left the bomb in a crate.

Scotty put his foot onto nothing but air. The motion came right at the time he was shifting his hands from one rung to another. He lost his balance and the other foot came off a rung.

"*What the . . . ?*" he mumbled.

For a few seconds he had only one arm on the ladder while he scrambled to regain his foothold. In an ornery fashion the tail of the ladder refused to cooperate. It flapped underneath him. His arm ached incredibly. Scotty was a tall, gangly young man already. He didn't need to try to make his arms any longer.

"*There!*"

He regained his balance. Forty feet above him, Dolan Yarnell was yelling something incomprehensible at him, probably something to the effect of "watch out" or "look out," something not too meaningful to the person who already had whatever he was supposed to watch out happen to him.

"Not enough ladder," were his words.

Indeed, there wasn't. He probably could have gotten enough ladder from the helicopter if he'd had enough foresight to realize he'd be descending the sheer face of Hoover Dam from a peephole window with ten miles of horribly angry water rushing down upon him.

He was nine, perhaps ten, feet short of ladder. There was no choice. Scotty mentally braced himself then let go of the rung and fell to the surface of the roof where he landed on his feet then immediately fell down on his backside. Back on his feet he staggered slightly, righted himself, then ran to the nearby crate. He put a hand on the face of the dam and looked up. He could feel the vibration from the natural disaster which was out there advancing toward the dam at speeds now reduced to ninety-five miles an hour.

He was going to drown or be vaporized. Not much of a choice.

It was 8:07 P.M.

Not thinking that Rostov would have boobytrapped the crate, Scotty ripped the top, then the front panel, then kicked the two sides down. The bomb rested on an aluminum cradle. It was an ugly thing. Scotty was oblivious to the wind snapping at his cheeks. His hands were almost numb from the cold, his fingers raw from the nylon and rough concrete. But his attention was solely on the bomb.

He didn't hear the dim roar up the canyon on the other side of the dam, nor feel the change in wind direction as the wall of water approached the head of Black Canyon. The water had overwashed the low coves that ring Fortification Hill to the west and rumbled on toward a promontory of land named Hemenway Wall. To the west the Wall gradually tapers off to a broad, gradually sloped area of campsites and summer homes along Boulder Beach. In the opposite direction the Wall forms the western cliff of the mouth of Black Canyon. The earth shook as the force approached, emitting a deep, continual, rumbling noise.

Scotty concentrated on the bomb. He pictured himself inside the Eads Bridge abutment and what the St. Louis BDU had done. This time there would be no rescuers from Scott Air Force Base. *He* was the Bomb Disposal Unit.

It was up to Scotty. All the pain, the accident, the stumbling after leads, the false chases, the empty feeling of not understanding—all of it was over. Either he defused the bomb or he didn't. Either the dam was saved or it wasn't. Either they captured the Soviets or they didn't. Either the electricity would be generated or it wouldn't. Either the United States would face down the Russians or . . .

The last option was too heavy to carry.

It was 8:08 P.M.

There was only one place to work, the arm of the bomb. His hands were bleeding as he grasped the head of the four-inch-wide stainless steel screwcap. He applied pressure.

It wouldn't turn!

Again he tried and again it wouldn't turn. Out of sheer release of energy he talked to himself.

"No! This can't be happening! I'm not coming all this way only to

fail! Wait a minute. Relax. Come on, Scotty boy. Relax. What's different here? Look at it! What's this?"

There was a half-inch screw in the middle of the cap. Was it there in St. Louis? He didn't know, couldn't remember. The screw was preventing him from opening the cap. He fumbled with it, trying to turn it with his thumbnail. Of course it didn't budge.

He stood up and hurriedly rifled his pockets. A dime. *Please have a dime, Scotty!* he thought.

"Come on, come on," he said impatiently.

There it was! A shiny Roosevelt dime.

It fell through his raw fingers onto the roof.

It was 8:09.

"Hurry!" he shouted to himself.

He reached over and picked it up. His fingers hurt. There was no time. It had to work the first time or it was all over. The dime fit into the head of the screw. He applied pressure. *It didn't turn!*

"No, no . . . the other way!" he berated himself.

Leaning on the dime he turned it counterclockwise to the left. It gave! The screw quickly loosened to the point where he could finger it out. It was four inches long. He dropped it onto the roof and immediately went to the larger screw cap of the three foot long detonator chamber. *Go for it!* The cap turned smoothly. It also fell to the surface of the roof, clanking as it bounced twice. The digital timer read 8:09, then in a blink it turned 8:10.

Scotty's heart jumped when it turned. Nothing. *He had at least another minute.* He saw no trip wires, just two wires which led from the timer to the detonator which in turn was embedded in the plastic explosive. Underneath there were small amounts of polonium and lithium which like lusty lovers waited to be joined. Pull the detonator? Disconnect the clock? The setup appeared to be one where the detonator was looking for electricity instead of a lack of it.

As carefully as he could, Scotty disconnected the right wire from the digital clock. No vaporization. Then the left. No vaporization. His brow dripped with perspiration even though the cold wind pushed 34°-air past his face. He pulled the detonator out from the plastic explosive and hurled it across and over the roof where it fell into the Colorado

Scotty stood up. His heart was seemingly beating at double time. He was out of breath as the rush of adrenalin surged through him. He looked up. He knew he didn't have much time. He also knew that if he was going to live he had to get back up that ladder, and he had to get back up in a hurry.

It was 8:11.

Sixty feet up the face of Hoover Dam he could make out the head and shoulders of Dolan Yarnell.

"Hurry up!" came the shout.

Scotty went over to the face of the dam and stood underneath the lightweight ladder. It had a mind of its own. It flapped irregularly against the dam, first this way, then another. Scotty jumped for the tail, trying to time its movement to his jump. He missed. Was he going to die, crushed by the tons of water which would overflow the dam in a matter of moments? Would he be swept away, perhaps the last victim of Khan's Ultimatum?

Scotty jumped again. This time his fingers touched the bottom rung but the ladder danced and feinted away.

The Glen Canyon discharge had passed completely through Lake Mead, its two-hundred-mile fall from elevation 3710 to elevation 1180 almost complete. The water would have to go someplace. Not only would it flood all the lowlands around Mead, it would have to find its lowest level. The lowest level would be on the downstream side of Hoover Dam. The crest of Hoover was at elevation 1236. The power plants were at elevation 690. Scotty stood at elevation 730. The ladder flopped against the dam at elevation 739.

The angry bore wave smashed across Boulder Beach, running well up the evenly-sloped terrain toward Boulder City. At Las Vegas Wash on the far western end of the lake the water covered highway 187 and rushed up the dry wash toward the shallow saddle between the hills. On the other side was a vast valley. In the basin of that valley was the darkened city of Las Vegas. As the water rushed toward the dam it was funneled into Black Canyon between the stone cliffs of Hemenway Wall and Sugarloaf Mountain, where the remaining wave was pushed back to two hundred feet high.

"You son of a bitch," he shouted to the ladder.

He couldn't reach it. *Use the bomb. Use the damn bomb*! It wasn't going to explode now. With the aluminum brace it weighed nearly seventy pounds. When death approaches, lifting or dragging seventy pounds is not a problem. And it wasn't. With one foot on the weapon and one foot on the roof Scotty launched himself for the ladder.

He caught it with both hands. His feet banged into the concrete wall of the dam. *Come on, grab it*! *There*! Now was the time he'd wished he'd followed through with his plans to get in shape, lift weights. Scotty had very little upper body strength, but somehow fear gave it to him.

He stabilized the ladder with his hands and arms. His feet were on the concrete wall. Right hand up one rung. *Pull!* Left hand up one rung. Left foot up the wall. *Come on, right foot!* His arms ached terribly. The wind now blew down-canyon from the rush of the advancing wall of water. The noise was tremendous. He had to get his foot onto the ladder's lowest rung.

"*Please!*" Scotty supplicated.

With a tug his right foot found the dangling rung, then his left foot got the one above it.

"*It's coming!*" was Dolan's shout from above.

It was 8:11.

Scotty climbed the ladder as fast as his arms and legs could move. The temperature of the air seemed to change, although the water temperature of the approaching wave was the same as the air, both frigidly cold.

"*Hurry!*" repeated Dolan.

"*I'm not going to make it,*" answered Scotty, his words lost down the canyon.

He was fifteen feet beneath the small portal. Dolan's arms were out ready to grab whatever he could of Scotty when he got in range.

"*I . . . can't . . .*"

— • —

The crest of the wave was slightly more than two hundred feet above the surface of Lake Mead. Because it was a bore wave, the height of the wave behind the crest decreased gradually, unlike a solitary or oscillatory wave, which has a parabolic structure. The water impounded behind Hoover Dam had no place to move as the wave approached. This had the effect of forcing the lower part of the wave to slow down. The upper part continued forward with momentum. The dam caused the wave to act like a typical wave approaching a shoreline. With more resistance the wave started to slow down. The topheavy wave then started to break. At a point fifty yards north of the four intake towers, the top portion of the wave fell to the forces of gravity and broke downward with tremendous energy. It smashed over the intake towers at the same time the water overflowed into both the Arizona and Nevada spillways. Water which had been forced up both canyon walls was now redirected to the crest of the dam. Both spillways were instantly filled above capacity. The two higher plumes of water flanked the huge wave which had broken near the intake towers. The crest of the dam, elevation 1236, was overwashed completely by water which tore through the canyon walls at elevation 1425 feet. Finding no support, the water then fell into the canyon below, crashing in spectacular fashion after falling nearly eight hundred feet.

— • —

"I've got you! Hang on!" said Dolan.

The dam went from vibration to shaking. It felt like the whole structure would collapse. Dolan grabbed Scotty's shoulders just as the mountainous wave overwashed the crest. It wasn't graceful but Dolan pulled Scotty straight through the window until Scotty's long legs fell and banged against the floor. Concrete dust filled the air in their close quarters. But neither minded. Getting up, the two men approached the portal. They were firsthand witnesses to an incredible sight.

The plunging water didn't just run down the face of the dam, instead it shot out at an angle. There was a thirty foot gap between the dam and the falling water. They were inside a waterfall, a Niagara on the Colorado. Scotty looked below to see the roof of the maintenance shed being destroyed by the countless tons of water. The roof of the building collapsed after the first thirty seconds. The water bounced and skipped off the top of the building. When the roof collapsed with the tremendous pressure, the water instantly filled the huge room, then quickly knocked the four-story front wall into rubble. Concrete blocks were scattered into the chaotic water and carried downstream as if they were cardboard.

Scotty turned and looked at Dolan, then reached out and offered his hand in thanks.

"I'm Scott Coldsmith. Call me Scotty."

"Dolan Yarnell."

"Are we going to make it, Dolan?"

"I don't know. Whatever happens, we don't have much choice, do we?"

"Thanks for pulling me out. I really didn't think I was going to make it."

"Sure you were. I was just there in case," Dolan said with modesty. "This isn't the best place to be. We're in the middle of the dam. If it goes, we're absolutely goners. We've got better odds at either one of the sides."

"My partner was on that side," Scotty said pointing to Arizona.

"Maybe he went up," said Dolan hopefully.

"Let's go," replied Scotty.

At the end of the short hallway was the injured, but now fully awake, Ted Dillon. With Scotty and Dolan on either side the trio made their way down the shaking hallway. The emergency lights went out. The hallway was a pit of darkness.

"Don't worry, I've got my flashlight," said Dolan.

Then he remembered. Holbrook's flashlight was dead.

— • —

"Who are those people?" Holbrook had asked.

J.J. began climbing the wooden steps up to the catwalk. Holbrook remained on the concrete floor.

"Soviet agents," replied J.J. tersely. "There's a man and a woman. My instructions are to bring the man back alive. His name is Alexander Rostov, hers is Katrina Tambov. Where does this go?"

J.J. looked down the narrow catwalk. A 40-watt bulb every one hundred feet provided dim illumination.

"Above us is the power plant for the Arizona generators. We're at the bottom level."

Holbrook caught up with J.J. at the top of the stairs and pointed to the huge pipe.

"That pipe carries water from the lake through the dam to each of the turbines. The turbines are off now, so the water is going straight down the pipe to an outlet downstream. This catwalk goes all the way to the end of the power plant and beyond to the control room for the outlet works."

"Where can they go?"

Holbrook furrowed his brow.

"Every sixty-two feet there's a stairwell that will take them up to the turbine galley then up to the generators. If they go up to either of those levels and reverse their direction, come back to a point directly above us, they could get back into tunnels and stairwells in the dam itself. If they don't, and decide to go straight, they'll end up at the control room for the outlet works. Short of that, there's a construction adit that leads to a dead end near the spillway tunnel and another that leads back to an entrance near the river."

Too many choices. The vibration from the advancing water shook the walls. The power plants were half-buried into the canyon walls.

"Come on, I'm going to need your help," said J.J.

The two men took off running as fast as they could go, Holbrook trailing. At each of the penstock gates the catwalk went through a doorway which was very much like a hatchway on a boat, requiring one to climb up and duck at the same time.

After the second lateral penstock J.J. stopped to listen for footsteps. He heard something, but directions were tough with the terrible acoustics, and the vibration from the oncoming wave was noticeable.

"Where do you think they went?" asked Holbrook.

"If I were Rostov and I expected an atomic bomb to go off in five minutes or be drowned by billions of gallons of water, I wouldn't head back. I'd probably go up, then try to find something which might go inside the canyon wall."

As he spoke, a shot rang against the arch-shaped steel passageway next to J.J.'s head. The shot came from someplace ahead. Then, through the dim light he saw her—the woman. The woman who had killed two children and a Park Service ranger in cold blood on a rainy night on a North Carolina beach . . . and the woman who killed at least one policeman in St. Louis. J.J. saw her head duck into the stairwell at the third penstock. They were going up.

The rock shook with the advancing water—the noise almost deafening.

"Up—they're going up," shouted J.J.

J.J. sprinted down the catwalk to the stairwell, then stumbled on the slippery steps, skinning his shin. Holbrook panted behind him. Where would they stop—turbine or generator level? J.J. bet on the highest level, the generators, and continued up the steps.

His reward was to see Rostov and the woman sprinting back toward the head of the Arizona generator alley. J.J. stopped and fired twice—both shots ricocheting off generator number two as he was off mark. J.J. never was a good shot.

The noise changed from a deep rumble to the drums of hell as the bore wave crashed down onto Hoover Dam, seven hundred feet above.

It was the end of the world.

The room shook as the water cascaded onto the top of the Arizona generator plant, which was mostly protected by being built into the canyon wall. However, about a third of the plant wasn't protected, and was now getting beaten by the debris-laden waters of Lake Powell. Below them, the path they had taken was under water. A wall of water rushed down the the large construction adit where Holbrook had been shot by Rostov, filling the cavernous hole within seconds. Water sought every crevice it could find, quickly rising and filling the catwalk area near the 50'-diameter penstock tunnel. Like a skilled dentist prodding a sore cavity with a pick, the pressurized water angrily sought to fill every crack it could. Water swirled into the stairwell and quickly started to fill it to the level of the turbines, rising at several feet per second.

Normally, water would rise inside to the level of the water outside—but this wasn't normal by any means. Outside, the torrent fell in a line which included the giant hole of the construction adit. This meant water was being forced by tremendous pressure into the hole. Water would rise in the Arizona generator facility until the pressure was released—until the dam collapsed or the ten miles of angry water passed over the dam.

— • —

"Shoot them!" Rostov yelled.

They were almost back to the dam. Rostov glanced at his watch. The bomb had failed.

It was self-preservation time.

As Katrina knelt and began firing, Rostov left her, and starting running down the long hallway which had been cut through solid rock, its walls wet with natural moisture. At the end would be a stairwell which would take him up the seventy stories inside the main body of the dam, and hopefully to safety. But as he ran, the loud rumbly noise became louder ahead of him. Several hundred yards ahead, the tunnel made a left turn. In an instant, swirling around the corner, came the leading edge of angry river water—water pumped up through the damaged maintenance shed and various holes. It was flooded ahead.

Rostov skidded and slipped to a stop and began furiously running in the opposite direction, back to the generator room. The water was moving much faster than he could run, but he didn't have far to sprint. Rostov came tumbling into the generator room just as Katrina had started to come after him.

"No—up there!" he shouted over the din.

Up there was anywhere they could go. Anyplace up. Near the junction of the A-1 generator a small construction adit had been built. The tunnel was eight feet tall, ten feet wide and had been used to provide tunnel crews easy access from the Arizona spillway to the dam itself. The distance from the adit portal in the generator room to the spillway was two-hundred-fifty feet, all inside the canyon wall—all uphill.

A tunnel was a tunnel, and it had to lead somewhere. At the moment, neither Katrina nor Rostov cared. All they knew was that they couldn't stay put. Run!

— • —

Before ducking to receive the gunfire from the Soviet woman, J.J. saw Rostov run for the hallway—then return not thirty seconds later. The two Soviets scrambled toward an unseen opening just as a torrent of water poured through the doorway.

"The water's rising!" shouted Holbrook.

His dam was holding up—almost *too* well. If it had been built a little bit more poorly, the water pressure wouldn't be driving the river water so high inside the building. At the same time the hallway ahead disgorged its muddy concoction, the stairwell behind gulped up water from below. The generator room was breached.

But what happened next was indeed something out of hell. A large boulder, scraped from a red canyon wall someplace between Page and Hoover Dam, smashed through the cement roof of the Arizona generator alley, destroying generator #3 and immediately flooding the

"Run!"

Run wasn't quite possible. Wade was possible. Slosh was possible. Run was not. Holding Holbrook's arm, J.J. went for the same hole that Rostov had ducked into.

"Where does that go?"

Holbrook couldn't answer, he was so fatigued.

"Go ahead! I'll follow you," he pushed at J.J.

Not minding Holbrook's suggestion, he helped the injured plant manager up and into the musty old tunnel.

Then the 40-watt emergency bulbs flickered and went out.

Up ahead there was a woman's scream as the tunnel was plunged into darkness.

— • —

"The lights are out!" Katrina cried.

Her scream of alarm echoed the length of the adit. Her hands groped the north side of the tunnel, her hands quickly cut by the sharp rocks. She stumbled twice. She could sense Rostov ahead of her by five paces or so. He was doing nothing to help her, just as he would have left her in the generator room if the water hadn't stopped him from escaping. She was a liability to him.

"Where are we going?" she screamed.

Katrina lost control. A month of physical and mental subjugation to Rostov had destroyed what had been a cool and calculating professional spy. Her fears were in total grip of her body. She couldn't see—her brain screamed for more information, reliable information. But the only things it was receiving were the sound of rushing water and footsteps, the raw touch of sharp stone, the slimy, silky brush from passing through ancient cobwebs, and the eerie feeling that there were animals in the tunnel—mice, rats. Self-preservation is a powerful control over wild fears, but it wouldn't be in control for long. Katrina was on the edge.

After a hundred uphill feet, Rostov stopped, Katrina bumping into him.

"Why have you stopped?"

"Quiet! Shut up!" he ordered.

She did as she was told. There were tiny things in the tunnel with them. The rats were leaving a sinking ship. Self-preservation was in all animals.

Rostov, his heart pounding from the exertion, his body lathered in sweat, strained to listen behind him. They were coming! The policeman was following them. Rostov blindly fired two shots down the dark hole they'd just come up. He held the gun high, shot, then moved his arm to the left and fired again, hoping that the bullet's trajectory would give him the best chance for a hit.

With the background of gurgling, frothy water advancing up the construction adit, Rostov heard an exclamation of some sort way behind them. Maybe a hit?

"They're coming," Rostov said in a whisper. "Keep going."

Hands in front of him, Rostov trotted the best he could. The air was old and musty, air that seemed . . .

Rostov ran into a wall, bounced, and fell down onto the tunnel floor. The wall was in front of him, not to the side.

"What—?"

Katrina stumbled into him and fell to her knees.

"Where?" Rostov said, his heart in his mouth.

"What's happened, Alex?" Katrina asked, afraid.

"Where's the tunnel?" Rostov shouted angrily, groping the rough cement in front of him. The texture was different than the solid rock of the wall. This was concrete—rough concrete. Rostov's hands searched for the opening, the path of the tunnel. His hands came upon the left tunnel wall of rock.

"No, no!" he shouted, fear in his voice.

Not knowing what was happening, Katrina was petrified. For the first time, Rostov's voice had the unmistakable edge of real fear—

terror. In the month they'd been together, she'd never once felt he was afraid of anything.

Back again across the wall Rostov went, hands feeling up and down the cement for an opening. He found nothing. They were going to die in a dead-end tunnel three hundred feet inside the cold Arizona rock of Black Canyon—drowned by slowly rising water, suffocated. It was a terrible way to die.

"There's no way out. We're trapped," Rostov said flatly, his fear now slightly controlled.

Panting, Katrina could hear the the sharp squeals of scurrying mice and occasionally feel one brush her leg. Then she felt the first dampness of the slowly advancing water slosh around her feet.

Katrina lost control of herself—she went over the edge, into complete hysteria. Wet, tired, defeated, scared witless—she began to sob uncontrollably. It was a wrenching, complete sob—her back and chest heaving with the crying and relentless release of emotion. She began to wail as she cried, the sound echoing down the rapidly-filling tunnel. Reaching into her pocket, she fumbled with the small case—the case containing her pill. There was no choice but to take it. She couldn't face the alternative. She couldn't die in this terrible tomb, buried alive—slowly tortured. The latch wouldn't open—she couldn't stop crying.

Latch open, she fumbled with the pill and dropped it. The pill made a tap-tap sound as it struck some of the concrete then was lost in the moisture of the floor.

"No-no-no-no-noooooo!" she cried, falling on all fours, fumbling around with the mice and muddy water.

She stood up, found Rostov and grabbed him.

"Give me yours! I must have it! Give it to me!"

Gone was any pretense at dignity.

Disgusted, Rostov struck her across the face in the darkness—hitting her in the neck and jaw—striking her so hard that she fell back down, hitting her head on the wall.

"I threw mine away," said Rostov.

— • —

"It doesn't lead anywhere. It's plugged with forty-two feet of solid concrete—has been since the spillway tunnel was finished in the 1930s. Once the spillway was done, there was no need for the adit—so it was plugged. They aren't going anywhere," said Winsloe Holbrook.

Behind them the generator room was slowly filling with river water. The boulder falling through the roof had been a blessing because water was now rushing through the generator room and back outside to the Colorado River. But the water level was still rising.

Sixty feet into the tunnel, wading in calf-level water, they could saw two bright flashes, then the sound—there was no time to tell Holbrook to duck. The bullets screamed past them and harmlessly down the tunnel.

"Stay on the side of the tunnel. He'll go for the middle, if he's got any left," warned J.J.

Slowly, they continued to wade. Then they heard the screams of Katrina Tambov.

"I think they've found the end," said J.J. with some satisfaction.

He would catch them both—whether he would live or not, was problematical—but he would catch them. The woman's screams were terrible, of fear that gripped her heart and soul. J.J. was afraid, but this woman was terrified. She had lost control.

Slap! He heard some angry words from Rostov, unintelligible. J.J. reached over for Holbrook, and softly pulled the plant manager down to his knees—then whispered in his ear.

"Get as flat as you can," J.J. said.

Holbrook lay prone in the muck, offering as little of a target as possible. Rostov wouldn't shoot that low, anyway. J.J. did the same, then shouted.

"Alexander Rostov, this is John Carteret of the FBI! Throw down your weapons! You are under arrest! It's over."

Rostov fired three times, each shot whistling over their ducked heads. Then his revolver clicked. He was out of shells. From the flash, J.J. could see that Rostov was only fifteen feet away, if that.

Then from behind a wave of water rushed over the top of them both, drenching J.J. and Holbrook and raising the water level in the tunnel to more than two feet—almost knee level.

This was it. J.J. wasn't going to die without first capturing his man.

"You son of a bitch!" J.J. muttered as he lunged forward, lurching through the water for where his mind's eye saw the last of the muzzle flashes.

Rostov was indeed reloading. J.J. heard the sound of the empty cartridge hitting the floor, then the click of the new one in place. The click and the collision occurred at the same instant. Rostov fired two wild shots which missed everything, ricocheting against the rocky ceiling and falling harmlessly into the water. Half-tackling, half-fighting, J.J. drove Rostov back against the cement plug. Katrina screamed.

"Help me!" said Rostov.

But there was no way for the woman to determine who was who.

J.J., his left hand firmly on Rostov's right, slammed the hand into the wall. Rostov's gun fell into the knee-deep water, gone forever. Free of the gun-worry, J.J. mustered every last piece of anger in his system.

"You son of a bitch . . . you son of—bitch!"

J.J. was a wild man, angry beyond reason. He had Rostov pinned against the wall and began to thrash Rostov's head against the concrete—bang, bang.

"You son of a bitch . . . you god-damned son of a bitch!"

J.J. slammed Rostov against the wall again and again and again. By the time J.J. realized he had to have Rostov alive, Rostov was either dead or knocked out. Rostov made a slurping splash as his body slid into the water.

J.J.'s breath came to him with difficulty in the heavy air.

"Alex?" came Katrina's voice. "Alex?" she repeated.

J.J.'s anger was not complete. This was the woman who killed two innocent children—and a dog—and a park ranger.

A god-damned dog!

Bile and hatred rose up in J.J. as he hit Katrina with a full fist, hard in the face—then followed with a blind swing which struck her in the chest, knocking her back against the rock and nearly out cold. J.J. had her under control and began to beat her mercilessly, senselessly— finally stopping when there was no resistance from the woman.

The two slime had been captured. Now, he had to keep them alive as long as he could.

"It's OK, Holbrook," J.J. said, obviously all in.

"The water's stopped rising," Holbrook offered, with hope.

Just then another wave belched up the tunnel, bringing the water above waist level.

"Here, help me with these two," said J.J. "Give me your belt."

While Holbrook undid his belt, J.J. did the same to the unconscious, but apparently alive, Rostov. With no grace, J.J. roughly tied Rostov's hands behind him. Katrina was groggily coming out of her beating when J.J. did the same to her arms with Holbrook's belt. Left unattended, it wouldn't hold them long—but attended, it would be a problem to escape.

"Can you take her? Hold her by the arms. If she . . . ."

A third rush hit them in the darkness, smashing up against the concrete plug behind, but did not fill the tunnel. There wasn't much room left, nor air to breathe.

"Whoa! Wait a minute! What's happening?" shouted J.J., holding onto Rostov.

Slowly but surely they were being pulled down the tunnel, back toward the generator room.

"Hang on to her!" shouted J.J. to Holbrook, who was having difficulty holding the Soviet spy, even though the woman was nearly a dead weight.

Rostov, on the other hand, was coming around. J.J. slapped at him roughly. The tunnel was draining!

"Don't go with it, Holbrook. Get your feet!" J.J. instructed.

The chest-high water soon became waist-high, then knee high. They were under control.

"Come on, you son of a bitch . . . move!"

J.J. could hardly believe the anger he had for these two slime. His emotions seem to go down, then back up every few minutes. He'd empty himself on the two of them, then relax, then fetch more from the seemingly bottomless well of hatred.

"When you die, Rostov—I hope it's slow, and I hope they put it on television. Are you all right, Holbrook? Keep talking to me."

"I'm OK. We should be back at . . ."

"Jesus Christ," J.J. exclaimed.

" . . . the generator room," finished Holbrook.

Indeed, they were back at the generator room—or what had been the generator room. A fifty foot section of the roof had been caved in—stars twinkled above. An hour before, J.J. had been sure he'd not see stars again. Coming from the pitch blackness of the tunnel to the natural darkness of the lightless generator room was almost like stepping into lighted room from a closet. Rostov and the Soviet woman had forms and faces—as did the tall plant operations manager—his pants now gone.

"Your dam held up, Holbrook—congratulations. Well done."

J.J.'s first instinct was to stay put—the first rule in any survival situation. Make camp and stay where you are. People will come to you.

"Do you think there might be a phone around here that might work?"

As he spoke the words, J.J. could see real lights coming from the end of the long hallway—flashlights bobbing in the hands of several people. One of them had to be Scotty!

"Scotty! Is that you?" J.J. shouted.

One of the flashlights started to move ahead of the others, the pace more of a lope than a run.

"We're all right! *"We've got them!"* J.J. shouted.

Scotty's happy shout of victory echoed down the hallway.

HOOVER DAM

It was 9:35 P.M. (MST). A very tired John James Carteret stood in Winsloe Holbrook's sixth floor office, wrapped in a heavy blanket. Scotty was crashed on the couch. Dolan Yarnell sat on the floor while paramedics attended to Nichols, who had managed to find the Nevada stairwell and climb up into the dam, and the injured Ted Dillon. Above them, debris littered the crest of the dam. A squad of FBI agents roughly led the captured Soviet agents into their jail on wheels. J.J. held up his hand for quiet as the connection to Washington was made.

"Mr. President . . . we have them," said J.J., smiling at Holbrook. "Hoover dam has held."

"Wonderful! Congratulations!" responded the president with genuine excitement.

"The names of the spies are Alexander Rostov and Katrina Tambov. Rostov has been in the United States for the last month. Tambov is the attaché to Dimitri Korz . . ."

"The UN ambassador?" asked the president, astonished.

"Yes, sir. The operation has been under the control of Korz while the spies were in the United States. There is no doubt that Korz has been taking his orders directly from the Kremlin," J.J. said, then became increasingly angry as he told the president of the Soviet involvement.

"The Soviets have been manipulating and orchestrating this whole thing from the beginning. They killed anyone and everyone who got in their way. The blood of innocent Americans is on their hands! I saw the bodies of two children, murdered up close. And four policemen in St. Louis. There can be no doubt, Mr. President, that Soviet leaders have been involved in this from the start. The sons of bitches killed . . ."

The president interrupted.

"Khan . . . what of Khan? And the bombs?" asked the president anxiously.

J.J. came back down, his anger temporarily abated.

"Khan is dead, as are all of his men. There were only four of them to begin with. The one called Aziz al-As died in St. Louis, apparently killed by one of the other Arabs. That's still a mystery. Khalid Rahman died in Dallas as a result of gunshot wounds in St. Louis. Khan's munitions expert, Bafq el-Rashid, was found earlier this morning in a motel in Gallup, New Mexico—dead from a shot in the face. At this point we're not sure, but we think el-Rashid died when Khan was captured. One of the Soviets will give us the information. Rostov said that Khan died when the bomb exploded at Glen Canyon," J.J. paused. "And the fifth bomb was put on a shuttle train at the Dallas/Ft. Worth airport. Rostov wouldn't give me the number of the train, but we'll find it. It's primed to explode in another two months," J.J. added.

"The Dallas/Ft. Worth airport!" the president exclaimed, incredulous. He'd flown through DFW hundreds of times. The thought was staggering.

"Yes, sir. By the way, what happened to the water? We thought we were going to be flooded for good. How'd . . ." J.J. asked.

"We followed your suggestion and dropped four hydrogen bombs in the Grand Canyon. It apparently has worked. A new lake is forming. Maybe we'll name it after you," suggested the president, only half-joking.

"Sir, you've got to get Dimitri Korz right away. Without his direct help and supervision, Rostov would not have been able to follow through. They wanted us to think that Khan was solely behind this whole thing. And they almost got away with it. Who would have known? Khan makes his pitch, the bomb goes off at Glen Canyon, another here at Hoover. Who would have known it was the Soviets? Who would have known?" asked J.J.

The United States had gone to the edge of abyss, leaned over, and had been very nearly pushed into a bottomless pit.

"You've taken care of things on your end, Carteret. I'll take care of things on this end. Don't you worry," replied the president, strongly. "Is your partner there? I'd like to talk with him."

"Want to talk to the president?" J.J. beamed at a now-alert Scotty, who picked the phone up quickly.

"Mr. President?" replied Scotty.

"Mr. Coldsmith, Bill Sessions tells me that without you, this case would not have been solved. He also tells me that you're new on the job. I find it incredible that we . . . the government of the United States . . . are occasionally lucky enough to hire people who aren't afraid to follow through, to go to the limit, to do what needs to be done. For that, I . . . and the American people . . . thank you, Scotty."

"Yes, sir . . . thank you," replied Scotty.

"Is the plant manager there?"

Scotty handed the phone to Winsloe Holbrook. As he did, dramatically, the lights came back on. Being in darkness for so long, the lights actually hurt the eyes—but they were welcome.

"Yes, Mr. President?"

"Mr. Holbrook, I—we—the country, needs the power from your dam. What condition is it in, and how long will it take to get the generators working again?" asked the president.

"The Arizona generator room was severely damaged by the overtopping, Mr. President. But Mr. Yarnell, the Power Operations Manager for Los Angeles Edison, says that the Nevada bank is in pretty good condition. Everything is wet, flooded—but not damaged by debris. We have to check the lines and transformers, but those are problems that can be solved. The physical plant seems to be in good condition, no major leaks—although I'm sure there has been damage to the spillways."

Holbrook realized he was getting into more detail than the president wanted.

"Sorry, sir—this is something that the more hands we put on it, the quicker it will get done.

"I want to thank each and every one of you from the bottom of my heart, Mr. Holbrook. Now you're going to have to excuse me, but I've got to go and kick some Soviet ass," replied the president smartly.

"Yes, sir. Thank you, sir."

Holbrook hung up, then turned to J.J.

"I've got to get to work, Mr. Carteret. I'm glad you're on our side," he said smiling, then shaking J.J.'s hand. Holbrook turned to Scotty.

"Thank you for saving my—our dam," Holbrook looked at Dolan Yarnell, then shook hands with Scotty.

"My pleasure," Scotty smiled.

As Dolan Yarnell and Winsloe Holbrook left to take care of the rebuilding of Hoover's electrical system, the two FBI agents looked at each other.

Had it been only this morning that they'd first met? Their lives had been forever changed. They were the best. From now on, accepting anything else but the best in life would be impossible. Whatever *could* be done, *would* be done.

With shameless affection the two men hugged each other. The case was coming to a close, but their friendship was just beginning.

WASHINGTON

"Status," ordered the president.

The participants hadn't left the room in twenty-four hours. They, like their counterparts in the Kremlin, were on the edge of history. Graham Atkinson's wife lay down for the second night without word from her husband. The D.C. snowplows still hadn't touched the rest of C Street except for the single path to their townhouse. The city was closed. Outside, the temperature never cleared 28. Inside the White House, the heat was on.

"Captain Silverek has cleared Teheran," reported Bulldog Russell.

"And his prisoners?" asked the president.

"The president of Iran is with them. We had fifteen casualties, sir."

"Very good," the president replied, grimly. "Those sons of bitches," he muttered. "Where are the Soviets?"

Russell went to the map and drew three lines; one from Afghanistan, a second from Ashkhabad east of the Caspian into Iran, and a third from Soviet Caucasus into the northwestern corner of Iran west of the border with Turkey. The third line broke into two dotted lines at the Iranian provincial capital of Tabriz.

"Our satellites photos show that the Soviet forces from Afghanistan are moving across the desert very quickly. They should reach the coastal cities along the Gulf within the next eight hours. Resistance is weak and the territory easy. The aircraft carrier *Seven November* is in position. We have six destroyers and the *New Jersey* in the area. We've scrambled planes from the *Nimitz* and *Kennedy*, but quite frankly, we're out of range for effective support. The Soviets have the advantage with the *Lenin* in near-support. The only thing we could effectively counter with are our subs, but . . ."

"We're not going to irradiate the Middle East," replied the president, impatiently.

"Yes, well . . . they've got the upper hand. However, we can respond. We must ask the Saudis for logistic support, I'm afraid," began Russell.

"Set up a line to the King," the president told an aide. "I want to talk to him in five minutes."

The president waved for Russell to continue.

"The Soviets are also doing well east of Teheran. They've moved several armored divisions within spitting range of the capital. Given what we've seen tonight, I don't think the Iranian government has much to defend itself with from the eastern flank. I think Teheran could fall, or at least be under siege by . . ." Russell looked at the clocks. The sun was rising in Teheran. " . . . by eleven A.M., their time."

"Do you have any good news, Jim?" asked the president.

"Yes, sir. The Soviets' attack into the Kurdistan province of Iran has been met with fierce resistance. We're seeing a strange thing occur along this line," Russell drew a north-south line from Tabriz to Baghdad. "Independent of nationality, we're seeing both Iran and Iraq field generals turning their attention to the invading Russians instead of fighting each other. This seems to be taking place on a front-by-front basis. I've never seen anything like it. Given that we've captured Waquidi, I think a call to Hussein could quickly turn things around. The Soviets would have to spend much more than they bargained for if both armies turn on them," said the tired Bulldog Russell.

"Do it!" ordered the president. "Damn!" he said, shifting in his chair. The heat was rising and everyone seemed to be clicking on all gears.

"What about New York, Bill?"

Bill Sessions put down the telephone.

"Mr. President, under your order, my men have just seized the Soviet mission to the UN in New York. Ambassador Korz has been detained."

From the speakerphone came Secretary of State Oden Bennett.

"Mr. President, I have notified our embassy personnel in Moscow to expect similar treatment. I must warn you, this is a dangerous precedent. Embassy personnel have always been immune to prosecution and seizure. This is . . ."

"Different, Oden. It's different. Thank you," the president abruptly turned to Earl Hardy. "Are the networks ready?"

"Foaming! Absolutely foaming! No one has told anyone anything. But, it's pretty tough to hide a fireball in the night sky . . ."

"And the lights," added the president.

" . . . yes, and the lights."

"Get me Moscow. I want to talk to that son of a bitch before I go on the air."

It was William Sessions who came up with the ball-breaker. Earl Hardy immediately picked up on it.

"Wait a minute, Mr. President. I have an idea. We're in the right, they're in the wrong. We've been attacked, and they're attacking. Yet, we both know the Soviets can cover anything with a blanket of disinformation. Three days from now they'll have half the world convinced that we had a nuclear accident, that *we* caused the whole problem!"

Sessions leaned over the president's desk and spoke earnestly.

"Mr. President, *use* television. You're good at it. *Use* it! The networks won't have any choice but to go with you, much as it pains them. We can have the Soviet agents sitting on top of Hoover dam in less than ten minutes. Hell, they may still be there! We can have Dimitri Korz under arrest and questioned. We have pictures of the water going through the Grand Canyon. But most important of all, *let the world hear your conversation with Gorbachev*. Call the BBC! Call Tokyo. Bring in the networks when we talk to the King of Saudi Arabia . . . even when we talk to Hussein! Get that Russian son of a bitch on the line and rip the hell out of him! *But let everybody hear it*! You won't have long, because even the Russians can pick up foreign TV. But you should have enough time to hang him."

The White House Situation Room was silent as Bill Sessions pulled back from the president's desk. He'd said his piece. Conversations between heads-of-state were private conversations, the talk of leaders making major decisions, not the kind of thing for eavesdropping. As Oden Bennett said, it was a dangerous precedent. No matter what happened, diplomacy would be changed forever.

Regardless of what happened, the Soviets were going to eat dirt.

At 11:26 P.M. EST, just as the nightly news programs were ready to close, the Great Seal of the United States appeared on television screens on all major commercial and cable networks, as well as European and Asian networks. The screens showed the president preparing for something. William Sessions provided the introduction.

"My name is William Sessions. I am the Director of the Federal Bureau of Investigation. I am in the Oval Office of the president of the United States in Washington, D.C. The president is preparing to talk to Secretary-General Mikhail Gorbachev, live. What you see is unrehearsed. The president's aides are preparing the hotline call. [pan to president's desk, aides scrambling] The voices you will hear are those of the president, Secretary-General Gorbachev and the two translators. [closeup of president and translator]

PRESIDENT: *Mr. Secretary-General, it has been only two hours since we have last talked. Much has changed.*

GORBACHEV [with superiority]: *My people tell me that much of your country is still in a blackout and that your bases are nearly defenseless. How have things changed?*

PRESIDENT: *We can see that your armies have covered a great distance across the eastern deserts of Iran. I demand that this illegal occupation be stopped. I am prepared to begin battle against your aircraft carriers in the Persian Gulf immediately. We are outnumbered, however we cannot let you have control of the Gulf.*

GORBACHEV: *This is all rhetoric, Mr. President. As I have said before, we are doing you a favor—punishing Iran for this terrible deed these terrorists have done to you tonight. You are in no position to do otherwise. In fact, my generals tell me that we could strike a killing blow to the United States within the next ten minutes. But, we are a generous people, Mr. President.*

PRESIDENT: *Two hours ago I accused you of complicity in the destruction of the Glen Canyon Dam. You and your spies have seriously damaged a vital national resource.*

GORBACHEV [anger]: *And I told you then I will not stand for this talk of spies! You and your American political lackeys see Soviet spies everywhere. There are no spies, except in your mind!*

PRESIDENT: *Yes, so you told me. Let me give you an update, Mr. Secretary-General. The dam at Glen Canyon has been completely destroyed. The explosions your spy satellites have seen verify my attempt to save the southwestern United States from destruction. This evening I was forced to detonate four hydrogen bombs within the area we know as the Grand Canyon. I am pleased to report to you that this was successful, although I am greatly saddened to have violated a beautiful act of nature. The water that was behind the Glen Canyon Dam is now impounded again. You will not be pleased to know that your attempt to destroy Hoover Dam has failed. [camera switches to Hoover Dam, Scotty and J.J. with Rostov and Katrina] The FBI has successfully captured two of your KGB agents, catching them in a direct attempt to sabotage the*

Hoover Dam by using the last of the five atomic weapons smug--
gled into this country by the Arab terrorist Zaid abu Khan.

GORBACHEV: *Preposterous!*

PRESIDENT: *We have irrefutable proof* [some commotion on opposite end of telephone] *that your spies were under the direct control of your ambassador to the United Nations, Dimitri Korz.* [camera switches to New York, 67th Street Soviet mission] *I have instructed the FBI to capture, detain, and question ambassador Korz. Short of attacking Moscow, I have no way of capturing the chain of command, Mr. Secretary-General, however I am confident that the decisions made over the last three weeks have come directly from your office. It was you who ordered the destruction of the Glen Canyon and Hoover dams. We have the people, your people, to back it up!*

Yes, much of the American West has been blacked out, however our bases are now on full alert, our silos ready to launch. You came very close to accomplishing your goal, Mr. Secretary-General. With both dams destroyed, the southwestern United States, including the populated cities of Los Angeles, San Diego, and Phoenix, would have been uninhabitable for years to come. The defense industry in the United States would have been permanently crippled. Hundreds of thousands of people would have died directly because of exposure to the elements. Nearly 20% of our water supply would have been wasted, flooding much of the Southwest. Yes, the catastrophe would have been total. You would have been able to pick your spots—free to pillage the country of your choice.

But not now, Mr. Secretary-General. Not now. I have received reports from various western cities that limited electrical service has resumed to priority locations. Yes, you have damaged us, but we are a resilient people!

[multiple conversations over telephone]

AMERICAN TRANSLATOR: *They apparently have picked up our signal and realize that we are on television. They have verified the capture of Korz and the KGB agents.*

PRESIDENT: *You will pay for this outrage, Mr. Secretary-General. Yes, you will pay. You will immediately cease your attack on Iran and remove your armies. The world will not stand for this level of duplicity. The Iranian government, Khomeini and Waquidi, attempted a heinous blackmail scheme, actually sending world-renowned terrorist Zaid abu Khan into the United States with atomic weapons bartered from other Arab sources. You, Mr. Secretary-General, not only knew of this attempt, but you fully encouraged it—even to the point of protecting Khan while he was laying his deadly traps! In fact, it was you who double-crossed Khan! You fully expected us to believe that it was Khan who destroyed the dams and that the world would recognize your takeover of Iran as justifiable retribution.*

Zaid abu Khan is dead. We have captured the president of Iran, Abdul Waquidi. He has confirmed what I have said. He is now on his way to American soil where he will be publicly tried for crimes against the United States. There will be further retributions to those who instigated this terrible plot, both from within Iran and in other Arab nations.

You will pay for this, Mr. Secretary-General. We, the people of the United States, demand that you make us whole!

We have proof of your crimes, Mr. Secretary-General. The world is now aware of your crimes. What do you intend to do? Is this what you meant by glasnost, Mr. Secretary-General? Is this what you meant by a new beginning? Is it?

AMERICAN TRANSLATOR: *Sir, the line has been disconnected.*

MOSCOW

The hotline room in the Kremlin had gone from confidence bordering on arrogance to near-tragic embarrassment and panic, all in the space of five minutes. Major General Bodnof had been the first to hear the terrible news.

The Secretary-General's personal conversation with the American president was going out live to the world! And he didn't know!

Bodnof had been bombarded with urgent telephone calls from foreign embassies, many not even encrypted. Bodnof's First Directorate had a staff whose sole responsibility was to monitor foreign television. At first they thought they were seeing some rerun of the American president's news conference, but were soon shaken to the boots. Bodnof had immediately told Viktor Chebrikov, who in turn called Gorbachev's of-fice directly. The call was answered by an aide who nearly threw up, knowing that he would have to be the messenger to deliver the terrible news to the Secretary-General. In the Soviet Union, the messenger of bad news was also subject to being shot.

Careers and personal lives were cascading to Siberia.

The aide had scribbled a note and had personally placed it on the table next to the hotline speakerphone. He had been forced to make a hand motion to get the Secretary-General's attention. Color drained, then flushed, Gorbachev's face as his emotions fell into the black pit of being discovered. There was no choice. It had never been his intention to launch a strike against the U.S., even though his generals had said it was possible. They weren't prepared for it. The Americans could probably launch an effective counterattack, enough to destroy everything of importance.

The mission had failed. Gorbachev was in disgrace. There were no excuses to be given, no velvet cover of disinformation to hide the issue. Blame was massive, and direct. Failure was complete. He would be lucky to survive the next forty-eight hours. Distribution of the blame was essential, more important than facing the American president. The generals could do what they wanted to with the army. Given no leadership and no authority, they would back off in a heartbeat.

When word reached the Iranian battlefronts that there was a major problem in Moscow, the sharp three-pronged Soviet attack was blunted by the realities of modern-day politics. No one in the entire chain of command, from Gorbachev to the last Red Army grunt, was willing to take responsibility. Without responsibility there was no resolve. Without resolve there was no fight. One by one, the tanks stopped and turned around. The war was over. They had been fifty miles from Teheran.

HOOVER DAM

While Mikhail Gorbachev concentrated on saving his life, a half-world away Scotty Coldsmith and J.J. Carteret returned to Hoover dam to watch a modern-day miracle.

"Can you believe it?" asked Dolan Yarnell.

The sight was hard to believe. Black Canyon south of the dam was littered with monstrous boulders. A pile of debris filled what had been the four-story maintenance building. Rocks of all sizes nearly filled the Colorado River downstream. While it would take a massive repair job to clear the canyon, Dolan Yarnell couldn't wait.

The president had asked for—no, demanded—electricity from Hoover dam. He got it.

At 8:28 A.M. (MST) on February 27th, almost twelve hours to the minute after the disaster, water flowed through the N-3 penstock, which turned the turbine, which created the magnetic field and generated the first pulse of electricity out of Hoover. Control of the load, heating the lines, and ramping of the power was handled by Dewey Humboldt in WAPA Phoenix, with Jim Green standing by.

"It's been a hell of a day," said J.J., absent-mindedly dropping stones into Lake Mead.

"Nice morning," replied Scotty, turning his face to catch the first rays of sunshine peeking over the canyon wall.

"What are you going to do now? Are you going back?" J.J. asked, turning to his young partner.

Scotty kept his eyes shut for a few seconds, his face and arms cut and bloodied from his climb.

"I suppose so. What choice do I have? It looks like I'm cut out for this kind of work," Scotty smiled, turning to J.J. "And you?"

"I can't go back, Scotty. I can't go back to the way things used to be. I . . . we've . . . been to the top. What am I going to do, go back to white-collar crime in Elizabeth City? There's nothing for me back there. I just can't . . . it's too comfortable. We've done something important here. You and I have affected the lives of hundreds of thousands of people . . . maybe millions. I've discovered I'm capable of doing more—of getting more out of life! I don't know where I'll end up, I just know I can't go back."

Scotty looked at his mentor with awe. J.J. had more balls than than he'd ever have, or at least it seemed that way. Scotty was actually looking forward to his job. He'd be a terror. He knew how to get things done now. Maybe he'd get his own rookie as a slave. He smiled at the thought.

"Maybe we'll work together again, sometime," Scotty said, turning back to Lake Mead.

J.J. continued to pitch pebbles into the water. No response was needed. They'd known each other for less than thirty hours, but he liked the young man. J.J. doubted if he would have been able to do what Scotty did, at any age. And, yes, it was a pretty morning. Below them, the faint hum of a single generator pumped life back into the dam and into the power grid of the United States. Soon they would receive the applause of a grateful nation anxious to make them both famous, at least for a week. The American people had an incredible capability of absorbing information, no matter how terrible. Soon there would be other stories, new information to replace the blazing headlines of today. Scotty and J.J. would never forget that morning. With a final sigh, J.J. threw his last pebble into the lake, then turned and slowly walked toward a waiting police cruiser. After a last moment of reflection, Scotty followed.